FOR HER EYES ONLY

FILE #05692-3 — A STEP AWAY by BJ James

Subject: David Canfield

Age: 38

Occupation: government agent, The Black Watch

Physical Description: Hair: brown   Eyes: golden brown
Build: lean, muscular, wide shoulders,
a bit under six feet

Special Skills: Reconnaissance. Elite agent.

Comments: The "best of the best." A man of conscience. Strong.
Silent. Iron control. Fiercely loyal. On a mission of revenge...
until Raven McCandless began to heal his tortured soul....

FOR HER EYES ONLY

FILE #05303-7 — DAWN'S GIFT by Joan Elliott Pickart

Subject: Creed Maxwell Parker

Age: 35

Occupation: former military/foreign diplomat

Physical Description: Hair: black   Eyes: blue
Build: 6'2", strong, muscled, broad
shoulders

Special Skills: Negotiation.

Comments: A man of secrets. Intimidating. Agile. Haunted. His
past and present are on a collision course. Will young beauty
Dawn Gilbert survive unscathed?

BJ JAMES'

first book for Silhouette Desire was published in February 1987. Her second Desire title garnered a second Maggie, the coveted award bestowed by Georgia Romance Writers. Through the years there have been other awards and nominations for awards, including, from *Romantic Times Magazine*, Reviewer's Choice, Career Achievement, Best Desire, and Best Series Romance of the Year. In that time, BJ's books have appeared regularly on a number of bestseller lists—among them, Waldenbooks and *USA Today*.

On a personal note, BJ and her physician husband have three sons and two grandsons. While her address reads Mooresboro, this is only the origination of a mail route passing through the countryside. A small village set in the foothills of western North Carolina is her home.

JOAN ELLIOTT PICKART

is the author of over eighty novels under various names, including Robin Elliott. She received the Best New Series Author of the Year award from *Romantic Times Magazine* in 1985, and is a two-time Romance Writers of America Golden Medallion (RITA) Award finalist. Her highly successful miniseries THE BABY BET continues in 2000 and 2001 in Silhouette Special Edition and Desire.

When she isn't writing, she has tea parties, reads stories, plays dress up—and the list goes on—with her young daughter, Autumn. Joan also has three grown daughters and two wonderful little grandsons. Joan and Autumn live in a small town in the high pine country of Arizona.

HIS
SECRET
LIFE

BJ JAMES
JOAN ELLIOTT
PICKART

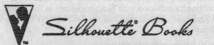

Published by Silhouette Books
America's Publisher of Contemporary Romance

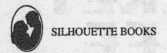 SILHOUETTE BOOKS

ISBN 0-373-21710-2

by Request

HIS SECRET LIFE

Copyright © 2000 by Harlequin Books S.A.

The publisher acknowledges the copyright holders of the individual works as follows:

A STEP AWAY
Copyright © 1992 by BJ James

DAWN'S GIFT
Copyright © 1986. Originally published as Robin Elliott

This edition published by arrangement with Harlequin Books S.A.

Visit Silhouette at www.eHarlequin.com

Printed in U.S.A.

CONTENTS

Dear Reader,

I've been asked to tell you the inspiration for this book. Actually, from my love of mystery, the concept of a clandestine government organization evolved first. From my own Scottish-American heritage came its venerable leader, Simon McKinzie. It seemed natural to call the organization The Black Watch in Simon's honor. And as natural that Simon's chosen must be men and women of abiding honor and great conscience. Caring citizens of extraordinary ability, who might falter beneath the weight of duty, but would never compromise principles. Traits reflected in the first agent and the first book of The Black Watch—David Canfield and *A Step Away*.

I hope you like both.

Enjoy!

BJ James

A STEP AWAY
BJ James

Prologue

"**B**astard. Prissy little..."

Simon McKinzie cut short the next expletive, hunching his massive shoulders against a cloying mist he couldn't escape. Like fog, it followed him, creeping into every cranny of the playground. From the look of the sky over the nation's capital, the worst was yet to come.

Shoving his hands into the pockets of his rumpled raincoat, in damp misery, he watched as Thomas Jeter picked his way through the deserted playground. When he'd chosen the park for this meeting, Simon had envisioned sunlight and laughing children. Safeguards for Jeter's neck. Next time, if, God forbid, there was a next time, he would check with the Weather Service. But now, with hands fisted, his bearlike body as hard as granite, he waited in the dreary June day.

Jeter, an elegant man dressed in sartorial splendor, halted before the big Scot. The mythical protection of a rope swing dangled between them. Setting a designer briefcase on a clump of grass, Jeter stood smirking up at the taller, older man. Like a gentleman farmer planning the castration of a prize bull past his prime, Simon thought. Except this bull wasn't quite ready to put out to pasture with his pride sliced open. Or his throat, or the throats of any of his men.

Jeter rocked back on his heels, using silence as a weapon. Simon looked back. The swing swayed lazily between them. A battle line, drawn by the whim of a summer breeze.

"Simon," Jeter said when the Scot made it clear he would stand all day as voiceless as the mist.

Simon's cold gaze stabbed down at the fashionable attire, the heavy cuff links glowing above the perfect manicure. Distaste burned in his hooded eyes.

Jeter tried again. "Good of you to see me." He gestured at the park. "Only you would think of meeting here."

Simon's lips curled, speaking more of loathing than a thousand words.

Jeter began to fidget. Simon watched him shrug his raincoat to the perfect drape over his jacket and shoot his cuffs the fashionable distance out of his sleeves. Then realizing he'd been intimidated without a word, Jeter forced himself to stop. In an attempt to establish control, he lifted his briefcase and snapped open its clasp. "I have information concerning one of your men."

Simon's gaze flicked idly to the case, then returned with unblinking precision to the bridge of the smaller man's nose. He let Jeter feel the weight of that stare, knowing his reaction was more subdued than expected. As he judged it would, Jeter's confidence bloomed.

Clearly, certain that his listener was hanging on every word, he spoke with perfect diction. "This is of grave concern, Simon. An urgent matter."

"Cut it out, Jeter," Simon said in a deep rumble. "And put your report away. There's nothing you can tell me about any of my men. Especially David Canfield."

Jeter froze. "How did you…"

Simon threw back his leonine head, smiling the smile that over the years had sent chills through any who threatened the deep cover of his organization. *His* organization. The special-intelligence organization conceived by a past commander-in-chief, but created by Simon. After fifteen years, it remained so highly secret, it had no recorded name, but among the few who knew of its existence, it had garnered a few. The Black Watch, Simon's Ladies from Hell—both for the strong and savage regiment of Simon's ancestral Scotland.

Members of his elite cadre, in honor of Simon, as well, called themselves simply, The Watch.

"How did I know you'd set your vicious sights on David?" Simon drawled. "Which reason would you like first?" Hand raised, fingers splayed, he ticked off his points. "Reason number one, your hunger for power, a need to control anything and everyone, including Simon McKinzie and his men."

Jeter opened his mouth to deny the accusation, but Simon silenced him with the narrowing of his eyes.

"Reason number two." A second finger folded. "Your fear of anyone who operates beyond your knowledge. You nose into every action, have an ear at every door—'' Simon smiled grimly ''—but not mine. Sticks in your craw, doesn't it?'' Before Jeter could respond a third finger dropped. ''Reason number three, you've been looking for a way to bring us down for years. A feather in your political cap to expose a threat to security, guilty or not. Right?''

Simon expected no answer. Finger number four dropped. ''David Canfield is the best of my men and, for the first time, he's in trouble.'' The fifth finger folded. The fist was complete. Simon reached between the ropes, resting his fist's weight beneath Jeter's chin. ''Reason number five,'' he said softly, each word like a silenced bullet. ''You're a vulture. David's the opportunity you've been looking for. You'd destroy him to get to me and The Watch.''

The fist pressed against the prominent cartilage in Jeter's throat. ''Hear me and hear me well. You won't touch David, and you won't use him to bring me down.''

Jeter couldn't stand his ground against the smoldering violence. He stepped back, holding the briefcase as a shield. ''This has nothing to do with you. The man's unstable. The weak link. A coward no one can trust. When his last mission went sour, he left his partner in a jungle.''

''Coward!'' Simon spat. The wet was forgotten, everything was forgotten but Jeter's accusations. God! How he hated these prim little bureaucrats who sat in ivory towers, lily-white hands folded in their laps while better men worked to keep the world intact. ''Listen and listen good. David Canfield did not leave his partner. Not while she was alive!''

''She was wounded and would've slowed him

down. We only have his word that he didn't leave her to die.''

"Not we, Jeter, *I*. *I* have his report. *I* shared his grief. *I* have his word. *You* have innuendo.''

"It's fact that he aborted an assignment and came out of the jungle when he could've finished alone. He's operated alone more often than not. Why not again?''

"There were reasons. Extenuating circumstances.''

"There are no extenuating circumstances for a man like Canfield. His sort are sociopaths, without conscience. He knows too much. With a few careless words, he can destroy everything we've spent years accomplishing.''

"We? Having trouble with your pronouns, Jeter?''

"Simon, you have to listen—''

"No,'' Simon interrupted, wondering how a biased, cliché-spouting idiot had weaseled his way into the ranks of those trusted with sensitive information. "I don't have to listen. You do. The last thing David is, is a sociopath.'' Simon wouldn't waste his breath spelling out for a cretin that conscience was one of the key requirements for The Watch and that David Canfield had more conscience than any man alive. Nor would he speak of his own remorse for using that conscience. With an edge of pain beneath the iron, he said, "David's never spoken carelessly. None of my men do.''

"They don't resign without warning, either, do they? But Canfield has.'' A sly smile twisted Jeter's features as he played his ace. "He's a malcontent. Simon, he can hurt you. Hurt The Watch. We have to silence him.''

"Silence him? To save The Watch?'' Simon's

hands gripped the ropes of the swing. "How do *we* silence him?"

"He could have an accident."

"Fatal, of course."

"Of course." Jeter's smile grew smug.

Simon watched it change, thinking the man should never play poker. The idiot considered his point taken, his prey caught. "Tell me one thing, Jeter. When did you decide I'd become a dithering idiot? Was it when you came to the learned conclusion that I'd do anything to save The Watch? Even betray one of my men?"

"No one would know that you—"

"Shut your lying mouth! If I agreed, once the...accident was done, you'd trip over your tongue to leak the truth." The laughter of a single child drifted from a distant hill, but Simon didn't hear it. His whisper was a cold warning of Jeter's mortality. "My men would know I sold David out. You'd see to it."

"No!" Jeter's spurt of confidence was shriveling. "No one will know."

"You're damn right, you son of a whore. Because it won't happen." Simon brushed the swing aside. Stepping closer, he grasped the silk of the smaller man's tie, drawing him onto tiptoes. "Do you know why, Jeter...? No? Then I'll tell you."

"For the love of heaven—"

"Shut up," Simon snarled. "I haven't told you your part in this."

"My part!"

Simon's grip silenced him. "From this moment, David Canfield's welfare will be your greatest concern. Why? It's simple. For your own survival. I have files, Jeter. Proof of every slimy trick you've pulled on your way up the political ladder. If anything happens to David, by accident or natural causes, you'll pay the price."

"You're bluffing. There are no files."

"I don't bluff," Simon said flatly.

Jeter abandoned the pretense of innocence. "There are others involved. Powerful men you wouldn't dare cross."

"Wouldn't I? Is it worth the risk to find out?" Simon hadn't thought that Jeter was in this alone. He was one of a breed, holding no elected office, wanting none. His sort were appointed in payment of political favors and fancied themselves the power behind the government. *They,* not men like David, were the conscienceless, running in packs, with no real loyalty beyond ambition. "Are you willing to give up everything to be the sacrificial lamb?"

Jeter's arguments deflated like a ruptured balloon. He shook his head, "No, I can't."

Simon's smile bared his teeth in a cold rictus. "Then we understand each other. David will be safe as a babe in his mother's arms."

"Yes."

Jeter's sudden capitulation to save his own neck, when only moments ago he was smiling as he planned David Canfield's death, infuriated Simon as nothing else had. "Can you imagine how hard it is not to break your dainty little neck? It would rid the world of one more slug."

Jeter was finally beyond words. He stared at Simon.

"No." Simon granted a reprieve, knowing this change of attitude wouldn't last beyond Jeter's escape from the park. Any who spoke so glibly of betrayal was a stranger to honor. The man was despicable, but Simon had a use for him as David's insurance. "Take this message back to the rest of the slime. Tell them I know who they are. Promise them from me that if anything happens, I'll find them." Eyes as cold as winter bored into Jeter's. "And not one will survive an hour longer than David Canfield.

"Now, go!" He shoved Jeter away, watched as the man clawed at an elusive rope for support, smiled as Jeter sprawled in the mud. "Get up. Get up and get out. I can't stand the stench of you any longer."

When Jeter was gone, Simon stood listening. Gradually, his anger eased. In his mind, he heard the sound of children laughing, innocent children, one of whom might grow up to be a man like David.

David Canfield. The man who made fact the cliché, "cream of the crop." He was the best of the best. Once, a young idealist with a smile that melted hearts. Not too handsome, too tall, too lean or too fat—nothing striking to draw the eye. The perfect chameleon...until he flashed his slow, lady-killer smile. Now, after fifteen years in the field, suppressing honor and gentleness, growing harder and more cynical each day, the smile had disappeared.

Simon shook his head like an angry bull. Sociopath! Just the opposite. David cared too much! It was the caring that made him the best. The caring that had nearly destroyed him. He'd become solemn and cynical. But hard?

"Never," Simon said in the darkening of the imminent storm. An idealist's way of coping. Of surviving. Scar tissue on wounds too awful to face.

He had never denied that he saw what he was doing to his best man. Each time he saw. "And, damn my soul, still I asked him for more." Now David was only a step away from going over the edge. "Or worse." A step away from becoming a rogue, an agent who takes the law into his own hands, wreaking havoc and sometimes death in the name of retribution. David meant to have the traitor who betrayed his mission and caused the death of his partner. The need, coupled with fatigue and remorse that had seethed for years, was driving him to the edge.

Simon sighed grimly, thanking God Jeter hadn't known how close he was to the truth. But, he promised himself, there would be no accidents, no hospitals where doors open only one way and luckless patients disappear. The psychiatrists wouldn't get David, nor the Jeters. Not yet, at least. It was a risk, a dangerous one, but Simon knew he owed David a chance to make peace with his conscience, his work, the world, and to heal himself.

"I know just the place for him to do it." Simon smiled as he added softly, "And the person to help him."

He felt a tug at his leg. A young voice asked, "Who you talking to, mister? Ain't nobody here but you and me. And we're gonna get wet in a minute, we don't go home ourselves."

"I think you're right." Simon knelt before the child who wore only a ragged shirt and faded shorts. "Where's your mother, boy? You shouldn't be in the park alone. You can't be more than six."

"I'm eight, and I'm alone 'cause I ain't got no mother. There's just my granny, and she's always drunk."

A street child, tough, smart, wise beyond his years, like David had been. The sort who fall between the cracks in society. Exploited then abandoned when they were trouble.

"But not David," Simon muttered, struggling with his own conscience. David had been snatched from the streets by the war, and from war by Simon. Now that he was a man with shattered beliefs, he would not be abandoned. "Never David."

"My name's Rico, not David."

Simon's grave expression eased. "Of course, it is." Reaching into his pocket, he fished out a five-dollar bill. "Take this. Buy yourself a decent meal. Don't let your grandmother spend it on liquor."

"No, sir, but maybe I'll buy her something pretty. Make her feel better. Then she won't have to drink to forget the bad stuff." With surprising wisdom, he added, "Can't forget anyway. Trouble's always waitin' when she sobers up."

"She won't forget, but maybe she can deal with it if someone who understands helps her."

"Like me?"

"Like you." Rain that had threatened throughout the afternoon began to fall in earnest. "Looks like we both better run." Turning the child around by his shoulders, Simon patted his head, saying, "Scoot."

He watched until the child faded from sight. His thoughts were of David. Of help and hope. Of a woman whose own life was once in shambles.

"Raven."

The sound of her name brought the illusion of sunlight and laughter and peace to a troubled man standing in the rain. Could she do the same for David?

"Yes."

Simon's decision was made. He would ask David for time. Time for David to make peace with himself and his job. Time for Simon to find the traitor in The Watch.

He turned and splashed to his car. He was going home to make two calls. First, across the city to David Canfield. Second, to the highlands of North Carolina.

To Raven McCandless.

One

David Canfield laid his night glasses aside and leaned back against a boulder. He relaxed, innate caution quieted for a moment. Clouds darkened the moon. He was a shadow blending into the mountain at his back, as much a part of it as the boulder where he sat. The sultry breeze that ruffled his thick brown hair and teased his somber shirt had died completely.

The granite was hard, and he wanted a cigarette. A filthy habit, a dangerous one. One that could buy him a bullet, cheating the medical profession of one more statistic. His smile was grim as he returned his attention to the valley.

An hour had passed since he had settled on this jagged rock overlooking the land below. In the fading light, he'd studied the terrain, the lake and the buildings. There were two cabins, as he had expected, built of weathered wood with bright tin roofs. Both structures were identical, sitting side by side on a tiny hillock beyond the lakeshore. The rise afforded an unimpeded view to the left and to the right. A wall of sheer granite towered at their backs.

The first McKinzies, proud, dour Scots seeking a home, had chosen well. For beauty, for defense. The valley was virtually impregnable—against an expected intruder—with the lake, the mountains and rough granite as its fortifications.

David had come to the valley under friendly duress. The only sort he tolerated, from the only person he'd allowed to exert it. This was Simon's valley, the older cabin had once been Simon's home, and would be David's for three months. He'd promised Simon that much, for The Watch, out of respect.

He'd come, for once doubting Simon's wisdom, and discovered he liked what he saw. From the mountainside, he had committed the valley floor to memory. He knew the number of stepping stones that wound through a wildflower garden and, in the forest beyond, noted a scattering of scarred trees, slashed by the claws of a bear. He found where the eagle nested. Like the eagle, he knew the rise and fall of the land. His gaze had followed the path from the cabins to the lake, losing it for a time beneath the night shade of a drooping hemlock.

He knew the valley like a finely drafted blueprint. It was the woman who was a mystery.

Reaching for his cigarettes, he shook one from the pack and struck a wooden match on the stone. There were no guerillas to smell the smoke or see the flame, yet he shielded its flare with his cupped hands. Drawing smoke into his lungs, he settled back. The match, by habit, he broke and tucked into the pocket of his jeans. Savoring the smoke, he turned his gaze to the newer cabin and its gardens.

What kind of woman would choose to live in such isolation? Who was she? What was she? Raven McCandless, spinster, friend of Simon McKinzie. Little more than name, rank and serial number...and Simon's good opinion. Spinster. The word evoked the image of a pinch-faced recluse with graying hair pulled into a cruel knot. A misanthrope with shades drawn, hiding from the world.

David rarely presumed. Like the telltale scent of tobacco smoke, presumption could be fatal. But Simon had been oddly reticent. His terse comments— "a special lady, the best kind of survivor"—left David little but presumption.

He smiled into the darkness, listening. The woman he'd presumed a recluse was swimming in the moonlit lake. Presumption shattered. He wondered wryly if the day might come when he preferred the pinch-faced recluse.

Grinding his cigarette out on the sole of his boot, he dropped the butt into his pocket. The last thing he needed was a woman. He wanted quiet and solitude. Perhaps, this night was a godsend. Pinch-faced misanthrope or siren, catching her unprepared would make her ill at ease with him, perhaps alienate her completely. Her disadvantage would be his advantage. Embarrassment and surprise for the lady who swam in the lake would assure his privacy.

Tucking the night glasses into their case, he made one more check of the valley and the lake. His eyes moved slowly, finding nothing amiss in the shadowed land. Quietly, he rose. A soft buzzing sounded from a deadfall behind him. Keeping his body rock still, with the barest move, he turned his head. "I hear you, friend."

Night in the southern Appalachians is not total absence of light. With accustomed sight, David found the rattler coiled and wary. Ancient antagonists, two battle-scarred loners, both too weary to fight. In the gloom, still and unsure, they waited. The beaded tail shivered. David heard the tentative buzz of warning, not anger.

"It's all yours, old fella," he said softly as he inched away. "I'm going to meet a lady."

The path he took was surprisingly easy. Unlike his trek into the valley from the winding, unpaved road, the underbrush was sparse. He was a ghost, gliding easily over rugged ground. Moving from boulder to precipice and down, he worked his way over the rock face with only the moon to guide him. Beyond the harsh wall of stone, on the gentler slope that led to the valley, a little-used trail eased his passage.

He moved quickly, sparing no glance to any of the valley but his destination. With the silent step that had saved his life in the jungle and in civilization, as well, he took up his vigil beneath the concealing cover of the hemlock. The dock that stretched from shore to lake gleamed like a silver track. Glittering water mirrored many bright moons as it lapped at its banks.

He felt the night, its stillness, the quiet. He breathed its fragrance, the scent of honeysuckle and evergreen. The woman who swam laughed, a contented note that drifted over the water like sweet music.

David frowned, disturbed by the sound. It was not the laugh of the woman, he presumed. When she walked from her cabin to the lake, the night glasses told him nothing, revealing only the back of a slender figure swathed in a flowing shirt.

She laughed again, melodic notes so clear, she might have been standing at his side. Something he couldn't identify stirred inside him. Watchful tension loosened for a moment before he gathered it back in. Annoyed with himself and the woman, he took a step nearer the lake.

A menacing rumble, a deep monochord joined by a second, stopped him short. His stare probed the darkness, distinguishing only the shape of stone and willow before the utter blackness of dense laurel. He knew what lay there, watching from the mountain as the huge dogs walked to the lake by the woman's side and took up their watch.

David's attention was riveted on the underbrush. No leaf stirred, no intrusion rustled the thick ground cover. Yet. One ill-advised move, *then* he would be dog meat. But for now, for the second time since coming to the valley, he was being warned away.

"So, now I know how the animal population feels about me." His eyes wandered to the lake as he considered the human element. She would be coming soon. He wondered again what manner of woman she was.

She swam well, barely rippling the lake's surface. The quiet seemed more intense with only the gentle splash of her stroke disturbing it. David could see the bright, ruffled water, but the swimmer was only a dark image. Not even the night glasses would pierce the depths of a lake. He knew little more than he had on the mountain. Only that she was a strong and graceful swimmer, and that her laugh was lovely.

A cloud drifted over the moon; shadows deepened.

The bright glitter of the water turned to a lightless black. He could not see her, yet he knew she was near. Then he heard the scrape of her nails on the dock, a cascade of water, the pad of her foot, and in an agile move, she was rising from the dock. For an instant, she stood poised. The still image of her body, lithe, full breasted, lean hipped, burned indelibly in his mind. Spinning slowly toward the lake, she rose on tiptoe, her arms lifted, her body stretching to the sky. Water spilled down her long, black hair and over her naked body, shimmering against her skin like carelessly strewed diamonds. She was a pagan worshiping the moon, a child stretching to grasp the silver globe, a woman paying homage to the night. A mystery.

Swaying, in a fluid move, she swept up her hair. Deftly, she twisted water from it then looped it over her shoulder. Plucking her white shirt, which was draped over a tree limb, she shrugged into it and stood looking out at the lake, listening to sounds only she could hear.

David watched, startled, entranced, his plan to surprise and disturb forgotten. His distraction was short-lived, for on its heels came the shock of unexpected anger. The consuming anger of grief, still too new, too vivid. He'd watched helplessly as a woman who loved life and wanted desperately to live it had died. As he'd held her in his arms, trapped in a war-torn jungle, the life she had treasured had ebbed away. Her death brought home to him how precious life was.

This woman, this Raven McCandless, who lived in sheltered peace, valued her life no more than to risk it for the careless pleasure of a sybarite. Helen Landon had postponed her peace and pleasure to serve

The Watch. Now that time would never come for her, and the thankless neither knew nor cared.

Hands clenched in anger, he stepped onto the dock. The woman froze, her hand caught in her hair as she'd tugged it from her shirt. If she felt panic or fear, it didn't show. She was as calm and untroubled as the night.

"Simon didn't tell me Raven McCandless was a fool." David's voice was low, his tone mild. Only the words were harsh. The dogs stirred in the darkness but remained silent. "But then, there was very little he did tell me."

Slowly she let her hair fall to her shoulders. "You're early, Mr. Canfield." Her voice, like her laughter, was lovely. There was no trace of fear or surprise as she added, "You weren't expected until tomorrow."

"I never do what's expected, Miss McCandless. It makes for longevity."

She nodded curtly as if she understood, and David wondered how much she'd been told of him. More, obviously, than he had of her.

"I've been swimming in the lake since I was fourteen, Mr. Canfield." She addressed his first remark without rancor.

"Alone in the moonlight?"

"Alone, and always in moonlight."

"Then you *are* a fool," he said bluntly.

She laughed, the same lyrical note that had drifted over the water. Pivoting on the pad of her foot, she swung about. The last tarrying cloud had swirled from the face of the moon and she was bathed in light as bright as day. "You're very like Simon." Her voice, like her face, was quiet, serene.

She seemed unconcerned that her shirt clung wetly to her body. She made no effort to hide the fullness of her breasts or the hard buds of her nipples. David realized in reluctant admiration that she wouldn't cringe or hide or pluck the transparent shirt from the body he had already seen.

"So are you," he said.

"So am I?" She raised a quizzical eyebrow.

David looked from her body to her face, into her dark gaze. He saw pride, courage and honesty. "Like Simon," he murmured, wondering for the first time if they were lovers. Simon was nearly twice her age, but what did age matter with a rare woman like this?

She stood calmly as he studied her in the light. Simon's special lady. Extraordinary. Exquisite. A woman like none David had ever encountered. Her black hair was swept back from her forehead, not in the puritanical knot he'd imagined, but in a loose, twining rope. Her face was a dusky oval, her features finely drawn. Her mouth made him think of roses. She was not only the most beautiful woman he'd ever seen, there was more, a special quality that reached beyond the surface. There was a serenity in her face and her smile that made men look and look again, wanting to lose themselves in the still darkness of her eyes.

He took a step, drawn to her as if she'd beckoned. The undergrowth rustled. The dogs made no other sound, but David knew he'd been given his last warning.

"Stop. Please," Raven cautioned.

"I know they're there."

Raven's gaze roamed the length of him. He was lean, his shoulders wide, his body muscled, but not heavily. He'd obviously walked in from the main road and down the mountain. No little feat. He'd come a day early to study the lay of the land. Naturally, he knew the valley and its inhabitants. She nodded. Of course, a man who never did what was expected wouldn't be taken by surprise.

"I mean you no harm. Nor them."

"I never thought you did." With a gesture from her, the dogs subsided.

She was a cool one. But neither serenity nor beauty were strangers to stupidity. "You take intolerable risks."

"What risks, Mr. Canfield, and intolerable to whom?" She met his heated look levelly.

David found himself wanting to goad her, to destroy the calm that surrounded her. His gaze moved deliberately over her body, lingering at the thrust of her breasts and at the flat of her stomach. Her body was lush and slender, curved and lean. An invitation.

She endured his blatant survey, still refusing to cringe and hide, refusing the hypocrisy of false shame. Unfounded rage blazed through him. He wanted to shatter the self-confidence that let her stand half-naked before him as coolly as if she were dressed in the finest clothes. Would she be so calm if she was trapped in a mosquito-infested jungle, or as confident if she had to live each day afraid it was her last? Would she be as serene sitting in a pool of blood, waiting for a friend to die?

Would Raven McCandless feel guilty for surviving when others hadn't?

Did it matter what she felt? Did anything matter beyond his promise to avenge Helen? Simon had three months to find the traitor in the ranks of The

Watch. David had given his word on it. Three months and he would be free of the pledge and the restrictions of The Watch. Free to find the betrayer, to make him die slowly, as Helen had.

"You risk your life, Miss McCandless, and it's intolerable to *me*."

"Why should what I do with my life matter to you?"

"It matters because I've seen people die who wanted to live. It matters because I lost a friend. A woman who treated life as precious, who never took any unnecessary risks."

"This woman, this friend, she died?"

"Yes." His voice hardened. "She died."

"I'm sorry."

"Don't be." There were worse things than dying. Sometimes, surviving is the hardest. But this pretty woman, living in her pastoral valley, wouldn't understand. She had no concept of torture and anguish. Nor of how, in the end, Helen had begged to die.

"Did you love her?"

David looked down at his hands, remembering the blood, hearing Helen's delirium.

"Mr. Canfield?"

Trapped in his thoughts, he hadn't known she'd approached him. He looked down at her fingers gripping his elbow. Her hand was rough and dry, the nails short. One was broken to the quick. Not the hands of a princess who never left her mountain fortress. Not the hands he expected. Not at all. "No," he said roughly. "I didn't love her."

Raven gave him a puzzled look. There was sadness in his voice, and grief, and something else she didn't understand. "Are you all right?"

"No, *Miss* McCandless, I'm not all right. That's why I'm here. Surely, your good friend, Simon, told you that." Shaking her hand from his arm, he wheeled about and strode from the dock. At its edge, he turned back, one foot on the ground, one on the weathered wood. His insolent stare swept over her. His eyes insulted, his mouth twisted in an unpleasant smile. "I'd appreciate it *Miss* McCandless, if next time we meet, you'd wear some clothes. My head may be a little screwed up, and I've lost a trusted friend, but I'm not blind, and I'm not a monk."

He turned on his heel, angry with the desirable woman she was, but oddly, angrier with himself for his arrogance. He couldn't blame Raven for the life she'd chosen. He had chosen. Helen had chosen. Her choice, in the end, had been fatal.

He stalked to the cabin he knew was his. The moon that had shone so brightly on his skirmish with Raven was darkened by a resurgence of clouds. The path was rough, needing all his concentration. Still, a part of his mind resisted, fascinated, intrigued, refusing to turn from Raven McCandless.

He stopped, straightened and stared at a flickering light. A lamp he couldn't see from the mountain burned cheerfully in a window, welcoming him to his temporary home.

Raven. Was there no escaping her serenity, her loveliness and now, her courtesy? He didn't doubt he would find the cabin cleaned, stocked and ready for him. And he had no doubt whom he should thank.

A part of him not yet hardened by the life he'd lived wanted to turn to her, to repent. Another part, stronger, unrelenting, would not. He resumed his walk, doggedly, following the light left by Raven. At the cabin's steps, he hesitated. Decency struggled to surface again and lost. Shrugging his shoulders against the silent rebuke of his damnable conscience, he climbed the stairs. Resisting the impulse to look back at the lovely woman he knew was watching, he stepped through the door into his dimly lighted sanctuary.

Raven waited until the light was extinguished before she turned away. Another backhanded slap. He'd had no time to familiarize himself with the cabin's interior, and certainly not enough to settle in. The lamp, flipped off immediately, was simply another insult. He was sending her a message, saying, "You did this, and I don't need you."

"Simon, what have you done to me?" she murmured. A chill, common in summer in mountainous altitudes, began to nip at her damp body. Crossing her arms against it, she closed her eyes, shutting from sight the dark cabin that seemed as brooding as the man.

Her life was in order, the valley, a quiet haven. She'd lived here alone for nearly ten years and had never been lonely. Simon first brought her to the valley, and in the end, it was he who had saved her sanity. Over the years, he'd given her much and never asked for anything in return. Now, he was asking, and she couldn't refuse.

"No." She opened her eyes. She *could* refuse. Simon would understand. Turning away, she walked to the water's edge. The valley and the lake were always lovely, but by moonlight, they were breathtaking. They were her peace and tranquility. Looking out at them, she could accept anything, even a stranger who was hard and cynical, who looked at her as if she should apologize for existing. Who ruffled her composure as no one ever had. Who set her heart racing with a roving look and a hurt, bitter smile.

She could refuse. Simon had left her that option.

Yet, she had known she wouldn't from the moment she saw David Canfield, standing like a satyr, lean and hard, dark eyes challenging. Even in darkness, she'd glimpsed the desperate weariness etched on his face, and in his voice, heard the hidden hurt, worn on his sleeve like a broken heart.

He was insulting and arrogant. He would disrupt the tranquil life she loved. And at the moment, he despised her. The next three months could be very difficult, but she wouldn't send David Canfield from the valley. For Simon's sake. For David's. For her own.

She faced the cabin. There was challenge in her own dark eyes as she met the blank stare of the cabin windows. David Canfield was an enigma. Simon had told her little, except that he was a friend as well as a colleague. A special friend who was hurt as she'd once been hurt.

"And bitter, perhaps even dangerous. To himself," she murmured. "But because Simon sent him, never to me."

Tomorrow, when there was no moonlight to play romantic tricks, perhaps she would see him as Simon's friend, no more. Then, if he would let her, she would do what she could. When his three months were ended, he would leave and the valley would be hers again.

The valley had never been lonely before. With the honesty that ruled her life, she knew she couldn't be sure it wouldn't be now. That same honesty would not let her deny the physical tug she felt beneath David Canfield's gaze. He wasn't a monk. His look alone would have told her that if he hadn't. He wanted her, and he hated himself for it.

They were strangers sentenced to a time together. He resented the enforced stay, and she— Raven shrugged. She had no idea what she felt or what she wanted. For the first time in a long while, she didn't understand herself.

Something cold and damp nuzzled at her. She looked down at a Doberman, black as night and as big as a calf. "Robbie. Did you come to see about me?" Kneeling, she wrapped her arms around his sleek neck and rested her head on his. "If I'm acting a little crazy, maybe it's because I am."

Another head, smaller than the first, snuggled beneath her arm. "Kate!" She laughed and tumbled onto the deck with the dogs. "I can't be completely crazy if you love me, can I?"

Like black phantoms, they danced about her, always ready for a game. David Canfield was not forgotten. It would not be that easy. He was simply pushed to the back of her thoughts as she rose to her feet and raced to her own cabin with the dogs in gleeful pursuit.

The sun was lifting over the mountains when Raven woke with a start. She'd slept past her usual time of rising by two hours, and still she was tired. Remembering it was the weekend and her days were her own, she relaxed. Her night had been long and restless, and she'd fallen into an exhausted stupor only an hour before dawn. A week had passed since David Canfield had come to the valley.

Her fears that he would disrupt her life were unfounded. On his first day, he walked out of the valley, bringing back his car and belongings. Then he virtually disappeared. There were signs of life in the cabin, a light here, another there, but no evidence of David. Raven settled into her own routine, working among her flowers in the morning, then driving over the mountain to Madison, to the college where she taught. Her evenings were spent on the illustrations for a book on wildflowers she'd written. When she was tired or restless, she relaxed at her potter's table.

She had convinced herself she'd put the interloper from her mind. Then, for an unfathomed reason, her thoughts were filled with David Canfield and his trouble. She thought of the woman who treated life as if it were precious, who never took an unnecessary risk. The woman he did not love. Somehow, Raven knew her death was the source of his pain.

Perceptions of death and loss dredged up old grief, and she'd spent the remainder of the night sweating and shivering, her eyes dry and burning. She hadn't cried since she was fourteen. Sometimes, she wondered if all the tears meant for a lifetime had been shed then.

Denied their release, she'd tossed fitfully in her solitary bed. Grief was finally exhausting and sleep, mercifully dreamless. In morning light, sorrows of the darkest hour were eased. The lost would always live in her heart, yet she'd learned to go on and not to hate—to see beauty about her and believe the world was good.

Simon taught her it was an insult to those she'd

lost to destroy her life with grief. She fought him, determined to punish herself for living. Then, gradually, she understood. Life ends, but so must grief, and the end of grief is serenity. Raven lived her life by this rule and only rarely forgot. Last night was the first time in a long, long while.

"But it's done now, and I'm stronger today than I was yesterday because of it."

Rising, she went to the bath to splash cold water on her face. Her next stop was the kitchen to make coffee. While it perked, she dressed for her run with the dogs. They would be waiting for her, sprawled before the door where they spent every night.

Tossing her sleep shirt aside, she drew on sweats, a T-shirt and worn, comfortable running shoes. Her hair was braided, requiring no attention. All that was left was collecting Robbie and Kate. She ran five miles with the dogs each morning. Running swept away the cobwebs of sleep and left her eager for the day.

She was out the door and down the steps with the dogs at her heels when she realized David was walking by the shore. She stopped short, surprised and disconcerted. He seemed contented with his solitude. With only a wave of acknowledgement, she headed in the opposite direction. She ran hard, her long legs stretching out in a ground-eating pace, exorcising disturbing thoughts of David from her mind.

Robbie caught her mood and picked up his pace, racing ahead faster and faster. Raven suspended all thought and ran for the sheer pleasure of running. When they made their turn and headed back, dodging over the worn trail, she picked up the pace even more.

The path David had taken was deserted. She felt a

flutter of distress. His troubles would only intensify if he shut himself away to brood. As she approached her own cabin, she saw he was sitting on its steps.

Winded and dripping with sweat, she stopped before him. Her heart was too full and her breath too short to speak. Resting with her hands on her knees, she wondered if the man planned to make a career of catching her at inopportune times. When she could straighten, she found herself looking into his solemn face.

"Are you all right?" He didn't touch her, but something in his expression said he wanted to.

Raven shrugged and managed a nod. Gradually, her panting slowed. "Why do you ask?"

"You were late. Then you ran as if demons were chasing you. I thought..." He shrugged.

He hadn't shut himself away as completely as she supposed. He was aware of her schedule. Raven was surprised. Concern had drawn him from his shell. Gathering her thoughts, she tried to reassure him. "I had a late night and overslept. There's nothing wrong, really, but thank you for—"

"Then you really are trying to kill yourself, aren't you?" He cut her off. The hard edges of his face had grown harder, the lines about his mouth deeper. His somber look became cold, angry censure.

"I beg your pardon?" She was startled by the change and puzzled by his accusation.

"Anyone who runs through the woods at the reckless pace you do is asking for a broken neck. Any fool who runs so hard at the end of a distance run is courting a heart attack. *If* she survives the woods."

Raven stifled a gasp. David's eyes moved with a look of satisfaction to the thrust of her breasts against

her shirt. She ignored the look. If this was mere concern, his anger must be something to behold. He was
goading her, spoiling for a fight. With as much dignity as she could manage she stood her ground, making a bid for peace. "I've been running the woods as
long as I've been swimming the lake. And just as
fortunately."

His look ranged over her, much as at the dock. His
eyes touched on her disheveled hair, her flushed face.
The sherry gaze traced the tilted line of her breast
beneath the sweat-soaked T-shirt, lingered as it had
before, then returned with painful deliberation to her
face. "Thank God, at least you don't run without your
clothes."

Don't, Raven warned herself, for his anger was an
expression of anguish. Solemnly, she quipped, "I've
been tempted, Mr. Canfield, but I'm deathly afraid of
chiggers."

A reluctant grin tugged at his lips, then he laughed,
a hearty, deep-throated laugh. "So am I, Miss Mc-
Candless. The little monsters leave a powerful itch."

Raven's laugh ebbed to a smile as she offered her
hand. "Shall we let our mutual fear be the basis for
a truce? This valley was never meant to be a war
zone, Mr. Canfield."

He rose from the step. There was no insolence in
the look that searched her face. After a moment, he
took her outstretched hand in his. "My name is David."

"And I'm Raven." In sunlight, she saw his hair
was deep brown, not black. He'd appeared taller,
broader, towering over her on the dock, but he was a
bit under six feet. With his anger disarmed, there was
still lines bracketing his mouth and furrowing his

brow. His days shut away in the cabin hadn't been restful. He was exhausted, and had been for a long time. Her tender heart forgot his hostility. "There's fresh coffee in the kitchen if you'd like some."

"No." He hesitated, then flashed a smile that startled Raven anew. "Yes! I'd love coffee that doesn't taste like black shoe polish."

"Yours?"

"How did you guess?"

"Deduction. Strong men like strong brew."

"Not that strong."

Raven smiled. "Then come in and sample mine."

Two

David sprawled in a chair in Raven's sunny kitchen, watching as she took earthenware cups from a cupboard. There was an economy of effort in her moves. Then he realized she was simply skillful with her hands. She pulled a pan of cinnamon rolls from their wrapper. Homemade, once upon a time, she said. Now fodder for the microwave. As the scent of spice swept over him, he knew it was delicious fodder.

Raven set the rolls on the table and sat in silence as David ate. When he picked up the fifth roll, she laughed. "You were starving!"

"I was working yesterday. Hunger keeps the mind sharper."

Raven wondered how many times, in how many places, he'd only had his hungry mind to depend on.

David looked into a cup marked by a dogwood

blossom. "How much do you know? What has Simon told you?"

"That you work with him. Secret and dangerous work that he never speaks of. Specifically of you, only that you're tired and troubled, in need of rest."

"Little enough, but more than Simon told me of you."

"There's little to tell."

He gave her a long look, and then he smiled. "I doubt that, Raven McCandless."

His smile was nice, but Raven was wary of their truce. She watched him over the rim of her cup.

"How did you meet Simon?" David asked abruptly.

"It's a long story. Too long."

"One you don't want to tell." He pushed back his chair and walked to the door of the terrace overlooking the valley. "Then tell me about the cabins."

"The original was built by the first McKinzies to come to the Carolinas nearly two hundred years ago. After it burned, the cabin that exists today was built on the site. I spent some time there with the McKinzies. After I finished college, I came back."

"And built your own cabin."

"Yes." Raven moved to his side. "The McKinzies scattered for one reason or another. Only Simon returns. His mother, Rhea, came here as a bride from Scotland, and he was born here. He loves the valley."

"That explains his occasional burr, and yours."

"The Scottish roll of the R. You have a good ear."

"When Simon comes, are you lovers?"

Raven went very still. Her eyes were glittering when she looked at David. "I love Simon, and I owe him more than I can ever repay, but we aren't lovers, Mr. Canfield.''

"Then he won't mind if I do this." David caught her braid in his hand, wrapping it about his palm, drawing her gently yet firmly to him. Something seethed in his eyes as his mouth closed over hers.

The kiss began like a punishment. The crush of his hand held the promises of bruises tomorrow. The thrust of his body was harsh and unyielding, but Raven stood pliantly, refusing to fight. Slipping the band from her braid with his fingers, he stroked the tangles from her hair. Murmuring something low and unintelligible, he drew her closer.

Raven's head was muddled, her heart racing. She was confused by the anger in him, bewildered by his tenderness. His kiss deepened, softened, tasting of cinnamon. She had never been held as he was holding her nor kissed as he was kissing her. No man had ever disturbed or provoked or intoxicated her as David.

As abruptly as he'd taken her in his arms, he released her. With his face close to hers, his hand still tangled in her hair, he murmured, "Did you know how much I wanted to do that the first night? The night I met the lovely, elusive Raven. I've watched you running over the mountain, with your cute little T-shirts plastered to you like a second skin. I've seen the way you move, confident, self-contained, as if there was no one else in the world.

"How many men have you driven mad? How many have you teased with your lush body and cool ways? Fire and ice. The cliché must have been intended for you. Were you born like Lilith, with the knowledge to tempt men? Or have you learned from experience that an untouchable woman is a dare?''

He ran a knuckle down her cheek and neck to the round top of her shirt. ''No man walks away from a dare when it's as beautiful as you.'' The tip of his finger rested at the hollow of her throat before dipping beneath her shirt to the cleft between her breasts. Before she could shake off her inertia to protest, he said softly, ''Be careful with your dare, pretty Lilith. You might run into a bad guy like me, who doesn't know the rules of your smug little world, who might not play by your rules.''

''Mr. Canfield...''

''Shh.'' His finger retraced its path, stopping this time at her lips, stroking them with a light touch. A reminder of his kiss. ''I'll see you later. Have a good day.'' He walked to the door with the step of a man accustomed to moving quietly and quickly. With the valley at his back, he paused. His eyes met hers, keeping them.

''My name is David,'' he said, and then he was gone.

''Have a good day! Sure,'' Raven muttered, ripping up a weed with particular relish. The dogs, lying in the shade with their noses buried between their paws, lifted their heads curiously. Raven didn't notice, and in a moment, they returned to snuffling in the dust.

''Fire and ice? Who? A matter of opinion.'' Plucking the last drooping passion flower from its vine, she glared at it accusingly. The irony of its name escaped her. ''Lilith, indeed.''

Shifting gingerly, she rocked back, folding her legs beneath her until her weight left her aching knees.

Looking along the garden rows boasting of neither grass nor weeds, she was astonished at how much she'd done. In the fever of unrequited temper, she'd done two morning's work in one. Brushing the hair that had escaped her braid from her face, she acknowledged the pristine condition of the garden for what it was—proof that her temper was not completely unrequited.

At least it was the garden that reaped the benefit of her rare loss of control. David Canfield hadn't had the smug satisfaction of witnessing a three-alarm spectacle, and her whirlwind invasion of the flowers had put his taunts in their proper perspective. Now, looking down at her favorite gardening shirt, faded and worn, and at jeans that had seen better days, she could laugh. "Lilith? Ha!"

She decided there was nothing like good, hard labor and unladylike sweat to improve one's mood. And she was definitely in a better mood. Pleased with herself and smiling, she started to rise and stopped. Suddenly, as much from the prickling at the back of her neck as from Robbie's perking ears, she knew that David was close. Her breath grew shallow. Her pulse throbbed in her ears. Every sense was heightened, remembering the strength of his arms about her, the desperate hunger in his kiss. The scent of wildflowers, sweet and heady, became the taste of cinnamon.

Kneeling there in the dust, with the sun burning down, she felt the rising flush of heat that had nothing to do with sun or with anger. The trill of sexual attraction, the man-woman awareness, was new to her. She wanted to deny it, but she was too much the realist to fool herself and too honest to try.

She'd been drawn to this stranger, who'd walked

out of the darkness with cruel words on his lips and pain in his eyes. He mystified and tantalized her. His challenging stare rocked her to the core, threatening everything she believed of herself. For whatever reason—because he was a man who had been without a woman too long; because he simply needed a woman, any woman; or because Raven McCandless excited him—he wanted her. It was in every look, every gesture, every harsh word. He wanted her, and it was tearing him apart.

He had kissed her. A kiss begun in anger, leaving no part of her unscathed. A kiss oddly tender beneath the anger. When he stepped away, she found she needed more. That need, not David's brooding hostility, nor his bitter arrogance, was the source of her malaise.

"And what do I do about it?" she asked as she smoothed the soil about a flower for the third time. Busy work, solving nothing, she knew as she forced herself to stop.

The valley was her home, she would not leave it. It seemed imperative, for many reasons, that David remain in the valley. He'd given his word he'd stay. They were locked into an intolerable situation that neither could change. Raven's only recourse was to make the best of it. She must ignore his resentment, hold her temper and conquer what was probably a naive fascination with a sophisticated man of the world.

Control. No matter what he said or did, that was the key to peace. Control, she repeated to herself in grim silence as, with a lift of her head, her gaze collided with David's.

He didn't acknowledge her. He simply stopped

where he walked by the garden's edge. His lean body was taut, his golden brown gaze brooding. Raven smiled at him, a smile meant to reconcile. David's look traced the line of her mouth with a lazy, intimate knowledge. Raven's smile faltered; her lips began to throb with the memory of his kiss. As if he could read her mind and was pleased by her discomfort, he smiled. It was only a subtle quirk of his lips, but she knew exactly what it meant.

He was goading her again, taunting her with his silence and his smile. He wanted to anger her, to splinter her composure. If she were male, he would pick a fight, going toe to toe, spending his rage. Then bloody and battered, happy as a clam, he would step up to the nearest bar and drink himself silly in celebration.

He was out of her league, but she would much prefer the toe-to-toe battle to this war of silent staring. Why should he stay when the valley was so abhorrent? No, she corrected, when *she* was so abhorrent. Simon would release him from his word if she explained how intolerable this was.

Intolerable for both of them. If he wanted a fight, then he would have it and control be damned. Raven tossed her newest resolution aside without a qualm. He was spoiling the valley with his antipathy, and he wouldn't go unchallenged. Anger, rare and white-hot seared her.

Her head snapped back, her gloves were stripped off and thrown like a gauntlet. Her knees hurt. Her shoulders were stiff. Her mind was one dark pain. She hadn't asked for this, any of it. The valley was more than mountains and water. Before David came, it was peace and security and, most of all, the absence of grief. It was her valley. Hers! He would not destroy it.

Anger serves thee not. Rhea McKinzie's voice murmured from the past.

Perhaps not often, Rhea, but this time, it will, Raven answered in her heart.

Before she could rise to charge into the battle she wanted, needed, he was crouching down to her. On his knees in the dirt, with his face only a little above her own, his hands cradled her head, his thumb stroked her cheek. Raven struggled to keep her anger, searched for the words of fury and found they were forgotten.

His eyes strayed to her mouth, lingered. His gentleness disconcerted her. He was as inscrutable as stone, kneeling in the dirt, holding her as if he'd discovered a mysterious treasure. His thumb ceased its stroking and moved over her temple to her forehead. His fingertips trailed down her cheek and jaw, tarrying at the base of her throat.

"What am I going to do with you?" he asked softly. "I came to the valley full of hate, with a burning need for revenge. I didn't want to feel. I didn't want anything or anyone. I'd given my word to Simon that I would put my troubles aside for these three months. I would come to his beloved mountains, I would rest and recuperate, but nothing would divert me."

Snapping a daisy from its stalk, he tucked it in her hair. His gaze was on the flower, concentrating on it. "I hadn't reckoned on Raven McCandless. Proud, strong, beautiful Raven, who beat me at my own game. I invaded your world and found you naked and wet from a swim. I wanted to shame you, yet you never flinched, never gave me that satisfaction. Perhaps the victory's yours, for you were driving me out of my mind. When I was cooler, I realized what I'd done, that I was the intruder in your valley, and I was ashamed.

"Shame isn't an emotion I'm familiar with or that I like. I tried to forget you, and found myself watching you, instead. I knew your schedule. That you're an early riser. Today when you broke your routine, I was certain something was wrong. I told myself you weren't my concern, that I didn't care. All the convincing in the world didn't work. Not even a walk by the lake. I had to know why you were late. I was coming to you when you came running down the trail as if the devil himself were after you. I thought—" he dragged a hand through his hair "—hell, I don't know what I thought. Then I was angry."

"At yourself for caring." Raven's voice was quiet. Once, she'd tried to hate those who made her feel enough to care. She was a long time learning that caring again wasn't disloyal to those who were gone.

"Yes." He didn't lie or evade. Somehow, Raven knew he never would.

"You kissed me to punish me."

"No, I kissed you to punish myself."

Raven nodded. She understood that, too. Compassion stronger than any anger constricted her throat. With her hand, she cupped his cheek. "David."

"Don't!" His grip was like a vise, dragging her hand away. "You don't know the kind of man you're dealing with. I'm only half-civilized. I've seen things and done things…" He loosened his grip, but kept her hand in his. "I've never dealt with a woman like you." Not a woman who looked at him as if she knew his grief and regret, as if she wanted to hold him and ease his anguish. Pity he could fight, but compassion unnerved him. "I don't understand you. I don't want to."

"Stay out of my way. I've apologized one time, and apologies don't come easy for an arrogant bastard like me. So stay out of my way. If you don't—" his gaze settled on her mouth hungrily "—if you don't," he continued hoarsely, "I won't apologize a second time."

"All right," Raven agreed mildly, not bothering to point out that he had come to her, that his apology was one she hadn't wanted. Oh, he was arrogant, all right, and calling him half-civilized might be stretching the point, but he was a good man.

She stood, looking down at him. "I don't know what burr you have under your saddle, but I know you've lost someone and I'm sorry." She stopped, crossing her arms over her breasts in an obdurate gesture. "There, that's not quite an apology, but it's as close as I'm going to come. Apologies come hard for naive, little provincials, too. So there won't be another." As if the digression hadn't occurred, she continued. "Losing hurts. This woman who loved life, maybe you weren't in love with her, but you cared for her. As a friend, a colleague, someone you respected." Raven hesitated, then played a hunch. "There's more to this. Your trouble isn't just the loss of a friend."

"Simon didn't tell me you were a shrink. Where do you hang your shingle?"

"It doesn't take a shrink. Living is more than existing. For some of us, it's sadness, and we become so familiar with it, we learn to see it in others."

"What would you know about living, locked away in a paradise where nothing ever touches you?"

You touched me, David Canfield, she thought.

"Is that why you leave the valley every day, Raven? Is there someone who touches you? Who makes you feel you're a part of the real world? Do you descend into the filth for a while, then come back to this?"

He was taunting her again, trying to drive her away with sarcasm. "Who are you trying to convince that you're a terrible person? Yourself? Me? If it's me, forget it. Heaven knows why, but Simon thinks you're worth salvaging. He sees something in you that you don't see, and at the moment, neither do I. But it's there. I have to believe it is, for Simon's never wrong."

"Simon's nearly twice your age."

"Don't!" She leveled a finger at him. "Don't you dare tarnish what I feel for Simon with your ugly insinuation."

"Then tell me what he is to you."

"The same as to you. A friend who saw something in me worth salvaging." She turned on her heel and without looking back, left him crouching in the dust. The dogs looked curiously from Raven to David before they followed her to her cabin.

David's anger vanished like summer smoke. He felt an irresistible urge to laugh. Not at Raven. At himself. She'd taken his arrogance and turned it back on him. She'd accepted his bitterness as natural, something to be endured, a thing that would pass. She'd been impervious to his insults—until they maligned something she held inviolate. Then she marched away, back straight, eyes flashing, leaving him crouched in the dust like a scolded boy. The thought of being bested by such an innocent drew a silent laugh.

"Hey, sweetheart," he yelled between stifled chuckles. "Your face is dirty."

A hitch developed in Raven's step, a little stutter in her feet. Then she stopped, fists folded at her side, back straight. One deep breath shuddered through her, then a second as she said without turning, "Thank you."

"And she marched up the steps and right out of my life." David had no idea he'd spoken aloud. Lifting a frosted bottle, he drained the last of the beer in three swallows. Leaning back in his chair, with his feet propped on the table before him, he squinted at the label on the dark bottle. "Hell, a man can't even get drunk without a woman." Raven had bought the beer, stocking the cabin with his favorite brand, compliments of Simon.

He wasn't drunk yet. Deep down inside, he knew he wouldn't be. The part of him that had spent too many years protecting his back wouldn't let him. "Even in paradise, I can't relent. Paradise." He shrugged and scowled, then tossed the bottle into the can by his chair, listening as it shattered over its predecessors. He considered going for another and decided it was pointless. Too many careful years.

From the floor, he gathered a sheaf of papers. He'd studied them for hours, checking the log of briefings against the traffic in the offices of The Watch. Who was in? Who was out? Who could've breached Simon's legendary security? The answer was always the same. No one. Only he and Helen and Simon were present the day the ill-fated mission was planned. The rest of Simon's people were scattered over the world on assignments.

"Who knew? And how?" Before coming to the valley, he'd studied the papers until he knew them from memory, and the answer was always the same. No one. Yet there had to be something in these records, something he was missing. Tomorrow, he'd call Simon to ask for other files. Perhaps they would hold the answer, and perhaps then he could concentrate.

He flung the papers aside. "Who do I think I'm kidding?" Sure he knew exactly what was in the papers, but he had gleaned little from them lately. For three days, since he invited her to stay out of his way, he'd thought of nothing but Raven.

Following the confrontation in her garden, Saturday had passed quickly as he busied himself with the chores a solitary man must do to exist. On Sunday, he copped a book from Simon's collection on law, reading only long enough to remember why he hadn't gone into law. For the rest of the day, he prowled the house and later, the trails. Once, he glimpsed Raven running, with Robbie and Kate dancing at her heels. On Monday, her routine began again and she left the valley, driving a four-wheel-drive vehicle with an exotic name that looked as if a hard breath would blow it off the mountain.

David, who'd spent the majority of his life alone, was inexplicably lonely.

Today was no better. The valley was filled with a hollow silence. As he had every day, he worked and studied, learning nothing, absorbing less. Then, desperate to put her out of his mind, he ran, blazing new trails over the valley floor and scaling the mountainside. Thorns tore at his clothing, leaves caught in his hair, a scattering stone bruised his ankle. He was a demon, ranging the land, unfeeling, uncaring, driving himself to exhaustion. When he stumbled back to the cabin, he was soaked with sweat, every muscle ached and his mind was at ease.

He'd worked then, managing to accomplish more than before. In telephone logs recording incoming and outgoing calls at the office of The Watch, he found one from Helen's desk to a strange number. A date? A doctor's appointment? David shrugged. It could've been anything, even a call made by someone else using her phone. Except, when he double checked the date, he found no one was in the office but Simon and Helen and himself. So she had definitely broken the rules and made a personal call. Not exactly a smart move, but it had been done before.

He had been making a note to have the number traced when Raven's ridiculous little car had clattered into the valley and it began all over again.

She'd hurried into her cabin, a bag of groceries in her arms. Next, she was in the garden, a basket over her arm, a pair of shears in her hand. She hadn't changed, and as she strolled the rows of flowers, she bore little resemblance to the woman he remembered grubbing in the dirt. In her slim, snug skirt and softly ruffled blouse, she was cool perfection, but strangely not ill-matched with the wild profusion of her garden. As he walked to the cooler to get his first beer, he'd wondered how many people Raven McCandless was.

From that point, the evening went downhill. He found himself lurking near the windows like a voyeur, catching glimpses as she loped across a meadow with Robbie and Kate, and brought a sheaf of papers from her car. Once, when she hauled a heavy box from the trunk and lugged it across the yard, he was tempted to offer his help. But with a particularly caustic expletive, he remembered he was the one who insisted they coexist separately. So he watched, feeling like a jerk as she struggled up the stairs and out of sight.

All right. Fine. It was nearly dark, she would stay in for the night. Out of sight, out of mind. The cliché was a joke and he knew it, but he'd settled down with one of Simon's books, this time a novel. He'd read the same page twice when he heard the soft slam of her door. The moon was full, and he hadn't a doubt where she was going.

She would wear a swimsuit in deference to his presence in the valley. "And look damn good," he had muttered, opening the second beer and the third, and then lost count. None had erased the image of her as he'd first seen her: lost in a rippling pool of mirrored moons; laughing like a child in secret delight; rising on the dock like Aphrodite, with her body silvered and shimmering with water. Breasts swaying gently with each move. Her waist curving delicately into the flare of her narrow hips. The fall of her dark hair as she rose, arms outstretched, worshiping the night like a pagan.

He sat, unable to work for every detail, every nuance and line was etched into his mind. "Everything," he muttered as he went for another beer after all, giving the label a baleful look, reminded of Raven's kindness.

Raven! Everywhere he turned, it was Raven. Lifting the bottle in a toast to the source of his misery, he gulped its contents down in one try. "In this, the year of our Lord, nineteen..." He couldn't remember the year, and knew he was farther gone than he thought. "In this, the year of our Lord, nineteen what-ever, David Canfield, spy *extraordinaire,* lost his mind."

He chuckled at his foolishness and was sober enough to wonder if tomorrow, when the hangover hit, would he still think it was funny. The retribution that awaited him sent him into a second fit of laugh-ter.

A sound cleaved through his laughter. He cocked his head as if trying to identify it, but he knew it was the sound he'd been waiting for, Raven's door closing quietly. Her swim was done. She was back, safe within the walls of her home.

David didn't realize until that moment how anxious he'd been. She was maddening and enchanting, and it worried the hell out of him that she swam alone in a lake that was cold on the hottest of days. It was absurd to worry. By her own admission, she'd been swimming in the lake alone at night long before he arrived. When he was gone, she would swim.

"So quit your worrying, fool." Before the words were out of his mouth, he knew he couldn't. Perhaps it was his punishment for coming into her valley like a raiding cossack, trampling over the tranquil life she'd made for herself. Maybe the loneliness he felt was the price he must pay for slapping a hand that had offered only friendship.

"That can be remedied." Then, "Of course, it can." Tossing the bottle aside, he made his decision. He brushed away the stench of beer and splashed wa-ter on his face. When his hair was carefully combed, he selected a fresh shirt and slid into it. No sense looking and reeking like a tramp when he wanted to make peace with a lady.

Before he could have second thoughts, he was out the door, down the steps and halfway across the adjoining yards. At her first step, he hesitated. It wouldn't work. She hated him. If she didn't, she should. His gaze fell on the rows of flowers, their colors muted, made more striking in the moonlight. They would be his peace offering.

When he knocked on her door, he carried a randomly chosen bouquet of Raven's own flowers. The door opened, slowly. He braced himself. It would serve him right if she slammed it in his face.

Instead, she stood framed by the light at her back, hands on her hips. She had dressed in a loose caftan, one of the one-size-fits-all sort. If camouflage had been her intent, the soft, clinging fabric defeated her.

"David," she said after an interminable time. "Are you going to come in, or do you prefer standing there all night?"

"I was afraid you might slam the door in my face."

"I was considering it."

"But you didn't." Her hair was still damp from her swim. Memories flooded his mind.

"No, I didn't." She smiled at him and moved aside.

David stepped past her and was assailed by the scent of baking bread.

"I suppose those are for me." Raven gestured to the haphazard bouquet.

"A peace offering."

"I see." She studied him solemnly, then burst out laughing. "Only David Canfield would be so arrogant as to bring me my own flowers as an olive branch."

Her laughter held the same note of delight that had once drifted over the water. David relaxed and let his gaze glide through the room, over the mildly cluttered desk and a lovely collection of pottery, to a small table before a window overlooking the lake. "Your table, it's set for two." Crystal and silver gleamed beneath the candle surrounded by flowers. David rarely bothered with possessions. His life and work forbade it, but he knew simple elegance when he saw it.

"It is, isn't it?" Raven looked up from arranging his flowers, her flowers, in a vase.

"You were expecting company."

"Not expecting. Hoping."

"I don't think you need worry on that score. If it tastes half as good as it smells."

"Are you hungry, David?"

He started to deny it, but decided that if this was to be a new beginning, he would be as honest as he knew how. "My cooking isn't exactly the greatest."

"Then join me."

Surprise leapt in his face. When he crossed the yard, the most he was hoping for was that she wouldn't slug him. "What about the guest you were expecting?"

"Hoping, David," she corrected as she set the flowers on a counter. "I was hoping you would join me for dinner."

"Me! Why?" He couldn't quite believe that she was standing there, more lovely than any woman on earth, asking him to sit at her table as if they were friends.

She looked at his flowers and smiled again. "Shall we call it my peace offering?"

"You knew I was coming over?"

"That was the last thing I expected. When you knocked at the door, I was coming to you."

I was coming to you. The phrase brought a vision that had nothing to do with dinner. He dragged his thoughts back from dangerous ground. "You're asking an arrogant, insulting bastard to have dinner with you?"

"No. I'm asking the man who brought me flowers." She put her hands on her hips, pulling the fullness of her caftan close to her body. "Are you going to accept my invitation?"

"If you'll tell me why you bothered."

Raven gestured eloquently, her bosom rising beneath the azure silk. "I think because I like you."

"Why in hell would you like me?" David asked, remembering the insults, the cruelties.

"Only God knows that, and maybe Simon. After all, he sent you here." Raven slid her arm through David's. "When I figure it out for myself, I'll tell you." With a smile that wiped the slate clean and signaled a new beginning, she led him to the table.

Three

David looked over the book he was reading, his gaze following his thoughts to Raven. For an hour, he'd tried to concentrate on a rambling tale of science fiction. The week, this night, Raven, disturbed him. Since the initial dinner, their first real step toward peaceful coexistence, their evenings had become routine. They began with dinner, followed by a stroll by the lake, then desultory conversation until Raven at her easel or he with his book began to droop and yawn.

Routines were dangerous. One became complacent. Restless caution grew tame. The edge that could mean survival was lost. He'd survived the streets, jungle warfare and The Watch by resisting routine.

Until now. Until Raven. She intrigued him. When his guard slipped, she made him comfortable. Mystery and comfort—an intoxicating mix more dangerous than routine.

Tonight, the routine changed. No aimless walk. No conversation. Raven was quiet, shunning her painting for clay. It was the first time she'd worked with the clay at a small, worn potter's table.

As he watched, her flashing fingers shaped the clay like magic. In a pool of light, with shadows playing over her features, she was pensive. The mass took form, and silent tension gradually vanished, as if the clay had drawn it from her. This quiet intensity, the channeling of her strength fascinated him. He'd known her for weeks, and each day, there were new facets, half revealed, half hidden.

It was the mystery that kept drawing him back. Each day, he promised there would be no more of such evenings. Each evening, after a day in the valley without her, he found himself waiting for the invitation he knew would come. And as ever, as tonight, he didn't refuse. Couldn't refuse, he admitted and looked away.

The room was like her. Warm, welcoming, a place to ease one's troubles. A room that gave but did not take. That, too, like Raven.

But what troubles could there be for her in her mountain paradise? he wondered as she set aside her work. "Finished?" he asked, admitting his vast ignorance.

Raven glanced up in surprise, as if she'd forgotten he was there. A shake of her head sent her hair tumbling over her shoulder. "It isn't finished. Tomorrow it will dry in the sun, after that, I'll paint it with a slip."

"Slip?" David laid his book down, more interested in the play of light over her face than in the answer.

"Clay in liquid form," she explained. The clay, smooth and nearly black, bore her signature, the flowering dogwood. "For this, I think, a white slip of kaolin."

"White on black?"

"White on white. Eventually. Before the slip dries, it will be polished with river stones. Then, perhaps I'll paint a design before it's fired, perhaps not. In the firing, the black clay will become white, the kaolin will stay true."

"White on white."

"Yes."

"If you paint it, what design will you choose?"

"The lines of the vessel determine its design."

"Sounds very artistic."

Raven shook her head again. "Not really. Only therapeutic. Working with the clay was one of many things Rhea McKinzie taught me. The table, the tools and the methods I use were hers. When she was troubled, she would sit for hours, working the clay, pouring her worries into it."

"As you did tonight."

Taking a wet cloth from the table, Raven rubbed it over her hands, cleansing the last remnants of clay from them. "Yes," she admitted. "As I did tonight."

"It's hard to conceive that a problem could create something such as this." He gestured toward the clay. The word *pretty* came to mind and was discarded. The work was too strong, too striking to be only pretty. *Handsome* was one description. *Masculine* another. Did her thoughts guide her hands? Was there a man beyond the valley that had driven her to pour her troubles into the clay as Rhea McKinzie had?

David felt something ugly and alien twist in his gut. "Is this man worth so much agonizing?"

Raven followed his gaze, as if seeing the vessel for the first time. It was solid and stark, and if clay could be attributed gender, it was masculine. David Canfield was surprisingly perceptive. "Both men are worth it."

The ugliness lashed at him. Irrational anger rose in his throat like acid, driving him to his feet. *Jealousy!* He drew a slow, deep breath to calm himself. It didn't work. Good Lord! It was true. He was jealous of a stranger. Two strangers. He had to know. "Why? Why do they matter?"

Raven was startled by the hardness of his tone. "The McLachlans are a fine family. Thanks to Dare, the eldest. He raised all three of his brothers. Half brothers," she corrected. "Alone and with unrelenting Scot stubbornness, he made them into fine young men. Now that very stubbornness is threatening to tear the family apart."

"What form does this destruction take?" David's drawl was laced with distaste. "Two men, or worse, two brothers, in love with the same woman?"

"I beg your pardon?" Raven lifted her eloquent hands, gesturing that she didn't understand.

David took a step closer. "That is how it goes, isn't it? The classic triangle, two men, one woman."

"A woman?" Raven was truly puzzled. Then, "I'm sure Jamie could have plenty of women friends or lovers, and so could Dare. But at the moment, their problem isn't a woman. I wish it were that simple."

"What could be more complicated than a woman?"

"Honor. Love. Ambition. One man's dreams for another. Dare's for Jamie. Jamie's a gifted pianist, but he wants nothing more than he wants to be a tree farmer like Dare. Dare won't hear of it. He's determined that Jamie won't throw away his talent. Both are so hotheaded, neither will even try to compromise. Jamie's young. This is his first year at the college. If Dare would just listen."

"Jamie is a student?" David interrupted. "And his brother, Dare, is a farmer?"

"Jamie McLachlan is eighteen. Dare is thirty-eight. He's the one who should be cooler and wiser."

"A student and a farmer," David said, then he chuckled. "A farmer and a student." The chuckle became laughter, the sound of relief. A pimply faced kid and a grizzled backwoodsman. Laughter dwindled into a grin as his eyes met Raven's.

"It isn't funny," she said mildly. "Dare's a proud man, and he wants more for Jamie than he had himself. He just can't see that Jamie doesn't want it. Not yet. Maybe never. If they can't resolve this or at least call a truce, their brothers, Ross and Robert Bruce, will be drawn into it."

"Why do you care so much, Raven?" Laughter vanished before the onslaught of more primitive emotions.

Raven hesitated. There was something different in his voice. She'd never heard him say her name in quite that way, a tone that made her breath catch in her throat and her mouth go dry. He was moving toward her, his steps deliberate. Nothing had overtly changed. He was the image of easy civility, but with every step, she sensed restless excitement, seething, barely tethered. The air was suddenly charged with it, prickling up and down her skin, setting her heart into a ragged rhythm.

"I care because a family is too precious to stand idly by and watch it be destroyed," she whispered, grasping absently at the original train of her thoughts. What was between them now had nothing to do with Jamie or Dare McLachlan.

He watched her watch him, seeing the tilt of her head, the lifting of her chin, feeling her eyes on his. At the table, he stopped. Her face was turned to him, away from the lamp where she worked. Only her hands were under the light. They were strong and rough, the nails short. Capable hands, talented hands. When she'd risen out of the lake, he had thought her hands did not suit her. Now he knew he was wrong.

Peaceful days and quiet evenings were forgotten, wiped from memory as if they'd never happened. The easiness, the comfort were gone. In their place was seething hunger and desire. "Did you think you would tame me, Raven? Draw me into your life. Feed me. Show me the kind of life I've never had. Will never have." He touched her hand, then drew away. "These aren't the hands of Lilith. Lilith could never have entranced me so."

He made a low, wordless sound. "Do you know how I felt when I thought you were troubled by a lover?" He didn't wait for her answer. He needed none, for it was in her eyes.

His chest rose in a slow, deep breath. His growl held no humor. "You have no idea, do you? Just as you hadn't known—" He broke off abruptly, only to begin again. "You were content sitting with me here, night after night. Too contented to know that you were driving me out of my mind.'' He traced the line of her cheek. His gaze locked with hers, seeing the knowledge in them. "But you know now, don't you?''

"I know.''

She didn't flinch, didn't blush, didn't look away. He wanted to annihilate that rigid control, to see her fevered with passion. "I've fought this, Raven McCandless. From the moment I saw you, I've fought it.

"Night and day. No matter what I did, you were in my thoughts.'' His hand slid into her hair, gathering it roughly in his fist. "There are times when the only way to win the battle is not to fight anymore.''

Then Raven was rising, willingly or with the pressure of his hand, he didn't know which. His mind was too full of the scent of her. He ached too much for the sweetness of her mouth to care.

He felt her shiver, heard the rush of a sigh. As his lips came down on hers, she murmured, "I was never contented.''

David's kiss was fierce, demanding. And Raven discovered she could no more reject his demand than she could escape the strong, warm prison of his arms. His hand in her hair tugged her head back, exposing her throat. His mouth was hot as it moved over her tender flesh. He drew her closer, and Raven gasped as every line of his body branded hers. Desire, rampant and new, swept over her. She moved against him, wanting more.

David went very still, not even daring to breathe. Raven turned her head only the little his grasp of her hair would allow. Her lips brushed his in a whisper-soft touch. A low groan shuddered through him, and he kissed her again. His lips slanted over hers, thirsting. Her mouth was sweet wine when she opened it to him.

Raven felt herself falling, spiraling down into a land where she'd never been. Where there were needs stronger than all she believed or thought or wanted. She was afraid, not of David, but of Raven McCandless. She was frightened, but fear was no match for his desperate lust or the desire that had needed only his kiss to awaken. Her hands caught in his hair as she met fury with fury, demand with demand and found them answered. He was wildfire, burning away the last shred of caution. She writhed in his arms, clung to him, whimpered when she could not be a part of him.

"Raven?" Shaken, he took a step back, holding her shoulders, keeping that little distance of sanity. His gaze touched the tangled hair, the bruised, pouting mouth, met the heavy-lidded look of desire. Her breasts rose in a ragged breath, but she didn't look away. She wanted him and couldn't hide it. As he'd wanted her from the first.

He'd tried to despise her for what she was, for the comfortable, parasitic life she represented. He had disavowed his male needs. Each day and each night, he had struggled, fighting himself, Raven and the inevitable. Yet, deep inside himself, he'd known.

He was wrong for her. She for him. He was a disciplined man. His mind ruled his heart and body. Reason over lust. But not now. He could no longer deny himself. He wouldn't fight a battle lost before it began.

Bending, he swept her from her feet. Spinning, he

walked to the door he knew led to her bedroom. His foot against it sent it splintering from its latch and colliding with the wall. Stepping inside, he spared no glance for the Spartan comfort that spoke of Raven.

He thought only of a woman more desirable than any. Setting her on her feet, he held her to him, steadying her as she swayed. As he brushed the tangle of her hair from her face, she smiled at him like a sleepy child. In the light of a lamp only as bright as a candle, her eyes were drowsy and full of trust. He almost left her then. He almost walked out her door, out of her valley and her life forever. Until he remembered the lake and moonlight and Raven rising from it like a goddess. Until he remembered her soft whisper.

I was never contented.

The last threads of sanity slipped beyond him as he reached for the first button of her shirt. His finger skimmed her skin in his task, feeling the throb of her heart in every part of her. "You're trembling."

"I know," she murmured, the words catching in a ragged staccato as the last button slipped free and his hands slid beneath the soft fabric to cup her bare breasts.

His fingers were rough, but his touch was gentle. Their slow, soothing stroke taking the weight of her softness, lifting, caressing, always stopping at the verge of her tender, aching nipples. The back of his hands trailed down her sides and over her midriff. His thumb raked the fold where breasts lay gentle over ribs. The fine down on his hands was like a thousand caresses, honing Raven's senses to a razor's edge. The slightest contact sent ripples of excitement quivering through her. He was teasing her. Tormenting her as she wondered wildly how torment could be so sweet.

Raven grasped his shoulders, her nails digging into the heavy muscles for support. Her body arched, her breasts lifted, offering their rose crests to his touch. But David denied her. With his palms, he followed the path he had before. Down her side and over her midriff. The hard, callused palms were hot. They burned a trail over her body, always teasing, never satisfying, driving her further into the madness. She had never needed a man to touch her as she needed David to touch her. She wanted to plead with him for more, but all she could manage was simply, "David."

With his eyes still holding hers, he brushed the long, flowing shirt from her shoulders. In a languid, unhurried motion he let it fall to the floor. Slowly, he stroked her throat, his hand sweeping over her naked shoulders and the sides of her breasts, stopping there, holding their swell. "Lovely Raven," he whispered. "Always so reserved, so untouchable. Until now. Tell me what you want."

Raven couldn't bear his gaze. Her lashes drifted over the dark mystery of her eyes. She was trembling when she cried, "I can't."

His thumbs moved over her breasts, circling the aureole, stroking the hard bud of her nipples. "Is it this, sweet Raven?"

"Yes." She arched against his hands. "Yes."

"Or is it this?" He leaned to her, taking her into his mouth.

Raven had no answer. Her head was thrown back, her curved body undulating with his suckling. The gentle nip of his teeth nearly drove her to her knees. Her grasp strained at his shoulders, her nails flayed his skin. Tomorrow, there would be blisters of blood, like banners, over his shoulders. But Raven didn't know the damage her desperate effort not to fall at his feet had done. "David, please."

His head lifted from her body. His eyes found hers again. As he wiped the sheen of sweat from her forehead, he said again, "Tell me what you want."

With her body cooling from his caress, Raven could only shake her head. "I don't know."

"Don't you, Raven?" He shook her gently. "We both know you're too old to play the innocent."

"I don't know. I don't."

"Stop. If I must play the game to have you," he said roughly, "then we'll play the game."

"No game." Coherent thought was beyond her now. "No game. I've never—"

"Don't." His hand closed over her mouth briefly. "Don't make a fool of yourself. I don't care how many lovers you've had. Not now," he murmured as anger added to the power of his desire. "Not ever."

Raven wanted to speak, to tell him his mistake, but as his head bent to her, she forgot everything but David. Then he was kneeling before her, sliding her jeans from her hips.

"You're a beautiful woman, Raven McCandless. Here." He stroked her breasts lightly, moving quickly away. "And here." He touched her midriff, trailing a fingertip over her navel to the lace of her panties. "And here." His hand moved lower. When Raven shuddered and swayed, he was rising to catch her. "Beautiful women need legions of lovers, worshipers at the shrine of beauty. Tonight, there will be only one."

When Raven was capable of thought again, she was naked, lying on her bed, waiting for David.

He had called her beautiful, cruelly and viciously, making it an insult. As she lay tousled and a little drunk with passion, he regretted his sarcasm. There was an untouched aura about her that even sultry sensuality couldn't tarnish. She was two people. The innocent who trembled as if his touch were her first; the proud siren who stood before him half-clothed, challenging every male instinct. Which woman was she? Either or both, for just this night, she was his.

Lifting the hem of his shirt, he ripped it from his body. He'd loosened his belt when he caught a glimpse of himself in the shadowed mirror over her dressing table. The man he saw bore little resemblance to the David Canfield he thought he knew. His hair was disheveled, his face flushed and grim: the cool chameleon of The Black Watch, driven to madness by a woman.

David was suddenly, unexpectedly afraid for her. Afraid of what a man who had never known gentleness might do to a woman whose life had been nothing else. "Raven." His voice was a rasp, his eyes on the stranger in the mirror. "Stop me. Tell me to go away, and I will."

"I can't tell you to go away." Her voice rose from the bed in a whispery rush.

"Then tell me you don't want me. Before it's too late."

"It's already too late." The truth. Always from Raven.

"I'm mad, Raven. I don't know what I'm doing or what I'm saying." He turned from the mirror, the sight of her sweeping everything from his mind. His hand went again to his belt. A zipper rasped, then he was naked.

He moved from the dark into the light, and Raven gasped. A sliver of moonlight slanted through the window, painting his body with a silver sheen. He was light and darkness. She hadn't known that beauty and such utter maleness could be the same. He called her beautiful, but it was he who was beautiful. Long, lean thighs rippled as he came to her. His chest heaved, drawing the flesh over corrugated abdomen and ribs. David lived hard, worked hard, expecting no reward beyond survival. His body, aroused and hungry for her, was testament to that life. To survival.

This, too, was survival, she thought as he stood by the bed, looking down at her. Without him, here, now, she would surely die. Raven laughed softly at her melodrama, a lovely, irresistible sound as she lifted her arms to him.

He let her draw him down to her, sinking into her embrace. He kissed her, stroked her, meaning to tease and torment. He wanted to drive her as mad as he, shattering completely the cool control. But there was no control to shatter. She was a whirlwind. Untamed, unpredictable, matching him kiss for kiss, caress for caress, tumbling fiercely with him over lavender-scented sheets.

Rising over him, she caught both his hands in one of hers. Holding them captive with only the strength of her wish not to be distracted by his touch, she explored his body. And she watched him as if she were just learning what would please and excite a man. Where her fingers trailed, her lips followed.

He felt the shudder begin in the pit of his stomach, spreading to every nerve and sinew. He was near the end. It was her torment that was complete. Clasping her wrists, he tumbled her to her back. With her hands pinned beside her head he kept them from their lethal forays. "Enough," he growled. Then more softly, "Dear God! Enough!"

"Enough," Raven echoed, her voice unsteady.

He came down to her, his hard body covering hers. He was trembling when he sought the final release. His brutal hunger would hurt her, and in a lucid moment, he knew he must be gentle. With agonizing care that was nearly his undoing, he let the searing heat of her enfold him slowly. Still, Raven recoiled and cried out.

David froze, the motion of his body ceasing. Knowledge, truth, but too late. When he would've drawn away, Raven arched against him and their joining was complete.

"No!" David cried. "Damn you, no." But even as he cursed her, she was drawing him down, moving against him until he was lost. "Damn you." The hoarse chant accompanied the pulsing of their bodies. "Damn you." Exquisite pleasure exploded within him. "Raven."

The moon moved beyond the window, but for the tiny pool of light beneath the lamp, the room was in darkness. They slept and woke, and, exhausted, slept again. Each time they came together, the fever in David grew torrid and Raven's response wanton. As dawn was breaking, sleep for once eluded him. He lay bound to Raven by the web of her hair, staring at the ceiling, wondering what in hell he'd done.

The night replayed in his mind. Every detail, every nuance excruciatingly clear. He saw her body trembling from his touch, and his fingers pulsed with the memory. His lungs were filled with her, his mouth with the taste of her kiss. His body ached in a most satisfying way from his use of hers.

Use. That's what he meant it to be. An exorcism, a cure. A victory. He'd been so certain, he hadn't listened, discounting her protests of innocence before she could make them. He'd been so cruel, so sure, and it hadn't mattered. She'd given herself to him with no restraints, with no questions of the past, no bargaining for the future. In the aftermath, in an unguarded moment, languid with pleasure, she spoke of love.

Love.

The word forced David from her bed. Raven stirred, reached for the space where he'd been, and whimpered in her sleep. He looked down at her, feeling trapped. He didn't doubt her. A woman of thirty, a virgin in a time when virginity meant little, would give it only to the man she loved.

He didn't want her love. Love was a burden, a trap. Sacrifice. He wanted no part of it. None! He wanted to snatch her from the bed and shake some sense into her. He wanted to make her hate him so much, she would forget this foolishness of love. With fists clenched and his naked body taut, he glared down at her. He wanted..God help him...he wanted to kiss her.

"Fool!" The word was a snarl as he snatched his clothes from the floor and stalked from the room.

Raven sighed, stretching every sore limb deliciously. She felt wonderful. No day was as beautiful. So this was what sex was all about. She laughed. If she'd known it was quite like this, she would've tried it long ago. No, she wouldn't, she amended, for she'd been waiting for David.

Rolling into the spot where he'd lain, she pretended she felt his warmth and wished he was with her.

Making love, she thought happily. It was truly that.

She stretched again, loving every ache from sleeping entwined. Though she hadn't wakened when he left her, she had known. Now, she wanted to find him. He'd been away too long.

"Whoops!" She swayed dizzily as she stood and clung to the tall bedpost. Can't be pregnant. Not this soon. Although she knew it was a very real possibility. Precautions were not an integral part of her life. And David hadn't been prepared. She glanced at the clock by the bedside. She could be six or four or three hours pregnant. She grinned beneath a blush at the thought of the times.

A sturdy little boy with David's sherry-colored eyes. A little girl to tease the solemn look from his face. A child. Fruit of their loving. Raven threw back her head and laughed, a happy sound drawn from a perfect world.

Scooping up her shirt from where he'd dropped it, she slipped into it. Not bothering with buttons or worrying that the garment barely reached her thighs, she hurried to David.

He was in her kitchen, sitting on the window seat, staring out at the lake with one knee drawn up, his wrist resting on it. In one hand was a cup of coffee. Dangling between the fingers of the other was a cigarette. She stopped in the doorway, reveling in the luxury of watching him.

He was combed and dressed, his shirt neatly tucked

into his jeans, his canvas shoes laced and tied. Untouched, she thought. As if last night never happened. She looked down at her rumpled shirt hanging open over her bare body. It had. She laughed giddily. Very definitely, it had.

He turned at the sound. Raven waited for him to speak. She smiled, but David's solemn face didn't change. Lifting the cigarette to his lips, he inhaled and exhaled slowly. Through a haze of smoke, he watched her. Raven felt that stare as if it were his caressing hand. Pavlovian desires. David looked; she responded. A conditioned reflex. A wonderful reflex.

"Good morning," she said at last, certain he could read what she was feeling in her face.

"Is it?" He looked away grinding the cigarette out in the ashtray beside him. When he looked back at her, a trick of the light turned his eyes cold.

"I thought…" She hesitated, shaking her head. She didn't know what she thought.

He stood, setting his cup aside, and moved toward her, slowly, stalking his prey. "What did you think, Raven?" He asked almost too softly. "That we would fall into bed, then live happily together forever? It doesn't work that way. Not for me. Love!" He said the word as if it were a curse. "A burden, lady, a trap. It puts responsibility and guilt on people who don't need it. Helen Landon died in a South American jungle because she thought she loved me. I didn't ask for it. I didn't want it." He was closer now, and Raven saw the light had nothing to do with the coldness in him. "Just as I didn't want anything from you except a quick tumble between the sheets."

Raven's throat was dry. She couldn't speak, but if she could, what would she say? She wanted to look away, but his hand suddenly cupping her chin prevented it. The utter contempt she saw in him turned shock to churning sickness. It took every bit of strength, dragged from the bottom of her soul, to face his scorn.

"You were good, baby. The best." His lips formed a cruel caricature of a smile as a finger trailed down the edge of her open shirt, drawing a line of fire that nearly took her breath away. His hand splayed over her belly. "Your little surprise means nothing to me. You sacrificed your precious virginity on the wrong man."

Anger did what shock and pain couldn't. She was glacially calm when she grasped his wrist, drawing his hand from her body. "You knew. I told you."

"A woman says a lot of things in the heat of the moment."

"Yes." She released his wrist almost nonchalantly. "Particularly when her teacher is as skilled as David Canfield. I won't be so naive next time, with the next man." She might have been standing fully clothed, speaking of something as unimportant as a minor disagreement. "I should thank you for the lesson in the etiquette of one-night stands, as well as for relieving me of the burden of virginity. You've taught me how good uncomplicated sex can be. You made me good because you're good," she parroted him. "The best yet, in my limited experience."

"Damn you!" His fists were clenched, not against the cool assessment of his performance, but in mercuric and unreasoning anger at the specter of Raven with another man.

"You've damned me rather thoroughly already," Raven said calmly. Turning from him, she walked to the door and opened it. "If you'll leave, I can get dressed. I have a great deal to do today."

She was magnificent, standing in the doorway. Proud, beautiful, so remote, he wondered if he'd imagined the woman who had been a flame in arms. A strange sadness—for the hurt he caused, for the love he didn't want—tempered his anger. "It would be best if I left the valley, but I gave Simon my word."

"And you always keep your word." She didn't mock him. She had too much class to stoop to mockery.

"Yes," he said simply. Then he felt compelled to add bitterly, "There were times when my word was all I had. If it's of no value, then neither am I."

"Keep your word. Stay in the valley, but leave me."

"Raven..."

"No apologies." She was as frigid as a winter night.

"No apology," he agreed. Wondering if it were not he who was damned, he stepped past her and out of her life.

Raven didn't watch him leave. She couldn't. Closing the door on the sight of him, she sagged against the wood. After a moment, the shaking stopped. With her palms flat against the door, she pushed away from it. Collecting herself, she straightened.

She'd been a fool. She faced the fact with the honesty that was as necessary to her life as her heartbeat. She'd given her body and with it, her heart, to a man who hated her. There were many things she would regret—her innocence, his enmity, her reckless assumptions. But not the giving. Never that. No matter how naive she'd been, a part of her knew no man would ever make love to her as David.

"No regrets," she murmured.

Never. Yet there was one thing she must know. Crossing to the telephone, she dialed a number. After a time, without preamble, she spoke into the receiver. "Simon, classified information of The Watch or not, I must know about Helen Landon."

As Simon began to speak, she settled into a chair to listen.

Four

Raven sat before her potter's table. The last of the natural light streamed through the open door. Her idle hands were folded loosely about a polishing stone. A white slip dried, unnoticed, on a clay pot. She'd begun with the intention of readying it for the kiln, but as with all her tasks of late, her hands grew still as her mind drifted. Simon spoke in her thoughts as clearly as he had days ago over the telephone.

Helen Landon? he had repeated, buying time, gathering his thoughts, as Raven had heard him do so often.

Yes, Simon, Helen Landon. She'd been patient. With Simon it was the only way. He would not be hurried.

Then David hasn't told you.

If he had, Simon, I wouldn't be bothering you.

Your voice, from the tone of it... It's not going so good, this thing with David?

She had paused, searching for an easy answer, then settled for blunt honesty. *No.*

I'm sorry, Raven. I didn't mean this.

It's too late for apologies, Simon. Just tell me about Helen Landon.

Then Simon began to speak, not of Helen, but of David as he'd been, as he was.

He was a special kid. Came from a hard-working middle-class family that if it had any luck at all, it was bad. The father's health failed. An expensive illness. Lost his business, his house. Moved to a poor neighborhood, taking nothing but his pride. The mother managed to provide the necessities with nothing left over for their only son's future. No training, no college. But they gave him a good home and instilled in him their old-fashioned ideals. He grew up tough in a tough neighborhood, but their teachings survived. Longer than either of them. David was alone and barely of age for the wind down in Vietnam. He was quick and responsible, and he moved up in the ranks. When he came to my attention, he was still new enough that he continued to cling to his idealism.

When Simon paused, the soft roll of his burr dying away, she prompted him, wanting to hear more. Much more. *He was special, an idealist, and you recruited him for yourself?*

For The Watch. He was the first.

And the best?

Yes, Raven. The best.

An idealist with a conscience. A rare breed for The Watch.

Rare and good. The Watch has a conscience, it must. Most just suspend it at times. But not David. It made him the best—and nearly destroyed him.

She had struggled with anger she had no right to feel. *You had to know what it was doing to him, Simon.*

I knew. I've watched the light go out of his eyes and the smile that could melt hearts disappear. And still, I gave him every ugly assignment.

Because David would do it and do it well, no matter what it did to him. Was it worth it?

Yes. Simon, unequivocally honest to the last.

It was worth a man's soul?

At the time, yes.

And now?

He was quiet for so long Raven had begun to think the connection had been severed. Then she heard a weary sigh and Simon was speaking again.

I wouldn't have done this to him if it weren't worth it.

A gentle rebuke. *I know, Simon. I think I only wanted to hear you say it.*

David's seen terrible things and done terrible things. It takes its toll on a man with his conscience.

As Helen Landon did?

She was young and new to the job, and a little starry-eyed, but she was good. David was the best in the business. As a rule, he worked alone, but this time, he needed a partner. They made a good team.

David said she loved him.

Yeah, I guess she did.

He didn't love her?

Raven had to ask, though she knew the answer.

What happened to David, the disillusionment, the

anger, was already brewing. Helen's death was only the catalyst. He would've regretted losing her, but another time, under other circumstances, it wouldn't have thrown him into a tailspin. People die in our business, Raven, and we grieve for a time, then go on.

How could this happen to him?

The answer to that, honey, is because he's David. Simon launched into a narrative of David and all he'd done. As if it were catharsis for his own soul, the story poured out. Raven was concerned, then she realized there were no particulars. Simon was not revealing confidential information. He spoke of accomplishments and their emotional toil, of burnout. He ended with David's last mission.

They were betrayed. The guerillas were waiting for them. Helen was taken prisoner. There was information she could have given them that would harm David.

But she didn't. Even when they hurt her. The love Raven knew he didn't want.

David took her from them. Then he stayed with her.

Until she died. The intolerable sacrifice, leaving unbearable guilt.

Weary regret had roughened Simon's voice. *David came out of the jungle alone.*

Raven hadn't needed specifics. No one had to tell her how terrible it was for Helen. For David, waiting, knowing why she was dying. For Simon who sent her.

It was the last straw, Raven. He turned his back on everything he believed in.

He's going after the one responsible on his own. Beyond the law, if he has to. And you can't stand by and let him do it.

No, if he does... Raven, David's only a step away from becoming a renegade. We can't let that happen.

Is that what you do, Simon? Take a man, a special man, exploit him, turn him into a machine. Then when he's in trouble, do you hunt him down like an animal?

Nobody's hunting David down. Not while I'm alive.

David's only trouble is that he feels guilty for living.

As you did.

Until you brought me here, and with Rhea, made me see that it wasn't wrong to live. Suddenly, everything had become crystal clear. *That's why you sent him to me, isn't it Simon? To do for him what you did for me.*

She'd heard only his breathing, harsh and slow over the phone lines. He was remembering a dear, dying friend bequeathing a child to him. She had waited, listening to the hollow silence until he found his voice.

Did I do wrong sending him to you, honey?

I don't know.

I can recall him. David keeps his word, but if I release him... Should I, Raven?

She couldn't humiliate herself by asking Simon to call David from the valley because of her foolish infatuation. Nor could she pretend she wanted it for David's sake, not her own. Her damnable honesty wouldn't let her.

No matter how she might want to twist and turn it, convincing herself and Simon that David should leave the valley, it was not possible. Her foolishness and his antagonism aside, David needed the valley. Simon was a wise man. He knew that his best agent needed the valley's peace to heal his mind and find himself.

She knew, more by what Simon didn't say than by what he did, that professional help for a man like David could be disastrous. He would be buried in the labyrinth of government hospitals and institutions and never be a concern again. She couldn't let that happen to David.

In the end, she'd gathered her courage and listened to what she wanted to believe was her conscience and knew was truly her heart. *Don't recall him, Simon. I can't help him, but time can. David's strong. He'll mend in spirit as well as mind. He needs the valley. Let him stay.*

Are you sure, honey?

I'm sure.

You'll call me if you need me?

I'll call.

Honey.

Yes, Simon?

Take care.

The conversation surfaced time and again. In the early morning hours spent in her garden. When she drove over the mountains to the college. But most of all, when the day was quiet, she thought of all that Simon had told her of David.

She heard Simon saying, *Take care.* And the echo of her answer.

"It's too late, Simon," she murmured aloud, running a finger over the drying slip. Once her carelessness with it would've disturbed her, but tonight, her mind was too full of David.

David, his face solemn, his eyes brooding. David, laughter transforming his features. His eyes heavy with passion, crying, "Enough!"

What had she been thinking when he took her in

his arms? Nothing. She was only feeling as she'd never let herself feel before.

"Let?" She laughed, a mirthless sound. With David, there wasn't a choice. It was simply there, full-blown and aching, beyond control. From the moment he'd stepped out of the darkness, a stranger with a stranger's needs, all she'd learned of protective detachment was threatened. Her world had changed forever beneath the look that turned moonlight into witchery.

Shock had given her brazen courage when she stood naked beneath the nebulous shield of her wet shirt, feigning an outward calm as his scorching stare saw what no man had. With every shred of her strength, she'd faced his challenge. Only when he'd left her, reeling from his insults, had reality crashed down about her.

She hadn't tried to hate him then, nor had she wanted to, for hate implies a compelling awareness. She'd wanted the protection of indifference. Then nothing he said or did could touch her. Aloof, she could be, and controlled, even distant, but she'd glimpsed hurt beneath his hostility, and indifference was beyond her.

When he took her in his arms, half in anger, she hadn't thought of consequences or the future. Had there been a future beyond that moment? God help her, no.

She hadn't thought David would be a part of her life beyond that time. She hadn't thought at all. She'd simply given her heart and body to him.

David wanted one, but not the other and she'd discovered they were one and the same. A package deal.

Raven shied away from an admission she was not ready to make.

"So, what do I do?" Drawing herself from her quandary, she began to clear the table of her tools, putting them away in a cabinet. The clay vessel was last. As she lifted it from the table, memories overwhelmed her. Of David watching as she shaped it. Of anger and enmity and passion.

"David." Her hands caressed the clay. Her skin flushed hot with her thoughts as she pressed its cool side to her cheek. A sound, a whispered breath, drew her heavy-lidded gaze to the open door.

He was there by the garden's edge, watching through the twilight. The revulsion she saw sent the clay slipping from her fingers, shattering into clumsy pieces. His icy focus never left her, only his mouth altered, his lips compressing into a grim line. Something was gathering beneath the habitual stillness of this rough, hurting man. Something Raven wanted to understand, but they were locked in a wasteland neither compassion nor lust could breach.

The fragrance of a summer breeze drifted lazily through the doorway, stirring Raven's dark hair. She brushed it away from her cheek, running her hand down the length of it, tucking it behind her shoulder. David's eyes left hers to follow its shimmering fall, and Raven remembered his hands in her hair, guiding her mouth to his kiss, tangling himself in it as he made love to her. Bound by it in sleep.

Everything blurred, and there was only the wanting.

Oh, God! Even his hate couldn't keep her from it. Trembling she waited until his uncompromising gaze took hers again, seeing the memory in them. In the hush, his breath rasped in his chest, his hands curled. His eyes were narrow slits, but in their dark glitter, Raven saw an answering hunger that neither hate nor contempt could silence. Primitive lust. Controlled by incredible effort.

The color drained from her face. She looked down at her hands, only their brutal clasp with nails scoring her palm kept her from reaching out to a man who would take her in hate. Wildly, she asked herself if she would go to him, giving whatever he asked, taking like a starving woman any crumb he would give.

"Yes!" She had no idea she spoke her shame as her breath became a racking shudder. God help her, yes. She would do whatever David asked her to do. Be whatever he wanted her to be. All he need do was touch her and she wouldn't have the strength to deny him.

From the far reaches of her mind, she heard Simon saying, *Take care.*

And her own answering, *Too late.*

It was too late the moment David had kissed her.

I love him! The words were startling at first. She'd never deliberately spoken them even to herself. I love him, she admitted again, and this time, there was no doubt. She was nearly giddy with the admission. The insanity of loving him she could cope with. Better than the shame of obsession.

Even as she knew his gaze was on her, hot and hard and full of the need he wanted to deny, she felt the resurgence of her confidence. She loved him and could deal with it. She wouldn't fool herself that it would be easy. But she'd loved before, not like this, not the love of a woman for a man, but love nevertheless. She'd lost before and very nearly not survived it, but she was older now. Perhaps, she would be hurt, perhaps, she would never love again, but she would survive.

With sudden clarity, the complexities were reduced to simple truths. Raven loved David. That was her problem. How he dealt with it was his.

When she lifted her gaze to his, the serenity of old was shining in them. There was a soft strength in her that nothing could extinguish.

David was caught by her gaze, held captive by her smile. He was barely aware of flowers dipping and swaying before a mischievous breeze. Why was he there, lurking in her garden, hoping to catch a glimpse of her? Why did he torment himself with memories of Raven, hair as black as night veiling her body, turning to him with an honesty he wouldn't believe?

She smiled at him across the night, and a knife turned in his heart. He had brought the ugliness of his life with him into her valley. When he had found peace, he had turned it to discord. When he had found innocence, he had taken it, discarding it like a cheap thrill. Her smile was his punishment.

His fingers curled around the head of a flower, crushing it. The scent of it—her scent—sang in his blood. Ripping the delicate bloom from its stem as if ripping her from his mind, he turned away.

When he was gone, Raven knelt to gather the shattered clay.

The sun struck midday as David drove down the mountain. Beneath shrinking shadows, one steep, hairpin curve plummeted into the next, zigzagging around and down. The sleek Corvette, his one folly, old enough to be a classic and well preserved, hugged the road and clung to curves. When the terrain flattened and twists became lazy bends, he leaned back, put the accelerator to the floor and let the beat of the wind sweep the clutter from his mind.

He'd been isolated too long. Ennui blunted his senses and warped his values. As the Corvette hurled through the gently rolling countryside, he convinced himself that the malady called Raven only needed perspective. She was beautiful, and the tragedy of Helen Landon had shaken him but not gelded him. He was a man with a man's needs, and Raven was there. It was as simple as that.

"The only game in town," he muttered, and hated himself the moment the words were out. It cheapened her, and she didn't deserve that. He cheapened himself by stooping to that way of thinking. Whatever Raven was, she wasn't a game.

Solitary farmhouses surrounded by lush gardens and close-cropped pastures gave way to the clutter of congregate living. David brought his speed under the sedate requirements and drove the streets of Madison, the little village that had grown up around Madison College, where Raven taught.

There were phone booths closer to the valley. He could've called Simon from any of them. But the wanderlust had seized him and without conscious plan, he'd found himself passing them by in favor of Madison.

The village was small, with no industry beyond that expected to serve the immediate needs of the college. Main Street circled a courthouse, and tucked along the street's length were the shops with quaintly refurbished facades. There was a richness here, a quiet sense of worth. A gallant old lady wandering into the twentieth century, teaching it the true meaning of *class*.

Beyond the cluster of houses, some old as the village itself, some new, lay the college itself. A luxuriant expanse of lawn surrounded it, with a forest at its back, and beyond that, the rise of mountains.

It was here Raven spent her days. Within its buildings, she taught her classes of horticulture and her specialty of wildflowers. In the peculiar camaraderie of the academic atmosphere, she interacted with her colleagues and with students and their families—like Jamie McLachlan and his brother Dare.

This was a part of her life David hadn't imagined. He thought Raven aloof, solitary. Yet, as he stopped, staring out at the buildings, he could see her standing before a lectern, speaking to a class. Or bending to a student, her braid tumbling over her breasts like a rope of silk. He'd never imagined Raven in a setting beyond her valley. Now, he knew she would do very well. Her quiet serenity would be appealing. The students would turn to her with their troubles, as Jamie McLachlan obviously had.

The McLachlans. Raven's troubled friends. Raven's caring. Raven rising from her potter's table. Raven in his arms.

Raven.

The sun bore down, turning the black car into an oven. David sighed. He'd come to Madison to make a safe call to Simon, not to moon over a woman he wanted desperately to purge from his thoughts. It was time to get on with his task. If anything could usurp Raven's memory, it should be the investigation.

Reaching for the ignition, he listened as the powerful engine roared. As he left the college behind and retraced the quaint streets, he reminded himself that Madison, with its aura of history and tradition, was not for the likes of David Canfield.

He found the perfect phone booth tucked on a side street beyond the sleepy bustle of the village. His coins clanked into the machine, the number was dialed, and on the second ring, the call was answered, as he knew it would be, by Simon. Dispensing with formalities, David went straight to the point.

"Anything new?" His voice rang hollowly in the cave of metal and Plexiglas. He listened as Simon outlined the progress of his own investigation. "That's it? Zip? Then we aren't dealing with an amateur. This guy's a professional, not just some fly-by-nighter looking for quick bucks. A mole so well placed, he might be anybody. He'll be dangerous, Simon."

A heavy motorcycle passed, the deep thrum of its motor obscuring Simon's answer. "Say again."

When Simon had finished outlining his strategy, David felt a little less cut off from the world he knew. "One other thing." He tugged the number from his pocket. "I discovered this in the telephone logs." He repeated the number. He wasn't ready to admit to Simon that he'd found it days ago and had forgotten it in his preoccupation with Raven. "When you trace it, get back to me. I can be at this number whenever you say." He rattled off the number listed above the dial. "It's small, but this could be the lead we need.

"Meet you at the what?" A second motorcycle passed, this one lighter, with an annoying buzz for an engine. The rider, like the first, had books strapped to the seat. College kids? Lunch break at Madison? David leaned forward, the receiver tight against his ear, a hand cupping the other. "What games?" He wondered why Simon suddenly wanted to make face-to-face contact when the telephone would suffice. "Highland Games? Is that where grown men wear skirts and if I yelled, 'Mac,' every damn man in the country would answer?"

He laughed. "I know, including you. How will I recognize you? Will you be wearing a skirt?" He held the phone away from his ear until Simon had finished his diatribe, then sobered instantly when he moved on to other subjects. "Raven's fine, Simon. Yes, I've seen her, but not today. It was yesterday. And yes, she is a special lady."

As if it were fate and some force had ordained it, while he listened to Simon extol Raven and her virtues, a young woman, slender, with midnight hair flowing down her back stepped from a shop. Her arms were loaded with books, a bag with the name of the shop emblazoned on it swung from her wrist. David's attention wandered from Simon. Would it be this way for the rest of his life? Would every slender, dark-haired woman be Raven in his imagination? Would every graceful walk be hers?

As she drew nearer, her features were blurred. He wiped the sweat from his brows and saw that the woman's hair was like Raven's because it was Raven.

"I'll be at the games. Just have the number." He cut Simon off in midsentence and replaced the receiver. The booth was like an oven, yet he stayed until she passed. Perhaps he intended to let her go, perhaps he was only gathering his courage to face her scorn. He didn't stop to analyze as he stepped from the booth.

"Raven." She stopped, and for an eternity, it

seemed she wouldn't turn. When she did, her face was composed, unreadable. He was suddenly at a loss for words, wondering why he'd brought this on himself. She tilted her head curiously, waiting with a maddening patience for his next move. "You left early this morning."

"I had some extra preparations to do for today's class." Her answer was noncommittal, giving him the barest essentials, nothing to ease his malaise.

In the bright sunlight, shadows of restlessness lay beneath her eyes. "Are you all right?"

"I'm as I was yesterday and the day before. As I will be tomorrow. Why do you ask?"

"I thought... I worried..."

"That I was pining away for my lost virginity?" She was so calm, so matter-of-fact, he wanted to shake her. Instead, he watched as she smiled again almost pityingly. "I'm not, you know. I don't regret it."

He felt as if his heart was in a vise, constricting the flow of his life. He struggled for a breath. "For the love of God, Raven—"

"What were you doing here, David?" she said, cutting him off.

He glanced at the booth and for a moment, his mind was blank. Then he remembered. "I was speaking to Simon."

"I see."

Sunlight glittered in her hair like black diamonds. David could feel its strands drifting over him as she'd learned his body with her lips. Like gentle rain that follows the thunder, he thought, and he lost the thread of his conversation. Raven was speaking, and he had no idea what she had said. "I'm sorry. What did you say?"

She laughed softly. "An apology, David?"

"A courtesy."

Her mouth quirked in a way that made him want to kiss it until it was swollen and sweetly aching. "Is there anything new with the investigation?"

"A lead, maybe." This was solid ground, something he understood. "I won't know until Simon checks it out."

"It must be hard."

"It's damn near impossible." Impossible not to forget every resolution, that this was a public street and his desire to sweep her into his arms.

"You must feel cut off from everything. I can understand how you must hate it."

She was talking about the investigation. The farthest thing from his mind. "Simon will do his best while I'm in exile."

"Is that how you see it, David? As exile?"

"No. Yes. I suppose I do."

"I know how it feels to be away from the place you want or even need to be. I'm sorry."

"Apology, Raven?"

She laughed, caught in her own trap. "No, only a figure of speech."

Her laughter died as they stood in the burning day. A child with a jam box on his shoulder scooted by them, the mellow refrain of a love song drifting from its speakers. A mournful voice sang of a love that almost was, then faded away. The town clock chimed three-quarters of the hour and fell silent.

"I have to go," Raven said. "I have an appointment."

"I'll carry your books." David took a step toward her and for the first time her control crumbled.

"No!" She backed away a careful step. "They aren't heavy and I'm sure you have something you should be doing."

"There's nothing." He advanced another step.

"David, no!"

He heard the thread of panic. He stopped, his hand outstretched until, feeling like a fool, he dropped it.

"I'm used to the books. They aren't as heavy as they look. I'm late." She backed away another step. "I have to go."

She turned abruptly and walked from him, head down, her books clutched to her breasts. She'd been the epitome of calm control until she thought he would touch her. Then she looked at him as if he were a rattlesnake.

"After what you've done to her, what did you want, Canfield? For her to fall into your arms?"

He watched her move, her body taut, the easy grace gone, and he knew that it was exactly what he'd wanted once. When she turned the corner and disappeared from sight, he felt a sense of loss.

Five

On Saturday, David rose early and dressed in khaki slacks and a light, knit shirt. This was the day he was to rendezvous with Simon at the Highland Games, set in a meadow high on a mountain side. It could take all day. Simon hadn't given David a time; he'd simply said "Be there."

In Madison, after the fiasco on the street with Raven, David had heard talk of the games. They were the topic in every store or shop. The biggest assemblage of clans was expected. The best athletes, the best dancers and pipers. Hotels and motels for miles around had been booked to overflowing for months in advance. He'd begun to understand how popular the event was.

He spent his evenings alone now. They were dull and endless as he systematically worked his way through Simon's library. Last night, he'd selected a number of volumes on the Scots, their tartans, their kith and kin, and their migration to America. As he steeped himself in their traditions, he learned that *mac*, the part of a great many Scottish names, meant simply "son." As did the more obvious *son*, tagged to end of names. Clan was the name given kinsmen united under a chief. Septs were an extension of the clans.

Highlanders, whether American or Scot, could trace their ancestry to a clan. Each clan had its distinctive tartan, or plaid. He read of their bloody history and stubborn survival. These macs and sons brought their pride and endurance with them wherever they roamed. The highlanders of the Carolinas were no exception.

Was Raven the descendant of a son of Candless? Was Simon son of Kinzie? David discovered his own second name was Scot. Sutherland, his mother's people—without a "mac" or a "son," but still a clan with a plaid of red and blue and green. He felt the pride of belonging before he shook it off and called himself a fool. He knew nothing of Scots or clans. He belonged nowhere and to no one. His interest was simply the studying he always did, readying for an unfamiliar situation.

Slipping his watch over his wrist was the last detail before leaving. Giving the room a cursory glance, he opened the door and stepped outside.

The sun was barely lighting the horizon, leaving the valley in unrelieved darkness. Raven hadn't come home last night. Her cabin crouched in the blackness as empty as a lost soul. The valley was dismal without her, and he wondered, as he had through the night, where she'd stayed and with whom.

"Why should you care, Canfield?" His voice was an intrusion in the hush of predawn. He missed her, dammit. Though they hadn't spoken in days, he missed her. Hell! he even missed the dogs.

With an angry fist, he pounded the railing by the steps, wondering why he couldn't get her out of his mind. If he didn't leave the valley soon, he would be a candidate for an asylum. With that bleak thought, he stepped into his car. As he made the two-hour drive, he rehearsed his argument for his release from his word and for his departure from the valley with the little grace he had left.

David moved with the crowd, letting its momentum take him through the gates, past booths with displays of Scottish food and wares, to the meadow. A thread of excitement ran through the people as they sprawled over the hillside on lawn chairs and blankets. A piper band struck up a tune. The shrill caterwaul of the bagpipes grated on his ears, then he caught the tune and the rhythm and decided he liked it. On the field below, men in kilts ran through practice paces, warming up for their events. But David searched the ever-changing crowd for Raven.

His eyes skimmed over the gathering so thick with the tartan, one could mistake it for Scotland. Would she be here? Wasn't every red-blooded Scot for miles around?

"*Ceud mile failte.* Welcome to the Highland Games." Simon stood at David's side, his burr more pronounced than David had ever heard. "It's a fine crowd, isn't it?"

"A fine crowd," David agreed. But where was Raven? Where was she last night?

"Have you ever seen the games?" Simon steered him through the mass, talking as easily as old friends who'd met by accident.

"Never."

"Then you have a treat coming." A band, dressed in velvet jackets and kilts and tall, furred hats, marched past in cadence. The leader called a signal, the pipes wheezed and began to play. "Do you like the pipes?"

"I could learn to."

"Last night, there was a piper's concert and the country dance. I should've told you, but I suppose Raven did."

"I haven't spoken to Raven." David caught Simon's quick, questioning look. "She wasn't home last night nor this morning. Maybe she was here for the concert and dance."

"I imagine she was. Have you seen her yet today?"

"Not today."

"You've quarreled."

"Yeah," David said shortly. "We've quarreled."

"I see." Simon, sometimes the diplomat, dropped the subject. The hand that rested lightly on David's shoulder tightened and steered him into the trees, beyond notice. In the protection of the shadows, he drew a small, white square from his pocket and held it out to David. "The name that matches your number."

David took the scrap from him. This could be the first concrete step toward finding the person or persons responsible for Helen's death. He unfolded the paper, read it, then looked back at Simon. "Jeter? The number called from Helen's desk belonged to Thomas Jeter?"

"An unlisted number."

"Helen had Jeter's unlisted number?"

"Someone who called from Helen's desk had Jeter's unlisted number," Simon corrected.

"There was no one except the three of us in the office at the time the call was made. I didn't make it. I know you didn't. Why on earth would Helen?"

"Maybe she had a thing for Jeter."

"A thing for The Watch's best enemy?"

Simon shrugged his bearlike shoulders. "Maybe she was returning Jeter's call. Maybe he had a thing for her."

"Yeah. Like a cold fish does for a flower."

"A strange analogy."

"A stranger alliance," David growled.

"If there was one." Simon didn't need to tell him that a full-scale investigation was underway nor that Helen Landon's most innocent contact would be probed.

"Who's heading it up?"

"I am, David. If Jeter's involved, then we know he wasted her to get to me."

"Enemy mine."

"Believe it. Before, it was only petty stuff."

It was on David's tongue to ask Simon to release him from his promise. It was the opportune time. If he left the valley, he could help in the investigation. He let it pass. Surprised, he shrugged, saying, "Why have you come, Simon? You could've given me the name over the phone."

"I wanted to see for myself how you are."

"Checking me out?" David asked. Simon wanted to be right, wanted to vindicate his decision not to slap him into the debriefing and treatment center. "Now that you have?"

"Now that I have—" Simon patted his shoulder "—let's go see the games. The opening ceremonies are about to begin, and there's Raven. Shall we join her?"

David turned, meaning to refuse, until he saw her sitting under the shade of an oak. She was dressed in a creamy blouse with leather laces at the neck and a dark, pleated skirt sashed with a length of plaid. Her hair was drawn back from her face in a loose coil low on her nape. She was composed and elegant. Untouchable. He wanted to slide the laces from her blouse and the pins from her hair and take the quiet elegance for his own.

He wanted things he couldn't explain, things he hadn't meant to want. He looked at her now and the slow burn of anger began. Raven was not alone. His eyes narrowed fractionally against the glare. His voice was guttural. "Who the hell is that?"

With a flicker of amusement, Simon glanced at David, then away. "The dark one with Raven? That's Dare McLachlan."

"The farmer." David stared at the broad-shouldered man who sat by Raven. There was a lean hardness about him that neither lacy ascot nor kilt could soften. The farmer leaned closer to Raven, hair as dark as hers brushing her cheek, as he listened to her low comments.

"Dare's a tree farmer," Simon elaborated. "You've met him, then, have you?"

"No," David said shortly. "What the devil is a tree farmer?"

"Christmas trees."

"Christmas trees?"

"The green things we hang tinsel on in December."

David ignored Simon's teasing. "He looks rough for a *tree* farmer." Dare McLachlan had the tight, watchful look David had seen on his own face many times.

"Don't kid yourself that it isn't grueling work."

A younger version of Dare climbed the embankment. With a swashbuckler's grand gesture, he kissed Raven's hand then dropped at her feet. David clenched his teeth as Raven's laughter drifted to him.

"That's Jamie. There's none like him, though he's a twin. Robert Bruce." Simon nodded to an astonishingly handsome boy with silver-brown hair slipping easily by Raven's side. "He's only seconds older than Jamie, and quieter. But when he's into mischief, he has no equal."

"The other brother?"

"Ross is Madison's pediatrician. He'll be along later. Where there's one McLachlan, there's usually four."

"Raven says there's trouble between Dare and Jamie."

"Not surprising. They're too much alike."

David looked doubtfully from Dare's still, somber face to Jamie's flashing grin.

"Dare was the master plan for Jamie at eighteen. He was a rascal, full of the devil himself. The pride and bane of his grandmother who raised him. She died when he was twenty, within the week, he discovered he had three half brothers. His errant dad reappeared, tried to establish himself as the true heir to the farm. Intended to sell it, pocket the money and run. The boy fought him, wouldn't let his dad set foot on the farm. Dare intended to keep it intact. He dropped out of college, took his brothers—that his dad was only too glad to give up—and raised them by himself.

"Ross was eleven. Robert Bruce and Jamie were less than a year. Of the four, only the twins have the same mother." Simon chuckled at his remark. "Of course, they would. They were a wild, motherless lot, and Dare became everything to them. A sobering experience for any daredevil."

"Jamie wants to be a farmer."

"And Dare opposes it. It figures. He wants his brothers to have what he missed."

"Whether they want it or not."

"No problem with Ross. He wanted to be a doctor from the first. Robert Bruce is a scholar. Jamie's another matter."

They were a handsome family, brawny and confident. The one aloof, brooding, the others with a hint of mischief in their slanting smiles. They were totally male, as comfortable in their laces and pleated kilts as in jeans and boots.

Dare touched Raven's shoulder and she didn't shrink away. David's envy fanned the flame of jealousy.

"If you can quit glowering, we might join them," Simon suggested.

"The blanket's already a little crowded."

"Won't be for long." Not bothering to wait for his consent, Simon led David past other blankets and clusters of lawn chairs to Raven. "When the games start, the McLachlans will be on the field. Dare throws the caber."

"Of course! The caber." David refused to ask.

"Simon!" Raven jumped to her feet. "Simon." There was a happy lilt in his name. "I thought I was dreaming." She flung her arms about him. "Why didn't you tell me you were coming? When did you arrive? How long can you stay?"

Simon laughed and kissed her forehead. "Taking it in order. You aren't dreaming. I wanted to surprise you. Just a while ago. Only today." He looked at her cheeks, flushed with the sun, and ignored the telltale signs of fatigue. "As beautiful as ever and still as popular with the boys, I see." As she stepped out of his arms, he nodded a greeting to the McLachlans, who had stood when she did.

"We nearly had a family feud deciding who got to bring her to the games, Simon." Jamie grinned at Raven. "To keep peace, we all did."

Dare caught a loose strand of Raven's hair and gave it a playful tug. "What Jamie isn't admitting is that we needed a referee, and Raven does it best."

"Is that what you want?" David stared pointedly at Dare's hand twined in dark silk. "A referee."

Tension crackled like summer lightning. Deliberately, Dare's level gaze met David's. "Among other things, Mr. Canfield." With a lazy caress, his gaze still locked with David's, his hand slid unhurriedly from her hair. "It is Mr. Canfield, isn't it?"

David only glanced at Dare's kilt, down and back, but it was enough. "It is *Mister* McLachlan, isn't it?"

"David!" Raven's shock was lost in Simon's laughter.

"You can't insult him that way, David." Simon was still chuckling. "Any Scot who's worn a kilt has heard that old saw. If you really want to make it a day for clichés, ask him what he wears under it.''

''What *does* he wear under it?''

Dare's lips quirked in what might have been a smile. ''Whatever I choose or don't choose.'' Eyes as chilled as a mountain lake took David's measure and dismissed him. Turning to Raven, Dare touched her cheek lightly, tracing it to the hint of a cleft in her chin. Ignoring her sudden blink of surprise, he leaned nearer, saying in a tender tone, ''I'll see you at nine for the Tartan Ball.'' His husky voice dropped a level. ''Look pretty for me.''

Without a glance at David and only a nod for Simon, he started down the hill toward the field.

Jamie's wicked laugh faded abruptly to surprise. Robert Bruce choked before he discovered an inordinate interest in a blade of grass. Even Simon made an event of clearing his throat. David was only aware that Raven's eyes were bright and glittering and her sun-flushed cheeks were brightened more by a blush.

''Canfield.'' Dare stood halfway down the incline, one foot on a small outcropping of stone. Oblivious of the watching spectators, he waited until David forced his attention from Raven. When their eyes locked, his shoulders tensed, the snowy silk shirt straining over them. His teeth flashed white in his tanned face. ''If you've a problem to work off, the wrestling is open to all comers.''

His eyes held David's for a fraction too long to be anything but a challenge. ''The stakes can be something we both want, Canfield. The first dance with Raven. If Raven agrees.'' He didn't wait for her comment. ''Scots are hospitable people. Perhaps we can find you a clan to represent.''

"My mother was a Sutherland," David said with a quiet dignity, and the challenge was taken.

"A good clan." For the first time, Dare's smile touched his eyes, and as quickly, it was gone. "Rob, Jamie." He was suddenly the brother patriarch, the chieftain of the McLachlans. "You have more to do than pester Raven." He waited while the younger McLachlans grudgingly admitted he was right, stole a kiss from Raven and said their goodbyes. With no more concern for David, Dare went with his brothers to the meadow.

Raven had stood quietly during the exchange, but her stillness was deceptive. She was disturbed by the attention caused by the bristling encounter. She was angry and puzzled. Angered by David, who rejected everything she was, who wanted to want nothing from her. Puzzled by Dare, who had little time for women, to whom she was a favored friend, no more or less.

David and Dare were men of different backgrounds but of the same mold. Terse, aloof, sober, single-minded. *Unreasonable*. While she wouldn't have expected geniality, she hadn't anticipated that in her company, they would bristle like stiff-legged dogs snarling over a bone.

It made no sense. They'd acted like children and had made her feel a fool. Only the smirks and twitters of those watching had kept her from stalking away.

The crowd watched now with a collective grin, waiting for the next comic episode. She had no intention of supplying them further amusement.

Raven reined in her temper, denying herself the wonderful pleasure of blistering David with it. Her smile was pleasant, her voice steady, but her eyes flashed as she tucked her arm through Simon's. "I've lost my escorts for the duration of the games. Would you care to join me?''

David opened his mouth but before he could snap out his objection, he heard Simon saying, "We'd be delighted." Then pointedly, "Wouldn't we, David?"

"No."

"Join me, David." Raven gripped his arm, her fingers digging into his flesh. Her smile curved over clenched teeth. "Pretend we're really one happy group. It's the least you can do after making a spectacle of us."

"I didn't make a spectacle. Your boyfriend did that."

"My boyfriend?" Raven's lashes fluttered down in weary disgust. Then regaining her equilibrium, with a subtle wickedness, she looked from David to the meadow. Her gaze searched for Dare and found him. As she watched him lift a weight, arms straining, muscles defined by sunlight and shadow, she murmured softly, "I wouldn't call Dare a boy."

Simon was having trouble with his throat again. David glanced at him but read nothing in his determinedly expressionless face.

"I'm tired of standing, and we're blocking the view. If you care to join me, David, fine. If not, fine." Raven turned to Simon. "You will, Simon? Please?" She stepped to the blanket, gathered her skirt about her and sat. With a Cheshire Cat smile twitching his lips, Simon joined her and, after a moment of indecision, so did David.

With his shoulders brushing hers, he sat stiffly through the opening ceremonies and the march of the clans. Though he reminded himself it was ridiculous, that he came from nowhere, belonged to no one, he felt an odd flicker of curiosity and pride at the passage of the Sutherland clan. With their standard high and kilts swinging, they marched to the beat of a snare.

Simon, who was enjoying everything immensely, leaned over to speak across Raven. "Your clan, David."

"Hardly," he retorted, lapsing into silence as the parade of tartans ended and the contests began.

The day grew hotter, the competition fiercer. The throng was enthusiastic and vocal. There was bedlam about them, but David hardly heard it. He was conscious of the brush of Raven's shoulder against his, of her stillness. The wildflower scent of her was driving him to desperation. She watched the games raptly, cheering a name that fell on his ears in a dissonant note.

The McLachlans were joined on the field by the fourth brother. Ross, like his brothers, was a varying version of the eldest and handsome in his own way. But it was Dare who commanded attention. Bared to his kilt, his body gleaming with a sheen of sweat, he went with seeming ease from one event to the next. David grudgingly admitted Dare was a superb athlete. He was among the best at throwing the weight, and putting the stone, both contests of skill and strength. Now it was time to throw the log that was the caber.

"Perfect," Raven said, judging Dare's throw.

"The red-headed guy threw it farther."

"Distance isn't the point, David." Her tone was cool and steady.

"Then what is the point? Why else would a grown man throw a skinned tree?"

"The goal is a 'twelve o'clock' throw, with the log landing perpendicular to the starting line."

"I suppose McLachlan's an expert?"

"As a matter of fact, he is."

"David," Simon interrupted. "I'd like something to drink, and these old bones are tired. Would you?"

With a look that asked since when did Simon have tired, old bones, David stood and walked away without a word.

When David was lost in the crowd, Raven turned to Simon, accusing, "You're enjoying this."

Simon's smile got the better of him, spreading over his craggy face. "I can't deny it."

"Would you tell me what's enjoyable about two grown men acting like children fighting over a toy?"

"You make a lovely toy, my dear."

"Stop it, Simon. You know that Dare has absolutely no interest in me beyond friendship. For some unfathomable reason, he was pretending."

"David's arrogance got his dander up. I know it, you know it, but David doesn't."

"This is ridiculous. David doesn't even like me. Why should he be jealous, no matter how strangely Dare acts?"

"Why, indeed."

Raven leaned away from him for a long, sweeping look. "You really are pleased with this."

Simon sobered. "Strange as it seems, David's being so disgruntled with Dare is a good sign. It means he's beginning to feel again. I don't fool myself that he's not a bit longer from total recovery, but it's a start. For a long time, he had no room for anything in his life but retribution. Helen Landon was the catalyst. Years of stress and guilt crashed down on him. She's become the focus of an obsession that could've been dangerous to the country as well as himself. Obsession clouds judgment. So does revenge. There's no room for the first in our business, and to survive, we must be above the other.''

"I don't understand."

"There are sensitive situations. One wrong move could bring disaster. David—'' Simon stopped, at a rare loss for words. He stared into Raven's eyes, willing her to understand what he hadn't said. "David became a threat. There were certain factors who wanted the problem solved.''

"These factors, they wanted David locked away?"

"No, Raven," Simon said gently.

Her hands were clasped in her lap. Fear shadowed her eyes. "Dear God," she whispered. "They want David killed!" She looked away, unable to bear the truth. "You sent him to the valley to buy him some time."

"Can you see why today has been good? It might've been unpleasant, but it was beautifully normal. I knew this could be hard on you, honey, but I believed David deserved a chance." He covered her hands with one of his. "God forgive me, I've played havoc with your life.''

He touched her chin, lifting her face toward him. He saw the loveliness frayed by strain. "I can send him away."

"Back to them?"

"Not yet. There are other places. Perhaps I should've sent him to one in the beginning.''

"But you didn't." Raven knew the "places," as Simon called them, were sanitariums where David's mind would be poked and prodded, and, even with the best of intentions, dehumanized. "You couldn't. Just as you couldn't send a fourteen-year-old girl.''

"No."

Raven remembered his gentleness with the wild, bitter creature she'd been. When he cupped her cheek to turn her face to his, she smiled.

Simon studied her features, his gaze moving slowly over them. Raven smiled, but there was always sadness buried so deep in her eyes that only those who loved her, as he did, could see. He wondered if he only imagined he saw a new sadness there, one too new and difficult to be hidden. "I came to see about David, but most of all, I had to reassure myself about you. About what I might've done to you."

"You haven't done anything to me, Simon."

He met her level gaze, probing for his own answers. His hand fell away from her face and onto the blanket. "Haven't I?"

"I'm a woman, not a fourteen-year-old girl. I made a choice." She lifted her head, looking to David, winding his way over the hillside. "Whatever was done, I did to myself."

Simon heard the courage and the pain. He heard resignation as well. "I can still send him away."

"No."

"Do you know what you're saying, lass?"

She watched David approach, soft drinks in hand. He paused. As if he heard a silent call, his head came up, his shoulders straightened. He turned to the field below and met Dare McLachlan's waiting stare.

Raven ceased to breathe. The crowd vanished. The clamor of voices faded. She was locked away from the world. Waiting. Waiting for David's answer to Dare's new challenge.

He was motionless, a somber figure against the backdrop of the color-spattered slopes. It's a game,

Raven thought. Only a game that men sometimes play. Dare was a friend. His challenge had nothing to do with her beyond that she was the reason for David's surly hostility. David, though it made no sense, couldn't bear that another man might have what he didn't want.

David wanted to walk away from her, and he'd tried. Perhaps now, he thought, by refusing this foolish challenge, he could. His diamond-hard stare burned across the meadow. He remembered Dare's hand on Raven. A cup nearly collapsed in the crush of his grip, spilling soda over his wrist. Almost imperceptibly, he nodded. Dare McLachlan, feet planted wide, bare chest heaving in a bark of silent laughter, nodded, too.

Raven sighed, reminding herself for the third time that it was only a game. It meant only that David hadn't conquered his desire for her. But even that was better than indifference.

Indifference offered no hope. Desire could become many things.

She was not smiling as she turned back to Simon, but he saw a difference in her. The bleakness was tempered. In a heartbeat, an emptiness was filled by hope and he saw the Raven of old. His worries were easing, his guilt lifting when she took his hand in hers.

"You've taught me to survive," she said. "Whatever happens, I'll be all right." She looked from Simon to David. "Don't send him from the valley. Not yet."

Six

The meadow, once lush and thick, had begun to wear thin when David walked onto it. The games had taken a toll on the grass, more so than on the athletes. These gladiators, who traced their lineage to the clans, were hard, tough men. They wore their plaids with a quiet pride. Jamie McLachlan had scrounged a kilt of the Sutherland clan. Careful not to give offense, David refused to wear it. He chose to wrestle dressed as he was, removing only his shirt and his shoes.

Excitement ran high among the clansmen. Dare McLachlan was a champion wrestler. This dark stranger was an unknown quantity. David heard muffled comments from the Sutherland clan, followed by an approving inspection. He had honed down to sinew and muscle. He looked like exactly what he was, cat quick, agile and strong. It promised to be a memorable match.

A hand came down on his shoulder, a deep, slightly burred voice asked, "Do you know highland wrestling?"

David looked into an austere face topped by auburn curls. The taller man offered his hand. "Patrick McCallum."

"David Canfield." He doubted there was a man on the field who didn't know his name. "I've wrestled, but not highland style."

"Dare asked me to teach you the moves and the rules."

David had seen this Patrick McCallum in the games. When Dare chose a tutor, he chose the best. David looked across the field to the handsome Scot and his brothers.

Following his thought, Patrick said succinctly, "Dare is nothing if not fair."

David wondered suddenly what he was doing here, facing a man simply to assuage his jealousy over a woman he didn't want. Dare McLachlan would be good for Raven. They would make a handsome pair. He remembered Dare's hand twining in her hair. Silk and iron.

No!

The word screamed like a jigsaw through his skull.

Patrick's voice intruded. "Step to the side, beyond the circle, and we'll begin."

David's schooling was short. Patrick McCallum wasted no words, and every move was instructive. When he was done, he considered David's ability. "What you lack in skill, you make up in strength and guts." His grim slash of a mouth lifted in a smile. "You've shown you've plenty of that by coming down to the field." Eyes, blue and piercing, narrowed. "Just don't make the mistake of taking Dare too lightly. Maybe he hasn't been the places you've been or done the things you might've done, but he's a hard man. He didn't get where he is with his forest lands reaching for miles by being timid. If he wanted something, he would be going after it, not wasting time with games."

The big hand fell on David's shoulder again. The voice was a low rasp, the burr of Scotland more pronounced. "Good luck, David Canfield."

David was given little time to ponder the red-haired Scot's enigmatic appraisal of Dare. There was information to be gleaned from the remark. Before he could think, he was in the wrestler's circle facing Dare. With a brief handshake and a curt nod, the match began. Hands locked, muscles strained, feet struggled for purchase. Body against body. Strength against strength. Skill against determination. Dare's grin flashed. David knew it was in sheer love of the game.

Time and again, they struggled. A stalemate unto exhaustion. Then error, miscalculation, advantage. David knew too late. He felt the crush of Dare's arms, the heat of his breath on his face. To the sound of a wild highlander's cry, David was slammed to the ground. The impact knocked the wind from his lungs and set the world spinning. As he lay on the ground, he heard the rustle of footsteps.

Breathing heavily, his magnificent body glistening with sweat, Dare looked down at David in stoic scrutiny. A grin broke over his face, and he dragged David to his feet. "Well done, Canfield." Rare praise, generously given. Bending, he picked up his shirt and slippers. When he straightened, he was abrupt. "Be at the Tartan Ball tonight."

"The program says by invitation."

"This is your invitation."

It had the ring of an order rather than invitation, but David said only, "Why?"

"Because Raven would like it." That said, Dare turned to leave the field.

"I won't wear a kilt," David called after him.

Dare turned back. "Maybe not this time, but you will. Next time."

"There won't be a next time."

"Won't there?"

"I'm leaving the valley in a few weeks."

"Then you're a bigger fool than I thought."

"I'm not a fool, McLachlan." The camaraderie born of combat faltered.

"Any man who walks away from Raven McCandless is a fool." Dare resumed his walk across the field, then dodged among tents erected by the clans and disappeared. David remained on the field. When he looked to the hillside, the crowd was breaking up. He searched for Raven among them. She was gone. He was alone, left to ponder the meaning of Patrick McCallum's remarks—and Dare's.

David stood in the shadows, listening. The music was a blend of old and new. There was the occasional piper's tune, but for the most part, the music was slow, rhythmic, instrumental. He'd had no intention in being here, meaning to leave as soon as he found Simon again. Instead, Jamie McLachlan found him—with an offer from Dare of a room for the night and a change of clothes for the ball. When he accepted, he told himself that it was only for the room, to give Simon and himself privacy and more time. But Simon was gone, flying back to Washington on a private jet, and David was lurking like a callow youth on the fringes of the festivities.

Raven was not hard to find. She was the center of a group that grew and shrank and shifted and changed. Only one thing remained constant. Raven. Her serenity was like a beacon. Every man, regardless of age, had managed to clasp her hand and kiss her cheek. When the music started Ross McLachlan, then Jamie, had led her to the floor. Patrick McCallum took her next. The big redhead held her much too closely, watched her too intently. David didn't doubt the Scot would have led her from the ballroom and into the night, keeping her until morning, if Raven agreed.

David shifted, at ease in his borrowed finery, but sickened by what he saw. It didn't matter that he told himself over and over again Raven was nothing to him. By the time Dare danced with her to a slow, sensuous tune, David was beyond telling himself anything.

Raven was a jewel in Dare's arms. She wore a slip of a dress so deeply red, it shone like the fire it emulated. Her hair was down, caught low at its curling ends with a matching rose of silk. The flower swayed at her back, drawing his eyes to the slender lines of her body. That body had been his once. Those lovely legs had wrapped about him, her arms had held him and all of Raven had been his.

Dare's head dipped to hers and lingered, as if he were whispering secrets. Then he laughed and spun her about, and Raven's gaze collided with David's.

Her cheeks were flushed, her eyes luminous. There was something magical about her. She was glittering stardust that would be gone with the rising sun. David had to touch her, hold her before the light took her. He stepped from obscurity onto the dance floor and muted incandescence flooded over him. The black of his clothing absorbed it. Only the band at his waist broke the somber lines. He seemed taller than his nearly six feet, and broader. His hair, a bit too long, gleamed against his collar. His features were craggy above the white ruffle of his shirt. If she was a flame, he was its shadow. As men were drawn to Raven, women found the man who moved among them irresistible. Their steps slowed, stopped, leaving their partners no other choice.

The chameleon of The Watch had never been so visible nor so oblivious. He knew only his need for Raven.

One by one, the revelers parted then turned as he passed them by. He moved with a dancer's step, slowly, prolonging the moment, keeping her forever in his eyes. In the heated throng, it was her fragrance that reached him first. Wildflowers. Until the day he died, he would remember wildflowers.

He had no idea when Dare moved aside, but Raven was in his arms and the music that had faded began again. Her clasp was warm at his shoulder and his nape; her body was cradled by his as she matched his steps. Her head was lifted, her face upturned. The arch of her throat was an invitation, the cleft of her breasts enticing, but it was her gaze, so dark, so deep, that held him.

Their feet barely brushed the floor. Moving in concert, arms entwined, bodies touching, their eyes spoke what their voices did not. David's hands slid the length of her back, stopping at the swell of her hip. His palm rested there, his fingers splaying over the gentle curve. He felt the music in her body and answered with his. Their moves were mated, every step, every breath. He was lost in her. Every thought was Raven, every beat of his heart as he danced with her, feeling the music, never hearing it.

Raven's fingers tangled in his hair, stroked free of the disarray she created, then tangled again. Her touch was electric, her gaze hypnotic. Her lips were parted, her breath shallow, yet her breasts rose and fell in a gentle effort to be free of the scarlet silk. Beneath the silence, there was a waiting passion.

He wanted to draw her closer and with a kiss, set that passion free. He wanted to set it soaring and with it, his own. He wanted to feel her flesh against his and hear her whisper of delight. He wanted to fall with her into a languid sleep and wake again and again to take her.

He wanted. Dear God, he wanted. But all he could have was a memory...of Raven, who made him forget for a while.

The music slowed, faded. They stood, arms entwined, gaze unwavering. A sound intruded and David remembered. The dance was over. For a moment, his hands caught in her hair, then he was stepping back, his arms sliding slowly from her. Inch by inch, his fingertips glided over fiery silk, memorizing her body beneath it. Reluctantly, for memory wasn't enough, his hands fell away.

His chest rose in a deep, shuddering breath. With the back of his knuckles, he traced the line of her face. Raven's lashes fluttered and drifted down, but not before he saw the look of pain. The little distance between them became a chasm.

He waited, riveted to the floor. When her lashes lifted and her gaze rose again to his, he saw her courage and strength. He smiled, a bittersweet smile, and turned away.

Raven watched him weave through the crowd, the rose from her hair crushed in his hand. When he was only a half-seen shadow, the flash of scarlet was still visible. The music began again and Dare was there, taking her into his arms. With a look of regret, he slid a hand through her hair to draw her head to his shoulder.

David paced the lakeshore beneath the full moon. There was a secret chill beneath the sultry air, and leaves scattered and rustled with his step. Leaves of the poplar tree, the color of the sun, that fell in Indian summer. Golden harbingers of the autumn that was to come.

Soon, the wildflowers Raven loved would be gone. Beautiful flowers with ugly names. Rare flowers, hidden from his blind eyes until she taught him to see. He looked to her cabin, to the small light that shone there. How many things had she taught him? How much had he absorbed by being near her, from watching, from listening? In the few precious halcyon days they'd shared, how had she touched his life so profoundly?

As he'd sat in silence, watching as she brought flowers to life on stark canvas, and even as he struggled with his lust for her, something in Raven reached out to him. Something stronger than man's needs. Something he had never known and thought he never wanted to know. No one word could describe it, for it was many things in one. Peace, honor, contentment—and what frightened him most.

Love. What did he know of love? What did he want to know? "Nothing," he said aloud, and even he heard the falseness in it. Once, that was true. So true that he'd hated Helen Landon more than he was grateful to her for her misguided sacrifice.

Truth flashed through his brain like neon in rain. He hadn't hated Helen Landon. He hated his shame for not caring as she did. He hated his indifference, that he hadn't truly known her. He hated the grief that haunted the dark corridors of a mind already filled with ghosts.

Once, his answer was to hide his emotions deeply in his subconscious. Helen Landon couldn't be so firmly tucked away. He was more aware of her in death than in life. She marked him indelibly with the stain of guilt and stirred the ghosts he thought quieted. In his desperation, he had acted irrationally, choosing revenge in an effort to diminish remorse. Revenge that would have been tragic—but for Simon.

Simon, friend, mentor, had sent his reeling wounded agent to the one person he thought could help.

"Raven." David turned. The cabin's light still burned, as it had into the night, every night, since the Tartan Ball. Raven. Working through her troubles at her potter's table. Troubles he brought to her life.

How had she grown so wise? What pain lay beyond the serenity? What in her life had given her the strength and courage he'd seen on a shadowed dance floor?

Like a marauder, he'd come into her valley, taking

her compassion, her kindness, even the gift of herself, and thrown them back in her face...an act of fear. Fear of feeling. Fear of caring for this woman when he hadn't for another. Yet he did feel and he did care. Never more than when she'd worn a dress of fire, her ebony eyes gentle on him. Every nerve had shrieked, and his heart had ached, and for the last time, he'd taken her in his arms. He'd wanted to dance forever, to hold her, keep her forever.

But the music had died and forever was done. When he let her go beneath the soft, shimmering lights, he'd seen himself mirrored in her eyes. A man who took and was incapable of giving in return. And Raven, a woman of towering strength and endless compassion, had understood.

In that moment, with the dancers about him, he'd seen the emptiness of his life and his future.

Now, suddenly, he couldn't face living the days left to him, unmoved and uncaring. The bleakness of it was more unbearable than the pain of caring. Because of Raven, the shackles and walls of a lifetime were tumbling, brick by brick, memory after memory. With some memories, he made his peace, with others, he could not. So he walked the shore, a man just beginning to understand, needing to sleep, but afraid of the dreams.

Once, they were only nightmares of a tormented subconscious, now, they were the purging of a soul. He dreaded the night, but he knew the dreams would make the healing complete.

Complete—and too late. The damage was done with Raven.

"I can still tell her that I'm sorry." Forgetting that

bastards like David Canfield didn't apologize, he began to walk to the light.

Raven was at her table, working the clay, molding it. She was dressed in slacks and a shirt of some rough, woven material trimmed with a coarse lace. In her concentration, she was in a world apart, untouchable. Once, he would have believed that nothing had ever touched her, that the calm within her had never been challenged. Now he knew it was not true.

Stepping through the open doorway he stood beyond the circle of light waiting for her to sense his presence. Her sure, deft moves slowed; her nimble fingers grew quiet. Drawing her hands from the clay, still unformed and rough, she folded them in her lap. With the gathering of her strength and her guard in place, her gaze lifted to him. For a fleeting instant, David wondered what it would be like to have her look at him always, as she had the night he made love to her.

Nothing in his life had been for always. Nothing ever would be. Always. The word was ashes in his mouth.

Raven did not let him see her surprise. The dance at the Tartan Ball, with its desperate silence that neither could find the words to end, had been so final. It was his goodbye, and hers.

Yet, after weeks of coexisting with only rare glimpses of each other, David was here. He was tired, she could see it in his face. In the end, the valley hadn't been kind to him. With a twinge of regret, she wondered if she shouldn't have asked Simon to recall him after all.

For all his weariness, a feverishness burned in him,

something that had drawn him to her. Quietly, for it was her way, she bided her time.

Abruptly, beginning in midthought, in a roughened voice, he said, "The terrible things you let me say to you. Never bothering to deny them."

"Would it have done any good to deny them?"

"I accused you of living an empty life, of being insular, selfish."

"It doesn't matter, David."

"You let me believe—"

"I let you believe what you wanted to believe."

"You could've told me."

Raven shook her head. "You were a stranger."

"I'm not a stranger now."

"What do you want to know?"

"How Raven McCandless came to be the woman she is."

Remembering how he had lain with her and loved with her, she wanted to tell him that he more than anyone knew who she was. Instead, she said, "I'm a woman, no more or less."

"It isn't that simple, Raven."

She sat, her spine erect, shoulders back. The slightest relenting would be her undoing. Silence ticked from one eternal second to the next. David folded his arms over his chest. A gesture that meant he would wait until she answered. "It's an ugly story."

"I've heard ugly stories before."

Raven sighed. She rarely spoke of her life. There was no secret in it. It was just too painful to put into words. Now, it was David who asked, and she couldn't deny him.

"McCandless is a respected name, but there was a

time I didn't think I deserved it. A murderess shouldn't bear the name of those whose deaths she caused.''

She braced for some expression of shock or disgust, but David's voice did not judge. "Your parents?"

"And my two younger brothers."

"You didn't kill your family, Raven." He said what he believed beyond a doubt.

"For a long time, I felt responsible. To a fourteen-year-old girl, it was all the same." She had turned away unable to face what she might see in his eyes. Now, as she risked a look, she saw he was standing as before, his face unreadable, waiting. There was no escape. He would hear the whole of it.

She didn't offer him a chair or waste effort on amenities that interested neither of them. Instead, she began to speak in a low voice, telling David things only Rhea McKinzie and Simon knew. "My father called himself a teacher. There were titles and degrees attached to his name, but Colin McCandless was husband, father and teacher, in that order. The degrees and titles were simply to make him better. Everything he did was to that end. His plan as father and teacher was to introduce his family to other cultures. We lived in Scotland, in France, in Austria and in other places. He taught in their universities. There was money. Not enough to be a burden or too little to be uncomfortable.

"That was the problem. Our lives were too ordered, our means too visible, their source too obscure. My father became suspect. A strange religious sect in a Middle Eastern country where we had settled, targeted him as a spy. Maybe he did small assignments for our government, or maybe he was exactly what he appeared to be. Whichever, he wouldn't have endangered us with anything serious.''

"Any meddling is deadly serious to certain fanatical religions," David interposed.

That was a truth realized too late. Far too late. ''We were going on holiday. My brother Douglas had chosen to go skiing for his tenth birthday. We were almost ready to leave for the airport when I remembered a book I wanted to read on the plane. They were waiting for me in the car when I came back from my room. Jamie, who was only two, danced in my mother's lap, calling for me to hurry. He wanted to see the snow.

"The sun was bright, as it was every day. As bright as mother's laughter. Douglas was trying so hard to be dignified. Dad reached for the ignition, and Jamie called me again. Except…except his tongue couldn't manage an *R*. He called me 'Waven' one last time, then everything stopped.''

"Jamie," David said softly, and Raven didn't need to be told that he'd made the connection between Jamie McLachlan and Jamie McCandless. If her brother had lived, they would've been of an age.

Raven had to move, leave the sound of her own voice behind. She wandered to the window. The night reflected her mood. Against a dark sky, ancient trees rose in black, jagged spires, the cavernous gloom beneath them as impenetrable as her soul had been.

She looked into the unchanging darkness. "When I woke, I was lying on my back. Flakes were drifting about me. For a moment, I thought we were already in Switzerland. It was hot. Too hot. My face hurt, and my back. I tried to get up and couldn't. I lay there in the snow. After a while, I realized it wasn't snow. Then I heard their screams.''

David's touch stopped her. As he turned her into his arms, she heard his voice, soothing, tender. Then he said no more, holding her until the pain passed. The stroke of his hand was peace in the storm. In another time, another place, she would've stood there forever. But it wasn't another time, or place, and after a while, she pulled away. With a wan smile, she turned again to the darkness beyond the cabin.

"When the bomb exploded, my father was thrown clear, but the rest of them—" She swallowed convulsively, then continued. "None of the doctors believed he could do it, but he waited for Simon. When he had Simon's promise to take care of me, he let go." Raven clutched at the lace on her sleeve, shredding it to confetti. "Then they were all gone. My mother, my brothers. My father."

"Simon brought you here, to his own mother."

"When I could travel. The burns, the concussion of the explosion, my guilt made it impossible for a while."

"Guilt, because you delayed the departure, because you weren't with them." David said the rest, sparing her that.

"Yes."

"Dying with them would've changed nothing, Raven." His conviction suggested a new understanding. "If they had a last thought, perhaps it was rejoicing that you weren't with them."

"I know that now, but it was a long time coming. The doctors wanted to put me in a hospital. Simon wouldn't hear of it. All I needed, he insisted was time and a good dose of Rhea McKinzie. They were reluctant, but he wouldn't take no for an answer." She smiled only with her mouth. Her eyes didn't change. "Nothing can sway Simon when he's certain he's right."

"We can both thank God for that."

As if she hadn't heard him, Raven began to speak of Simon's mother, Rhea. "She was already a very old woman, for Simon was a child of middle age. She was strong and so wise. With an iron will and infinite patience, she taught me that it wasn't wrong to survive when my family hadn't. That was the first step and the hardest. Then she taught me that love was a precious gift to be given unselfishly with no guilt attached. She made me understand that love given might not find an answer, but must be accepted and cherished as the treasure it is.

"You called it a burden, an unwanted sacrifice, a waste. Love is never a waste. I know that now, but for too long, I felt as you do. No one could get close to me. Despite Rhea's teaching, I wouldn't let them. For a while I left the mountains, trying to escape her truths, living awhile in a village in southern Arizona."

Raven the innocent, who had loved no man until him. David ached to touch her in more than compassion, but knew he'd lost the right. "It doesn't snow in southern Arizona."

Raven wasn't surprised by his observation. David was kinder, more intuitive than he thought. He knew that each snowfall would, for a horrible moment, be ashes and the shriek of the mountain winds would be the cries of her family. "When Rhea fell ill, I came home. I realized then I could roam the world in search of peace and I would always fail, for these mountains are my peace. I haven't cried since I was fourteen, not even when I lost her, but I found my strength, if not my tears.''

"When it snows and the wind blows?"

"I cope. When I can't, there's Dare."

"Alisdair McLachlan." Who, in Patrick McCallum's cryptic words, wouldn't waste time on a game if he truly wanted something. "Dare." *Who wouldn't waste time on games if he wanted Raven.* He was near when she needed him, and David was grateful. "A friend."

"Only that. Always that." Glad for the change of subject, she said, "He regretted his behavior at the games. Out of sheer devilment, he wanted you to think there was something between us. When he realized he liked you, he wanted to make amends. The Tartan Ball was his way."

"He didn't understand that it was too late for us." Too many cruel things had been done; too many said. Not even gentle Raven could forgive them.

"He understands now." *Dare understands that I love you,* she thought, *and that I won't try to keep you.*

"Raven, I didn't know."

For a crazy instant, she thought David had read her mind, then she realized he was speaking of her family. "There's no reason you should."

"I should have known you weren't as I tried to paint you. Hell." He ran a frustrated hand through his hair. "When I let myself be honest, I knew you were the fairest, least-selfish human being I've ever known." He'd come to apologize, but it was too late and not nearly enough. Instead, he could tell her that Simon had been right in sending him to her.

He wanted to turn her from the window so he could take her in his arms, but her grief had passed. He could touch her pain, but never again her joy.

"I'll be going from the valley soon. I think Simon will agree that my time here has served its purpose. I won't go empty-handed. I'll be taking the lessons I learned from you." Raven shook her head, but David stopped her denial. "I've learned that love is anger as well as joy. That it is its own punishment, its own reward. That it can be tears as well as laughter. True love expects nothing.

"Most of all, I've learned that those fortunate enough to love and be loved are blessed."

God help him, he would give his soul to hold her, giving himself to her, not just pretty words. His fingers curled into his palms. "I've learned more of the meaning of love by living here in the valley than I did in a lifetime beyond it." He touched her then, briefly, letting his fingers slide over her shoulder. Her head was bowed, the fall of her hair hiding the little he could've seen of her face. "Simon was a far wiser man than I knew."

Raven heard his footsteps taking him to the door. Before he left her, there was one more thing he should know. "David, love is forgiveness. Even when forgiveness isn't needed."

She heard his slow deep breath, could imagine his chest rising with it. Then after a moment, she knew she was alone.

Seven

"No!"

David bolted upright in his tumbled bed.

"No." Sliding his hands through his hair roughly, he tried to force the last vestige of his dream from his mind. He had dreamed little since coming to the valley. Now, in the week following the Tartan Ball, they'd become constant.

In the dark of night, when he succumbed to exhausted sleep, his life in The Watch poured from his subconscious, each dream a progression, each filled with destruction and the turmoil of greedy men. Each night, he walked amid squalor and starvation, unscathed, unable to help. He dreamed of betrayal, of a faceless woman. She called to him, but he didn't answer. She was hurting, and he didn't comfort her.

At last, he'd seen her face. Raven's face, with ash drifting over it like dirty snow. Raven, not Helen Landon. Raven, who had known tragedy and grown strong and serene.

Raven, who hadn't loved a man until—

He drew a cigarette from a tattered pack on the bedside table. A match scratched against the cover and exploded into flames. With a grimace, he bent to it and discovered his hand was shaking. When light from the match died, he leaned against the carved wood of the headboard, closing his eyelids. The fragile membrane was a shutter for the eye, but not the mind. With a will of its own, that wayward part of him turned to the woman who had been a flame in his arms.

In a room much like this, she had come to him, giving her greatest gift, herself. To him. Not to Dare McLachlan, who had been in her life nearly forever, who was there in her need. Not to the handsome, dashing Patrick McCallum, who would turn any woman's head, whose violate look made no secret that, were she willing, she would be his for a while. That was Patrick's way with women.

David felt a hot surge of anger at McCallum—for his lust, for the impermanence—then had the good grace to be ashamed. Like himself, Patrick was not of the valley. A man of the world, the big Scot had fallen under Raven's innocent spell. But Patrick hadn't tasted of her delights. He never would, for Raven would only give herself to the man she loved.

She loves me.

The words were a whisper in his mind. An echo of what he had known for so long. As with the wildflowers, he'd been blind until she taught him to see.

"She loves me."

And love is never a waste.

He was on his feet, spilling the covers from his bed. In his left hand, the forgotten cigarette. In his right, the rose she'd worn. He didn't recall taking it from the bedside table where it had lain every night since the Tartan Ball.

The flower nestled like a jewel against his flesh, recalling the touch of silken skin, the scent of wildflowers and silence. He remembered the mating of their steps, like the mating of their bodies. He remembered ebony eyes, luminous, gentle, holding his. But most of all, beneath the decorum, he remembered the waiting passion. Waiting for his touch, his kiss. Only his.

"Dear God! She loves me."

Love is forgiveness.

He was halfway to the door when he remembered that the rose was still in his hand and that he wore nothing. Another time, he would've laughed at the idea of calling naked on a lovely woman, but not tonight. Stubbing the unsmoked cigarette in an ashtray and laying the rose carefully in its accustomed spot, he scooped up his discarded khakis. He was too impatient to bother with belt or shirt or even shoes.

The clock in Simon's library struck the hour. Two o'clock, but she would be awake. Weaving his way through the familiar darkness, David stepped onto his porch.

Darkness. Unrelieved darkness. Her cabin was dark. For the first time in weeks, she wasn't working into the morning. God help him, her cabin was dark and not even the fickle moon would light his path to her.

A sense of helplessness swept over him. He wanted to go to her, to wake her. To make love to her. But he couldn't. For the first time in days, she was getting the sleep she needed. His hand came down with a crash on the rail.

"Fool!" His voice floated through the silvered night, and there was no one to deny him. She'd been waiting for him. Waiting for him to believe and to come to her. Looking at the darkened cabin, he knew he was right.

His heart contracted, and the blackness of night lay like a mournful omen about him. The windows of her cabin were empty, staring eyes. Unwelcoming. At last unwelcoming. Raven had waited until she thought the waiting was useless, and now it was too late.

He had closed the door between them many times, or had tried to. But Raven never had. She hadn't once shut herself away from him, until tonight. There was a finality about the darkened cabin that sent a shudder down his spine. He mourned the easy silences, the soothing comfort, the gentle elegance. They would never be his again.

God! What a slow-witted, slow-acting fool he'd been. Perhaps this, whatever it was, with Raven wouldn't have lasted. Perhaps they were too different for it to last for always. But he would have had today and tomorrow and the tomorrow after that. Instead, he had nothing.

Nothing.

Sickened, he stood poised at the steps, torn by the need to wake her. To ask for a little while. He wouldn't be greedy. She had given him so much. He wanted only a little, just for a little while. Then he would be gone from her life, a stronger man because of her, and she could love again.

He yearned to take that first step to her, but for the

first time in his life, he understood what he would be asking.

As a night bird called and was answered by its mate, David turned to his own dark cabin. A splash at the lake stopped him. Hand on the door, head bowed, he waited. A night hunter? He heard the steady rhythm. For a time it ceased, and he thought, perhaps, he had imagined it.

Then again, the imperceptible splash. The lazy ripple of water. Raven. Swimming in her beloved lake.

Like a sleepwalker, he crossed the rough path. A soaring wind rustled the treetops. Skinny pines swayed and bowed. Over the mountain, too distant to be a danger, lightning flickered a promise of rain. On some level of consciousness, David was aware of it, of everything, but it didn't matter. Nothing mattered but Raven.

A stone clattered under his foot and Robbie rose from the underbrush, and at his side, Kate. Robert Burns, Raven's favorite poet. Katharine Hepburn, her favorite actress. Faithful guardians, keeping watch.

He couldn't see it, but he knew that both wagged their stubs of tails and flicked their ears. In his time here, they hadn't become playful with him as with their mistress, but because Raven accepted him, they had accepted him. And like her shadow, they were quiet, unobtrusive, ever present.

Beneath the hemlock, he waited, as he'd waited on his first journey into the valley. Kate came to him, snuffling at his hand until he scratched her ears. Next came Robbie, but standing aloof, never unbending enough to ask for affection. David smiled grimly. Were all males alike? Was it part of the masculine mystique to be above the need to be loved?

"Then we're fools, Robbie. Great, hulking fools."
The dog shivered, struggled with himself but didn't
relent.

Water lapped against the dock and David thought
no more of Robbie or fools. It was time. She was
near. He stepped from the protection of obscurity. The
dock stretched before him. Putting one careful foot
before the next, he paced its length. At the water's
edge, eyes closed, he listened, not daring to watch.
After a time, he opened his eyes and she was there,
fingers grasping the edge of the dock, water surging
from one last, glorious dive into the depths of the
lake.

Golden eyes met ebony and held. As if he were
watching himself from afar, David saw his hand
reaching toward her, waiting uncertainly, hungrily, for
hers. His heart stumbled beneath her dark, searching
gaze. Then her grip relaxed on the rough boards and
her hand was lifting to his, palm to palm, fingers
clinging.

Amid a cascade of water, he lifted her from the
lake. She was naked as he'd known she would be,
and more lovely than he remembered. He didn't
speak; he couldn't. He could only hold her to him,
reveling in the swell of her breasts against his chest,
the molding of her body to his.

"I hoped you would come." Her breath was sweet
and warm against his shoulder, sending a lightning of
its own through him.

"I thought I was too late." His whisper was roughened with fear.

"Never." She shook her head and was silent.

"Your cabin was dark."

"You could have come in the darkness to me."

"I did. The darkness of my own personal hell."

She drew away, unmindful of her nakedness, thinking only of David. There was a haggardness about him that suggested that he had, indeed, been through a private hell. But beneath it, there was a look, if not of peace, then its beginning. "And now, David?"

The night was a translucent veil, teasing, then revealing. She was magnificent, and his for the taking. But not until he wiped the look of concern from her face. He would see her smile as he drew her down to him. "It's done. I've made peace with the memory of Helen Landon at last."

"Love is a gift," he said, echoing Raven, not verbatim, but better, in his own words, making the thought more truly his. "Perhaps not to be returned in kind, but to be treasured." He touched her face, tracing the line of her cheek to her mouth, lingering there. "Simon knows magic." He kissed her, softly, slowly, with only his hand and his lips touching her. "Its name is Raven."

Raven trembled. "You really are all right?"

"More than I've ever been in my life." His voice was low, the roughness gone from it. "If it truly isn't too late."

Raven heard the strength and beneath it, the need. Turning her face into his hand, she kissed his palm. "Make love to me, David. Here by the lake where we first met."

"You're cold. You're trembling."

"Not from the cold, but still, you can warm me."

"Yes."

"Make the night more beautiful, David."

"The rain is coming."

"Not for a long time," she murmured, letting herself be drawn to him, knowing that his token resistance had been only that. A token. The prolonging of an exquisite need that would find an even more exquisite fulfillment. As their bodies met and her hands went to the snap at his waist, she murmured again, "Not for a long, long time."

When David woke, the night had changed. The moon that had been hidden behind the gathering clouds peeked through. Giving its blessing, it shone over them. The breeze that played among the treetops dipped now to the earth. It skimmed over their naked skin, turning their warmth to chill. Not even the reflected heat of Kate's black-furred body as she lay by David's side, or Robbie at Raven's, could deter it.

David looked down at the woman who slept in his arms. She was lovely. Her skin was tawny and golden against the vivid bath sheet beneath them. She was honor and goodness and magical peace amid a breathless, beautiful passion. He didn't understand how there could be peace as well as passion, would never understand. Like the tides of the sea and the moods of Raven's mountains, after the furor, there was tranquility, the time of holding her, of filling his mind and heart with the sight of her. Raven, with hair of midnight and spirit of sunlight, an exotic flower lying in guileless abandon against a field of blue.

He could watch her sleep forever, would wish this cherished interlude wouldn't end. Like the elusive stardust he'd imagined, it was not to be. Thunder, the passion of a mountain storm, rumbled, no longer in the distance. The threat of rain was reality.

Slipping his arm from her, he knelt over her, and gathering her again to him, rose to his feet. A massive

Doberman rose on either side and walked with him the length of the dock. The rhythm of his step woke her. Drowsy, with her head against his shoulder and her lips brushing his skin, she asked regretfully, "So soon?"

"Only a change of scene."

"The rain."

"Yes, the rain," he answered, though there was no need. She was asleep again. At the dock's end, he paused and turned. It hadn't changed. Somehow, he'd thought it would. Ridiculous! As ridiculous and sophomoric as making love in the open on hard, splintered wood. Tomorrow, he would feel every one of his thirty-eight years in every muscle. But that was tomorrow. The night was not yet over, and making love to Raven was never ridiculous. Anywhere, anytime.

Anywhere. Anytime. Yet he chose his cabin. Not because it was closer or because the rain was imminent. In a way he couldn't explain, making love to her in *his* bed, just for the remainder of this one night, made her his as nothing else could.

It wouldn't last. He didn't expect it to. Neither did Raven. When she took his hand, by mutual and unspoken consent, they'd agreed to take what was given them, to treasure it for the little time they had.

Much, much later, when his need was quenched, if not sated, he sat by the bed, watching her sleep, memorizing the way her hair grew in a swirling pattern over her ear; how the corners of her mouth lifted in a sleepy smile; how the cleft of her breasts deepened as she tucked her arms about her. When she stirred and frowned at finding herself alone, he murmured softly, "I'm here, Raven."

When she reached for him, drawing him back to

the bed, he knew a flicker of regret for the tiny seconds he'd wasted away from her. Then, when she rose above him, with her hair falling like a torrent of silk over him, there was no thought of anything but Raven.

Raven turned from her easel and looked into David's unwavering gaze. With a gesture that was not quite self-conscious, not quite comfortable, she asked, "What?"

"Nothing." David didn't smile, but his expression was calm, marked by contentment.

Though she'd come to expect his gaze on her and reveled in the softness she saw in this hard, brutal man, she had never grown accustomed to it. Could never take it for granted. He unsettled her. His look never failed to set her heart racing and her body throbbing. Her question had been simple reflex. A moment to gather her scattered wits. To rein in the desire a look or gesture could ignite.

Her life in the past three weeks, the last of David's sojourn in the valley, was a confusing mix of tumult and accord, of tenderness and brutal truths, of laughter and pain. The wildness in their coming together, utter sexuality, triggered by an uncalculated gesture, a look. The consuming desire that took her beyond thought or reason. The melding of bodies, joining in a fevered pitch, rising in a blaze that exploded in spangles of sunlight. Of love.

Each time, when she thought she couldn't bear it, couldn't live beyond it, the contentment came. And she discovered she lived, that her heart still beat in her chest, that only her soul had soared with his— when he was a part of her and she of him.

Because of the loving, it would always be so. No matter that he would be leaving soon, it would forever be so.

Survival, contentment, but never surfeit. Never that, for no matter how devastating and impossible, there was always the desire for more rippling barely beneath the surface. Rippling and surging, as now, with only a look from David. Perhaps such consuming hunger for a man's touch made her wicked or wanton, but Raven didn't care. These were days of enchantment. And if they never came again?

She wouldn't think of that. Tomorrow would come, but not yet. His eyes were on her, his book lying unopened on his lap. His body was taut beneath a surface negligence. Her own gaze swept him, languid with invitation.

"Nothing, David?" she murmured, letting her gaze dwell on the sudden rise of his chest as his breath caught.

"Only that I like to look at you," he said, so softly, she barely heard. There was pleasure in his tone, and more. "I've never known a woman as graceful or as lovely."

Raven's eloquent hands were quiet. Her head bent almost demurely as she had to look away from his tenderness. There was something he wanted to say, that he hadn't the words for, but her heart was nearly too full to keep still, her need too great to wait. Yet the tenderness from which her look had fled soothed her, drawing back her gaze like a flower to the sun. David *was* her sun.

"Raven." Her name was a caress. "You've given me the only peace I've ever known."

Raven smiled, and David saw her absolute serenity.

He had always seen it, though he hadn't known how to value it. Now he knew of her loss, of her pain and guilt, and of the childhood horror that had robbed her of her tears. In the aftermath of tragedy, she found not bitterness and hate, but a gentleness and compassion.

She was serenity, but at a price.

He'd seen ugly things and had thought himself strong until he found Raven and discovered the real strength of survival is forgiveness. Forgiveness of oneself for surviving.

Peace. If she'd given him that, her job was done, her promise to Simon discharged. A man at peace with himself would become a whole man, sure, confident, rational again. If her love went with him from the valley? It was a gamble she'd taken and would never regret. Not one kiss or caress or even estrangement. Not when the look in his eye turned her blood to liquid fire that only he could cool.

Once, she hadn't believed peace and passion could abide together. Now, she knew that only a man at peace with himself and his world could give himself so completely. Her breath quickened. Her lashes fluttered to the sudden flush of her cheeks, then rose, revealing eyes filled with exquisite need. "Peace is sweeter...after."

Before she could finish her appeal, David was answering. His book fell in a heap on the floor. His chair clattered against the wall. As it overturned, he was across the room, sweeping Raven into his arms and striding down the hall. The carpet before the open door was a mighty temptation, but the look in her eyes promised repeated delights, and he wanted to surround himself with all that was Raven. The whole cabin was her. Every board, every fabric, but nowhere was it as vital as her bedroom.

It was her sanctuary, and no man but he had been there. He wanted to revel in the knowledge, to lie with her and let the scent of her drive him to madness. He wanted to tumble with her, skin caressing skin, and feel the crisp, sun-dried sheets at his back as flesh sought flesh.

Their time was growing short. But for this little time, they could forget.

From that moment, David stopped counting his time with Raven in days or even hours. It was as if he had a stopwatch in his head that could freeze a moment or a second. He was a thirsting man storing water for the drought, except his store was a heady wine too precious to measure.

During the long hours she was away at class, he busied himself in any way he could, always avoiding the clock. Because of the season, the days were growing shorter. She left in darkness and returned in darkness, making their time in the sun all the more precious. At day's end, always in her bed, always with her head pillowed on his shoulder, his last thoughts were of Raven.

Raven, dancing in a swirl of golden leaves. Raven, bending over a lowly dandelion he wouldn't have seen or thought beautiful, until she taught him what beauty was. Raven, who laughed now as if laughter was her breath. Raven, who teased him and banished his somber looks. Raven, who forbade him to brood. Raven. Always and everything, Raven.

* * *

"You've been quiet tonight," he said into the darkness over her bed.

"I know." She turned her cheek into his shoulder, her lips brushing his chest.

"Something wrong?" Tell me, he wanted to say. Tell me what dragon to slay, and I'll slay it. Or what right must be done, and I'll do it. But he didn't, for he was the dragon, he was the wrong. The wrong man, the wrong time, the wrong place. Nothing he could do would ever right it. Guilt, black and overwhelming, streaked through him. For pleasuring himself with her with such abandon. For taking the gift of herself and giving nothing in return. For allowing something as hopeless as it was wonderful to continue.

As if she sensed the sudden change in him and understood the blackness of his mood, she shifted, sliding her body over him. She wore the poet's shirt of rough, creamy cotton and frothy lace, his favorite. He liked the feel of her skin beneath it. Pearls beneath sand, satin under homespun, that teased him until, in a fever, he would draw it from her. But he didn't tonight. Her face was too solemn, her eyes too dark.

"Don't!" she demanded fiercely. "Don't spoil what we've had with regret. You were the first, but don't ever think that I didn't know what I was doing. I went into this with my eyes open. Don't scowl at me, and don't spoil the little time we have left with thinking this was wrong because it had no future. I learned long ago that not everything beautiful has a future."

"Raven." He tried to tell her that her first man should have been her last. The one and only love of her life. She was that kind of woman. It was what she deserved after the heartache of her youth. He wanted to tell her he was sorry he had robbed her of that. He needed her to understand that beautiful things could last—but not for him. He tried, but she shushed him with a kiss of such startling intensity, he fell silent at last.

"Don't even think that I would have been denied any of this. Not one moment. If there is a man out there somewhere for me someday, and if it matters that I loved you first, then I don't want him. And his wanting me would be a lie."

"No." Any man would want her, and he would never be a lie.

"Yes!" Planting her hands on either side of him, she lifted her body from his, affording a very enticing view of her breasts beneath her shirt. "There are times in our lives that make us what we become, or will become. If that man of the future does not love the woman you've made me, he won't love me at all."

"Then he'll be a fool," David said, and he knew he was speaking of himself.

"Yes," Raven agreed with such conviction that after a moment, she laughed. "If you take that as it sounded, you must think you've created a simpering idiot with a monstrous ego."

"I took it exactly as you meant it. You aren't an idiot, Raven. You're only kind and generous to a fault." When she protested, he shushed her by drawing her head to his chest, stroking the dark strands of her tangled hair from her face until she was quiet and relaxed against him. "All this began because I said you were quiet tonight. You never told me why."

"I wanted to ask a favor."

He felt the tension start again in her shoulders. He waited for her to continue, when she didn't, he said, "It must be pretty important if you're worried over it."

"I haven't worried as much as anticipated your answer."

"Is it something so serious?"

"I don't think so."

"But I will?"

"You will. You're going to say no in the mistaken idea that it's for my sake, for the protection of my reputation."

He was thoroughly puzzled, but one thing was true. He was concerned about her reputation. About what his stay in the valley had done to it. After the fiasco of the Highland Games, his solution was to stay out of public notice. His calls to Simon were made now at out-of-the-way phone booths. The few purchases he needed to make were never made in Madison. After the ball, he'd made certain he was never seen again with Raven. Perhaps it was too little, too late, but it salved his conscience at least a little.

"What is this favor?" He stroked her taut body. "I'll do anything, if I can."

"Jamie's recital. It's tomorrow in the college auditorium. Since the Highland Games, he admires you tremendously. It would mean a great deal to him, and to me, if you would come."

"No." David's body was suddenly as taut as Raven's. "Surely you realize that's impossible."

She pulled away from him. "It isn't, but suppose you tell me why you think it is."

"*This* is why!" he said almost angrily. "Anyone can take one look at us and know."

"They know already, David." She lifted her arms. The full sleeves of her shirt drifting from her wrists reflected the slanting light of the moon like glistening snow. The neck of her shirt dipped low over the fullness of her breasts. Its lace framed the lovely slope, slipping dangerously toward a darkened nipple that peeked through its coarse, loose weave. "What do you see?"

He saw a woman who knew the pleasure of love. A lovely, desirable woman. He wanted to lean forward and capture with his mouth the impudent nipple that played hide-and-seek with its shadowy veil of lace. As he felt the mounting desire that could sweep away even the blackest despair, he murmured hoarsely, "I see a beautiful woman."

Raven met his gaze levelly, refusing to give ground. "You see a wanton. A woman discovering the pleasures of an affair. It's obvious, isn't it? In the way I move, the way I speak, the look in my eyes. It consumes me and elates me."

"Yes," David admitted. Anything else would be a lie.

"Have you fooled yourself into thinking that my friends haven't seen the change? That they don't know what brought it about? Do you think that what's inside me switches off when I'm away from you? There's magic here." She rested the flat of her hand on the bed where she had lain with him so many times. "Magic that all the world can see."

"Why confirm what they only suspect? Let suspicions remain suspicions. It will be easier for you when I'm gone."

Anger flared; her face hardened. "I won't say I'm proud of this, David." Raven rose from the bed, facing him in the little light that found its way through the window. "But no one has made me feel ashamed. Until now. Until you."

She turned away, moving with an unnatural stiffness to the window, her shoulders hunched as if her world had turned sordid.

Suddenly, the room that was his world seemed too much. More than a bastard deserved. The bed, her bed, was cold and empty without her. He hadn't meant to hurt her or make ugly something she treasured. He only wanted to protect her from himself, from the harm he'd done. But wasn't it too late for that?

David remembered the Tartan Ball and the look in Dare's eyes as he stepped aside for David. Dare knew even then, the wise man that he was, that he couldn't protect Raven from some things.

David was on his feet, crossing the room to Raven as he had before, as he would again. At the window, he drew her lovely, unresisting form against his nakedness. In the poet's shirt, she was, indeed, a pearl beneath sand, satin under homespun. He would give anything to wipe the look of sadness from her face. Anything. But Raven wanted very little and for a moment, before he brushed the thought away, it rankled that it was so little.

"Raven." His voice was rough, unsteady. "Sweetheart. Smile and I'll go anywhere for you. Siberia or hell. Even Jamie's recital." She was so still, he had the sinking fear she wouldn't accept his clumsy entreaty. Had he made one more thing too ugly to survive. Then she was turning to him, promising him in a voice that trembled that Jamie's recital wouldn't be as cold as Siberia or as hot as his second choice. The look of disillusionment was not completely gone and her smile was tentative, but when her arms wound about his neck, he knew she was still his Raven.

He led her to her bed like a saddened child. Trying to reassure her, he tucked the flowing shirt chastely about her, and then the covers, before slipping in beside her. For the first time in his life, David Canfield understood completely how caring was more than passion, more than desire. In Raven's bed, he discovered there were untold pleasures in comforting a hurt, beautiful woman, and in holding her. Holding her until she finally slept.

Eight

The sound of voices lifted and soared as David stepped with Raven into the back of the auditorium. Madison was a small college, but its needs were handsomely met by an endowment made by a wealthy family. What was once their summer estate was now the college campus. On a misty summer morning, Great-great-great-grandfather Madison had found his bride among the locals. He never forgot or let his family forget. In their generosity, Madison provided amenities much larger colleges lacked. One was the concert hall that took David by surprise.

"Listen." He grasped Raven's arm, drawing her to a stop, forgetting the implications of this public appearance. "Listen to the sound. I'd wager a whisper can be heard in the back row as well as it is in the first."

"What the Madisons do, they do well." Raven

continued to the aisle where three brawny men sat. The McLachlans, as striking in contemporary dress as in kilts.

"Dare. Ross. Robert Bruce." David addressed them after each greeted Raven with a kiss. There was no time for more as the lights dimmed, signaling the recital was about to begin. David sat on Raven's right while Dare was on her left, with the younger McLachlans beyond. David hadn't the opportunity to assess the reaction to his presence. When the lights went out and Jamie strolled to center stage, he forgot to care.

The transformation was astounding. Imp had become virtuoso, distinguished in black tie and tails. Every move sure, every note perfect, Jamie's music was passionate and pastoral, powerful and subtle. Sounds that recalled rippling water and the crash of the sea. The whisper of the wind through tall pines, the majesty and solitude of the hills. Jamie played faultlessly, and when Raven's hand slid beneath his, David closed his eyes and listened. There were only he and Raven and Jamie's music.

Too soon, the recital was done, and the audience surged to its feet. There was an encore, and another, and a third, then Jamie, with a familiar rakish smile, begged off.

The crowd began to move to the doors. Ross and Robert Bruce excused themselves to speak with friends. Dare was engaged in conversation with a formidable dowager. As the hall grew quiet, David rose, with Raven at his side. He hadn't spoken since the lights had gone down. Now, he breathed a single word, "Jamie?" Then, "I'll be damned."

"You aren't sorry you came?"

David turned to find her gaze on him; her eyes were shining. He wondered if she'd watched him throughout the program as she did now. Anyone who saw her would have little doubt of her feelings, and David knew with a trill of pride that the look was for him. Lifting her hand to his mouth, he brushed a kiss to the back of her fingers. "I'm not sorry."

"David, Raven, if you can tear yourselves away, it's time. The reception's already begun." Dare's dark face was lit by a grin, a mix of pride and amusement.

"Is it?" David didn't look away from Raven.

"The custodian will be closing the hall shortly. No," Dare corrected as the lights went out. "The custodian *is* closing the hall."

"And Jamie's waiting." Keeping her hand in David's, Raven led the way from the auditorium.

The reception hall was small but done with the Madisons' style. As Raven was drawn into the crowd, David stepped back to watch. These were her friends, her people. How would they accept her now that her life included him?

"They don't care, David." Dare was at his side, a flute of champagne in each hand. "Those who matter are glad Raven has finally found someone."

"Am I that obvious?"

"That you're worrying about what will happen to her when you leave? Yes, my friend. You're that obvious."

"I have to go." David waited for a comment. When the man at his side made none, he continued. "I wouldn't fit in here. After a while, I would make her more unhappy by staying."

"Keep talking, maybe you'll convince yourself, if no one else."

David forced his attention from Raven, slender elegance in a tightly belted dress that drifted about her like amethyst smoke. Dare offered David a glass of champagne. His dark coat and light, ruffled shirt were much like the one he'd lent to David the night of the Tartan Ball. "Dare." David's grip on the flute threatened the fragile crystal. "Will you help her?"

"I'll be here, but there are some things I can't make easier for her."

"She's a strong woman. She'll forget me."

"Yeah. When pigs can fly and fools learn the word *can't* is a self-imposed limitation. You say you can't stay in the valley. Jamie says he can't leave." Dare broke off, watching his laughing, young brother, surrounded by a bevy of adoring girls. "Look at him. He's happiest when he plays, but hasn't the sense to know it."

"When he's older, he'll know where his happiness lies."

"As David Canfield does?"

Not even the gentleness of Dare's tone softened the scalding sarcasm. Before David could refute it, his arm was taken by a tall, thin woman with a mass of white hair caught in a chignon at the nape of her neck.

Ice blue eyes peering through a lorgnette impaled him. "So, this is the young man who's put the roses in our Raven's cheeks?" She was crisp, blunt, reminding David of his third grade teacher.

When Dare attempted an introduction, she cut him off with a regal gesture. "I know who Mr. Canfield is, and you can tell him who the old biddy is when she leaves."

"Old biddy, Dean Madison?" Dare dared not laugh.

"The old maid of the founding family, who didn't have the good sense to take what she wanted for the little time she could as Raven has." The lorgnette dropped to her bosom. Without its distortions, David saw her eyes were lovely. "I knew your scalawag of a boss, Mr. Canfield. He was a student at Madison for a while. That Simon thinks highly enough of you to send you to his home speaks well of you. If you don't decide to rescind your resignation in your... ahh...former employment, come see me. Madison College could use a man of your experiences."

"As what, ma'am?"

"As an instructor, of course. Do you think I would waste your talents in criminology and diplomacy and skulduggery as a security guard?"

"My talents?" David smiled in spite of his efforts not to. "Are you so sure I have them?"

"Positive. Simon was your teacher, wasn't he?"

"Yes, ma'am."

"Checkmate. Dare," she addressed the man at David's side, "not one word to Jamie about *not* becoming a tree farmer. In fact, put him to work. So long that he can hardly find time to sit at the piano. So hard that when he does, all he can do is fall asleep."

"Give him what he wants," Dare said with a touch of irony.

"In spades. Mr. Canfield?"

"Dean Madison?"

"I'll be waiting." The regal back turned. They'd been instructed and dismissed.

"I feel like I did when Miss Halmer paddled my hand with a ruler in the third grade," David muttered.

"For me it was Miss Addison, fifth grade."

"Is she always like this?"

"Always."

"Lucky school. Lucky students."

"Yeah. You ready to brave the mob and give our compliments to my young genius?"

"Before you put his nose to the grindstone?"

"In spades."

"I liked your friends." The Corvette streaked over the road, its headlights brightening their path like day. David felt Raven's smile rather than saw it. "I know very little about music, except whether or not I like it. I think Jamie could make me like scales."

"He was pleased you came."

"Your Dean Madison offered me a job."

"She doesn't know."

David looked from the road. Raven was subdued, the gaiety he'd seen at he concert and reception dimmed. "What doesn't she know?"

"That this is your last week in the valley."

David slowed his speed. Leaving his left hand on the wheel, he slid his right hand into Raven's. She didn't move away, but beyond a smile, she didn't respond. The remainder of their journey was made in somber silence. It had begun. David felt it, the unconscious drawing away. The way of the mind and heart to soften a coming blow.

"I spoke with Simon today."

Raven looked up from her potter's table. She had recovered her composure after the concert and was again his tranquil companion by day, his passionate lover by night. In the evenings, she worked at her pottery.

"How is he?"

"He's well, but there's no break in the case. A lead, a phone number, hasn't gone anywhere."

Raven folded her hands in her lap. "How do you feel about the past now?"

David shook his head. Laying aside his book, he went to the window. "As if it all happened to someone else. That Helen Landon died for a man who shouldn't exist anymore."

"Are you sure he does?"

"I'm not sure of anything."

Raven waited. She couldn't help him now. His choices must be his own, uninfluenced by anyone.

"There's more," he said, breaking the silence.

"Something that troubles you."

"Helen Landon's family has planned a memorial service. They've asked that I come."

"Where?"

"Tennessee."

"Will you go?"

"It's not very far away from the valley. A day's drive." He shrugged and fell silent.

Raven left the table, going to join him at the window. "It's hard facing people who've lost someone. Would you like me to go with you?"

"Would you?"

She touched him then, laying her hand on his shoulder. "Wherever you need me."

His hand clasped hers, drawing it to his lips, and she went into his arms. "Thank you," he murmured as they looked over the valley together.

"Young man." Her voice was as peremptory as Dean Madison's, but the wizened old lady with skin of wrinkled leather and thinning brown hair pulled into a punishing knot, bore little physical resemblance to her. She was perched on the edge of her wheelchair like a fledgling robin who might fly or tumble to the ground. "Come here."

David went to her, kneeling in the grass at her side. Raven felt a surge of pride as she watched him lean patiently over the old woman, listening as if she imparted the greatest knowledge. He had that talent. A way of giving his unwavering attention in an aura of grave interest, then, in a trice, of striking one breathless with a smile. When he relaxed and forgot, no woman was immune. Not even this one, who looked as impervious as shoe leather.

Raven moved nearer, over the grass of the cemetery, trod by Helen's departed mourners. She waited for the moment David would smile and this ancient woman of Tennessee fell under his spell.

"She was a wild one." Raven heard the old, quavery voice. "She did foolish things, then more foolish ones to cover them. She was slick. Not many saw her at it. But I did before they shipped me off to the home. I did, sitting in my corner, in my chair. She thought my mind was as dead as my legs, or she just didn't care that I saw her playacting."

"Children do that, Mrs. Landon. Your granddaughter was no different than other children in that."

"She was, Mr. Canfield. She was."

"Why did you decide to speak to me about this?" David asked, more to humor the lady than for any other motive.

"I sensed a sadness in you. Maybe our Helen caused it with her foolishness, maybe she didn't. There was a mystery in her death. In all the years I knew her, any mystery involving Helen was created by Helen.'' The old woman looked into David's eyes. ''There's an investigation going on. Mr. McKinzie informed us of it today. Look into Helen's activities. Maybe your answer will be there, maybe not.''

''You didn't like your granddaughter, did you?''

''I didn't like her scheming, but I loved her. That's why I don't want her to be the reason for hurt.''

''Time's up, Mrs. Landon. Your son said to give you just five minutes with this gentleman, then to take you back to the convalescent center,'' said a brawny young man.

The old woman sent the nurse a withering look. ''Convalescent! Humph! How do you convalesce from old age?''

Ignoring her mockery, the man in whites propelled chair and woman to a waiting van. On its side was a cheerful logo aimed at making growing old and infirm a joyful experience. As the lift raised the chair into the van, the dark eyes of the old woman never left David. Not until the doors were shut and the van moved away.

''You heard?'' David asked as Simon joined them.

''It matched the version she told me.''

''What do you make of it?''

''A crazy old lady who hated her granddaughter.''

''Crazy like a fox.'' Raven spoke for the first time since the memorial service ended and the family gathered about David. She had bided her time, standing near but apart as they spoke to him in earnest tones, asking quiet questions with poignant need in their faces. Then, their goodbyes said to child and friend and sister, they'd gone. The last to leave was the old lady. ''She loves her granddaughter.''

''Honey—'' Simon put an arm about Raven

"—we can't investigate the ravings of every senile old woman."

"Not everyone, and not senile. Don't make the mistake Helen made. Don't assume her mind is as dead as her legs."

"You really think we should take her seriously?" This from David.

"What other leads do you have after all these months, Simon? David?" Raven waited as they got her point. Then, softly, "What other choice do you have?"

Simon addressed David. "What are your plans now?" His younger companions understood the unspoken—now that your exile is over.

"I'm going back to the valley with Raven for a few days. And you?"

"Back to Washington." Ruefully, Simon added, "To investigate our newest lead, as our lovely sleuth here suggests. In fact, my plane should have taken off ten minutes ago." After kissing Raven and brushing David's hand aside for a bear hug, he tossed them a jaunty wave, along with, "I'll be in touch."

Raven walked with David over the hillside to the Corvette. They were alone, removed from the bustle of the city below. Sunlight slanted through the trees, and crickets chirped in their rustling leaves. The air was so clear, it shimmered. The scent of woodsmoke whispered in the breeze. Colors were muted now, but soon, the sprawling forests would be dressed like gypsies.

Autumn, the beautiful end of summer. An ending, yet a season of riches. By drawing away from David, abandoning the best of times in fear of their ending, she had almost lost her autumn.

Almost. Her arm about his waist tightened, her step moved with his. She would remember this loveliness, how it surrounded her as she stood by the man she loved when he needed her. When he needed her, she thought, for a while.

"Raven. Thank you."

"It wasn't as difficult as you expected."

"Only because you were with me."

Raven stopped, linking her hands with David's. "There is an inn in a little glade along the way home. Even if she might have been as foolish or foolhardy as her grandmother thinks, I'd like to drink a toast to Helen there. No matter what else she did, she kept you safe." Raven's face was thoughtful. "We could be there by sunset."

"A toast to Helen," David agreed, "at sunset."

David's few days in the valley with Raven came and went, yet he showed no signs of leaving. Raven did not question it in the long, glorious days they spent together. Nor did she leave the valley. David did not make his expected journeys to one of a number of isolated phone booths, and for Raven, the daily trips into distant Madison ceased.

Though she'd worked at the college through fall registration and afterward, assisting the freshman class in orientation, her classes had ended until spring. These autumn and winter months she would devote to text and drawings for her book.

But in these special days with David, neither the book nor her drawings nor even her pottery could draw her from him. These were their halcyon days, days of happiness, of memories that must serve a lifetime. There was no looking ahead, no mourning for the time that was coming. Raven discovered that when one lived each day as if it were the only day, the day of reckoning did not exist.

This is paradise, David thought as he sat on the dock, a fishing pole wedged between the gaps of its planking. He glanced at the pole occasionally, not to see if a fish had taken his lure, but daring one to interrupt him. A cool breeze skimmed across his bare chest and ruffled his hair. He lifted his face to the sky, for once letting his attention wander from Raven.

He heard her laugh, and closing his eyes, let the sound drift with the wind over him. It was a lovely sound. The loveliest in the world. "David." He heard her voice and decided he was wrong. That was the loveliest sound, his name, with the laughter beneath it. "If I waited for you to catch our dinner," she continued, "we'd starve to death."

"No, we wouldn't. We could always make rock soup." He opened one eye and let the sight of her fill him. Other women might be dowdy in a tattered shirt and cutoffs that were even more disreputable, but not Raven. There was nothing that Raven wasn't pretty in, and turning it around, Raven was pretty in nothing. The illusion made him grin.

"You're thinking wicked thoughts, I can tell." She plucked a worm from the can beside her and made a show of nonchalance, but nothing hid the telltale flush that crept up her throat and over her cheeks. As she baited her hook and threw it again into the water, her lithe ease turned to clumsiness and the blush deepened. When David chuckled, she rounded on him. "What's so funny?"

"You are. I am. Everything." He looked at her, at

the dock's edge. This was where he'd fallen under her spell. "I had forgotten." As he was likely to do of late, he spoke his thought aloud, and when she looked askance, he added, "I'd forgotten how to laugh. But now that I've remembered, it's addictive. The more I laugh, the more I want to."

"You've grown lazy, too," she retorted, but a teasing tenderness lurked beneath the words. "It's been so long since either of us has been out of the valley, our cupboards are nearly bare. It's fish tonight or nothing."

"You're forgetting rock soup." He had no fear of starvation. He knew from experience that beneath her magic hands and with the help of a well-stocked freezer and cellar, a little of this, a dab of that, a sprinkle of this herb and a leaf of another, she could produce an ambrosia worthy of the gods.

"What on earth is rock soup?" Reeling her line in, she inspected it and found a wily fish had managed to pick it clean while evading its barb.

"Didn't your mother tell you of the poor soul who had nothing but water and a rock for his soup until he enticed others to add their food to the pot for a share? At least, that's how I think the story went."

David chastised himself for mentioning her mother, for bringing painful memories into their perfect world. When Raven only laughed, saying her mother was an accomplished storyteller, but she seemed to have missed that one, he relaxed, if only a little. He was reminded of something he needed to speak of to Raven, an issue that weighed on his mind, one he'd skirted for days.

Sitting as he was, his head resting against a weathered post, he watched her cast and reel and cast again.

She was an expert, putting the line exactly where she wished. Only, the fish were not cooperating today. The muscles in her arms flexed, then tensed with the drag of the line. With a shake of her head, she began to reel in again.

She was a far cry from the spinsterish thirty-year-old he'd once envisioned. Even farther from anything he'd branded her. But for the spill of her loosely bound hair and the sway of her breasts beneath the shirt, she could have been a young boy. A lissome athlete whose every move was unstudied vitality. Except today. Today, there was an inner quietude, a thoughtfulness ever present within the teasing and the banter.

Her line bobbed and pulled taut for an instant, then went slack again. Raven reeled it in, secured the reel and hook and put them away. "The fish have something on their minds other than feeding. As you suddenly do." Hands on hips, she surveyed the man whose smile had faded.

"Raven, there's something we need to talk about."

"Yes, I think there is," Raven agreed, and when he offered his hand, she took it, letting him draw her down beside him on the dock. Sitting with her hand still in his, she waited for him to speak.

"When I first came to the valley, I did a lot of thoughtless things. I was careless, criminally so." With his thumb, he stroked the tender flesh of her wrist, feeling his pulse joining with hers. "I've made mistakes in the past, and borne the consequences. But this time, there's more than myself to consider."

Raven stirred, started to speak, then subsided. He needed to say what he felt he must.

"We have loved well, but not always wisely." He

faltered, his mind on the times that the sweep of passion overwhelmed them. When wisdom was forgotten. "There were times when you weren't protected."

"But not many," Raven offered quietly. When David had discovered she was inexperienced, he had discreetly assumed the responsibility of her protection. And, yes, there were those times when neither considered it.

"One thoughtless act could be enough. You've helped me put my life back together. The price mustn't be your own."

What would you do, David, if our passion were fruitful? Would you stay in the valley? Would you stay with your child and me? The question trembled on the tip of her tongue. She wanted desperately to know. Did such answers matter when his concern was unfounded? "We weren't always wise," she said in a low voice. "But there's no baby, David." She looked to the horizon. "I'm not carrying your child."

Instead of satisfaction at having his intuitions confirmed, David felt a moment of piercing disappointment. Disappointment turned to anger. Anger became loathing. He hadn't the right to wish that this lovely woman, who had given her love, would give life, as well.

"I thought not," he said at last. "But I had to be sure."

"There's nothing to keep you in the valley."

"No." He waited for the elation, the joy of freedom. This was what he wanted. Wasn't it?

Drawing Raven into his arms, his cheek resting against her hair, he stared blindly at the horizon and wondered at his sense of loss.

* * *

The telephone jangled in the darkening twilight. David's hand went immediately to the receiver, lifting it from its cradle to keep the phone from ringing a second time and waking Raven. Though he was completely alert, it took him an instant to comprehend the message delivered in a hurried, broken voice. In shocked tones, he murmured assurance and his thanks. He replaced the receiver gently, but when he turned to Raven, he found her watching him.

"What's wrong?" Their lovemaking that had filled the late afternoon and the sleep that followed were forgotten in her concern.

He didn't have time to cushion the blow, so he said what he must abruptly, "That was Simon. There's been a break in the case. He's been shot."

Raven's hand flew to her throat. There was not enough air to breathe. "Is he..."

"He'll live," David said tersely. "Thank God the bastard who shot him doesn't know that. He does know where I am, Raven."

"Now he's coming after you," she whispered. "He has to before you find the same clues Simon did."

"Us. He's coming after us. He's traced me to the valley and you."

"Then what can we do?"

"Simon was ambushed and left for dead. He was unconscious for hours. His assailant has that much time on us. He could be anywhere."

"He could be here already," Raven said. "Watching us."

"Or the road."

"Do we stay here or do we go?"

"We go."

"If he's watching the road, we'll take the trails."

She wasted no more time with questions. Sliding from the bed, she threw off the poet's shirt and slipped into jeans, a heavy shirt and boots. David was only a button or two behind her when she straightened, saying, "I'll pack what food we might need for a few days on the trail. You see to the rest."

David allowed himself a moment to watch and admire her single-minded purpose, the economy of motion, then turned to his own tasks.

Nine

Nine

Darkness would be their shield. Until they left, David
told Raven, they would keep their usual schedule.
Moving carefully through their preparations, they
avoided being silhouetted against the windows, yet to
any watcher, displayed no undue caution. They
laughed and talked as on any night. Only David heard
the disquiet in Raven's voice.

She went to the door, opening it only a little, looking for her dogs. They were not in their accustomed
place. Perhaps they were off on a rare foray into the
forests. Whatever the cause of their unusual absence,
Raven refused to let her worry distract her.

David felt sympathy and admiration for her. She
loved the massive Dobermans as much as she loved
any human, but she faced this new trouble with the
courage he'd come to expect. She went once more to

the door. His heart lurched in regret as she closed it futilely. She was pale as she resumed her packing.

As he checked off their supplies against a mental list, David was pleased by her grasp of the situation. Her understanding of their needs. She'd gathered dried fruits from her cellar; they needed no preparation, and were light to carry. There were canned goods and water and a bedroll. Their departure could be as simple as walking out of the valley to safety, or they could be cut off completely, left to rely on trails in a lethal game of hide-and-seek. The trip over the mountain would take days. Raven planned for every possibility.

David regretted that their only weapons were assorted knives gathered from her kitchen and a rifle she kept for emergency use. With his service revolver, a powerful weapon that was never beyond his reach, their armament was little enough but would have to serve.

"Raven," David called when he was certain nothing remained to be done. She looked up from braiding her hair. "It's time."

Raven nodded and went to her bedroom, where she turned on the lamp by her bed. She waited there while David saw to the doors and extinguished the lights in the rest of the cabin. Then he joined her in the bedroom. Together, they waited the time normally needed in preparing for bed. At last, David nodded, and Raven turned out the lamp.

"This is it." In the darkness, he sensed her drawing near. He didn't ask if she was frightened. Only an idiot wouldn't be frightened when faced by a stalking killer. Her hand on his arm, steady, lingering briefly, signaled she was ready.

Moving like a cat, with Raven in his wake, David left the bedroom and crossed to the front door. He hesitated. "This may be a fool's exercise. There might be no one out there."

"He's there," Raven answered in a calm voice. "Or if not, he will be. He can't risk your finding the same clues Simon has. When he realizes he hasn't taken you by surprise, he'll suspect Simon survived and revealed his identity."

"Jeter," David said, giving a name to a faceless enemy. "His name is Thomas Jeter."

"Then we must act on the assumption that Jeter is out there waiting for you. For us."

David was so still, so silent, Raven wondered what thoughts were weighing on his mind. She waited patiently, giving him space. After a time, she touched his shoulder. "David?"

"I know." He covered her hand with his. The heat of it warmed the cold coil of dread. "I know," he whispered. "But first, this."

One hand slid about her waist, the other cupped the back of her head. His lips were on hers, tenderly but with a building hunger. There was an urgency in his kiss and in the intimate caress of his tongue. His arms were steel about her, melding the softness of her curves to the hard planes of his body. Clutching fingers drove into her flesh and were like a vise against her skull. Hunger and need and fear for her were in the devouring kiss. He was as desperate as he'd ever been. He wanted to draw her closer, to keep her safe at any cost.

When he drew away, his hands framed her face. "Promise me that whatever happens, you'll stay out of harm's way." Memories of another woman, of another place and of foolish sacrifices rushed in a tide of horror through his mind. "Promise me."

Raven understood his apprehension. As much as she could without a blatant lie, she promised, "I won't do anything foolish."

He held her a moment longer. Sighing, he released her. "I'll have to settle for that."

Raven bent, shouldering her small bag of supplies. David touched her face one more time and felt the brush of her lips as she turned her mouth into his palm. He had to struggle against the need to draw her back to him simply to hold her. A breath shuddered through him, shattering the silence that had fallen. His hand fell away from her face, his fingers flexing into fists. Enough time had been wasted. Too much. Abruptly, David signaled it was time to go.

Words were no longer necessary, and neither spoke again. David opened the door only enough to slip through. He moved in a crouching run to the railing at the side of the porch. As Raven slid beneath the rail, only a fraction behind David, she was thankful she'd changed into sneakers rather than the hiking boots. Boots would have been sturdier for the climb, but when quiet was of the utmost importance sneakers were better.

She followed David across the yard, praying that the dogs wouldn't choose this time to return and give them away. She realized by the path he was taking he intended to travel in a wide circle, merging with the road at a point beyond danger.

Despite the hint of chill in the air, sweat poured down her face and into her eyes. A spot between her shoulders prickled and burned, waiting for the slamming force of a bullet. Running a pace behind David, she wondered if this was how his life had always been, waiting for the bullet that had his name on it.

At the forest's edge, under its black canopy, David straightened. By his soft sigh of relief, Raven knew he'd been dreadfully worried by this mad dash over open ground. Allowing her a second to catch her breath, he began the circle that would lead to the road.

"No." She caught his arm. "This way."

"We'll try the road first. The supplies were just in case—"

"We aren't going to the road. We aren't going to try."

"Raven, I have to get you to safety."

"Until Jeter's stopped, there is no safety for me." Before he could argue, she stated the obvious. "You've said he'll know Simon warned you. The next and obvious deduction is that I know, as well. Neither of us will be safe again, David. Not until Jeter is caught."

"I have to get you out of here," David said doggedly.

"And risk losing him?"

"That doesn't matter."

Raven felt a lift of pleasure. She concerned him more than the revenge he'd wanted. David had never said he loved her, but she wondered, hoped that he did—at least a little. But that was to be savored another time. The issue now was life or death. "It matters to both of us. We have to stay in the valley and draw him out. To end this once and for all. If we don't, neither of us will have any peace again. I don't want to live my life looking over my shoulder."

"Raven, we haven't the time to discuss this."

"He'll come after me, David. So why not use me as a decoy?"

"No!" He grasped her arms, his fingers digging into her. "Dammit, Raven, I've already been responsible for losing one life to this man. I won't be for another. I won't lose you. I can't!"

"You won't," she said, wondering if he understood what he was saying. Aware of it or not, he was saying that he loved her. "There's a ridge on the mountain. From there, we can see and be seen. Yet it will be easily defended. I only intend to let him catch a glimpse of me. To draw him to it. The rest will be up to you."

"And if I fail?" he asked bleakly.

"You won't fail. We have too much at stake." It was the only way. He had to see that. He couldn't let Thomas Jeter slip away. For their safety. For Simon's.

"All right," he agreed at last. "We'll go to your ridge, but at the first sign of trouble, you're leaving."

"Alone?"

"Yes. Alone."

"We'll circle this part of the lake," she said quickly. Then, before he could demand another promise she wouldn't keep, she answered, "I'll lead."

David fell into step behind her. She knew these mountains better than he, and from the equipment she possessed, he knew she'd camped in them.

A quarter of the way around the lake, they began the ascent. They climbed steadily for two hours. David guessed that by day, without hampered vision, it could've been done in half the time. Near the crest of a ridge, trees began to thin, then disappeared. Raven led him to a natural meadow that was tiny and grassy and strewed with granite.

"This should do," she said, laying down her pack as she faced the valley.

David joined her at the precipice. She was right. Their view of the valley was unobstructed. As was the valley's view of the ridge. For the first time, he thought her plan would work. If he could get Raven away, it would be perfect. The mountain at their back was rugged, but she was expert enough to take herself over it and down, out of danger.

"No." Her voice was low and firm. "I know what you're thinking. I'm not going, David. We're in this together."

"I can handle Jeter better if I don't have you to worry about."

"That won't work. I'm here to stay. You won't be able to draw him out if I'm not."

David felt his temper rise at her stubbornness. "Since you have all the answers, would you care to enlighten me?"

Raven's own temper flared, but this was the time for cold logic, not fiery encounters. Giving herself time to cool down, she went to her pack and unzipped it. From it, she drew a can and a belt. With an object in each hand, she said, "I'm going to bring him to us with a careless mistake. One you wouldn't make. He'd suspect a trap, if you were alone, but with a clumsy novice, he wouldn't."

"I'm listening."

But not convinced, Raven knew. "The morning sun will strike this mountain full force by seven. Any bright object will catch its rays."

"The flash will be seen in the valley," David mused.

"A carelessness Jeter wouldn't believe for a moment from you." Raven was repeating herself, but she had her point to make. "One glimpse of me and he'll think he's found you, that he has you because of my stupidity."

She was right about the sun. Grudgingly, David admitted it. "It might work."

"If it doesn't, there's another probability."

"Robbie and Kate."

"They'll find me." Then almost under her breath, she added, "If they're able."

David went to her, sinking with her to the grass. He wrapped his arms about her, murmuring into her hair, "They will be able, Raven. Jeter isn't the prissy, clumsy fool we thought, but I doubt he's the sort who could take on two Doberman pinschers."

"If they're alive, they'll find me."

"Leading Jeter straight to us. That's more his style, to watch and follow."

Raven didn't believe a word, and neither did David, but it was something to hold onto. A comforting fantasy to keep her mind from the other alternative. Pretending her dogs were alive and well, she left him to begin setting up their fireless camp. When David recalled his experience with the rattler on a shelf of granite, she agreed the boulders would provide good cover in the light of day, admitting she preferred the open meadow by night.

Since this was to be a cold camp and neither was hungry, she finished quickly. The last thing to do was to set the guard. David insisted that he take the entire watch. Raven refused.

"Dammit, Raven," he exploded. "I didn't say I didn't trust you to do this. I said you needn't do it."

"I say that I do, and I *will*." She was unperturbed

by his exasperation. "Contrary to what you want to believe, you need the rest more than I. Our lives may rest on the speed of your reflexes. Even David Canfield, man of iron, must understand that. Take the first watch. I'll relieve you in three hours."

As she walked away to her bed roll, David felt an urge to laugh. He'd been bested with admirable ease. He didn't doubt she could do as she said, and do it well. He watched as she settled into her bedroll and turned on her side. In a moment, her breathing grew shallow and easy. Her lashes lay like shadows against her cheek. Her single braid fell over her breast. David wondered if her sleep was genuine or feigned.

"You're quite a woman, Raven McCandless," he murmured, and took up his watch.

"David." He was shaken awake. He hadn't intended to sleep at the end of his watch. Glancing at the risen sun, he realized he had. Raven crouched beside him. "He's here."

Flinging back his covering, David went to the precipice. Below a man was moving cautiously over the valley floor. "Jeter! And you can bet your last dollar he's armed."

David whirled about. Raven's can was already set on a misshapen jut of stone. The label had been peeled from it. Shadows cast by the morning sun were slowly shrinking away from it. In a matter of minutes, it would glitter in the autumn morning. He turned to Raven, studying the serviceable shirt, the heavy jeans, the bright, buckled belt that flashed and dimmed with every sunlit move. A beacon, summoning Jeter.

David's heart was suddenly pounding, his chest throbbed with its force. The sound of a rising wind and the call of a jay were lost in the thunder of his heartbeat. Fear churned in his gut. Not for himself, but for her. "Take off the belt, Raven."

Her lips moved, but the sound was swept away by the wind. "For God's sake, Raven, take off the damn belt. For all we know, Jeter could be a sharpshooter, a sniper. All it would take would be one bullet." His chest heaved. His eyes closed. "Take off the belt... please."

Raven was startled by his intensity. Then slowly, her fingers moved to the buckle and the belt fell to the ground. David stared down at it, watching it wink in the sun. When he looked at her, she saw relief in his eyes. Relief and something that made her spirit soar.

"You've done your share." David's tone was strained. "Now take cover. It's unlikely Jeter will be here before nightfall. Just in case, I want you out of the line of fire."

Raven didn't argue. He needed total concentration. All his senses must be attuned to Jeter. "You'll let me know if you see any sign of Robbie and Kate?"

He nodded but didn't answer. His face was bleak, and Raven knew then that he thought the dogs were dead. Perhaps they were. They'd never strayed this long before. But she couldn't believe they weren't coming back. She had to hope they were still alive.

She moved to obey, the forlorn slope of her shoulders tearing at him. As she climbed a small, grassy incline, he called after her. "If this doesn't work, get out. Take the roughest trail and don't look back. Jeter won't know these mountains like you do. Promise me you won't waste time here."

She stiffened, listening, her back ramrod straight.

When he fell silent, she shuddered, her body bending forward as if she'd been struck. As quickly as it had come, the weakening was gone. Her voice was low but steady. "I won't look back."

She threaded her way through the scattered granite to a fortresslike formation of stone and hillock, then disappeared. The meadow was empty. David was alone. He moved to the edge of the precipice, his thoughts solely on the man who prowled the valley floor.

Raven knelt by David in the twilight. She'd stayed out of sight in the long, anguished hours of watching, leaving her position only to bring David food and water from their meager supplies. She offered water now. He took the cup, his fingers brushing hers, and drank. It was warm and metallic, but quenched his thirst.

"Anything?" she murmured as she took back the cup.

"Nothing for hours."

"Do you think he knows we're here?"

"He knows, Raven. He was smart enough to bury himself under Simon's nose. He's smart enough to find us. It's just a matter of time." David touched her cheek, wondering if he would ever hold her in his arms again.

Raven's hand closed over his wrist. Her lips touched the taut flesh at her fingertips. She smiled, a little wistfully, and stood. David heard her footsteps whispering through the drying autumn grass, but he kept his attention on the valley and the trails leading to their mountain refuge.

"Robbie!"

He heard her cry and spun from the long slab of granite that served as his post. Every instinct jarred with a sudden sense of wrong and danger. "Raven! Don't!"

His warning came too late. She was racing heedlessly over the meadow toward the black dog that half crawled, half stumbled toward her.

"Raven!" David called again, but too late. Even as he spoke, a shadow materialized from the underbrush. Arms closed about her like a vise. A Jeter that David had never seen whirled to face him. The gun in his hand was pointed directly at Raven's head.

Blood drenched the shoulders of Jeter's shirt and ran in crimson rivulet's down corded arms. Robbie's blood, not Jeter's. He'd carried the wounded dog up the mountain beyond them and then down. A certain lure to draw Raven into his grasp. David felt bitter respect for the cunning mind and brute strength needed to execute it.

Raven was pale and taut and silent. A gory sleeve crushed her back against Jeter. Her throat was smeared with Robbie's blood.

Jeter grinned and motioned for David to drop his gun. A haze of rage as red as blood screamed in David's brain. Like a savage, he wanted to streak across the clearing to rip the offending arm from Raven. He wanted to destroy the man who dared to touch her, violating her goodness with his treachery. A taunting smirk told him Jeter wanted it, too. The man wanted to gun David down in that wild, mad rush.

Then, what chance would Raven have? David's fingers opened. The revolver fell at his feet. Deliberately, he blanked Raven from his mind, focusing his attention on Jeter. The man had gotten to the clearing, close enough for a shot, two shots, and he hadn't taken them. The little bantam wanted to strut. He wanted his moment of glory. He meant to gloat before he did what he'd come for. David hoped to turn that need into a chance for Raven.

Forcing himself to relax, David measured his opponent. Jeter was built like a small tank. The powerful, compact body had been concealed for years by skillfully fashioned suits. A sardonic smile tilted the grim slash of David's mouth. "My compliments to your tailor."

"He had his uses." Jeter dismissed the reference to the strength he'd kept hidden.

"Had?"

"Past tense. Like your beloved Scot."

The arrogant bastard thought he'd beaten Simon. It was a slim chance, but it was the only one David had. His laugh taunted. "It takes more than a cheap traitor to do in an old fox like Simon McKinzie."

"Don't waste your breath. I saw him."

"Simon might have been down, but he wasn't out. Who do you think warned us? Who knew where I was but Simon?"

"Anybody could've found out. I did, by tracing this little lady's call to Simon. She was with you at the services for that simpering fool, Helen Landon."

"Who was looking for me, Jeter? Except the man who must be sure his link to Helen Landon was never discovered?" A vague motion caught at the edge of David's peripheral vision. Not Jeter, whose gestures were dramatic and calculated, nor Raven, inanimate and mute. Something moved beyond them, but David couldn't risk a look. "Simon got too close for comfort, didn't he? And you couldn't be sure how much

I knew. You had to get both of us." He let a jeer creep into his words. "Except you failed with Simon."

"You lie!" Jeter's voice took on an edge of uncertainty.

"Do I?" There was movement beyond Jeter again, the sway of grass, a shivering shadow.

"Enough!" Jeter's voice slashed through the meadow. "I'm tired of this little game. Move to the ledge, Canfield."

David hesitated. Jeter jerked Raven's head back by her braid, jamming the barrel of his gun viciously into the soft curve of her chin. In the failing light, David saw a thin trickle of blood at the corner of her mouth.

Jeter's eyes never wavered. "Move."

"No, David!" Raven's cry was garbled from the brutal pressure.

Another blow like the last could easily crush her throat. He had no choice. Stepping closer to the ledge, he ignored the yawning chasm below. "It was you all along. You used Helen, didn't you?"

"This discussion's over. You're first over the ledge. After a while, the little lady will join you." Jeter clucked his tongue in mock remorse. "Climbing accidents are so sad."

"Simon will know better."

"Simon's dead!"

"Then who warned me?"

"Shut up!" Jeter was cracking. Pulling Raven roughly against him, he used her braid to bend her head at an impossible angle. Her strangled moan had David whirling from the precipice. He didn't care what Jeter did to him. It didn't matter, so long as he bought time for Raven. He felt the ricochet of a bullet and heard Raven call his name in anguish. He braced to attack as a bolt of black lightning streaked from the underbrush.

One hundred twenty pounds of snarling fury drove Jeter to the ground. He lost his hold on Raven. As he clawed at her, Robbie's glistening fangs closed like a steel trap, shattering his wrist. Jeter shrieked and struggled to turn the gun on the wounded dog as David kicked it out of his hand.

Like a mad thing, Jeter flailed at the dog. "Robbie!" Raven's command cut through the frenzy. No more was needed. The battle was done. Robbie backed off, limping to his mistress with the last of his strength.

David spared a glance for Raven, assuring himself she was unharmed. She was down and there was blood on her—Robbie's blood. With a grateful heart, David bent to deal with the fallen Jeter.

The moon was rising in a black sky still streaked with the fading fire of the sun. That beautiful aura, when day met night, held no magic for David as he crossed to Raven. She was a grave image in the pale darkness, only her hand moved lovingly over Robbie's still body. Moisture-laden grass cushioned the sound of his steps, yet he knew Raven heard. She heard, but still, he called her name. Only her name.

"Raven."

When she looked up at him, smiling a sad smile, he crouched by the great dog, his hand like hers stroking the heavy fur. After a time, she leaned her cheek to the sleek, dark head cradled in her lap. Robbie stirred and licked her hand. The meadow was hushed, even the wind was still. When she straightened, her eyes were dry.

"He's gone," she murmured, and David heard the grief locked inside her.

"Yes." But Robbie would never be truly gone as long as Raven lived. David looked out over the valley, remembering the bitter man he'd been. Understanding at last the man he'd become. He thought of the past and of Helen Landon, and felt neither anger nor guilt. Whatever Helen had done, for whatever reason, she'd been instrumental in bringing him to Raven.

And here on this hillside, in the name of love, he would've done what was needed to protect this magnificent woman and asked nothing in return.

When the night grew chill in the higher altitude, he rose. After seeing to Jeter, who was trussed uncomfortably like a mummy, he built a fire and brewed the sweet, dark chocolate Raven had packed. When it was done, he took it to her. She wouldn't drink it, but the heated cup could warm her hands.

Sitting beside her, he drew her back, into his arms. Her sigh—soft, weary, yielding—told him all she hadn't said. With his lips against her hair, he held her and dared to dream of a future. Tomorrow, he would take Jeter down. Then Robbie and Raven.

He would be needed in Washington for a while, but when he was free again, he would come back to the valley.

Ten

"**H**ave you heard from Raven?"

David shook his head, avoiding Simon's probing stare. He moved to the window that overlooked hospital grounds. Simon would be here for a few more weeks of therapy, then he would be going to the valley to convalesce. David had been assured by harassed doctor after harassed doctor that, though Simon's recovery was slow, it would be complete.

Now David shrugged his shoulders with a nonchalance that fooled exactly no one. "I haven't heard from Raven since she was in Washington to see you."

"Then why are you wasting time here?" Simon growled. "Jeter's put away. We know what he was and for whom. I have the solemn oath of the government involved that his contacts will be, shall we say...removed. He was small potatoes. Wheeling and dealing in penny-ante stuff. A disgruntled, self-important government official looking for a quick buck and a little glory as he climbed the ladder to power.''

"Helen Landon paid for his ambition." David hit the window with a force that threatened it. "He destroyed her, with my help.''

"Your conscience should be clear about Helen. She was exactly what her grandmother said, a foolish manipulator who got in over her head." A sad frown flitted over Simon's face. "She was my mistake.''

"How do you figure that?" David faced Simon again, the tensions of the city, The Watch, his old life were there again in his eyes.

"Poor judgment. Poor screening. Some of her outstanding qualifications blinded me to important flaws. Flaws that outweighed any qualities." Simon sighed heavily, and David heard the self-recrimination. "Things I should have seen.''

"Simon…''

"Jeter tripped himself up. He got impatient, cocky. He pushed for your dismissal. A dismissal that was to be fatal. In his zeal, he said some things. Things he shouldn't know. Suddenly, Helen's grandmother wasn't a senile old woman. Everything she'd said made sense.

"Helen wanted to shine. To get ahead. She used Jeter to create a situation. He'd been approached by some comic-opera colonel, had a little information, precious little, that he traded. When she saw her blunder, it was too late.''

"Simon.''

"Let me finish, dammit!" He wheeled his chair closer to David. "I should have seen it long before I did. The number you found…''

"Could've meant anything."

"The bastard had to spell it out for me. I thought he only wanted me. Instead, he betrayed the country, as well. I underestimated him. Worthless files aside, when I added two and two and finally arrived at four, he was already there, with a gun, to silence me. You were next. He'd traced Raven's call and seen her with you at Helen's memorial service. It was that easy for him.

"Perhaps I'm as flawed as Helen was." From the confinement of his wheelchair, Simon looked tired. Illness etched his face, aging what had once seemed an ageless man. "My error almost cost you your life."

"You can't know when every slime takes it into his head to slide over the line, Simon. There aren't enough hours in a lifetime to watch them all. Jeter was a lone wolf hidden in the pack and just obvious enough in his underhandedness to avoid suspicion of more serious involvement.

"As for Helen, she was a damned good agent until infatuation and hunger for glory blinded her. *She* almost cost me my life, not you. Then she gave it back to me. If there's a debt to be paid, she paid hers. Now it's Jeter's turn."

"It will be a long time before he sees the light of day. If ever." Simon's tone altered, softened. "That's it, then? You've come to terms with what happened?"

"I've put it into perspective."

"And your damnable conscience?"

"When a man comes to terms with his conscience, is he still a man?"

"Not a man like David Canfield." Simon offered

his hand. When David took it, he covered it with his left. "Good luck, David. Have a good life. When you get to the valley, kiss Raven for me and tell her that I'll thank her in person in a few weeks."

"Then you know."

"That The Watch has truly lost you? Yeah, I know. But who would choose The Watch when a woman like Raven is waiting for him."

"Is she? I brought a lot of pain to her life. There were times when I was worse than a bastard."

"But you love her. I saw that for myself at the games. And she loves you, David."

"She did. A lot has happened that could've changed that."

"Not Raven."

"I haven't heard from her, not in weeks, Simon."

"She had her own grief to work through. Robbie, and then finding Kate."

"Both taken out by a scope shot." David's voice was flat, bitter. "Only Robbie took a while to die."

"It was ugly, David, but she won't fold. She's made of stronger stuff than that. This has been rough on you, too. Raven wouldn't want to pressure you. She's giving you space to decide, to choose."

"I don't need space. I know what I want. I want Raven and a life in the valley."

"Then why are you standing here with me, David? Go to her."

"We both know there will be times when I'll be difficult to live with. No one can wave a magic wand and make my years in The Watch disappear. Is it fair to ask her to struggle with it?"

"The choice is Raven's. Let her make it."

"Yeah." David smiled wryly. "Dean Madison offered me a job. Can you see me as a college professor?"

"I can see you as anything, David Canfield."

"If I have Raven." He realized he still held Simon's hand. He squeezed it, surprised at the returning strength he felt. Someday, when Simon was ready to listen, David would tell him how much he'd meant to him. He'd remind this rough, kind man that he'd saved his sanity—and his life. And with his warning, the life that mattered. Raven's life. David would tell him. Not yet, but soon. "Be well, my friend, and wish me luck."

When David was in the open doorway, framed by its dark wood, Simon called after him, "You don't need luck."

"We'll see."

Simon chuckled. "Were you ever this afraid when you faced the bad guys?"

"I've never been this afraid in my life." David smiled a rueful, lopsided smile and, with a salute, began the long walk down the polished hospital corridor. The echo of Simon's chuckle and then his laughter followed him into the morning.

Raven leaned her head against a piling of the dock, listening to the quiet. The afternoon sun was warm on her face.

Indian summer, a time she loved, the mild, clear days that came like a gift in autumn. A time she was most at peace with herself, her world. But no more. She was restless, unsettled, and had been for days. The valley with its deep dark nights and its flaming days hadn't appeased her.

She had risen this day in a fever, dressed, redressed

and dressed again. Nothing felt right. Her skin ached. A futile hour spent at her potter's table produced nothing, achieved nothing. Her gaze had strayed too often with her thoughts to a telephone that did not ring.

How was Simon? Was he well? Were his friends about him? Was David?

David.

Always David.

Her heart had pounded in her throat like a drum. The air in the cabin stifled. The strictures of her clothing became unbearable. She'd found herself dressing again, her hand going to the poet's shirt. David's favorite. The soft fabric had drifted over her bare body like a cloud. Lace caressed and revealed—but there was no one to see.

The path to the lake had drawn her. Shimmering water whispered a silent invitation. She had thought she would swim, remembered David's quiet worry when she did. Instead, she'd drowsed the afternoon away, sitting on the dock, one foot trailing in the cool water, one curled beneath her on the weathered wood.

She missed Robbie and Kate, but in the long, silent weeks, the keen edge of grief had mellowed. She would have other dogs. Someday.

A footstep whispered on the dock and was still. She couldn't turn, couldn't breathe. A breeze teased gleaming curls that escaped from the loose coil pinned at the crown of her head. They tumbled about her throat and shoulders and the swell of her breasts. Fallen leaves of scarlet danced over the dock, rustling and murmuring enticing secrets, leading Raven's gaze to David.

Not the David she'd known, but the man who had

first come to the valley, distant, troubled, handsome in his own way. He wore dark, close-fitting trousers with shallow pleats. Token obeisance to current fashion that mattered not one whit to him. His shirt was turquoise, a deep, rich color captured in luxurious silk. The comfortable elegance of the wise and seasoned traveler—the sophisticated mantle of his world. In the glinting sun, a new dusting of silver at his temples hinted of that world's tribulations.

Handsome, distinguished, forbidding. David, but a stranger. An untouchable stranger.

Raven drew a long, anguished breath and looked away from his fathomless eyes. The sound of his footsteps began again, the tap of leather heels, a slow, measured pace bringing David relentlessly nearer.

She meant to rise, meeting him on common ground, and no matter the hurt, keeping her pride intact. Before she could move, he was there, feet planted implacably, waiting for her.

Raven lifted her head, her eyes traveling the length of him deliberately, seeing at close range what she hadn't seen from afar. She was shocked by the man beneath the veneer of elegance. He was handsome, yes, always to her, and distinguished. But not forbidding. He was not an untouchable stranger. He was a man with his heart in his eyes.

His gaze never left her face as he leaned to her and, with a familiar, courtly gesture, offered his hand. Water lapped at her toes, a cricket chirped in a nearby shrub, the shrill cry of a hawk rose over the valley floor—sounds of the valley magnified by its silence and unheard.

Slowly, with a soaring heart, Raven lifted her hand to his. Palms met, fingers clung. Sun-warmed flesh held fast. Then he was drawing her up and to him, spinning with her in the sunlight. Holding her as if he would never let her go. Kissing her. Muttering low, sweet words. Kissing her again. "I was afraid."

"That I would swim alone?" She wanted to hear what she had seen in his eyes. The words. The truth.

He drew the pins from her hair; his hand burrowed in the spill of black gossamer. His voice was husky, rough. The admission of fear, the truth, was not easy for him. "I was afraid you wouldn't want me."

She touched his face, then because she couldn't bear the anguish there, she laid her cheek on his shoulder. "I want you, David," she murmured into the pulsing heat of his throat. "I'll always want you."

He drew a long, slow breath, his chest shuddering with it. His hand slid down her body, holding her to him as if she were fragile, easing the ache of his lonely weeks away from her. When he could trust his voice, he said, "It won't be easy. I'll be difficult, moody, though I won't mean to be."

"Because the memories won't just stop," Raven murmured. "Because in all your years in The Watch, you've never been able to feel that the face of the enemy is the same, whether man, woman or child. Wicked or kind. Vigorous or infirm."

"My weakness."

She stepped away, able to meet his gaze, needing to. "Not your weakness, David. Your strength."

"I came to the valley to find a place of peace, but you became my peace and my strength. I love you, Raven." Her eyes were shining, the look in them enough to bring the strongest man to his knees. She was beautiful. She had never been so beautiful, and it was for him. Yet he felt incomplete. A look was not enough. Dear God! Not nearly enough. "Tell me."

Raven went utterly still. Shock turned her tawny skin pale and her eyes darker than night. She spun about, turning her back on him, moving away. At the dock's edge, she rested one hand on the piling, the other at her breasts. Her back was straight and proud, but her head was bowed.

He wanted to go to her and take her back into his arms. The valley was home now, and none of their differences mattered. This proud, brave woman was his love, the love he would've died for. Only one thing mattered. "Tell me." His voice was raw and aching with his need for the words he'd thought he never wanted to hear. Need became hunger and hunger, desperation. Control that had spun to a fine, thin thread finally snapped. "Dear God! Raven, tell me."

When she turned, her head lifted. Tears glittered on her cheeks. "I love you, David." A smile so lovely, it nearly destroyed him barely curved her lips. "I love you."

She was his sunlight, his hope. When she smiled at him through her tears, he knew she was more than his love. She was his life.

"Raven." His hands were white-knuckled fists. He wanted her. He wanted her with him always. He wanted to spend his life hearing that soft whisper, basking in her love. But had he misunderstood? Was it too late? Had he done too much? Was the danger of loving him unbearable? Her tears, so lovely, so rare... He had to know. Was love enough?

He was hurting. He was desperate. But most of all, he was more than afraid. The chameleon, the proud, lonely man of The Watch was terrified. She was his life. Had he lost her?

A tear trembled on a lash and tumbled down her cheek. With a fingertip, he caught the crystalline drop. It held his world. "Raven?"

If her smile was lovely, her quiet serenity was breathtaking. Her lips brushed his skin where her tear had lain. "I never expected to be so happy. I never thought you'd need to hear that I love you."

David shivered, his body swaying. This was how it was to love. It was pain. It was enchantment. And tears could be joy. His voice was rough and tender. "Simon didn't tell me it would be like this."

"No."

"I think he knew."

"Yes."

"Our oldest sons, Simon first? Or should it be Colin?"

"Simon, I think, and then Colin. After that, I'd like a David."

David laughed. It was a beautiful sound. "In that case, my love, we'd better begin." As quickly as it had come, his laughter faded. "Oh, God! Sweetheart. I thought—"

"Shh." Raven's hand was on his shoulder, and when he opened his arms, she stepped into them. "You couldn't lose me. You never will."

His fingers twined in her hair, binding her to him. His body convulsed against hers. He wanted the words. He wanted to hear her say that she loved him. He knew that he would, over and over again, now that she knew he needed them.

The quietude of the mountains surrounded them as they embraced in the sun.

Raven didn't know how long he held her. He needed her; he loved her. Only that was significant.

When he moved away, his arms still linked about her, his eyes were dark, glittering gold. "Before we begin our little Scots, shouldn't we attend to a little thing called marriage?"

"Later, love." She rose on tiptoe to kiss him. The poet's shirt slid temptingly from her shoulders. "Much later."

His marauding gaze was a caress, his voice a whisper as he drew her slowly nearer. "But not too much later. I don't think it would be wise."

"No." Raven chuckled delightedly at her wonderful, proper renegade and let her shirt of cotton and lace drift from her body.

"David," she whispered when he was only a step away, "I love you."

* * * * *

*Also available in August 2000
from BJ James,*

The Return of Adams Cade,
Silhouette Desire #1309,

a MAN OF THE MONTH *title
and part of BJ James miniseries*
MEN OF BELLE TERRE.

Get 2

HOW TO GET YOUR
2 FREE BOOKS AND FREE GIFT

1. Peel off the 2 FREE BOOKS seal from the front cover. Place it in the space provided at right. This automatically entitles you to receive two free books and an exciting mystery gift.

2. Send back this card and you'll get 2 "The Best of the Best"™ novels. These books have a combined cover price of $11.00 or more in the U.S. and $13.00 or more in Canada, but they are yours to keep absolutely FREE!

3. There's <u>no</u> catch. You're under <u>no</u> obligation to buy anything. We charge nothing – ZERO – for your first shipment. And you don't have to make any minimum number of purchases – not even one!

4. We call this line "The Best of the Best" because each month you'll receive the best books by the world's hottest authors. These authors show up time and time again on all the major bestseller lists and their books sell out as soon as they hit the stores. You'll like the convenience of getting them delivered to your home at our discount prices...and you'll love your subscriber newsletter featuring author news, horoscopes, recipes, book reviews and much more!

5. We hope that after receiving your free books you'll want to remain a subscriber. But the choice is yours – to continue or cancel, anytime at all! So why not take us up on our invitation, with no risk of any kind. You'll be glad you did!

6. And remember...we'll send you a mystery gift ABSOLUTELY FREE just for giving "The Best of the Best" a try!

MIRA®

SPECIAL FREE GIFT!

We'll send you a fabulous mystery gift, absolutely FREE, simply for accepting our no-risk offer!

Visit us at
www.mirabooks.com

Books FREE!

The Best of the Best™—Here's How it Works

Accepting your 2 free books and gift places you under no obligation to buy anything. You may keep the books and gift and return the shipping statement marked "cancel." If you do not cancel, about a month later we will send you 4 additional novels and bill you just $4.24 each in the U.S., or $4.74 each in Canada, plus 25¢ delivery per book and applicable sales tax, if any.* That's the complete price, and — compared to cover prices of $5.50 or more each in the U.S. and $6.50 or more each in Canada — it's quite a bargain! You may cancel at any time, but if you choose to continue, every month we'll send you 4 more books, which you may either purchase at the discount price…or return to us and cancel your subscription.

*Terms and prices subject to change without notice. Sales tax applicable in N.Y. Canadian residents will be charged applicable provincial taxes and GST.

If offer card is missing write to: The Best of the Best, 3010 Walden Ave., P.O. Box 1867, Buffalo, NY 14240-1867

BUSINESS REPLY MAIL

FIRST-CLASS MAIL   PERMIT NO. 717   BUFFALO NY

POSTAGE WILL BE PAID BY ADDRESSEE

THE BEST OF THE BEST
3010 WALDEN AVE
PO BOX 1867
BUFFALO NY 14240-9952

NO POSTAGE
NECESSARY
IF MAILED
IN THE
UNITED STATES

Dear Reader,

The first line in *Dawn's Gift* is "He was home." But while Creed Parker has returned to the farm where he grew up, the ghosts he carries within him from the secret life he has led for so many years keep him from finding the inner peace he so desperately needs.

It is the gift of Dawn Gilbert's love that heals Creed's broken spirit and makes it possible for him to be truly home at long last.

I hope you enjoy *Dawn's Gift,* and that you will know that you truly can go home again if that is where your heart belongs.

Thank you all for the wonderful support you've shown me over the years. You are the ones who make all the hard work worthwhile.

With warmest regards,

Joan Elliott Pickart

DAWN'S GIFT
Joan Elliott Pickart

(originally published as Robin Elliott)

For Iona Lockwood and Virginia Conrad,
who shared their beautiful trees with me.

One

He was home.

Creed Parker stood at the end of the narrow dirt road, his gaze sweeping over the land, then coming to rest on the small two-story frame house nestled among the tall trees.

The old place needed a coat of paint, he mused, and the front steps were sagging, but oh, damn, it looked good. The whole farm did. Yeah, he was home.

Creed took a deep breath, filling his lungs with the early-morning air, sifting through the scents that assaulted him to see which he could still put a name to: honeysuckle, dew-soaked grass, overripe fruit on moist soil. And the sounds: squirrels chattering, birds singing, a cow or two bellowing in the distance.

He nodded in approval, then started off again, walking slowly down the road to come to the front of the house. The door would be unlocked, he knew that, but he didn't want to go in, not yet. The last streaks of dawn were giving way to the blue sky of August, with its golden sun and white clouds. The chores had begun an hour before. The house would be empty.

Creed swung his suitcase onto the wooden porch, then headed around the side of the house, his step quickening. An urgency engulfed him, a need, and he began to sprint toward the barn, his long legs covering the distance of the back lawn, then passed the chicken coops, to come at last to the weather-beaten building that was devoid of paint.

In the doorway he hesitated, allowing his eyes to adjust to the dimness. And then he saw him.

"Dad?" Creed said.

Twenty feet away a man stiffened, his back to Creed, then he slowly turned to face him.

"Creed?" he said. "My God, boy, is it really you? Creed?"

"Yeah, Dad, I...I'm home."

"Praise the Lord. Five years. It's been five years!"

In an instant they were moving, meeting in the middle of the expanse, holding each other in a tight embrace. The son towered over the father, was bigger, stronger, tightly muscled. His hair was thick and black, with streaks of gray at the temples, while the older man's was receding some and totally gray. Eyes were matching blue, but yet, they were different. The father's eyes were warm, gentle. The son's were cold, like sentinels guarding the path to his soul.

"Creed," the man said, then stepped back, gripping his son's arms as his gaze took him in from head to toe. "You're tired."

"I was up all night."

"It's more than that."

"Yeah, Dad," he said, taking a deep breath, "it's more than that."

"Your room is just how you left it. Get some food, sleep."

"I have to unwind a little. Okay if I wander around first?"

"This is your home. You do what feels right. I gotta get these cows milked before they holler to the next county. I'll see you up at the house later."

"All right," Creed said, turning and walking to the entrance of the barn. He stopped with his back to his father. "Dad?" he said, his voice low. "Thanks...for not locking the door."

"It'll always be open for you, son. Welcome home."

Creed nodded and left the building, knowing his father was watching him go. With his hands shoved into the back pockets of his jeans, Creed went through the long, neat rows of vegetables that were ready to harvest. His broad shoulders clad in a blue chambray shirt brushed against tall stalks of corn, then he went farther to the grazing pasture, and beyond to the woods. He blanked his mind, and drank in the sights, sounds, smells of all he saw.

He was home.

Creed's wandering took him through the woods to the old swimming hole where he'd played in reckless abandon as a boy. His blue eyes flickered over the calm water, as the memories crept in on him and he stood quietly in the peaceful surroundings.

A sudden noise brought him instantly alert. He coiled, tensed, his eyes darting in all directions as he moved swiftly, silently, to the safety of the trees. He heard the breaking of twigs, the rustle of leaves, then...then the lilting sound of a woman's laughter danced across the air like tinkling wind chimes.

She emerged from the shadows of the trees to stand in a patch of sunlight at the edge of the water, lifting her arms to embrace the warmth brought by the passing of the dawn. Her hands floated down to untie a blue ribbon from her hair, causing the honey-colored cascade to tumble to her waist in silken beauty.

Creed's breath caught in his throat, as the woman slid the knee-length terry-cloth robe from her slender body and dropped it to the ground. She was naked, her skin the shade of a soft, velvety peach, the gentle slope of her hips and buttocks, the satiny length of her long legs, declaring her to be woman, feminine, the counterpart to Creed, the man.

His heart thundered in his chest, and a section of his mind questioned what he was seeing, wondering if he had imagined the vision of loveliness before him. But then she laughed again, that delightful, free, happy sound, and he knew she was real. She moved into the water, then floated on her back, the fullness of her bare breasts swelling above the surface. Her eyes drifted closed, and an expression of serenity settled over her delicate features, her lips holding a tiny smile.

A surge of guilt swept over Creed as he realized he was watching what wasn't his to see. But, oh, Lord, she was beautiful, like a nymph, a mermaid, a gift that had come with the dawn. He felt the heat in his loins, the stirring of his manhood, as his mind went further; saw him take her in his arms, kiss the moisture from her skin, then lower her to the carpet of grass and bury himself deep within the honeyed warmth of her, making her his.

"Damn," he muttered. He had to get out of there. But who was she, this gift from the dawn? He'd leave now, grant her the privacy she assumed she had, but he had to find out who she was, where she'd come from. Was there a man waiting for her to return? Children? Surely she hadn't ventured far clad only in a robe, so she must be from a neighboring farm. Was she a wife and mother, out of his reach, beyond his touch? He had to know.

After one last lingering gaze, Creed turned and made his way back through the woods with expertise, breaking no twigs beneath his feet, causing no noise despite his large frame. He left no evidence, no trace that he had ever been there, but *he* knew. Oh, yes, he knew.

Creed looked for his father when he passed by the barn, but there was no sign of Max Parker. At the back door of the house, Creed hesitated, remembering his one-week stay of five years before. They had buried his mother, dear, loving Jane Parker, and the house had been filled with friends and neighbors bringing food, reminiscing about days gone by. Max had been consumed with grief, moving through the house in a daze, and Creed had left him like that, in the care of the neighbors. He'd had no choice, he'd had to go. Had to go back to a life, a world, his father knew nothing of, and Creed didn't want him to know.

Creed wrote to his father, just as he had done when his mother was alive. Letters of lies, of make-believe, of fantasy. He related stories of exotic cities across the globe, of beauty, splendor, excitement. He searched his imagination for descriptions of magnificent homes, parties, high fashion, anything and everything he could bring into crystal clarity on paper. But none of it was true. None of it. He was Creed Maxwell Parker, thirty-five years old, only child of Max and Jane. And he was a man with secrets.

He pulled open the screen door and stepped into the yellow-toned kitchen. The gray linoleum creaked under his weight as he walked across the room, his gaze lingering on the stove where his mother had prepared the meals while he'd been growing up. Nothing had been changed in the living room, and he retrieved his suitcase from the front porch. He would take on the memories within those walls later, when he was rested. He was too tired now, just too damn tired.

The stairs leading to the upper rooms groaned under Creed's two hundred pounds, and the banister was loose beneath his hand as he gripped it. He felt suddenly uncomfortable within his own body, as if he were too big, too strong, should not be allowed to subject the old house to who and what he was.

"Get some sleep, Parker," he said, entering a bedroom. He tugged off his shoes, tossed his shirt over a chair and stretched out on the double bed. He sighed deeply, shut his eyes and in the next instant was asleep.

Dawn Gilbert placed a noisy, smacking kiss on the cheek of the gray-haired woman who was kneading bread on the kitchen table.

"Won't do you any good," the woman said, striving to add a stern note to her voice. "I know you've been skinny-dipping in Parkers' pond again. Max ought to run you off with a shotgun."

"He doesn't even know I'm there," Dawn said. "What smells so good?"

"Cherry pies. If you can bring yourself to put some clothes on instead of just that robe, you can carry one over to Max. Oh, and pick up his mending if there is any."

"Oh, good," Dawn said, laughing. "I get to do my Little Red Riding Hood number through the woods again with my basket of yummies. One of these days a handsome wolf is going to jump out at me."

"And what would you do with him if he did?"

"I'd think of something, Aunt Elaine," she said, wiggling her eyebrows.

"Phooey. You'd turn tail and run. You talk a fancy story, Dawn Gilbert, but you're a skittish colt when it comes to men. You've got half the males in Wisconsin tromping to the door, and you hold them all at bay."

"I'm being…selective. Better to have no man than the wrong man. That, unfortunately, I learned from experience. You see before you an older, but ever so very wiser, woman. My next husband is going to be perfection personified. A real wingdinger of a guy."

"Do tell," Elaine said, laughing softly.

"Oh, yes. In the three years since my divorce I've created the most incredible man in my mind. I'll get dressed. For all I know, he's waiting for me in the woods this very minute."

A short time later, Dawn was dressed in jeans, tennis shoes and a cotton blouse, which she tied beneath her breasts, exposing her bare stomach to any breeze she might encounter during her trek through the woods. The temperature was climbing, the humidity high, and she'd braided her hair into two pigtails to keep the heavy tresses off her neck. With a wicker basket containing the cherry pie slung over her arm, she set off in the direction of the Parker farm, a mile away.

"So much for my handsome wolf," she said when she emerged from the woods. "Guess he's on sabbatical. Yoo-hoo, Max!" she called, not really expecting a reply.

In the kitchen, Dawn placed the pie on the table, setting the empty basket next to it. Max Parker left any mending he had on the chair in his bedroom, and she dashed up the stairs. She was as comfortable in that house as she was in Aunt Elaine and Uncle Orv's, and Max himself seemed like part of her family.

"Blue room," Dawn said, passing the first open door. "Green room," she said, at the second door, then stopped dead in her tracks.

There was a man on the bed in the green room.

"Oh, good heavens," she whispered, staring into the room.

She moved cautiously forward, halting by the edge of the bed and peering at the sleeping figure. One word, one thought, came to her mind: *Beautiful*. He was absolutely beautiful. His hair was a raven glow with streaks of gray at the temples. Temples that were part of a tanned, rugged face with a straight nose and square chin, accompanied by very sensuous lips. His neck was strong, shoulders wide, arms corded in muscles and, oh-h-h, that chest! Now *that* was a chest. Curly black hair swirled over bronzed skin, and the steely muscles were in perfect proportion to his arms. Flat belly, narrow hips and, yep, nifty thighs pressed against the faded material of his jeans. Head to toe, the man was beautiful.

But, Dawn thought, who was he? There was a suit-case on the floor. Was he a friend or relative of Max's? Or—oh, geez, some bum who'd found the door unlocked and wandered in for a snooze? Were bums that beautiful? Maybe she'd better go find Max and tell him there was a beautiful bum sleeping in the green room, just in case he didn't know.

After one more appreciative appraisal of the sleep-ing man, Dawn turned to leave, her leg brushing against the edge of the bed. In the next instant she screamed as viselike fingers closed over her arms from behind, lifted her off her feet and flung her onto the bed. A hand gripped her throat as her body was covered by a crushing weight. With wide, terror-filled eyes, she stared up into a face that was only inches from hers.

"What?" Creed said, shaking his head slightly to clear the fogginess of sleep. "It's you! The gift...the woman...dawn. Oh, I'm sorry," he said, rolling off her and getting to his feet. "Did I hurt you?"

Dawn struggled to sit up, tugged her blouse back into place and gingerly checked her neck with her fingertips.

"Who are you?" she asked, relieved her vocal cords hadn't been smashed flat. "How do you know my name? Why are you in Max's house? Forget it," she said, scrambling off the bed. "I'm getting out of here!"

"Hold it," he said, grabbing her arm.

"Get your hand off me, Buster," she said, her voice trembling. Had that sounded tough? Brave? In control? Oh, Lord, she was scared to death!

"You're scared to death," the man said, dropping

his hand. "I really do apologize. I didn't mean to frighten you. I'm Creed Parker, Max's son."

Dawn squinted at him. "You don't look like Max. Well, sort of, but you're a lot bigger. Anyway, Creed Parker is in some foreign country being a fancy diplomat."

"I came home," he said quietly.

Dawn looked directly up at the man, who held her gaze unflinchingly. Her dark brown eyes locked onto his icy blue ones, and she felt pinned in place, unable to move. Then she realized that she was no longer frightened, but instead, rather fascinated by this tall man who claimed to be Creed Parker. His voice was deep, rich, appropriate for his size, and a tiny section of her mind wondered what it would be like hearing him speak gentle words of love.

Slowly the web of fascination began to build as her senses reacted to every aspect of him. There was an awareness of his raw virility, an acute remembrance of every steely muscle she had scrutinized, a whiff of heady male perspiration. A strange tingling started in the pit of Dawn's stomach and crept through her, dancing across her breasts, causing them to ache, showing itself finally in a warm flush on her cheeks.

And still she didn't move.

Had seconds, minutes, hours passed? She didn't know. She saw only blue eyes that were slowly changing, sending a message now of something different. The cold, icy stare had become one of desire. This man wanted her!

"How did you know my name?" she asked, taking a step backward and forcing herself to pull her gaze from him.

"I don't know your name. In fact," he said, a slow

smile creeping onto his face, "I should be the one demanding to know why you're in my father's house."

"But you said it. I heard you say my name. Dawn," she said. Oh, that smile! It softened his rugged features, made him appear younger. Crinkling little lines formed by his eyes. Eyes that were a warmer blue when he smiled.

"Dawn?" he said. "You're kidding. That's incredible. Your name is really Dawn?"

She frowned. "I've never had anyone get so charged up about it before but, yes, I'm Dawn Gilbert. I'm Elaine and Orv's niece. I brought a cherry pie over to your father, then came upstairs to pick up his mending. Are you positive you're Creed Parker?"

He chuckled, the sound seeming to rumble up from his chest, and it caused a shiver to travel down Dawn's spine.

"Creed Maxwell Parker, ma'am," he said. Ah, man, she was lovely, he thought. He was hoping to somehow find out who the mermaid had been, and here she was, standing a few feet away from him. Her last name was Gilbert, so she probably wasn't married. When he'd looked into her brown eyes, his mind had skittered to the thoughts he'd had of making love to this exquisite woman. He'd called a halt to his mental ramblings, before his body gave evidence of his desire, which would have probably scared her to death again.

"Well," she said, throwing up her hands, "it was rather startling meeting you, but welcome home."

"Thank you. I hope I didn't hurt you."

"No, but do you always wake up so violently?"

"No," he said thoughtfully. "I've been known to wake up very lovingly."

"I'll bet," she muttered, turning on her heel and starting toward the door. "See ya."

"Hey, you're not leaving, are you?" he said, following her out into the hall.

"Yes," she said, peering into Max's room. "No mending. 'Bye, Creed."

He leaned his shoulder against the wall and crossed his arms over the broad, bare expanse of his chest. When Dawn reached the top of the stairs he spoke.

"Dawn?"

"Yes?" she said, turning her head to look at him.

"When I said, 'dawn' before, I was referring to the time of day."

"Oh," she said, lifting a shoulder in a shrug. "Whatever."

"Which was when I first saw you this morning."

"You saw me this morning?" She stopped speaking as the meaning of his words sank in. "You've got a lot of nerve, Creed Parker!"

"Hey, I was on Parker land, and along comes a trespasser to the old swimming hole. I was minding my own business, then—"

"Don't you say another word!" she yelled, her cheeks crimson. "I'm going to tell your father on you! I wish you'd go back to China or wherever you came from. And take a slow boat!"

Dawn ran down the stairs, the sound of Creed's laughter following her as she dashed into the kitchen, grabbed the basket and went out the door.

Creed walked to the bedroom window and brushed back the curtain. His grin grew wider as he watched Dawn stomp toward the woods, her braids flapping against her back. She was gesturing wildly with her hand, and he had the distinct impression she was on a tirade of uncomplimentary statements against one Mr. Creed Maxwell Parker.

"Dawn," he said, letting the sound of her name roll off his tongue and echo through the room. Lovely. She was absolutely lovely. And she was a very desirable woman. Whew! Was she ever! She was five feet six or seven to his six feet two, and would fit next to him like heaven itself. Those legs. Those long, satiny legs of Dawn's would wrap around his and... "That's all!" he said, flopping back onto the bed, as desire rocketed through him.

He'd been too long without a woman, Creed told himself. That was why he was overreacting to Dawn Gilbert. Granted, she was beautiful and feminine, but he was getting a little crazy! No, maybe not. There was something special about her, something that had attracted him the moment he'd seen her by the swimming hole. Lust? Well, yeah, but more than that, a strange tug at something deep within him.

"Ah, hell!" he said, drawing his hand down his face. Why was he wasting his mental energies thinking about her? He had enough problems to deal with. He hadn't just come home, he'd run. He'd turned his back on it all, and run. He was empty, drained, shaken to the core. And tired. Just so damn tired.

With a groan, he rolled over onto his stomach, gave way to his fatigue and slept.

Dawn was still sputtering with anger when she flung open the back door and stalked in, startling Elaine. The mile hike through the woods had not cooled her fury one iota.

"A sneaky snoop," she said, plunking the basket on the table. "What he did was not the behavior becoming a gentleman. And furthermore, smashing me to smithereens on his bed wasn't very nice, either!"

"I take it you met your handsome wolf?" Elaine said calmly, as she sat at the table shelling peas. "Sounds like you had an interesting trip. Who is this man who has you all in a dither?"

"Creed Parker," Dawn said, collapsing in a chair.

"Creed is back? My goodness, what a surprise. Max must be so happy. Why were you in Creed's bed? Never mind, it's none of my business."

"I wasn't in it, I was on it, through no choice of my own, thank you very much. You would not believe that man's reflexes. One minute he's dead to the world, and the next he's murdering me!"

"You're exaggerating, I'm sure. You probably went barging in where you didn't belong, as per usual. That Creed is a good-looking fella, don't you think?"

"I didn't notice," Dawn said, examining her fingernails. "He was all right, I guess. You know, average."

"Oh? Then he's changed a great deal since he was here five years ago for Jane's funeral. That Creed was a handsome devil. Tall, strong, hair as black as Satan himself."

"There's a dab of gray at his temples," Dawn said absently.

"Wide shoulders, and—"

"Forget it!" Dawn said. "I'm not having this conversation. I'm going to go clean out the chicken coop." Luscious lips. Lips that would claim hers as

he wrapped those arms around her and... "Chickens.
'Bye," she said, hurrying out the door.

"Welcome home, Creed," Elaine said to the empty
room, as she laughed in delight. "Oh, yes, welcome
home."

Creed stirred on the bed, opened his eyes, then inhaled the aroma of food that drifted up from down-
stairs. The gnawing emptiness in his stomach reminded him that he hadn't eaten since the day before.
His eyes widened as he glanced at his watch and saw
that it was nearly six o'clock. He'd slept the day
away. After a shower in the bathroom at the end of
the hall, he pulled on clean jeans and a black knit
shirt, then walked slowly down the stairs to stand in
the quiet living room.

What would he say to his father? Creed asked himself. Max had already sensed there was something
wrong, had seen the weariness in his son that went
beyond the need for sleep. But Max wouldn't pry, nor
push. He was a man of few words, who respected the
privacy of others. If Creed wished to talk, Max would
listen, but the decision would be Creed's to make.

"Smells good," Creed said, entering the kitchen.

"Fried chicken," Max said. "I've learned to cook
since your mother's been gone. I was beginning to
wonder if you were dead to the world till morning."

"I'd have starved by then. Want some help?"

"Can you cook?"

"No," Creed said, smiling. "But I can set the table."

"Fair enough."

Creed completed his chore, then carried dishes of
food to the table. The two men ate in silence for sev-

eral minutes, Creed emptying his plate, then refilling it.

"This is the best meal I've had in a long time, Dad," he said finally.

"Not as good as your mother's, but I manage."

"You've said in your letters that you're doing all right here alone."

"I miss my Jane, son, but I've got a parcel full of memories to keep me company. I tend my land like I've always done, and life goes on. I like to believe that when I go to my maker, Jane will be there, and we'll be together again."

Creed shook his head. "Incredible," he said. "You have such inner peace. I envy you that."

"Why envy what you can have for yourself?"

"It's not that easy."

"Never said it was. I went through a bad spell after I lost your mother, had trouble finding a purpose, a reason to get up in the morning."

"I should have been here."

"No, Creed, you had your own life to lead. The pain was mine to deal with. I worked my way through it, and found the peace you're talking about. It's there for any man, if he wants it bad enough."

The men looked at each other for a long moment, then Creed averted his eyes and concentrated on his meal. He filled his plate for the third time.

"Gonna have room for cherry pie?" Max said, chuckling. "Elaine sent it over. The Gilberts have been mighty good to me over the years."

"Who's Dawn Gilbert?" Creed said, causing Max to look at him in surprise.

"Where did you see Dawn?"

"I saw her when…she came upstairs for mending

or something. We talked a bit. She wasn't sure I was your son at first."

"Dawn's a joy to have around," Max said, laughing softly. "She's spread a lot of sunshine in the three years she's been at Elaine's and Orv's. Thought I mentioned her in my letters, but I guess not. Anyway, she's like a daughter to the Gilberts, makes up for them never having children."

"Yeah, but who is she? Where'd she come from? There was never a niece visiting the Gilberts when I was growing up."

"That's 'cause Orv is the black sheep of the family. Way back when, he walked away from the Gilbert family money to be a farmer. They cut him off without a penny and pretended he didn't exist. Dawn is the daughter of Orv's brother. Elaine and Orv didn't even know she existed until she showed up on their doorstep three years ago. Sorry sight she was, too."

"What do you mean?"

"It's not my place to be telling Dawn's business, Creed."

"You can't start and then stop. What do you mean, she was a sorry sight?"

"Well," Max said, frowning, "it's all behind her now, so I guess it can't hurt to tell you, long as you don't mention it to her. Dawn was married a couple of years to a rich fella her father was grooming to take over the family business. Thing was her folks thought the man was just dandy, could do no wrong, but he mistreated Dawn."

"What do you mean?"

"He beat her, son."

"Damn," Creed said, smacking his palm on the table and getting to his feet. He walked to the back door, bracing his hands on the frame and staring out the screen. A hot fury churned within him as he pictured Dawn, saw the gentle slopes of her body, the silken dew of her skin, heard the lilting sound of her laughter. That bastard! his mind roared. He'd like to get his hands on the man who'd hurt Dawn. Lord, what she must have suffered. So, she'd run. She'd come to the farm to seek solace, rebuild her life, find her peace. Everyone around him, it seemed, had found their peace.

"Want some cherry pie?" Max said quietly.

"What? Oh, yeah, sure," Creed said, returning to the table and sitting down. "I'm sorry. I guess I overreacted to what you said, but the thought of some guy abusing Dawn like that is heavy."

"Yes, but it's over, done. You saw her, Creed. She's full of life and happiness. She's twenty-six now and has her whole future ahead of her to do with as she wishes. She's been mighty content on the farm. Walked away from that high society falderal and never looked back."

"And men? Is there, well, someone special?"

"Nope. They flock to her like bees to a pretty wildflower, but she treats 'em all the same—friendly, goes here and there with 'em, but nothing serious. She says she's waiting for the cream of the crop this time 'round."

"She deserves the best," Creed said, drawing a line on the table with his spoon.

"That so?" Max said, a smile tugging at the corners of his mouth.

"Yeah, that's so," he said gruffly. "Where's this fancy pie you're raving about?"

As the pair ate huge slices of the delicious dessert,

Creed glanced up at his father. How could he do it? he wondered. How could he sit there as if having his son across the table was an everyday occurrence? He had to be curious as to why Creed had suddenly arrived, how long he planned to stay. And it had to have upset him to know Creed was troubled.

"I'm not being fair to you, am I?" Creed said. "I pop up unannounced, with no explanation as to why."

"This is your home. I'm your father. You don't have to explain anything to me. Sometimes, though, it does a man good to talk, to cleanse his soul by sharing what's eating at him. I'm here, Creed. I hope you know that."

"I do," he said, his voice hushed, "and I'm grateful. But I can't tell you about it," he said, shaking his head.

"Don't rush it. You're tighter than a role of baling wire. Give yourself a chance to rest, relax. Take one day at a time for now."

"Yeah," he said. One day at a time, and each one had a dawn. Dawn. There she was again in the front of his mind. She'd been through hell, and put her life back together. And so had his father. Did he, Creed Parker, have that kind of strength? First, a man had to care about the tomorrows, and right now he didn't give a damn. Oh, yeah, he'd run, all right, to get back home. Thing was, there was nowhere he could go to escape from himself.

"Well, I've got cows to milk," Max said, getting to his feet.

"I'll do it for you."

"No, you take it easy your first day back."

"I'll clean up the kitchen then."

"Fair enough. Just put all the dishes in that fancy

dishwasher you bought your mother. There's no food left to tend to.''

"Guess I made a pig of myself," Creed said, smiling.

"Well, your mother used to say you're a big man, with a big appetite and a heart to match."

"I don't know about that. Mothers see what they want to see."

"Could be," Max said, nodding. "I agree with her, though. 'Course as your father, I look a bit further."

"To what?"

"The truth, or lack of it. I'll see you later," Max said, going out the door.

Creed spun in his chair and watched his father walk across the back lawn. What had he meant by that parting statement? he asked himself. How much did Max really know about Creed's life, where he'd been, what he'd done? No, there was no way he could have found out. He was sensing something was different about his son, that was all.

"I had no right to come here," Creed said under his breath. "It would break his heart if he knew the truth. But I had nowhere else to go!"

With a weary sigh, Creed got to his feet and began to clean the kitchen. When he was finished, he rewarded himself with another slice of cherry pie.

Dawn walked across the back yard and settled onto the grass, leaning her back against a tree. Conversation at dinner had centered on Creed Parker, and his image seemed determined to dance before her eyes. Aunt Elaine and Uncle Orv were obviously delighted that Creed was back, though neither could hazard a guess as to how long he'd be staying. They recounted the youthful antics of the rambunctious Creed, and laughed at the memories of the mischievous little boy.

Creed had joined the army after high school, according to Uncle Orv, then later became a diplomat in the foreign service. The Parkers apparently hadn't been disappointed that Creed hadn't stayed on the farm, Dawn mused. But knowing Max as she did, she could see that he'd want his son to be happy. But was Creed really happy? There was something about his blue eyes. They were cold, like ice chips, wary, watching for... Oh, she was being silly! She didn't even know Creed Parker.

"His body I've been introduced to," she said merrily, recalling his startling reaction after she'd woken him from sleep. And, oh, what a body. She'd felt every hard contour of him that she'd so thoroughly gawked at while he slept. Goodness, he was...male. He was also a tad frightening. Didn't diplomats go around in fancy suits attending parties? Creed had reflexes that were unbelievable. He'd sprung at her like a panther, like a man trained, conditioned to a completely different type of life. "Oh, stop it," she said aloud. "Your imagination is working overtime, Dawn Gilbert."

Oh, good grief! she thought. Creed had seen her swimming naked in the pond. Those blue eyes had swept over her. How had she measured up to the women in the fancy countries he'd been in? Oh, who cared what he thought? He'd had no right spying on her like that. Of course, she had been on Parker land, and bathing suits had been invented for a purpose, and she *had* enjoyed every minute of looking *him* over when he'd been asleep.

"That's enough time spent thinking about you,

Creed Maxwell Parker,'' Dawn said, getting to her
feet. ''For all I know, you'll be gone tomorrow.'' Oh!
she fumed, marching back to the house. Why was the
thought of Creed's disappearing as quickly as he'd
come suddenly so depressing? Darn it, what was it
about that man that made it impossible to push him
very far from the center of her thoughts?

Two

The sound of voices woke Creed the next morning, and he bolted up on the bed, instantly wide awake. In the next moment he realized where he was and relaxed, moving slowly off the bed and walking to the window. He stood out of view due to his nakedness, and brushed back the curtain.

The acres of neat rows of vegetables had been descended upon by swarms of people carrying bushel baskets. Their voices and laughter danced across the early-morning air as the sun crept above the horizon. It was harvest time on the farm, and it was dawn.

Creed sank back onto the edge of the bed and ran his hand down his face. Dawn. He'd dreamed about her. He hadn't expected to be able to sleep at all after the hours he'd rested during the day, but he hardly remembered putting his head on the pillow.

And then he'd dreamed of Dawn. She had been

intermixed with faces he wished to forget, had floated in and out of familiar surroundings he never wanted to see again. She had smiled at him, tossed the honey-colored cascade of her hair and held out her hand, beckoning him to come to her. Over and over he had reached for her, but she'd been just beyond his touch. Each time, he had been pulled back to where he didn't want to go, had been set upon by those who haunted him. He had struggled against their crushing weight, calling to Dawn, then suddenly she had been gone, disappearing into a misty fog.

"Damn!" Creed said, pushing himself to his feet.

In the shower, Creed gave himself a firm directive regarding Dawn Gilbert. He had to quit thinking about her! He hadn't come to the farm to become mentally consumed by a woman. He was there to sort through the jumbled maze in his mind, the turmoil in his soul. He stood in a dark tunnel of self-doubt, emptiness, and desperately needed to find himself. There was no room for a woman in his thoughts or his bed. Physical work was the key; the pushing of his body until he was better equipped to take on the raging war in his head. He'd gotten himself into this living hell alone. He had to face it in the same manner—alone. Visions of beautiful Dawn would no longer be allowed to intrude.

Dressed in jeans and a tan T-shirt, Creed walked down the stairs and into the kitchen.

"Creed!" Elaine said. "Glory be, it's good to see you. Give me a hug."

Creed smiled and opened his arms to the woman he'd known all his life.

"Hello, Elaine," he said, hugging her tightly. "It's great to see you."

"Let me look at you," she said, stepping back. "Same as ever. Too handsome for your own good. That gray in your hair just adds to your sexiness."

"Oh, yeah?" he said, chuckling. "Max didn't tell me it was harvest day. Guess you're here to cook up a storm. Mind if I have some of that coffee?"

"Help yourself," she said, moving back to the counter. "I'm just making up a batch of sandwiches. Harvest isn't like the old days, when we went from farm to farm helping each other. Those workers are all trucked in from Madison from a big commercial outfit. We feed 'em lunch, that's all. Used to be a grand time of year when everyone came together, moving from land to land, the womenfolk cooking for hours on end."

"Yeah, I remember," Creed said. "It was like a big family."

"With all you youngsters getting into mischief," Elaine said, shaking her head.

"Hey, not me. I had a permanent halo around my little head. I was a joy to raise. Never caused my folks a minute's upset."

"Drink your coffee, Creed," Elaine said, laughing, "before your nose grows out to the wall. I suppose you're hungry."

"Those ham sandwiches look good. A couple of those and the rest of this cherry pie, and I'll be all set."

"Not a farm boy's breakfast, but it'll do. Here you go."

Creed sat down at the table, ate one of the sandwiches, then started on the second.

"Orv over here?" he asked.

"Yes, he's out there supervising with Max. This

outfit will be at our place tomorrow. Dawn's in the back yard making lemonade for the workers.''

"Oh," he said, taking a bite of sandwich. Dawn was there? If he looked over his shoulder out the door he'd get a glimpse of her? Damn it, no! He'd settled all that twenty minutes ago. Dawn Gilbert was invisible where he was concerned.

"You met Dawn, I hear," Elaine said pleasantly.

"What? Oh, yeah, she came with the pie yesterday. Max told me she's been with you for three years."

"And every day's been a blessing. She's brought a lot of joy to our lives, as though she were our own daughter. I hate to think of her leaving us."

"Leaving?" he said, stiffening in his chair.

"Well, it's bound to happen. She's a lovely young woman who should have a family of her own. One of these days, she'll find the right man and move on."

"Not all women marry," he said, relaxing again. "If she's happy with you and Orv, likes the simple life here, she might just stay on indefinitely."

"Wouldn't be right," Elaine said firmly. "Dawn has too much love stored up inside her. She's meant to be a wife and mother."

"I understand she tried the marriage road once," Creed said, immediately feeling the knot tighten in his stomach.

"Max told you about that?"

"I pushed him a bit. You know Max, Elaine, he doesn't fill his time talking about other people's business. I just wondered how Dawn came to be here. Seems to me, she'd have every right to be down on men."

"She was at first, I suppose. She was like a frightened bird, not knowing where to go, who to trust. She reminded me of a flower, opening its petals one at a time, very carefully. Now she's a lovely blossom, full of life and happiness.''

"What do her folks think about her being here?"

"We called them when she came, felt they had the right to know she was safe. They haven't contacted her since. It's hard to understand people like that. Dawn filed for divorce, took back the name Gilbert and put it all behind her. She cried her tears—many, many tears—then learned to smile again."

"Some people can do that," Creed said quietly. "My father is another one who's worked through his troubles and started over."

"You do what you have to in this life. So, tell me, Creed, how long are you going to be home? Knowing Max, he didn't ask you."

"No, he didn't," he said, picking up his dishes and carrying them to the sink. "You sure do make a great pie, Elaine."

"I know when I'm being told something is none of my business," she said, pursing her lips together.

"Elaine, I don't know how long I'll be here."

"Well, each day will be a blessing for Max. He's missed you, Creed."

"He understands that I couldn't get away. I was on the other side of the world."

"But now you're home."

"Yeah," he said, his dark brows knitting in a frown, "now I'm home. Well, I'll go hunt up Max and Orv, and find out if I can make myself useful."

"See you later."

Creed stepped out the back door and filled his lungs with the fresh morning air, again putting names to the scents that reached him. His eyes flickered over the

sky, then to the woods on his right. With a defeated
sigh, he slowly turned his head, knowing whom he
was seeking, knowing whom he would see.

Her back was to him as she stood under a large
shade tree twenty feet away. She was dressed in cut-
off jeans that hugged the slender slope of her hips
and curve of her buttocks. A red cotton blouse was
tied under her breasts, exposing part of her back to
his view. His eyes traveled the entire length of her,
seeing the heavy braids, then lingering on the satiny
expanse of her long legs.

His mind gave him a direct order to walk across
the lawn in search of Max and Orv. The feminine lure
of Dawn Gilbert bade him to journey in her direction
instead.

Actually, Creed decided, it would be a good idea
to see Dawn, talk to her for a few minutes. He'd met
her when he was bone-weary, not really himself. Now
he was rested, he would get things back in their
proper perspective where she was concerned. She was
a pretty woman, but not terrific enough to throw him
so off balance. Strange how a man reacted when he
was out on his feet. He'd get this thing settled about
Dawn right now.

With a nod of his head, Creed strode across the
lawn.

"'Morning," he said, as he came to where Dawn
stood.

"Creed," she said, looking up at him. "Goodness,
you startled me."

And then she smiled.

Ah, hell! Creed moaned silently. Her smile was like
sunshine. She was beautiful. Beautiful! How could he
look at her lips without thinking about kissing her?

She had such soft-appearing lips, and her skin, her hair, were almost calling out for his touch. Oh, good, great, he thought in dismay. He sounded like a lunatic!

"Creed?" Dawn said, frowning slightly. "Is there something about lemonade that makes you uptight? You've got an awfully fierce expression on your face."

"What? Oh, I was just trying to figure out what you're doing."

"Making lemonade," she said. Oh, dear heaven, she thought, could he hear her heart thudding? The way that T-shirt stretched across his chest was sinful. She was going to pass out right into her tub of lemonade. Creed Parker was too much to take so early in the morning!

"Think you have enough?" he said.

"Enough what?" she said, blinking her eyes once slowly.

"Lemonade. I've never seen it made in a laundry tub before."

"Works great," she said, stirring her brew with a broom handle. "I scrubbed it to within an inch of its life. Then I multiplied the recipe a zillion times and, ta-da, enough lemonade for the harvest crew. I'll put it in those milk cans, and lug it out to the edge of the fields."

"The army could use you," he said, leaning his shoulder against the tree. "They're into cooking in quantity. I'm not sure they use broom handles, though."

Dawn laughed, the lilting reasonance causing Creed to jam his hands into the pockets of his jeans. The dream flitted before his eyes and he wanted, needed, to reach out his hand and touch her, reassure himself that she was really there. Damn it, what was wrong with him?

Dawn rested the broom handle against the edge of the tub and reached for a bucket of sugar that sat on the ground.

"I'll get it," Creed said.

In perfect synchronization it seemed, Dawn dropped to her knees as Creed hunkered down on the other side of the bucket. As her hands closed over the rim, his covered hers, then their gaze met and held.

Warm, Creed thought. Her hands were warm, soft, so delicate beneath the rough calluses of his own. She hadn't disappeared as she had in the dream. "Dawn," he said, hardly above a whisper.

The sound of her own name spoken in that husky timbre caused Dawn to draw an unsteady breath. The heat from Creed's hands was traveling up her arms, across her breasts. A wondrous yearning began deep within her and crept through her, as she was held immobile under Creed's compelling blue eyes.

Oh, what would it be like to be kissed by this man? her mind asked. Just kissed? No, more than that, much more. Creed held a promise, a gift, within the tightly muscled magnificence of his body. He exuded a blatant sexuality, a maleness, an announcement of power and strength. Never before had she been so acutely aware of the intricate differences between man and woman. Never before had she rejoiced in her own femininity. Never before had she desired anyone the way she did Creed Parker.

"What are you doing to me?" she asked, hearing the quiver in her voice.

"Dawn, ever since I saw you by the swimming

hole I... No!'' he said, pushing himself up, then raking his hand through his hair. "You want all of this sugar dumped in there?''

"What?''

"The sugar!'' he said gruffly.

"Creed?'' she said, gazing up at him questioningly.

"Dawn, don't,'' he said, his voice strained. "Don't look at me like that. I see desire in your eyes. And confusion, along with an almost childlike innocence and trust. For God's sake, don't trust me!''

"I'm not a child!''

"Damn it, lady, do you think I don't know that? I ache with the want of you, Dawn Gilbert, and I don't intend to do a damn thing about it. I don't need this kind of trouble. I'm not going to bed with you!''

"Well, who in the hell asked you to?'' she yelled, scrambling to her feet. "You're taking a lot for granted here, Mr. Parker. I have never in my life met a man with such an overblown ego. Maybe your fancy foreign females drool all over your tight T-shirts and sexy jeans, but I'm totally unimpressed. I wouldn't sleep with you if you were the last—''

"That's it!'' he grated, hauling her to him by the upper arms and bringing his mouth down hard onto hers.

In the next instant the kiss gentled into a soft sensuous embrace, as Creed gathered Dawn to the hard wall of his chest, his arms folding around her in a protective embrace. Of their own volition it seemed, her hands crept upward to link behind his neck, her fingers inching into the thick, night-darkness of his hair. She parted her lips to receive his questing tongue, which dueled, danced, flickered over and around hers.

Creed had the irrational thought that he was drowning. He was being swept away on a tide of passion that he had no wish to escape from. The taste, the feel, the aroma of the woman in his arms was sweet torture, agony and ecstasy, heaven and hell. An eternity had passed from the moment he had seen Dawn until now, until this kiss.

A soft moan penetrated the hazy mist of Dawn's mind, and a sense of panic washed over her as she realized she didn't know if the passion-laden sound had come from her or Creed. Dear heaven, what were they doing?

"Creed!" she gasped, pressing her hands against his chest.

He lifted his head and looked down at her, his eyes a smoky blue, sending a readable message of desire. With a shuddering breath, he trailed his hands down her arms, then stepped back, his gaze never leaving hers. A crackling, sensual tension hung in the air, nearly palpable in its intensity.

"If I said I was sorry," Creed said, his voice gritty, "I'd be lying."

"Creed, I don't want any apologies."

"Hear me out," he said, raising his hand, then shoving both into his back pockets. "Something is happening here, with us, that I don't understand. I've never experienced anything like it before. It could be old-fashioned lust, I suppose, but I have a feeling it might be a hell of a lot more than that. Thing is, Dawn, whatever it is, I'm walking away from it."

"Why?"

"Why?" he said, with a bitter-sounding laugh. "Because you deserve better than this, than me."

"You don't even know me, let alone what I deserve."

"I know you. Dawn, I told you not to trust me, and I meant it. Just because I'm Max's son doesn't guarantee that I'm anything like him. Max is a warm, giving, loving human being."

"And you, Creed? What—who are you?" she said, wrapping her hands around her elbows.

"I wish to God I knew," he said, his voice flat.

And then she saw it.

The pain.

Deep in the blue pools of Creed Parker's eyes, Dawn saw a haunting depth of anguish. Her breath caught in her throat, and she lifted her hand toward him before she realized she had moved.

"No!" he said, then turned and strode away in the direction of the barn.

Dawn pressed her fingertips to her lips, and blinked back her sudden tears. She wanted to run after Creed, comfort him, soothe away his pain, chase into oblivion the demons that stalked him. He *was* a warm, giving, loving human being. He was! His kiss had been sensuous, his strength tempered with infinite gentleness. She had felt his muscles tremble as he strove for control as he'd held her, so safely, so protectively, in his arms.

What had happened to Creed? Dawn mused, absently pouring the sugar into the tub. What had caused the happy, mischievous little boy to become a haunted man? Had he been hurt by a woman, by love? She had known the pain of that kind of betrayal, and hers had been accompanied by physical abuse as well. No, she didn't think it was a woman. She just didn't think so. The turmoil Creed was suffering seemed to be directed at himself *from* himself. She wanted desperately to help him, but how?

"Oh, my," she said, sighing deeply, "I think I'd better just concentrate on my lemonade."

Creed headed around the side of the barn, avoiding contact with Max and Orv. Sweat ran down his back and his heart thundered in his chest. His eyes darted in all directions, wary, watching for any signs or clue that he was in danger. Every muscle in his body was tensed, coiled, ready.

"No!" he said. "No, I'm home. Home!"

He drew in a shuddering breath, then leaned against the side of the barn, resting his head on the weatherbeaten wood, and closing his eyes. His heartbeat quieted. The smells of the farm inched into his senses, the sounds of his youth, of a time past. A time of inner peace.

He'd felt it, that peace, when he'd been holding Dawn Gilbert. Everything had faded into oblivion but her—the sweetness of her mouth, her special feminine aroma, the softness of her body pressed to his. Dawn had replaced the ugliness within him with the very essence of herself. He'd taken from her, and given nothing in return.

"Stay away from her, Parker," he said aloud, pushing himself away from the barn. He'd tried to tell her that she deserved better than what he was. But then she'd pressed him for an answer as to who *was* Creed Maxwell Parker. The emptiness, the black void within him had hit him like a ton of bricks. So he'd run again. Like a scared kid, he lit out to hide behind the barn. "Damn," he said, shaking his head.

Creed walked slowly around the side of the building, then uttered a colorful expletive at what he saw. Dawn was pulling an obviously heavy milk can through the thick grass in the direction of the fields. Creed took off toward her at full speed.

"Damn it, Dawn!" he said, when he reached her.

"Damn it, Creed!" she yelled. "Quit sneaking up on me every two minutes."

"That can is too heavy for you!"

"Says who?" she said, releasing her hold and placing her hands on her hips.

"Me!" he said, moving in front of the can.

"Oh, is that so! Well, guess what, Mr. Macho, I got along perfectly fine around here before you showed up. I'm very capable of hauling this milk can from here to there. Now move out of my way!"

"No!" he said, crossing his arms over his chest.

"I'm warning you, Parker!"

"Don't push me, Gilbert!"

"And don't you dare holler at me. I thought diplomats were diplomatic! You probably screamed your way around the world. Get away from my milk can! This is the United States of America, and I have my rights! I—"

"You're done," he said, and in the next instant he picked Dawn up and flung her over his shoulder, circling her legs tightly with his arms. "Cute tush," he said, giving it a friendly pat.

"Put me down!" Dawn shrieked, whopping Creed's back with her fists.

His throaty chuckle only infuriated her more, as he set off across the grass in the direction of Max and Orv.

"Creed Maxwell Parker, put me down!"

The two older men looked up in surprise as Creed and his cargo descended on them.

"Hello, Orv," Creed said calmly. "Long time no see."

"The blood is running to my head!" Dawn said. "My teeth are falling out!"

"Mighty good to have you home, Creed," Orv said.

"Help! Uncle Orv! Max! Help!"

"What do you think of our fancy harvest crew, son?" Max said.

"They sure work fast," Creed said, nodding. "Seems like a real efficient outfit. I understand they're doing your crops tomorrow, Orv."

"Yep."

"I'm going to strangle this barbarian with my bare hands!" Dawn said, giving Creed a solid whack on the rear.

"Out for a stroll?" Orv said, his shoulders shaking with laughter.

"No," Creed said slowly. "I need you two to baby-sit this brat so I can tote those milk cans down to the field."

"Aaak!" Dawn screamed. "Don't you touch my milk cans!"

Dawn grabbed one of her flying braids in her hand, and in the next instant, pulled Creed's T-shirt free of his jeans. She danced the end of the silky hair across his bare tanned back and giggled in delight as she saw the muscles jump.

"Dawn!" Creed said. "That tickles, Get out of my pants!"

She wiggled the braid with vigor.

"Oh, man!" Creed said, laughter rumbling up from his chest.

"Wanna place any bets?" Max said to Orv.

"Nope. I'd say it's a pretty even match."

"Think you're right," Max said, his blue eyes alive with merriment.

"Dawn! Cut it out!"

"Put me down!"

"I give up," Creed said, swinging her off his shoulder and setting her on her feet. "You're a wicked woman."

"Don't speak to me, Parker," she said, stomping away. "I'm going to go wash out my laundry tub."

"Don't go near my milk cans," he called after her.

"Oh, Lordy, you've got hell to pay now, boy," Orv said, laughing heartily. "She's got a temper on her, our Dawn."

"Don't worry about a thing," Creed said, striding off toward the milk can.

"Wouldn't have missed that for the world," Max said.

Creed carried the milk can to the edge of the field, then retrieved the other from beneath the tree. Dawn was hosing out the laundry tub, and ignored Creed as he picked up the second can. Her stormy expression caused him to whoop with laughter, and she gritted her teeth. His mission accomplished, Creed strolled back to the tree and watched as Dawn continued to spray the tub.

"I might mention," he said, "that if you have any ideas about dousing me with that hose, you'd do well to reconsider your diabolical plan."

"Oh, now, Creed," she said, ever so sweetly, "do

you actually think I would do something like that? Me?''

"It crossed my mind," he said, chuckling.

They looked at each other, then burst into laughter, the engaging sounds mingling together in the summer air. Then Creed's expression grew serious, and he reached out to trail his thumb over the smooth skin of her cheek.

"You're quite a woman, Dawn Gilbert," he said, his voice low.

"You make a great caveman," she said, a breathlessness to her voice. Tearing her gaze from his, she continued, "I guess this is clean. I'll put it back in the barn."

Dawn walked over to shut off the water, then turned to see Creed holding the laundry tub in one hand.

"Here we go again," she said.

"Let's call a truce," he said, smiling at her. "I'll tote it, you show me where you want it put."

"Okay," she said, throwing up her hands. "I know when I'm licked."

They walked in silence for a few moments before Creed spoke.

"You're happy here with Elaine and Orv, aren't you?" he said, more as a statement than a question.

"Yes, very happy. It's totally different from the way I was raised. I was a very spoiled little rich girl."

"It's hard to imagine you like that."

"Oh, I was a classic case. Finest clothes, best schools and absolutely no sense of identity, who I was. I followed my parents' rules to the letter, never questioned a thing."

"Including their choice of a husband for you?"

Dawn looked up at him in surprise. "You know about that?"

"I asked because I was interested in who you were, how you came to be here. I'm sorry for prying into your business, but I really wanted to know more about you."

"It doesn't matter," she said, as they entered the barn. "It was a long time ago. I feel as though it happened to someone else. The laundry tub goes over there in the corner."

Creed put the tub in place, then returned to the center of the barn where Dawn stood.

"But why the farm? Why did you come to the Gilberts'?"

"I don't know. I'd heard my parents talking about Uncle Orv once, and tucked it in the back of my mind, I guess. When I left Chicago—no, ran from there—I came here. Elaine and Orv took me in, and have given me so much love. This has been the happiest three years of my life."

"How did you do it? Forget the nightmare you'd been through."

"I'll never really forget it, Creed. In fact, it's important that I remember in a detached sort of way, so I never take for granted how much I have now. It took me months to really get over what had happened. And during those months, I cried. The tears were always close to the surface, ready to spill over. Aunt Elaine told me to cry whenever I felt the need, and I did. My tears were a cleansing thing, just like when a soft spring rain comes to the farm. And then? I stopped crying, because it was over, finished, and it was time to start fresh."

"Incredible," Creed said, shaking his head.

"Men have been taught that they shouldn't cry when they're hurting, and that's wrong. They go out and get drunk, or punch somebody in the nose, but it doesn't solve a thing. There's no shame in showing emotions, Creed. Tears can wash away a lot of pain."

He looked down at her, a deep frown on his face. "Tears aren't always the answer," he said.

"But many times they are," she said, her voice hushed.

The dim light of the barn cast flickering shadows over Creed's face as Dawn gazed up at him, searching, seeking some clue as to what he was thinking. She could not clearly see the message in his blue eyes, as he stood statue still before her. It wasn't until he exhaled a rush of air that she realized he had been nearly holding his breath as he listened to her softly spoken words.

"Dawn," he said, then opened his arms to her.

With no hesitation she moved into his embrace, relishing the strength of his muscle-corded arms that folded around her, savoring his aroma, the heat emanating from his body, as she rested her head on the hard wall of his chest.

And then he held her.

Simply held her.

Dawn's eyes drifted shut, and a soft sigh of contentment whispered from her lips as she and Creed stood perfectly still, close, nestled against each other in a seemingly endless stretch of time. All sounds and smells disappeared into a hazy mist. For Dawn, there was only Creed.

Then slowly, tiny sensations of desire began to stir within her, kindling the ember of need to a rambling fire that licked throughout her. She trembled in

Creed's arms, and he pulled her closer, his own arousal evident as he fit her more tightly to the rugged contours of his frame. In an unspoken message, sent and received, she lifted her head as he lowered his, and their lips met, parted, tongues joining, as passions soared.

She circled his neck with her arms, pressing her mouth harder, harder, onto his. Her heart beat wildly against her ribs, as their labored breathing echoed in the quiet building. Creed's hands slid up to cup the sides of her breasts, his thumbs inching inward, stroking, bringing the buds to taut, throbbing awareness. The kiss grew more frenzied, urgent. He groaned deep in his chest, his muscles trembling as he strove for control.

"Dawn," he said, moving his hands to her waist.

"Oh, Creed," she said, taking a shuddering breath. "You make me feel so..."

"I know. I feel the same way. It's different from anything I've ever felt. I want you, Dawn. I want to make love to you so much, so very much."

"And I want you to make love to me," she said quietly, looking directly into his eyes. "I've never said that to a man before. I know I was married, but it's as though this is the first time for me. I do want you."

He cupped her face in his hands and gazed at her, a gentle smile on his face.

"Dawn's gift," he said. "That's you. My gift from the dawn. I desire you like no woman before. But until I work through some things I have to tackle, I can't make love to you. I just can't. I'm not rejecting you, I'm protecting you, from me."

"But..."

"Yeah, I know you can take care of yourself, make your own decisions. So, okay, I'll rephrase it. This isn't the right time for *me*. Dawn, I may never get myself squared away. It may be too late for me. When I hold you, kiss you, you're all that matters. But when I step back I have to face who, what I am, mixed up with the fact that I don't know who I am at all." He stopped speaking and moved away, raking a restless hand through his hair.

"I don't understand. Creed, what happened to you? What are you running from?"

"Myself," he said, his voice hushed. "I'm running from myself, which I'm discovering is impossible. I shouldn't have come home, but I had nowhere else to go. My father senses that I'm troubled, but I just can't tell him why."

"And me? Will you talk to me? I'll listen, Creed, you know I will."

"No. The problems are mine to solve."

"Do you think it's a sign of weakness to share, to ask for help? I don't think I would have survived if it hadn't been for Elaine and Orv. Whatever it is, Creed, you don't have to suffer through it alone. I'm here. I'll—"

"No!" he said sharply.

"All right. I won't try to push myself on you. But please, Creed, talk to Max. You said yourself that he realizes something is wrong. If I can see the pain in your eyes, then Max can see it, too. Go to your father."

"And say what?" he asked, his chest heaving. "That somewhere along the line I misplaced his son, lost his precious boy halfway around the world? Tell him...that it was all a pack of lies? The letters. All those letters were a bunch of bull, don't you understand? How proud my folks were of their son the foreign diplomat. Pages and pages I wrote about fancy parties, homes, important people I'd met, and none of it was true!''

''My God,'' she whispered.

''Is that what you want me to tell Max? I can't. I won't break that man's heart. He lost his wife. I can't tell him the son he knew is gone, too!''

''You're not gone! You're standing here. You're home!''

''No, Dawn,'' he said, his voice suddenly low and flat. ''The body, the shell is here, but Creed Maxwell Parker no longer exists. There's nothing left inside of me. I'm empty, drained, living in a black tunnel of hell. I have nothing to offer you, or Max, or anyone. I'd only take.''

An amalgam of emotions assaulted Dawn as she stared at Creed—emotions of helplessness, frustration, of wanting to bring comfort to this man who was suffering but who would accept no assistance. An ache seemed to settle over her heart, a heavy weight that caused an actual physical discomfort.

If only he would cry, she thought. She'd hold him so close, hold him while he wept because... Oh, dear heaven, no! She wasn't falling in love with Creed, was she? Whatever this jumble in her heart and mind was, surely it couldn't be love!

Three

"**D**awn?" Creed said. "Are you all right?"

"What?" she asked. "Oh yes, I'm fine."

"I realize that all I've done is talk in circles, but it's the best I can do for now."

"I understand. I didn't mean to pry," she said, managing a weak smile. Lies? All those letters to Max hadn't held a word of truth? If Creed wasn't a foreign diplomat, then what was he? *Who* was he? Dear heaven, what had he done to be filled with such pain?

"I've frightened you, haven't I?" he said, raking his hand through his hair. "I can see it in your eyes. You look just like you did when I jumped you in my bedroom yesterday. I'm sorry, Dawn. I've said more to you about myself than I should have. I had no intention of dragging you into this, upsetting you. I don't suppose you could just forget what I said about those letters I wrote to Max?"

"Forget? No, Creed," she said, shaking her head, "that's impossible. But you have my word that I won't tell anyone."

"I appreciate that. Look, I'm going to hunt up some tools and see if I can fix the front steps of the house."

"All right. I'll go see if Elaine needs any help with the food for the harvest crew."

"Aren't you going to thank me for carrying those milk cans to the field for you?" he said, smiling at her.

Dawn burst into laughter. "No, I am not, Mr. Parker! Your display of machismo was totally unimpressive."

"Well, shucks, I tried. You got an interesting ride out of the deal, you know. You're the prettiest, softest sack of potatoes I've ever toted over my shoulder."

And what a gorgeous shoulder it was, Dawn mused. "I could have lived without it," she said, smiling. His back was tan, taut, had actually rippled when she'd flicked her braid over his smooth skin. Beautiful. "Well, I'll see you later!"

"Dawn?"

"Yes?"

"Thanks."

Their eyes met in a steady gaze, and Dawn instantly felt the tingle of desire begin deep within her. A part of her mind registered a flash of anger that she was so susceptible to Creed's blatant sexuality, his vibrant masculinity. But another section of her thoughts rejoiced in the new, strange, wondrous sensations he evoked throughout her. She felt alive as never before, so aware of her own femininity.

She had responded to Creed's kiss and touch with

an abandon that both shocked and pleased her. She'd come alive, really alive, in the circle of his arms. Had she actually offered herself to this man? She, Dawn Gilbert, who gave chaste kisses at her front door, had boldly told Creed she wanted him to make love to her? Yes, she'd done it, all right.

Question was, would she have gone through with it? Made love with him? Or had she subconsciously known there were people tromping around outside the barn, that she and Creed were not really alone? Good grief, why didn't she know herself better than this? Since meeting Creed Parker a facet of her had surfaced that she'd been unaware even existed! What was this man doing to her?

Creed suddenly cleared his throat and averted his eyes from Dawn's, breaking the sensual spell that had once again woven itself around them like silken threads.

"I'll get started on the steps," he said.

"Okay. 'Bye for now," Dawn said, hearing the slight tremor in her voice.

She hurried out of the barn, then slowed as she walked toward the house. The summer sun caressed her skin and she took a deep breath, feeling as though she had returned to familiar surroundings from an unknown place. And, in a way, it was true. Creed had swept her away on a tide of passion, as well as evoking within her temptestuous emotions of physical wanting, needing, and an urge to help and comfort him. Her calm, pleasant existence was being turned topsy-turvy due to the arrival of Creed Maxwell Parker.

When Dawn entered the kitchen, Elaine immediately burst into laughter.

"Well, thanks," Dawn said. "I didn't know I was so funny looking."

"I have never in my born days seen such goings-on out a kitchen window," Elaine said. "Creed kissed you one minute, and the next? He threw you over his shoulder and marched away. I was laughing so hard, I had tears running down my cheeks. Mercy, the two of you together are something."

"You were watching out the window?" Dawn said, feeling the warmth of a blush on her cheeks.

"Certainly. It was more fun than I've had in ages. I was disappointed when you went into the barn. Couldn't see a thing from here."

"For Pete's sake," Dawn said.

"That Creed is quite a man. I remember when he was in high school, and the girls used to swarm all over him. I imagine he's had his share of women while he's been flitting around the world."

"Am I supposed to be getting a message here?" Dawn said, frowning.

"Oh, honey," Elaine said, sighing, "I don't know what to say. My heart was singing with joy when I saw Creed kissing you. But then, well, I realized I still think of him as the Creed I watched grow from a boy to be such a handsome man. Truth is, he's been away a long time, could very well be someone I don't know at all. There's just something about him.... Well, I've said enough."

"What do you mean, there's something about him?"

"His eyes, honey. He used to have warm, laughing eyes, blue as the sky, like Max's. But now? There's something different about Creed's eyes, a winter chill,

icy, cold. It's as though the life has gone out of him.
I guess I'm not making much sense.''

"Yes, you are,'' Dawn said quietly.

"I love that boy like he was my own, but I love
you, too, Dawn. Tread softly until you're sure you
know what you're doing. Remember, Creed hasn't
said one word about being home to stay. He's vague
on the subject, says he isn't sure how long he'll be
here. I don't want you hurt, Dawn. All right, now you
can tell me to mind my own business.''

"I love you, Aunt Elaine,'' Dawn said, kissing her
on the cheek. "Don't worry about me. I'm not the
naive child I was when I arrived on your doorstep
three years ago. I'm all grown-up now, know who I
am, and what I'm doing. I appreciate your concern,
but it really isn't necessary.'' Oh, ha! she thought.
What a bunch of blarney! Nice spiel, and used to be
true. Right up until she'd seen the beautiful bum
sleeping in the green room. "What can I do to help
you with the food?''

Dawn chatted with her aunt as they prepared lunch
for the harvest crew, striving for a lightness to her
voice, a relaxed air of normalcy. In actuality, she was
shaken to the core, as the endless questions about
Creed screamed in her mind. And with them came the
unknowns about herself.

At noon, Max and Orv carried the trays of sandwiches, fruit and pies to the field. Elaine announced
she'd serve lunch in the kitchen in exactly ten
minutes, and instructed Dawn to find Creed. Dawn
walked through the house to the front door, then
stopped, her breath catching in her throat as she saw
him.

He had removed his T-shirt and his broad, tanned

back glistened with perspiration. The faded jeans rode low on his hips as he bent over, sawing a section of wood he had propped on a crate. The muscles in his back, shoulders and arms bunched and moved with the steady rhythm of the saw.

There she stood, Dawn thought ruefully, gawking at Creed Parker again. She was either thinking about him, leaping into his arms or staring at him like a love-struck teenager. Love-struck? No! She absolutely, positively was *not* falling in love with this man. In the first place, love didn't happen this quickly. Did it? No. Physical attraction? Yes. But love? Certainly not.

And secondly, she mentally continued, since she was basically a nice person, she was simply concerned because Creed was troubled. A great deal of her preoccupation with him could be chalked up to her maternal instincts. Oh, really? She hadn't felt like his mother when he'd been kissing her, that was for sure! And when he pinned her in place with those icy blue eyes of his? She was a goner. She was also going to wear out her brain if she didn't take time off from the jumble in her mind. Enough was enough.

Dawn pushed opened the door, which creaked on its hinges, and in the next instant gasped in shock. At the movement behind him, Creed dropped the saw, then wheeled around, crouching low as one arm shot out in front of him, his other hand flying to the back of the waistband of his jeans. It had been executed in the quick, smooth, powerful motion of one conditioned, highly trained, moving with a sixth sense. And Dawn saw it all.

Creed straightened his stance as she stepped out onto the porch. He planted his hands on his hips and stared up at the sky, taking a long, weary-sounding breath before he looked at her again. She stood statue still, eyes wide, her heart racing beneath her breast.

"Creed?" she said, her voice hushed. "You were reaching for a gun, weren't you?"

"Let it go, Dawn," he said, his voice low, flat.

"No! I could tell that what you just did was as natural to you as breathing. It's just like what happened in your room yesterday. Why do you have reflexes like that? Why would you automatically go for a gun when you heard a noise behind you? Why, Creed?"

"Damn it," he roared, "give it a rest! I told you I had no intention of discussing my personal life with you, or anyone else, and I meant it! I can't erase what you just saw, but I sure as hell don't owe you an explanation for it!"

"No. No, of course, you don't," she said, clasping her trembling hands behind her. "It's none of my business."

"Ah, man," he said, running his hand down his face.

"I, uh, just came to tell you that lunch is ready," she said, turning toward the door.

"Dawn, wait."

"Yes?" she said, facing him again.

"Give me some time to sort all this through, okay? I know it's not fair to shut you out one minute, then pull you into my arms the next. And, oh, yes, Dawn Gilbert, I do want you in my arms. Could you trust me. No, forget that. Why should you trust me?"

But she did! Dawn realized. She had no reason to, but she did trust Creed. She didn't know who or what he was, but at that moment it didn't matter. He was asking for time and trust, and she would give it to him. Why? She didn't know that, either. She certainly didn't know a heck of a lot!

"Fair enough, Creed," she said. "I won't push you for any answers."

"Fair enough?" he said, smiling slightly. "You sound like Max."

"Yes, I guess I do. He's an important part of my life, just like Elaine and Orv are. You're coming in for lunch, aren't you?"

"Yeah, I'll wash up, put my shirt on and be right there. Am I asking too much, Dawn? You're giving me time, trust, keeping my secrets from Max. Is it too much?"

"No, Creed, it's not. I don't know why, but it's not."

They stared at each other for a long moment, then Creed nodded. Dawn walked slowly into the house.

Lunch proved to be a jovial affair, with everyone giving a slightly different slant to the tale of Dawn, Creed and the milk cans. Laughter echoed in the Parker kitchen, and Dawn decided she had never seen Max look happier.

"Peach, apple or cherry pie?" Elaine said finally.

"Yes," Creed said.

"Land's sake," Elaine said, "he's got a hollow leg."

"I bet good farm cooking tastes dandy after those fancy foreign foods you've been eating, Creed," Orv said. "'Course, there's no gold-edged plates to eat off of like you diplomats are used to."

Dawn looked up quickly at Creed, but he appeared calm and relaxed.

"I'll rough it," he said, smiling.

"You sure rubbed elbows with important people," Elaine said, putting the dessert on the table. "Did you ever wear a tuxedo with a ruffled shirt?"

"Yes," Creed said, taking a big bite of peach pie.

"Did the women have beautiful gowns and elaborate hairstyles?" Elaine asked.

"Everyone decked out in their finery for embassy affairs," he said. "The waiters wore white gloves, and served champagne in crystal glasses on silver trays. Classy."

"Mercy, imagine that," Elaine said wistfully.

Lies, Dawn thought. It was all lies! Creed wasn't a diplomat! How easily the fabrications flowed off his tongue, how at ease he was spinning his fantasies, creating stories of the glamorous life he had led. But where had he really been, and what had he been doing? With a gun.

"Dawn?" Elaine said.

"What? Oh, I'm sorry. I was daydreaming."

"I asked you if you wanted some pie."

"No, thank you. I'll help you clean up here, then I'd better get home and tend to my babies."

Creed's fork halted halfway to his mouth. "I beg your pardon?" he said.

"Cute little buggers," Max said. "Dawn's babies are real dolls. Win your heart in a minute."

"I didn't realize you had..." Creed started. "You left your babies alone?"

"Well, I can't tote them everywhere I go," Dawn said, picking up one braid and studying the end of it. "I have a right to a little freedom, you know."

Creed scowled.

Max, Elaine and Orv dissolved in a laughing fit.

Dawn blew on the end of her braid with an expression of innocence on her face.

"Okay," Creed said, a slow grin tugging at his lips. "I know when I've been had. What's the deal, the con?"

"To what are you referring, sir?" Dawn asked, raising her eyebrows.

"Your babies," he said, grinning at her.

"Oh, them! Little dolls, just like Max said. I have a reputation all the way to Madison for making beautiful babies. Cute ones, too."

"I'd like a picture of your face, Creed," Max said, blue eyes dancing. "Close your mouth before you catch flies."

"He had it coming for the milk cans," Dawn said. "All right, Creed Parker, I will now take pity on you, since you're slightly outnumbered. Dawn's Dolls is my business. I sew handmade baby dolls with complete wardrobes, and sell them in shops in Madison."

"No kidding?" Creed said. "I'm impressed. You'll have to show me your babies."

"Be glad to," she said. "They're sweet."

"Yeah, real dolls," he said, laughing. "You had me going there for a minute."

"Can't you picture Dawn as a mother?" Elaine said.

"I most certainly can," Creed said, looking directly at Dawn. "Oh, yes, I can see Dawn with a child. It was the part about leaving them over there alone that threw me. She'd never do that. Right, Dawn?"

"No. No, of course, I wouldn't," she said, meeting his gaze. He could see her with a child? No man had ever said that about her before. Most saw her as a

pretty decoration, an object to show off on their arm.
What kind of father would Creed make? "Time to
clean up," she said, getting to her feet. "And, Creed?
Be sure and hose out *your* milk cans very thoroughly
when you bring them up from the field. That lemonade is sticky stuff."

Max, Elaine and Orv started laughing again.

Creed went back to scowling.

The meal completed, everyone dispersed. Creed
tugged on one of Dawn's braids as he passed her, and
told Elaine she made the best pies in the state of Wisconsin.

"It's good to have him home," Elaine said to
Dawn. "There was laughter in this house today, just
like when Jane was alive."

"How did she die?"

"Pneumonia. She always was a frail little thing,
and Max and Creed used to take such good care of
her. She caught cold that winter and, well, we lost
her. Max was beside himself with grief."

"Did Creed come home when he heard his mother
was ill?"

"It was all rather confusing. Jane was in the hospital in Madison, and Max was phoning the State Department over and over, asking them to get a message
to Creed. They kept telling Max someone would call
and let Max know when Creed could get here. You
would have thought they'd have given Max the number of Creed's fancy embassy or whatever it was.
Anyway, Max never heard a word, and he'd call
again. But Jane died before Creed got home. He arrived the morning of the funeral."

"I see," Dawn said quietly.

"Creed could only stay a week. He came to me and Orv and asked us to take care of his father, said he was very worried about him. 'Course, we were planning on watching over Max, anyway. Oh, my heart did ache for Creed. He never had a chance to say goodbye to his mother, his father was in terrible shape and he had to pack up and go."

Go where? Dawn wondered. *To do what?* Hadn't Max ever questioned why it had been so difficult to locate someone as visible as a diplomat for the United States government? No, not dear, sweet Max. Trusting Max, who took everything at face value and passed no censure.

"Creed made plans to visit several times in the past five years," Elaine went on, "but something always kept him from getting home. Now, here he is without a word beforehand saying he was coming. I guess working for the government is very unpredictable. 'Course, he wrote all the time, even phoned now and then. I'm sure you can see how much having him here means to Max. I just wish…"

"Wish what, Aunt Elaine?"

"That I didn't sense such a change in Creed, see the difference in that boy's eyes. Maybe I'm being foolish, but I think he's uneasy about something, troubled. Max must have noticed, but he'd never say a word to Creed. No, Creed would have to go to his father and bring it all out in the open. I just can't help but worry about Creed, though. And I worry about you, too."

"You worry about everyone, and I love you for it," Dawn said. "Look, perhaps Creed is just tired, needs a vacation. I'm sure that being a diplomat is a very high-pressure career. Maybe you're just imagining some of the distress you sense in him.''

"Maybe," Elaine said, nodding. "I hope so. Well, let's get these pies covered. That Creed sure made a dent in each one. That boy knows how to eat!''

And she was learning how to lie, Dawn thought dismally.

After the kitchen was cleaned, Elaine said she'd check if the harvest crew had gotten enough to eat.

"I'll see you at home," Dawn said, then turned as loud hammering came from the direction of the living room.

"He'll bring the roof down," Elaine said, going out the back door.

Dawn wandered into the living room, purposely clearing her throat as she entered to warn Creed of her arrival. She did not, she decided, wish to witness another display of his razor-sharp reflexes.

"'Lo," Creed said, glancing at her over his shoulder.

"Goodness, you're busy."

"Just tightening up this banister. It's nice to know I haven't lost my touch with a hammer and saw.''

And his touch with a gun? Dawn asked in her mind. She had to stop thinking about it. The whole thing was beginning to drive her crazy!

"So," Creed said, "are you off to tend to your babies?"

"Yes," she said, smiling, "duty calls."

"Dawn's Dolls. How did you get started on such an unusual endeavor?''

"By accident, really. When I came to Aunt Elaine and Uncle Orv's, I was a lost soul, if you will. I won't go into all the boring details, but I had no self-esteem, no sense of purpose, direction. I followed Orv around the farm, but I was as useful as an extra foot. The first time Elaine sent me out to gather eggs, I ended up flying out of that chicken coop screaming my head off because a chicken came after me. Oh, my,'' she said, laughing softly, ''I was a dud.''

''And?'' Creed said, chuckling. ''Elaine sent you right back in and said to show that chicken who was boss.''

''Exactly. The chickens are my full responsibility now. And, I will have you know, I was the one who got the best price for Orv and Max's hogs last year.''

''Good for you.''

''Anyway, I still had a lot of time on my hands. My fancy schooling was useless on the farm. One day, Elaine asked if I'd help her with making some new kitchen curtains. Me, who had never sewn a stitch. Turned out I had a natural flair for it. We were going to Tuckers' farm for a cookout for their little girl's birthday, and I started playing around with fabric scraps Elaine had in a box. I made a cute little doll all decked out in a party dress. Amy Tucker adored it, and I had such fun making it.''

''And you were on your way.''

''Yes. I experimented with differed styles, then decided that no two of my dolls would be the same. Each would be unique. Word spread, and Amy's friends all wanted one. Then I got terribly brave and took some into Madison to a boutique. They accepted a half dozen on consignment, and they sold in a week.''

''Whew!''

''Now I have orders from three stores and several others have approached me, but I have all the business

I can handle. I've turned one of the bedrooms into a workroom, and I go to it. It's very rewarding, not just financially, but…''

"I understand, and I think it's terrific. I admire you, Dawn, for the way you've gotten a handle on your life, found yourself, your direction."

"Thank you. I owe a great deal to the love and support I got from Elaine and Orv. Max, too. He's been wonderful to me. I insist on paying room and board to Elaine and Orv."

"Uh-oh."

"Tell me about it. Elaine sputters every month when I give her the money, then stuffs it in the cookie jar. I don't think she's touched a penny of it in the past couple of years."

"She loves you like a daughter. Elaine wouldn't feel right taking money from her own family."

"Well, I give it to her anyway. It makes me feel better, but there's really no way to repay someone for their love."

"Except by loving them in return," Creed said quietly, turning to face her.

"Have you ever been in love?

"With a woman? No."

"But there's been a lot of women in your life."

"There has?" he said, smiling at her.

"Oh, come on, Creed. You're a good-looking man, and I'm sure women have been chasing you for years. Why am I standing here puffing up your ego?"

"Okay, so I've had my share of women. But I've never been in love. Have you?"

"No."

"Not even with your husband when you first married him?"

"No. The Dawn Gilbert who married him is someone I no longer know. When I marry again, I'll be in love, absolutely bonkers for the guy," she said, laughing.

"He'll be a lucky man," Creed said, his voice low. Dawn being held, kissed, touched, made love to, by someone other than himself? Dawn growing big with another man's child? Damn it, he didn't like the sound of that. Not one little bit! Oh, yeah? Where did he get off having such possessive thoughts about her?

"You certainly switch moods fast," Dawn said. "You look like you're about to punch somebody in the nose."

"What? Oh, I was just thinking about something. So, where are you going to find this dreamboat of yours?"

"Around," she said breezily.

"Change the subject," he said, frowning deeply.

"Why?"

"Because I'm the guy you said you wanted to make love with!" he said, none too quietly. Dawn jumped in surprise. "I don't want to stand here discussing the jerk you're going to marry!"

"He's not a jerk! Oh, this is stupid! He doesn't even exist!"

"Good. Keep it that way," he said gruffly, slamming the tools back into the box.

Dawn opened her mouth with every intention of giving Creed Parker a piece of her mind, then shut it again. Goodness! she thought, how possessive he sounded.

"Forget I said that," Creed said. "I don't have any claim on you."

Oh, darn, Dawn thought.

"Yes, damn it, I do!" he roared in the next instant. "You respond to my kiss, my touch. There's something happening between us, Dawn, and it's not just lust. I desire you, but it's more than that. I... Ah, hell, forget it."

"Again? Would you kindly make up your mind? I can't keep up with you. It's like having a conversation with a Ping-Pong ball."

Creed glared at her, then rested his arm on the end of the banister as he ran his other hand over the back of his neck. A slow smile inched onto his lips, then widened into a grin.

"I've been called a lot of things in my day," he said, "but never a Ping-Pong ball."

Dawn burst into laughter. "Oh, Creed," she said, "you and I, together, are exhausting."

"You and I, together," he said, pushing off the banister and closing the distance between them, "are a glimpse of heaven itself." He cupped her face in his large hands. "When I kiss you, Dawn, I don't want to stop. My mind goes further, sees us making love, becoming one. Oh, yes, there is something very special happening between us."

"Creed, I can feel it, too."

"Thing is, I can't promise you that I'll find my answers, my inner peace. I just don't know. Dawn, I don't want to hurt you, but I could, don't you see? If I find no escape from my dark tunnel, I'll have nothing to offer you. Nothing. If you tell me to stay away from you, I'll understand, and I won't touch you again."

Not touch her again? Dawn's mind echoed. Not kiss her, hold her, make her feel alive, feminine, filled with wondrous sensations? Walk away from Creed as though his emergence into her life had held no significance, had been nothing more than a fleeting fancy? No! It was too late for that! If he left her now, this very minute, she would miss him, want to see his smile, want to be gathered into the strong circle of his arms, and press her lips to his.

He held the power to shatter her into a million pieces, should he disappear as quickly as he had come, for he had already staked an unnamed claim on her. She should order him out of her life while she still possessed a modicum of reasoning. But she couldn't, and she knew it. She was probably a breath away from falling in love with this man, who had frightening secrets and inner demons to fight. In battles there were winners and losers, the victors and those defeated. If Creed lost against the foe that stalked him, then she would also lose, for he would leave her.

But it was too late to weigh and measure, view pro and con, right and wrong. The directives from her mind were intermingled with those from her heart, and her heart spoke with the louder voice.

"I can't tell you to stay away from me, Creed," she whispered. "I just can't."

With a moan, he gathered her into his arms and brought his lips to hers. Her hands splayed over his back, feeling the corded muscles beneath the T-shirt, as their tongues met in the sweet darkness of her mouth. It was as though he were stealing the breath from her body, and replacing it with the heat emanating from his rugged frame. It created a liquid fire of need, of desire, that rambled throughout her.

"You'd better," Creed said, taking a ragged breath, "go tend to your babies."

"My who?" she said, her voice unsteady. "Oh, yes, my darling dolls. I've got to finish the order for—"

"Shh," Creed said, as his head snapped around to stare at the front door.

He moved swiftly to the window, staying out of view as he brushed back the curtain. Had they come after him already? he thought, his jaw tightly clenched. Damn it, had they found him so soon? He'd covered his tracks, made it appear he was headed for Greece, then circled back.

"It's one of the harvest crew trucks," he said under his breath, then silently cursed. He'd done it again. He'd reacted on instinct, and Dawn had witnessed it. He was going to turn around and see the fear in her eyes, the questions, the doubts. She deserved explanations. She had the right to know who it was who kept pulling her into his arms, kissing her, stirring her hidden desires. But how could he explain what made no sense to himself? What could he say that would make it all disappear, bring a smile back to her lips, the warmth to her dark eyes? Nothing.

Creed turned slowly, postponing the moment when he would see in Dawn's eyes, on her face, what he knew would be there.

"Well," she said, a little too loudly, "I'm off. I'll never get that order completed on time if I don't get to work. The banister looks great, Creed. Max will be pleased with it, and the front steps, too."

"Dawn, I—"

"No, don't," she said, shaking her head. "Let me pretend I didn't see that. I said I'd give you time, and I will, but the questions are screaming at me, and I don't know where to put them. So much is happening

so quickly, that I'm probably having a nervous break-
down, and I don't even know it. I really need to go
home, be alone for awhile.''

"I understand.''

"Creed,'' she said, her voice trembling, "did you
bring it with you? The gun? Is it here in this house?''

"Yes,'' he said quietly, "it's here.''

"Good.''

"What?'' he said, obviously confused.

"Whoever you thought was outside that window, I
don't want them to hurt you. I really couldn't handle
it if they hurt you,'' she said, blinking back sudden
tears.

"Oh, Dawn, they…''

"I've got to go,'' she said, turning and running
from the room.

"Ah, man,'' he said, "what am I doing to her?''

Halfway through the woods on the way to the Gilbert farm, Dawn sank to the ground and leaned her
back against a tree. Her legs were trembling so badly
they refused to hold her, and her heart raced beneath
her breast. She felt as though she were caught in
quicksand, unable to free herself. Her breath came in
short gasps, and she pressed her fingertips to her
throbbing temples.

The situation was worse, far worse, than Creed just
running from himself. He was also fleeing from people who wished him harm. When she'd asked him if
he had his gun, she had thought only of his safety.
She hadn't cared if he'd done something wrong, if
those pursuing him had every legal right to do so. She
hadn't cared! She couldn't bear it if something happened to him! Oh, dear heaven, was she really in love

with Creed? Was it love causing these tempestuous emotions within her? How was she to know?

"Oh, God," she said, sinking her face into her hands, "I can't deal with all of this." Why had he come back? Why couldn't Creed have just stayed wherever he'd been, written his letters to Max, let them all go on with their lives as they were? He had no right to... But yes, he did. This was his home, Max was his father. Creed could not be held responsible for her reactions to him, the instant attraction, the pull on her senses, the heightening of her passion. She had gone into his embrace willingly. He had given her the opportunity to walk away from him, and she'd refused.

She would grant him the time and trust she'd promised to him.

Four

At midnight, Dawn gave up her futile attempt to sleep, and walked to the open window of her second-floor bedroom, her gaze lingering on the star-studded sky. The sound of a cricket's serenade filled the night, and an owl hooted in the distance. The smells of the farm intertwined, hanging heavy in the hot, humid air.

The Gilberts' home was almost identical to the Parkers' in size, the farms themselves both 125 acres. The friends grew the same crops, had fifteen dairy cows each, kept chickens and raised hogs for market. But now there was a sudden and disturbing difference between the two stretches of land. The Parker farm had Creed.

Dawn sighed as she lifted her hair from her neck, hoping for a cooling breeze. The image of Creed danced before her eyes, and she knew that no firm mental directive would chase it away. Through the afternoon hours while she worked on the dolls, the thought of Creed had hovered in her mind. Through dinner, then the evening, he had been there. When she crawled between the cool sheets of her bed, he had stayed close, so close that her breasts grew taut beneath her nightie at the remembrance of his kiss and touch.

Creed Maxwell Parker was home. And Dawn Gilbert knew beyond a shadow of a doubt that she would never be the same again.

Her gaze shifted to the woods that separated the two farms. "Good night, Creed," she said. "Sleep well, my love." With a shuddering breath, she wrapped her hands around her elbows, as tears blurred her vision.

She was in love with Creed Parker.

In the quiet of the summer night, there was no escape from what she knew to be true. She loved him. She loved a man of secrets, of lies. A man with icy blue eyes that spoke of a pain that was ripping him to shreds.

But those eyes were warm pools of blue when he smiled at *her*, smoky with desire when he wanted *her*. *She* brought him from the shadows of his demons, and made him laugh. He considered himself a man alone, but he wasn't, because she loved him. Together they could face the demons of his past, beat them, be named the victors, then look to their future. Together.

Creed cared for her, she knew he did. That message was clear each time he took her in his arms. He might even be in love with her, but he was ignoring the whispers of his heart. Oh, yes, she would give him time and trust, but with them would be the strongest power known to humankind: love. She didn't care who Creed was or what he'd done. It didn't matter, because he was home now, safe. And she loved him.

A gentle smile formed on Dawn's lips as she moved back to the bed and slipped between the sheets. Creed's image seemed real enough to touch, and with that thought, she slept.

In the rosy glow of first light, Dawn made her way through the woods to the swimming hole. In spite of her few hours' sleep, she felt alive and carefree, bursting with energy. Her senses seemed strangely alert, magnifying the sights, sounds, smells around her. Her skin tingled, her eyes were sparkling. She was in love, and it was glorious. Her laughter danced through the air, clear, uninhibited, the resonance of one whose joy came from within.

At the edge of the water, she dropped her robe to the ground, relishing the warmth of the rising sun as it caressed her naked body. She pulled the ribbon from her hair, then moved into the pond.

His gift from the dawn, Creed thought, as he watched from the trees.

He'd slept restlessly, tossing and turning through the hours of the seemingly endless night. He had not been beleaguered by images from the past, but instead had seen only Dawn, heard her laughter, felt the heat of desire course through him as he remembered the feel and taste of her mouth on his. Awake and unable to tolerate the confines of his room, he'd tugged on jeans and a T-shirt and left the house, walking through the woods in the eerie first light. Standing by the swimming hole, he replayed over and over in his mind the moment he had seen Dawn Gilbert. A splash of color caught his eyes, and he reached into the grass to retrieve the blue ribbon she had taken from her hair. He smiled, then placed the ribbon in his pocket.

At the sound of Dawn's approach, Creed had moved to the cover of the trees to watch her in the morning ritual. It felt right, good, that he stood guard over her while she swam naked. He belonged there, protecting her, because she was his lady, he was her man.

In the serene setting of the quiet woods at daybreak, Creed Parker knew he was in love with Dawn Gilbert. He took the knowledge unto himself slowly, sifting it through his mind, his heart, then his soul, savoring the warmth it brought to each section of his being. Savoring the peace. No ghosts were allowed entry as he drank in the sight of the vision of loveliness before him, the only woman he had ever loved.

Creed moved out of the trees and walked to the edge of the pond. Dawn was floating on her back, her eyes closed and a smile on her lips. He spoke reverently, a husky timbre to his voice, as he said aloud the name of the one who had captured his heart forever.

"Dawn."

The hushed sound of his voice enfolded Dawn almost like a cloak of velvet caressing her, comforting and exciting her in the same breathless moment. Creed was there. If she opened her eyes she would see him standing before her so strong, so ruggedly handsome, so magnificent in his male splendor.

Dawn slowly lowered her feet as she lifted her lashes to reveal her brown eyes that glistened with sudden tears. A soft smile formed on her lips as Creed extended his hand toward her, his icy blue eyes transformed into warm, tender, welcoming pools the color of the sea.

She walked toward him, their gaze meeting as she rose from the cool water, the moisture clinging like dewdrops to her satin skin. The wet cascade of her hair tumbled to her waist and fell across the full mounds of her bare breasts, as she placed her hand in Creed's and stood before him.

For a seemingly endless moment they simply stood there, hardly breathing, as pulses skittered and heartbeats quickened. Then Creed cradled her face in his large hands, brushing his lips over hers, then kissing her cheeks, forehead, before moving to the slender column of her throat. She gasped in pleasure as he filled his hands with her breasts, then lowered his mouth to draw first one then the other rosy bud into the darkness. Tilting her head back, Dawn closed her eyes to savor the sweet torture of his tongue and teeth working their magic on the soft flesh. The seductive rhythm was matched by the pulsing beat deep in the core of her femininity.

She gripped his powerful shoulders for support, as a moan escaped from her lips. Creed lowered her slowly to the plush grass, stipping off his clothes before stretching out next to her.

"Beautiful," she said, her voice whisper soft. Her gaze swept over his magnificent, bronzed body. His manhood was a bold announcement of his need, his want of her. And she loved him. "You are so beautiful, my Creed," she said.

"You are the beautiful one," he said, his voice gritty with passion. "You are my gift from the dawn. Now you are giving me yourself, Dawn's gift. Your name is so right. Dawn is a beginning, a newness, a fresh start. That's what you are to me.''

"Oh, Creed," she said, lifting her arms to his.

In a languorous journey, he kissed and caressed every part of her lissome body. His lips trailed a heated path over her skin, that was matched by the liquid fire of need within her. She, too, explored the exquisite mysteries of Creed's taut, muscular body, marveling at his perfection, anticipating the sensual promise of what would be hers. As his hand slid to the inner warmth of her thighs, she moved restlessly, her breathing erratic, cheeks flushed.

"Creed, please!"

"Yes!"

His mouth sought her breasts once more, then moved to her lips in a searing kiss. Then with a smooth thrust of power he entered her, filling her with his maleness, as she arched her back to bring him closer. The raging rhythm of their bodies thundered in a synchronized tempo—harder, stronger, building a tension of ecstasy.

"Creed!"

"Don't be afraid. I'm here. Hold on to me."

Dawn called to Creed again as the spasms rocketed throughout her in rippling waves. She dug her fingers into his corded arms to keep from floating into oblivion. An instant later, he shuddered above her, chanting her name, then collapsing against her, his energy spent. He pushed himself up on trembling arms to gaze at Dawn's face.

"Oh, Creed," she said, placing her hands on his cheeks. "I have never experienced anything like that. It was wonderful."

"*You* were wonderful," he said, kissing her tenderly.

He moved away, then tucked her close to his side, sifting his fingers through the damp, silken threads of her hair. Oh, how he loved her, wanted to cherish and protect her for the rest of his life. But to declare his love was to speak of a promise, a commitment, a future that they could share. And offer Dawn what? His ghosts, his emptiness, his search for himself?

Only when he was with her, was he complete. When he stood alone, he was a shell, held captive in his dark tunnel of confusion. To use Dawn as his only link to life, to inner peace, was wrong. He would continually take from her, drain her, give her nothing in return. Until he was whole, he had no right to speak of his love for the delicate creature he held in his arms. Their lovemaking had been like none before, a joining not only in body, but to Creed, in heart and soul as well. He must beat the foe, and the foe was himself.

"I'd like to stay right here all day," Dawn said, bringing Creed from his reverie.

"So would I. We've created a world of our own. Dawn, there's so much I want to say to you, but I can't find the words. Just know, believe, that what we shared was more important to me than I could ever begin to tell you."

"I understand, because I feel the same way. Creed, I know you have things you have to settle within yourself. But as you're sorting it all through, I think it's only fair that you know that I love you."

"Oh, Dawn," he said, tightening his hold on her.

"I'm not asking anything of you, Creed. My love for you is, well, mine. I don't care what you've done

in the past, because I love you for who you are now—
for who you are in regard to myself.''

"But, Dawn, I..."

"I will be here if you want to talk about whatever
it is that is causing your pain, but I won't push you
for answers if you choose not to give them. You are
loved, Creed Maxwell Parker. You are so very, very
loved.''

With a throaty groan, Creed brought his mouth
sweeping onto Dawn's. The ember of desire burst instantly into a raging flame of passion that carried them
above reality, as they once again became one. Sated
at last, they lay close.

"We'd better make an appearance or our families
are going to send the Marines looking for us,'' Creed
said finally.

"I don't want to move."

"Up, my lady,'' he said, reaching for his clothes.

"Are you coming over to our place? The harvest
crew is probably there by now.''

"No, I told Max I'd plow the fields. It's been many
years since I've driven a tractor. I hope I don't run
into a tree.''

"There are some things you never forget how to
do,'' Dawn said, stretching leisurely.

Creed chuckled, then got to his feet to dress. Dawn
pulled on her robe, then rose to stand in front of him,
where she was the recipient of a long, sensuous kiss
that left her trembling.

"See you soon,'' Creed said, close to her lips.

"Yes,'' she said, drawing a steadying breath.

Creed watched until she disappeared among the
trees, then he turned and walked slowly away in the
opposite direction.

* * *

Dawn's fervent hope that Elaine would be somewhere other than the kitchen was not fulfilled. The older woman looked up from where she sat working at the table the minute Dawn entered through the back door.

"I was getting concerned about you," Elaine said. "You usually aren't gone this long when you sneak off to Parkers' swimming hole."

"I lost track of time. I'll get dressed and be right back to help you make food for the crew. Won't take me a minute. I just need to rinse out my hair and—"

"Dawn, what's wrong? You're babbling."

"Wrong? Why, nothing. Nothing at all. Everything is fine. You do worry so," she said, kissing her aunt on the cheek.

"Do I? Max is here. He said Creed was nowhere in sight this morning."

"Oh?"

"My dear child, I don't want to see you get hurt. I realize that you and Creed are attracted to each other, but tread slowly, be sure you're listening to your mind as well as your heart. I came right out and asked Max if he thought Creed was troubled about something. Max said yes, but he won't approach Creed about it. Oh, Dawn, Creed won't even say how long he's staying. Don't you see? He could pack up and be gone tomorrow."

"No!" Dawn said, shaking her head. "He won't. He wouldn't just disappear. Not now."

"Oh, Dawn," Elaine said, sighing, "I knew it the minute you walked in that door. You made love with Creed."

"I'm *in* love with Creed," she said, lifting her chin

to a determined tilt. "That makes a tremendous difference, Aunt Elaine."

"And Creed? Does he love you?"

"He cares very deeply for me, I know he does. Creed and I are not children. We know what we're doing."

"No, you're not children. Their hurts can be soothed by a hug and a Band-Aid. The pains adults suffer are far greater. I don't want that to happen. Not to you, not to Creed. I love you both."

"We're fine, really we are. I've never been so happy. Creed is everything and more than I'd ever hoped to find in a man."

"Is he? Just how much do you actually know about him?"

"Enough to have fallen in love with him. I'll get dressed," Dawn said, hurrying from the room.

"Oh, Dawn," Elaine said quietly, "I do worry."

In her room, Dawn refused to replay in her mind the conversation with Elaine. Nothing, *nothing*, was going to destroy the memories of the lovemaking shared with Creed. Her body still hummed with the sensual joy of having been kissed, touched, filled by the man she loved. He had shown her the true meaning of the coming together of man and woman, a splendor like none she had ever experienced before. She had waited a lifetime for Creed, and now he was there.

But for how long? her inner voice asked. No! She wouldn't dwell on that, nor on what plagued Creed, brought the icy emptiness to his blue eyes. He had spoken of the dawn and of her, as beginnings, fresh starts. So be it. The past was just that...in the past. But was it? Whom had Creed been expecting when he'd gone for his gun, and when he'd peered out the window at the sound of a vehicle? Who, what, stalked him? Would he ever be free to love her? Would he?

"Stop thinking!" she said, marching down the hall to the shower. "Just love Creed Maxwell Parker, and stop thinking!"

While Dawn and Elaine prepared the food for the harvest crew, an uncomfortable silence fell between them. For the life of her, Dawn could not come up with one thing to say in the form of idle chitchat that would draw her aunt's thoughts from the subject of Dawn and Creed. She knew Elaine was concerned about the outcome of Dawn's love for Creed, and Dawn was distressed to realize she was causing the dear woman such upset. But it took only a whisper of a thought of Creed Parker for Dawn to feel the warm glow once again within her.

At noon the food was carried to the crew, then Dawn packed a lunch for Creed in the wicker basket and set out through the woods for the Parker farm. The chugging sound of the tractor reached her as she crossed the rear lawn, and billows of dust marked the place in the field where Creed was plowing. She walked to the edge of the freshly turned earth, and waved her arm in the air as Creed swung the tractor back in her direction. He acknowledged her presence with a fist punched straight upward. Dawn laughed in delight.

His lovely, lovely Dawn, Creed thought, willing the lumbering machine to go faster. Their lovemaking had been incredible. What they had shared could not be put in mere words. The physical had been inter-twined with the emotional, and he'd never experienced anything like it before. Ah, man, she was something, his Dawn. He loved her.

At the edge of the field, Creed shut off the tractor and swung to the ground in a smooth motion. He grabbed his shirt from the back of the seat and strode toward Dawn.

"Hello," he said, brushing his lips over hers. "I'll do a proper job of kissing you after I hose off this sweat and dirt. What's in the basket?"

"Lunch," she said. Creed was glistening with perspiration, creating rivers of moisture through the layer of dust on his broad, bare chest. He was, she decided, beautiful. "Are you hungry?"

Creed chuckled low in his throat. "What's on the menu?" he asked, wiggling his eyebrows at her.

"This and that," she said, batting her eyelashes, "and that and this."

"Sold!"

By the tree where Dawn had created her tub of lemonade, Creed turned on the hose and drenched his torso and head. As Dawn watched the intriguing play of muscles in his arms and back, a tingling sensation swept along her spine, and she swallowed heavily as desire rambled unchecked within her.

Oh, goodness, how she loved this man!

Creed turned off the water, then reached out his arm and circled Dawn's waist, pulling her up against him.

"You're all wet!" she said, flattening her hands on his chest.

"But I want my first taste of lunch," he said, then claimed her mouth with his.

The kiss was long and sensuous, and Dawn was trembling when Creed released her. Her cotton blouse was damp from being crushed to his chest, her breasts clearly outlined beneath the thin material. Creed's eyes swept over her, and the buds of her breasts grew taut, aching for his tantalizing touch.

"Ah, man," he said, "what you do to me."

"What you do to me," she said, taking a steadying breath.

"Food! Give me food before I ravish your body right here under this tree."

"Can we vote?" she said, smiling up at him.

He laughed, then slipped on his light blue shirt, leaving it unbuttoned and hanging free as he pulled her down next to him on a dry patch of grass. As he ate a thick sandwich and drank lemonade from a jar, Dawn watched his smile disappear, then change into a deep frown that knitted his dark brows together. Minutes passed, and Dawn began to chew nervously on her bottom lip.

"A Ping-Pong ball," Creed finally said, causing her to jump.

"Pardon me?"

"You said I was like a Ping-Pong ball, because I went back and forth. That's what's happening in my mind now. I keep having this tug of war with myself. A part of me feels it's very unfair to you to be involved with a man who is keeping secrets from you. Another section says that my problems are mine, I created them, I have to solve them. To dump them on you, tell you everything, is not right, either. Damn. I don't know what to do, Dawn, I really don't."

"Creed, I..."

"I guess I have to face the fact that I have a fear of losing you after having just found you. You said that you love me as the man I am in regard to yourself. The only Creed Parker you know is the one who's here on this farm, with you, kissing, holding, making love to you. What about the other Creed? If you came to hate that side of me Dawn, what would become of your love?''

"Hate you? Creed, I love you! My love isn't conditional, only encompassing the good times. There is nothing you can tell me that is going to change how I feel about you."

"You don't know that!"

"Yes, I do!"

"Damn," he said, raking his fingers through his damp hair. "I'd be taking from you again, asking you to be a part of my dark tunnel. I thought, hoped, that by coming home I could settle things within myself, figure out where I got lost, know who I really am. If only I could explain it all to you in a neat package with everything straightened around in my head. But the void is there, that emptiness. I'm filling it with you, and not coming to terms with the ghosts like I'm supposed to. That's wrong, don't you see? I don't deserve your love, Dawn, not in the shape I'm in now."

"Then talk to me, Creed. We'll battle this thing together. It's all bottled up inside of you, and it's ripping you apart. What better person to share it with than the woman who loves you?"

"I should be protecting you, cherishing you, not dragging you through this garbage. Your love is a gift and I don't want to lose it."

"Which is better? For me to know the truth, or guess about what is bothering you? I'm human, Creed. There's times when it sneaks up on me, frightens me. I've seen your razor-sharp reflexes, and I've seen you automatically reach for a gun. I also know there's someone, or a lot of someone's, after you. I push it all away, concentrate on you, us, then I see the pain in your eyes and it rushes back on me. Ghosts take up too much room. They're there, hovering around, seeming to get bigger, stronger. Oh, Creed, please! Tell me everything. Tell me!''

The play of emotions that crossed Creed's face spoke of his inner struggle, his desperate effort to sort through the jumble in his mind. Dawn stared at him intently, sending mental messages to him to take her into his arms and talk to her, bare his soul, allow her to help him.

Please! her mind begged. *Please, Creed!*

He rolled to his feet in a smooth, powerful motion, then shoved his hands into his pockets, his back to Dawn. His shoulders were set in a tight, hard line, his neck a thick column as he held himself rigid. The tension emanating from his rugged body seemed to work its way into Dawn's, causing her to shiver as she watched him. Seconds, then minutes ticked by, and an ominous silence fell. Hardly breathing, her heart thundering beneath her breast, Dawn waited, her gaze riveted on the tall man before her.

Creed drew a deep, shuddering breath. "No," he said, "I can't do it. It would be like describing a bad movie to you, then announcing I don't know how it ended. Better for you to have none of the facts, than just some. The piece of the puzzle that's missing, is me. This isn't going to work, my being here."

"What are you saying?" she whispered, a knot tightening in her stomach.

"I'm using you, Dawn. I'm using you and your love to bring me inner peace. I'm still running from myself. I've got to leave, go somewhere else, so I'll have to face this thing head on.''

"No!" she said, scrambling to her feet as quick tears filled her eyes.

"Yes," he said, turning and gripping her by the shoulders. "It's the only way. We have no future together until I'm a whole man again.''

"Don't leave!" she cried, tears spilling over onto her cheeks. "Oh, please, don't do this.''

"I have to! We can't survive this way. I'll work it out somehow, then tell you everything. You'll have a choice then, Dawn, as to whether you still want me. I can't ask you to stay with me until I have something to offer you. If I find Creed Maxwell Parker, I'll come back and explain it all to you.''

"And if you don't find yourself, your peace? What then?" she said, choking on a sob.

"I'll contact you, let you know, but I won't step back into your world again, Dawn.''

"No, no, no!" she said, wrapping her arms around his waist and burying her face in his chest.

He circled her shoulders with his arms and pressed his hand to the back of her head, holding her tightly.

"I'm so sorry," he said, his voice strained. "I've made you cry. I've hurt you. The last thing I ever wanted to do was hurt you. I've taken so much from you, and given you nothing in return.''

"That's not true. It's not! You've shown me what it means to be in love, truly happy. You're treating me like a child, who has to be shielded from anything unpleasant. I'm a woman, your woman, and I love you!"

And he loved her, Creed thought. He had to leave, because he loved her. Her tears were caused by him.

He'd made her cry. He had no right to make Dawn cry. In his own way, he was abusing her, just like the scum she'd been married to.

"Listen to me," he said, tilting her head up and looking into her tear-filled eyes. "I've got to do this. I'm going to finish plowing the field, then go tell Max. You said you'd give me time and trust. You meant that, didn't you?"

"Yes, of course."

"Time and trust, Dawn," he said, lowering his lips to hers.

Dawn returned the kiss feverishly, wrapping her arms tightly around Creed's neck. An irrational part of her mind told her that while she held him, he couldn't leave her, while she kissed him, he couldn't go. She leaned against him, molding herself to him, clinging to the man she loved as tears streamed down her face.

Creed lifted his head, then cradled her face in his hands.

"Don't cry anymore," he said, his voice gritty with passion. "Please don't cry anymore. Those aren't cleansing tears, they're tears of pain, and I caused them."

Dawn took a deep, wobbly breath before she attempted to speak. "You're right," she said, "I'm falling apart here. I said I wasn't a child, but I'm acting like one. I'm supposed to be helping you, not adding further concern. You do whatever you must, and I'll wait. I will wait, Creed. Time and trust? Yes, you have them. And my love. Forever."

"Oh, Dawn."

"You'll leave tonight?"

"Yes. I think that will be easier on everyone."

"What about Max?"

"He probably knows something is wrong, but he won't ask for an explanation. My silence is kinder at this point."

"Will I see you before you go? Oh, damn it, Creed, I hate this! I hate everything about it! I want to stamp my foot and throw a tantrum, do something, anything, to keep you here."

"That's better," he said, smiling at her. "Get mad as hell, Dawn Gilbert."

"I am!"

"Good! You'll do okay angry, rather than sad. You can pop me in the chops if you want to."

"Don't tempt me," she said, then sniffled as she brushed the tears off her cheeks. "How can one man make me so happy and so miserable at the same time? My life would be so much simpler if you'd turned out to be a beautiful bum sleeping in the green room."

"What?"

"Nothing. I don't suppose you're going to tell me where you'll be?"

"No."

"Didn't think so," she said, sighing.

"I'll— Someone is coming through the woods," he said, his head snapping around.

"Don't you dare do your superman reflexes number, Creed Parker! I've had all I can take for one day."

"When you get mad, you don't mess around," he said, grinning at her.

"You'd better believe it."

Suddenly a figure emerged from the trees, running at full speed. Creed frowned and moved Dawn behind him, as the young man came barreling up to where they stood.

"Creed Parker?" he said, gasping for breath.

"Yeah."

"Mr. Gilbert sent me for you. I'm part of the harvest crew. It's your father, Max. He's collapsed. Mr. Gilbert thinks it's a heart attack."

"Damn it!" Creed said, then took off at a run toward the woods.

"Dear heaven, no!" Dawn said. "Not Max!"

In the next instant, Dawn started running in the direction Creed had taken. Her own anguish was forgotten, her thoughts now focused on dear, loving Maxwell Parker.

Five

The University Hospital in Madison was a beehive of activity, but the four people waiting for news of Max Parker's condition were oblivious to the hubbub. In a designated area near the emergency room, Dawn, Creed, Elaine and Orv sat in numbed silence.

By the time Dawn had made her way through the woods to the Gilbert farm, Creed had placed an unconscious Max in the back seat of the Gilbert car. Orv sat next to his dear friend while Creed drove the forty miles into Madison. Dawn and Elaine followed in the pickup truck, neither speaking as Dawn drove above the speed limit.

And now they waited.

Dawn watched as Creed pushed himself to his feet and walked to the window, bracing his hands on the frame and staring out. His jaw was clenched so tightly she could almost feel the pressure. The tension emanating from his rigid body seemed to crackle through the air. She longed to go to him, wrap her arms around him, tell him his father was going to be fine. But there was nothing she could say to erase the horror of the moment. She herself was a breath away from bursting into tears at the thought of anything happening to Max.

Dawn pressed her fingertips to her temples, drew a deep, steadying breath and waited.

Why? Creed thought fiercely. Why Max? No, that wasn't fair. There weren't answers to questions like that, no blame to be placed. Unless... Had Max's concern for Creed's obviously troubled state of mind brought on this attack? Had he done this to his father with his selfish act of coming home like a frightened boy? Should he place Max's name next to Dawn's as people he had hurt by his arrival?

"Damn," he said, running his hand down his face. He shouldn't have come back. But if he'd stayed away, he wouldn't have discovered Dawn. No, he shouldn't have come back. But what if Max's heart attack had been inevitable, and Creed had been halfway around the world when his father needed him? Or had the attack been Creed's fault? Damn, the Ping-Pong ball was bouncing back and forth in his mind again. Back and forth. Pounding against his brain.

"Mr. Parker? Creed Parker?" a man said.

"Yes," Creed said, spinning around as the others got immediately to their feet.

"I'm Dr. North," the gray-haired man said, coming forward and extending his hand.

Creed shook the doctor's hand absently. "My father?" he said. "How is he?"

"I won't mince words. He's very ill. He's had a massive heart attack, and is in critical condition."

"Oh, God," Dawn whispered, clutching Elaine's hand.

"All we can do," the doctor continued, "is see what happens in the next twenty-four hours. We can't ignore the fact that this isn't Max's first heart attack, and there's already been damage done to—"

"Wait a minute," Creed said. "What do you mean, this isn't his first attack?"

"Max has been my patient for over a year. He came to me complaining of chest pains and fatigue. I ran tests, which indicated he'd had a mild heart attack. I wanted to hospitalize him, but he refused."

"Did you know about this, Orv?" Creed said.

"No, son. Max never said a word."

"I don't understand this!" Creed said. "Why would Max keep something so important from us?"

"Easy, Creed," Orv said. "Let the doctor finish."

"Well," Dr. North said, "there isn't that much to say. Max saw me once a month, and I began to detect a general weakening of his heart. There really wasn't anything I could do, except advise him to rest the moment he felt tired. In all honesty, this attack doesn't surprise me. I just wish it hadn't been so severe."

"Could stress, worry, have brought it on?" Creed said, a pulse beating in the strong column of his neck.

"Don't do it, Creed," Elaine said. "You're looking to blame yourself for this and you shouldn't. Max has been a happy man since you got home. You're not responsible for what happened."

"No one is," Dr. North said. "The heart's a muscle, and Max's is damaged, worn out. He knew he was running a risk by refusing to be hospitalized last year, but he said he was staying on his farm where he belonged. I had to respect him for that. He knew what he wanted to do, and he did it. That's all I can tell you. Now, it's wait and pray.''

"May I see him?'' Creed said.

"Only through the window. If he holds on for the next twenty-four hours, I'll move him to the cardiac care unit, but for now he's in isolation, where someone will be with him every minute.''

"Okay,'' Creed said, taking a deep breath. "Thank you.''

"I'll keep you posted,'' Dr. North said.

"Yeah,'' Creed said, as the doctor left the room.

"Oh, Creed,'' Dawn said, blinking back her tears. "None of us knew that Max was ill.''

"I know,'' Creed said, extending his hand to her. "Come here. You're white as a ghost.''

"It's such a nightmare,'' she said, moving to his side. Creed circled her shoulders with his arm and held her tightly. "Max has got to be all right. He just has to, Creed. Oh, I'm sorry. I'm acting like a child again. I want to wave a magic wand and make all of this disappear. Well, I'm not going to fall apart. I just wish there was something I could do.''

"You're doing it,'' Creed said quietly, "by loving him, caring so deeply.''

"Creed,'' Orv said, "as much as I want to stay, I'd best get back to tend to the farms. There are chickens and hogs to feed, cows to be milked.''

"I can't ask you to take all that on,'' Creed said. "That's double work.''

"I'll help him,'' Elaine said. "We're better off busy than sitting here stewing. You call us if there's any change in Max's condition. If we're outside, keep phoning until you reach us. You can stay here with your father, and put your mind at ease about the chores. Dawn, are you coming with us?''

"No, I'm staying."

"Dawn, no," Creed said. "There's no point in it. Go on home and get a good night's sleep."

"I'm staying," she said firmly, looking up at him. "I want to be here."

Creed studied her face for a moment, then nodded. "All right," he said. "I can see that your mind is made up."

"We'd best be getting back to the farms," Orv said.

"Call us, Creed," Elaine added, squeezing his hand.

"I will, and thank you both."

"We love Max," Elaine said. "It's as simple as that."

Creed watched as Elaine and Orv left the room, then looked down at Dawn.

"I'm going to see Max through that window," he said. "I'll be back in a few minutes."

Dawn nodded, then sank onto the sofa as Creed walked away. How quickly things can change, she thought ruefully. For reasons of his own, Max had kept the facts of his ill health to himself. Like Creed, Max had secrets, had chosen not to share what he knew. The Parker men were strong, independent and, yes, stubborn. She loved Max as she would a father. She loved Creed as a man, *her* man, the extension of herself. And at any given moment, she could lose them both.

"Don't you cry again, Dawn Gilbert," she said

aloud. "Creed has enough problems without you blubbering. Knock it off."

Creed stared through the isolation-room window, his eyes flickering over the elaborate equipment surrounding his father's bed. Max looked so small and old, he mused. He'd seemed to weigh nothing at all when Creed had lifted him into his arms to carry him to the car. Why hadn't Max told him about the heart attack of the year before? Didn't a son have the right to know that his father was ill? No, not really. Max was a man, not just a father. A man with decisions to make as he saw fit, just as Creed had done. And Maxwell Parker was a helluva of a man.

"Be tough, Dad," Creed said softly. "Fight like hell."

Creed walked slowly back to the waiting room, then stopped in the doorway, looking at Dawn where she sat on the sofa. A handful of hours ago he'd told her he was leaving. And she'd cried. Now her tears were for Max. So much love radiated from her. She was so giving, trusting. Well, now he was staying, because Max needed him. His own inner struggles would go on hold, all energies directed toward his father.

"Creed?" Dawn said, glancing up and seeing him in the doorway. "How is he?"

"I don't know," he said, walking to the sofa and sitting down next to her. "The same, I guess. They've got him all wired up to machines. He's lying there so damn still, and he looks old, Dawn. Old and tired."

"I hope you're not blaming yourself for this. Your coming home was a joyous time for Max. His eyes have been sparkling ever since you came. I just wish he'd told us about the first heart attack."

"I can understand why he kept it to himself. For the first time, I'm stepping back and viewing Max as a man, not just my father. We're more alike than I ever realized."

"Stubborn."

"True," he said, smiling at her, "but loveable. Right?"

"Oh, yes," she said, leaning her head on his shoulder, "very, very loveable."

Creed picked up her hand and laced his fingers through hers. "I'm sure it goes without saying that I'm not leaving tonight. I guess I'll never really know if my coming back in the shape I'm in moved the timetable up on Max, but at least I'm here now, when he needs me. When my mother died, I left him high and dry. I haven't been the greatest son in the world."

"Max is very proud of you, Creed."

"No," he said, his voice hushed, "Max is proud of who he thinks I am, who I present myself to be. His son, the foreign diplomat, deserves Max's praise, and that person doesn't exist."

"Oh, Creed," Dawn said, sighing.

"Enough of that. It's dinner hour and we'd better get some food. Dawn, I really think you should go back to the farm. It's going to be a long night."

"No."

"Don't accuse a Parker of being stubborn, Gilbert," he said, getting to his feet and pulling her up beside him. "You win first prize in that category."

"Have I been insulted?"

"No," he said, brushing his lips over hers, "you've been kissed."

"I was? I missed it."

"Pay attention this time," he said, lowering his mouth to hers.

The kiss was long and sensuous, leaving them breathless. Creed drew in a deep breath, let it out slowly, then went to inform the nurse on duty that he would be in the cafeteria if they needed him. The meal consisted of tasteless food and little conversation, their thoughts never straying far from Max.

Later, Dawn swallowed her tears as she stood by Creed's side and looked at Max through the window. Dr. North appeared, informed them there was no change in Max's condition, then Creed called Orv to convey the message.

The long night began.

An almost eerie hush fell over the hospital as the lights were dimmed slightly and the visitors disappeared. New faces appeared at the nurses' station as the shift changed. The emotionally draining day played its toll on Dawn, and at midnight she curled up in the corner of the sofa and dozed.

A restless energy surged through Creed and he paced the floor, finally stopping to stare out the window at the lights of the city. As he jammed his hands into his pockets, his fingers closed over the blue ribbon he had found in the grass by the swimming hole. He pulled it free, then gazed at it in the palm of his hand.

Exquisite pictures of Dawn and their lovemaking replayed in his mind as he ran his fingertips over the satin material. What was to become of them? His plan to leave had been a difficult choice, but the right one, and now it was impossible for him to go. The course of his life had come to an abrupt halt, then headed in a different direction when Max had been struck down.

The danger lay, Creed realized, in his knowing that he could find peace within himself when he was with Dawn. A peace not earned, fought for and won, but given to him as yet another of Dawn's gifts. And it was wrong. He would once again be living a lie, presenting himself as someone he was not. He must resist the urge to seek solace in her love. To be worthy of Dawn's love, he had to be complete, a total entity unto himself, so he could give as well as take. Only then could he tell her that he loved her, wanted to be with her always as her husband, father of children they would create together. Only then. And it might never come to be.

Creed shook his head and frowned, then placed the ribbon carefully in his pocket. He walked to the sofa and stood watching Dawn sleep, a gentle smile tugging at his lips. Once again he saw the enchanting combination of child and woman, sensuous woman. With her hair in those thick braids, she appeared far younger than her twenty-six years, but the lush curves of her body, the full breasts pushing against the cotton blouse, gave testimony to her maturity.

Creed was filled with a coiling need, not just one of physical desire, but more. He desperately wanted to regain control of his life, right the wrongs, set everything in order. As it was, nothing was in its proper place, no section of his existence functioning as it should. His father lay close to death. His lady, his love, was unobtainable to him. He himself was an emotional wreck. A frustration, a cold fury, were building within him, bringing beads of sweat to his brow. He wanted to rage against the injustices, use his strength to beat them into submission, restore peace where there was chaos.

"Mr. Parker?" a nurse said from the doorway, bringing Creed from his thoughts.

"Yes. Has my father's condition changed?"

"No, no, your father is the same. I thought you might like these blankets and pillows."

"That's very kind of you," he said, taking them from her.

"You really should try to get some sleep. I'll wake you if there's any news. You're not going to do him any good by jeopardizing your own health."

"You're right. Thank you."

Creed tucked a pillow beneath Dawn's head, kissed her on the cheek, then placed a blanket over her. She stirred, then settled back into a deep sleep. He slouched into a leather chair and stretched his long legs out in front of him, crossing them at the ankles.

What the nurse said made sense, he supposed. There was no telling what tomorrow held, what there would be to face. Yeah, he'd better get some sleep.

He leaned his head back, closed his eyes and drifted off into a light, restless slumber.

The sound of voices woke Dawn and Creed at the same time, and they both sat up, not knowing where they were. Dawn groaned. Creed stood and stretched his neck back and forth, mumbling a few well-chosen expletives.

"Max," Dawn said, coming out of her foggy state.

"I'll go check on him right now," Creed said.

"Well, well," Dr. North said, coming into the room, "you two look worse than Max does this morning. Doesn't say much for this swanky hotel you stayed in."

"How is he?" Creed said.

"He had a good night, woke up for a minute or two and is resting comfortably. I'm pleased. His condition is stable at this point. I'm going to have him moved to cardiac care this morning. There's no reason to wait any longer. Max isn't out of the woods yet, Creed, but so far, so good."

"Thank God," Dawn said.

"When can I see him? And I don't mean through a window," Creed said.

"The immediate crisis is over," the doctor said. "Now we'll monitor him very closely, and also get a true picture of how much damage was done to his heart. You can sit with him later today, if you like. I'd suggest you go home, then come back. You look like you spent the night here, and that might upset Max."

"Oh, okay," Creed said, running his hand over his beard roughened chin. "I guess I could pass as a..."

"Beautiful bum," Dawn said, smiling at him.

"I'll see you this afternoon," Dr. North said.

"Thanks, doc," Creed said.

"That's great news about Max," Dawn said, getting to her feet. "Isn't it?"

"Like the doc said, 'so far so good.' I guess these things are hard to predict, so they take it one step at a time. Come on. We'll go home and get some decent food. No sense eating the junk in this place if we don't have to."

"All right."

"By the way," he said, pulling her close, "you're nice to wake up to. You do realize that we just spent the night together."

"Relatively speaking," she said, smiling up at him. "I must look dreadful."

"You look lovely," he said, lowering his mouth to hers. In the next instant, he jerked his head up again. "Uh-oh," he said. "I forgot about my beard. I'm going to scratch you. Pretend I kissed you good-morning."

"I don't have that vivid an imagination," she said, circling his neck with her arms. "I'd like to order one kiss, please, beard and all."

"Comin' right up," he murmured, then claimed her mouth. "Home. Now," he said, when he finally released her.

"'Kay," she said breathlessly, her heart racing.

Creed went to see Max once more through the window, while Dawn returned the blankets and pillows to the nurses' station. The fact that the curtain was drawn over the window brought Creed striding back down the hall with a deep frown on his face. He looked, Dawn decided, like an angry grizzly bear.

The morning air was remarkably cool, but the traffic was bumper to bumper as Madison's work force spilled onto the crowded streets. Creed maneuvered the old truck with skill, plus a patience that surprised Dawn. He continually waved drivers in ahead of him and voiced no objection at the snail's pace at which they were moving. The good ole farm boy in him, she mused, surfaced at the strangest times.

That thought caused Dawn to frown. So much had happened so quickly, that it had not yet occurred to her to look much further than the fact that she loved Creed. Her deepest hope and prayer was that he would calm his inner turmoil, then come to love her as she did him. And if that happened? What then? Years before, Creed had left the farm and its way of life to join the army. The traditional order of son stepping into his father's shoes to tend the land had not been followed. Creed had chosen a different road, one that had caused him pain, left him floundering.

And the future? What did he see for himself? Where would he want to go? He was highly trained, Dawn thought ruefully, for something that required split-second reflexes and carrying a gun. Wonderful. Not quite what was needed on the farm. Creed looked so right, so natural, behind the wheel of a pickup, riding a tractor, walking through the woods. That did not indicate, however, that he wished to spend the rest of his life on the Parker farm.

And Dawn? She'd had her fill of city life, society, falderal, plastic smiles. Each time she went to Madison to shop or conduct business for Dawn's Dolls, she registered a rush of relief when she returned to the Gilberts'. The farm was her home, her haven, the place where she could be herself, accepted as she was. She loved the slower tempo it offered, the sights, sounds and smells. There was meaning, purpose, in growing the crops, an indescribable joy at witnessing the birth of a calf or a litter of piglets. There were ongoing promises of tomorrows as new life sprang forth. The farm wasn't a place, it was a way of life. A way of life Dawn never wished to leave.

"Oh, dear," she said, sighing.

"Problem?" Creed asked, glancing over at her.

"What? Oh, no, I was just thinking."

"There's a store a few miles up ahead that opens early to cater to farmers. I need to stop and get something."

"Okay," she said. "Naturally you assume that my female curiosity will get the better of me and I'll ask what you suddenly need from the store."

"Yep."

"Forget it, chum."

Creed just chuckled.

Dawn lasted exactly three blocks.

"Darn it," she said, punching him in the arm, "why would a man who is probably half-starved and has spent the night in a chair, have an urge to go shopping?"

"Paint."

"Paint," she said, nodding. "Paint?"

"I'm going to paint the outside of the house. It looks pretty shabby, and it'll be a nice surprise for Max. No, don't say it, Dawn. I realize there are no guarantees that he'll live to see it, but it's something I want to do…either way."

"I understand," she said, smiling at him warmly, "and I think it's a lovely idea. In fact, I'll help you."

"Oh, yeah? Have you ever painted before?"

"No, but how tough can it be? Stick the brush in the paint, slap in on the house. Big deal."

"Oh, man," he said, laughing and shaking his head. "I'm headed for trouble here."

"We'll be a great team, you'll see."

"We *are* a great team," he said, his voice low. "What we have, what we've shared, in such a short period of time is more than some people have in years of being together. You're very important to me, Dawn. I want you to know that it meant a great deal to have you with me last night. I've been alone for so damn long, and I'm glad I've found you. I just wish… Well, one day at a time for now. There's the store." He loved this woman so much, he mentally tacked on. For the remainder of his life, he would love her.

Dawn's sigh was wistful. Such beautiful words, she mused, so full of promise, creating images in her mind of marriage, babies, endless years of happiness with Creed, working by his side to nurture their land and their love. Their love? No, he'd never said he loved her, there really were no promises, and the future was a foggy blur. All she had was each moment wherein she breathed with Creed. For now, it would have to be enough.

Inside the store, Creed headed for the section displaying paint, then with Dawn at his elbow he studied the color chart.

"What color do you think you want?" she asked.

"I don't know. Not white. It's always been white. Dingy, drab, dull, boring white."

"Goodness, I didn't think it looked *that* bad."

"Hey, wait a minute," he said, digging into his pocket and producing the satin ribbon. "Blue. A light, delicate shade of blue, just like this. What do you think?"

Dawn stared at the ribbon in Creed's hand. What did she think? That she'd shatter into a million pieces if this warm, tender, wonderful man left her. That he had depths that he himself was not fully aware of. That the same hand that knew a gun, found room for a pretty blue ribbon that had been hers. That she loved Creed Parker with every breath in her body.

"Hello?" Creed said.

"I think that blue would be very nice," she said, tears prickling at the back of her eyes.

"I'll go so far as to paint the trim white. Yeah, it'll be great. Max will love it."

"I'm sure he will," she said softly.

The supplies were purchased and loaded into the

back of the truck. Creed found a pay telephone and called the hospital while Dawn waited in the truck. A sudden weariness swept over her, and she leaned her head back and closed her eyes.

Creed slid behind the wheel and turned the key in the ignition.

"They're moving Max to the cardiac care unit now," he said, driving out of the parking lot. "I told the nurse that if he woke up to tell him I'd be there this afternoon. She said that only immediate family can visit him."

"They won't let me see him?" Dawn said, lifting her head. "I'm like family, and so are Elaine and Orv. That's not fair! I love Max, and that must mean something to the people who make those stupid rules!"

"Hey, easy. You're getting all strung out. I'll talk to the doc about it, okay?"

"But what if they say no? Max has been like a father to me. I've seen him every day for the past three years while you were off God knows where and—" Dawn stopped speaking as she saw Creed's jaw tighten and his eyes narrow. "Oh, Creed, I'm sorry. I didn't mean that the way it sounded."

"I know I haven't been a terrific son for Max," he said tightly. "I don't need you to remind me of that fact."

"I said I was sorry! It just all caught up with me. I'm tired, and hungry and so worried about Max. I wasn't insinuating that you haven't been a good son."

"Weren't you?" he asked, his voice low.

"No! Max's world centers on you, and you know it. Every time he got a letter from you he'd bring it right over for all of us to see. And when you'd call he'd be smiling for days. He's proud of you."

"Of who he thinks I am!" Creed said, smacking his palm against the steering wheel. "The letters were full of lies, remember? You do remember that, don't you, Dawn? Or have you conveniently forgotten, so it makes it easier for you to be with me, allow me to kiss you, touch you, make love to you?"

"Stop it!" she yelled. "You're the one consumed with guilt over your lies, the life you led, whatever it was. Why don't you test our love, Creed? Mine, Max's, Elaine and Orv's. Why don't you tell the truth?"

"Oh, good, great!" he said, with a snort of disgust. "Just gather everyone around the kitchen table and calmly announce that Creed Maxwell Parker, whom you all know and love so very, very much, is a killer!" *No!* his mind screamed. *Not like this! He hadn't meant to tell her like this!*

Dawn felt as though she'd been struck by a crushing physical blow. The air seemed to swish from her lungs, and a roaring noise echoed in her ears. Her entire body was heavy, as if it belonged to someone else and wouldn't move under her command. She opened her mouth, but no sound came out as she stared at Creed.

Killer? her mind repeated. Creed killed people with that gun he carried? That was ridiculous. What an asinine thing for him to say. He certainly had a strange sense of humor at times. Creed wasn't a killer, for heaven's sake. It was impossible. She loved him. "Oh, dear God," she whispered, then a nearly hysterical sob escaped from her lips.

"Dawn, please," he said, glancing over at her pale face, then redirecting his attention to the traffic. "I'll explain everything, all right? I had no intention of dumping it on you like that. I'm so sorry! We'll be home in a bit, then I'll start at the beginning. Dawn?''

"What?" she said, shaking her head slightly. "Were you saying something?"

Creed drew a shuddering breath. "No," he said, "nothing."

Dawn hardly remembered the remaining drive to the farm. A heavy silence hung in the truck, an oppressive silence, that made it difficult to breathe. She clutched her hands tightly in her lap and concentrated on taking air into her lungs, then letting it out, telling herself that if she failed to accomplish the ongoing task she would suffocate. Her head pounded with a steady cadence, adding further confusion to the jumble in her mind. Fragmented pictures danced before her eyes—scenes of Creed smiling, holding out his arms to her, then Creed gripping a gun, his features hidden by shadows, his expression unreadable. Bodies floated down in slow motion, bodies with no faces, no names, dead bodies. And Creed had killed them.

"Dawn, we're home," Creed said quietly, placing his hand on hers.

She stared down at the strong, tanned fingers, covering hers. They warmed her icy skin, and the heat traveled up her arms, creating a tingling sensation as it went, stroking her, waking her from her semitrance.

"Creed?" she said, lifting her lashes to look at him.

"Yeah, babe, it's me. Let's get you inside, okay?"

"Oh, Creed," she said, flinging her arms around his neck as tears spilled onto her cheeks, "hold me. Please hold me. I'm so frightened. So frightened, Creed!"

He gathered her close to his chest, pressing his

hand to the back of her head as she buried her face in his neck. He held her as if to never again let her go. She was there, in his arms, but he was alone. Incredibly alone. The emptiness twisted like a knife in his gut, the pain racking his mind and body. Every beat of his heart thudded a single word in his brain. *Killer.*

He'd lived with the truth, suffered the agony of the truth, but never before had he spoken it aloud, heard his voice fill the air with the truth. The word itself was lethal. He had seen the devastating effect it had had on Dawn, the horror, the disbelief, and, oh, Lord, the fear that had swept over her. And she was clinging to him, trembling in his arms like a frightened child, a broken bird, so fragile, vulnerable. What had he done to her?

Creed's head snapped up as the front door of the Gilbert house was pushed open and Elaine came out onto the porch. He lifted his hand to motion her forward, and she hurried to the truck.

"Creed? Dawn?" she said, pulling open the door. "What's wrong? Is it Max?"

"No, he's doing okay. He's stable, and had a good night," Creed said, taking Dawn's arms gently from his neck. "Dawn is just worn out, needs some food."

"Come on honey," Elaine said to Dawn. "Breakfast, a hot bath, then bed. Emotional fatigue is worse than physical. Let me fix you a decent meal, Creed."

"No, thanks, I'll go on home. I'll bring the truck back later after I unload the paint."

"Paint?" Elaine said.

"I'm going to paint the outside of the house for Max. Blue. It's going to be a pretty blue. Elaine, take care of Dawn. She's been through…a lot."

"Of course I will."

"I'll be going in to see Max this afternoon. The doc isn't promising anything yet. I'll keep you posted."

"Creed?" Dawn said.

"Here now," Elaine said, "you come along with me, Dawn. Sure I can't feed you, Creed?"

"No, I'll get something at the house."

"We've been praying for Max," Elaine said.

"I know you have," he said, smiling slightly.

He crossed his arms over the steering wheel and watched as Dawn slid off the seat and walked into the house with Elaine's arm around her shoulders.

Don't go! his mind echoed over and over. Dawn, don't leave me, let me explain, let me tell you how it all happened. Dawn, please!

With a hand that was visibly shaking, Creed turned the key in the ignition and drove home, the silence of the house beating against him when he entered.

Dawn vaguely remembered eating, taking a warm bath, then allowing Elaine to slip a nightie over her head and tuck her into bed.

"I feel like a child," Dawn said.

"Doesn't hurt anyone to be fussed over a bit when they need it. You'll be good as new once you've had a nap."

"Will I?" she asked dully.

"Honey," Elaine said, sitting down on the edge of the bed, "I know you're worried about Max. We all are. We don't want him to be taken from us because we love him. But death is a part of life. If we lose him, we'll have to have faith, believe that it was meant to be."

"Death," Dawn said in a near-whisper. "There's all kinds of death, Aunt Elaine. Some are peaceful, gentle, coming at the end of full and happy lives. Other deaths are violent, horrible, deliberately brought about by a...a killer."

"Land's sake, what gruesome talk. Now you shut your mouth and your eyes, and get some sleep. I wish I had insisted that Creed eat. He looked terrible. You two put in a rough night. Well, food and rest, and you'll both be fine."

Nothing was fine, Dawn thought, as Elaine left the room. Nothing at all.

After shaving and showering, Creed pulled on clean jeans, remembering to take the blue ribbon from his pocket and place it on the dresser. He stared at it for a long moment before turning and striding from the room. He consumed several cups of coffee while finishing the remainder of the peach pie, then unloaded the paint from the back of the truck. And through it all, the Ping-Pong ball in his head went back and forth between thoughts of Dawn, then his father.

In the living room, he collapsed on the sofa and stared unseeing at a spot on the wall. Memories of his youth crept in around him: of his frail, gentle mother, of the laughter that had echoed within those walls. Oh, he'd been a handful, with his boundless energy and quick, mischievous mind. He'd given everything his maximum effort: schoolwork, chores, his love for his parents, the pranks he'd pulled. Life had been for living and he'd enjoyed it to the hilt.

Then the world beyond the farm had beckoned to him with its mysteries and undiscovered adventures.

And so, he'd gone. With the blessings of the two most important people in his existence, he'd left the farm to take on the excitement of the unknown. As with everything else before, he'd plunged in at full steam. And then...

"Ah, hell," he said, getting to his feet, "not now. I've got to get some sleep."

Dawn's image followed him up the stairs, down the hall, settled next to him as he stretched out on the bed and laced his fingers under his head. He welcomed the desire that surged through him, the heat of it, the ache; it said he was alive, not just an empty shell masquerading in a man's body. He loved Dawn, wanted, needed her, and she could very well be lost to him forever.

The anger, frustration, began to build within Creed again, causing his heart to thunder, his pulse to race. He turned the rage inward on himself, for losing control of his life, for forgetting who he was. He moved the past years through his mind and frowned deeply at the chilling memories. As the knot in his gut tightened, he came to the present, to Dawn, to the brutal way in which he had flung the word "killer" at her with no regard for her feelings.

A strange, bitter sound erupted from his lips. How did one soften the title of "killer"? It was, *he was* everything it implied. Oh, sure, he'd told Dawn he would explain it all, how it had happened. Would she listen? What in the hell difference did it make? He didn't, couldn't, accept the truth about himself, so why should she? It was right that he should lose the love of Dawn Gilbert, because he'd never deserved to have it in the first place. He'd taken Dawn's gift of love and crushed it, destroyed it.

With a strangled moan, Creed rolled over onto his stomach. As if knowing he could bear no more, his mind went blank, giving way to sleep.

Six

"Elaine?" Creed said, entering the Gilbert kitchen.

"Oh, hello, Creed," she said, from where she was cooking at the stove. "You look much better."

"I slept for an hour. I brought the truck back. How's Dawn?"

"Quiet. She came down a few minutes ago and said she was going to work on her dolls. Are you leaving to go see Max now?"

"No. I called the hospital and they said they were running some tests on him, then he would have to rest. They asked me to wait a couple of hours before I came. Did Dawn say anything about this morning?" Creed asked, running his fingers through his hair.

"I figured there was more wrong with Dawn than just being upset about Max. Now, seeing you, I know there is. You frown any deeper your eyebrows are going to grow together. What happened between you and Dawn, Creed?"

"It's complicated, Elaine. I should never have come home, I guess. No, that's not true. Max needs me, and I'm glad I'm here. But Elaine, I never intended to hurt Dawn. I swear I didn't. She's the most wonderful woman I've ever met and I...I care a great deal for her."

"But?"

"Yeah, but," he said, leaning against the kitchen counter. "I'm not in a position to offer her a damn thing."

"Because of what's troubling you?"

Creed's head snapped up, then he straightened his stance and shoved his hands into his back pockets.

"Now, don't get in a snit," Elaine said. "Dawn didn't say a word to me. I knew the minute I saw you that something was wrong. You forget, Creed, I've known you since you were born. It's your eyes. They're different—cold, empty, hurting. You're a man carrying pain inside him, and those of us who love you can see that."

"Max, too? He definitely knows?"

"Of course he does. He's your father. He's waiting for you to come to him if you want to talk about it."

"Oh, no," Creed said, staring at the ceiling, "I've brought nothing but trouble."

"By bringing joy to Max by your being home? By making me and Orv mighty glad to see you? By bringing a glow of happiness like I've never seen before to our Dawn? That's what you've brought us, Creed."

"There are things you don't know."

"I realize that. But there's not been a problem

made that couldn't be handled by love. Maybe not solved completely, but accepted, worked through. I think you're forgetting that.''

"There's some things a man has to do alone.''

"Maybe. Maybe not. Dawn's in her workroom upstairs.''

"She probably prefers not to see me.''

"You won't know unless you ask.''

"You're a tough lady, Elaine,'' he said, smiling slightly.

"No, I love you like a son, and Dawn like a daughter. I want to see both of you happy.''

Creed looked at the older woman for a long moment, then nodded and walked slowly from the room. Elaine pursed her lips together, wiped a tear from her cheek and continued cooking.

Upstairs, Creed went down the hall, glancing through the open bedroom doors. Then he saw her. Dawn was sitting in a rocking chair by the window, staring out over the farm. She was rocking slowly back and forth, a baby doll clutched to her breasts. Her hair was loose, a shimmering cascade of beauty tumbling to her waist, and she was wearing a long lightweight mint-green robe.

Creed stood in the doorway allowing the sight of Dawn to wash over him, cool his fury, ease his pain. The vision of loveliness before him was his love, his life. Had he lost her? Was it too late to reclaim what they'd had, then move tentatively forward? Was he destined to lose his lady and his father at the same time?

Creed moved into the room to stand by the rocker.

"Dawn?'' he said quietly.

"Creed," she said, not looking at him, nor halting her back-and-forth motion in the chair.

"Would you rather I left you alone?"

"Who did you kill, Creed?" she said, turning her head to face him.

"It's a long story."

"Damn you!" she shrieked. "Who did you kill?"

"Men who were trying to kill me! That's how it's done, how the game is played. If you're quicker, smarter, luckier, you stay alive. If not, you're dead. The ones who took me on are dead!"

"Dear Lord," she whispered, "what kind of man are you?"

Creed backed away from her and took a deep breath. "I don't know," he said, his voice hushed. "I just don't know."

Dawn swallowed the lump in her throat as she saw the haunting pain settle on the icy pools of Creed's blue eyes. His voice was flat, weary sounding, and his shoulders slumped slightly as if their burden was too great to carry. Her fear and confusion were nudged aside, and replaced by love, tenderness, the want and need to comfort.

"Talk to me," she said. "Tell me everything. Make me understand."

"What I don't understand myself? How can I do that?"

"You're not alone anymore, Creed. I love you. It's unimportant whether or not I *should* love you, because it's too late to turn back. I'm asking you to tell me who you are, because I have a right to know. If you care for me at all, you'll tell me."

"Oh, Dawn," he said, "how can I say it in such a way that you won't hate me? I had such lofty ideals, such a sense of pride in what I was doing. I don't know where it all went wrong, when I changed, how I lost myself.''

"Come sit by me," she said softly.

Creed gazed at her, their eyes meeting, holding. Before he realized he'd moved, he pulled the chair from near the sewing machine and placed it in front of her. He hesitated a moment, then swung his leg over the seat and sat down, propping his elbows on his knees and lacing his fingers loosely together. Staring at his long, tanned fingers, he began to talk.

"I was in intelligence in the army," he said quietly. "I was a natural for it, had some kind of uncanny sixth sense. After Vietnam I was approached by a man named Curry about joining a special, secret branch of our government. They'd been watching me carefully, and decided they wanted me. I became an agent, an operative, a highly trained…killer.''

Dawn's hold on the doll tightened. "Go on," she said.

"I told my parents that I'd left the army for the diplomatic corps. And they believed me. My assignments for the first few years were lightweight stuff— making contact with deep-cover agents, quiet exchanges of smuggled documents—nothing fancy. Then, a deal went bad. I was set up by a double agent, who I met with in a back alley in France. He had two other men with him and they jumped me.''

"Oh, Creed.''

"I killed them," he said, his voice flat. "It was them or me, and I shot them. I couldn't believe it. I just stood there staring at those dead men. Three days later Curry found me drunk out of my mind in a cheap hotel. I didn't even remember how I got there. I told him I was finished, done, that I couldn't handle cutting men down in cold blood.''

"What did he say?''

"What you'd expect, I suppose. That I'd only done what I'd had to do, that I was a top-notch agent, my country needed me to continue in my role, the whole nine yards. I bought it because I needed to believe it to save my sanity. That was six years ago. I got tougher, more dangerous assignments, went undercover and didn't surface for months at a time. I pulled the trigger on that gun again and again, and then I lost count. *And every time, it got easier!*''

Unnoticed tears slid down Dawn's cheeks as Creed stopped speaking. He continued to stare at his hands as a chilling silence fell over the room. Seconds, then minutes ticked by. Dawn wanted to pull Creed into her arms, declare her love, offer it as a shield against the horrors of his past. But she didn't move, nor speak.

"About a month ago,'' Creed said, seemingly unaware of the pause, "Curry showed up and said the two of us had a special, top-priority assignment. The wife of a high-ranking foreign official was being held for ransom, and we were to get her out of the hands of the terrorists. We found them easily enough, because they were three young, stupid hotheads, who didn't know what they were doing. So stupid that they'd killed the wife right after they'd kidnapped her.''

"Dear heaven,'' Dawn said, "why?''

"I don't know,'' he said, taking a deep, shuddering breath. "Curry and I came flying through the front door, and he shot two of them as we came in. I stood there, Dawn, with my gun pointed right between that kid's eyes and I froze. He couldn't have been more than eighteen, and he was begging, pleading with me not to shoot him. They hadn't meant to kill the woman, he said, but she'd screamed and one of them had hit her too hard. The kid was sobbing, Curry was yelling something at me, but I couldn't move. Everything just stopped.''

Creed got to his feet and walked past Dawn to the window, bracing his hands on the frame.

"I knew at that moment it was over," he said, his voice strained, "because I couldn't figure out what I was doing there. The black tunnel, the emptiness settled over me. The face of every man I had ever killed flashed before my eyes. Killed because I was a killer, and I suddenly didn't know how it had all come to be. I lost myself somewhere, didn't know who I was. I turned and walked out of that room, and the next day I told Curry I was quitting.''

"Did he try to talk you out of it?''

"Hell, yes. He said to take a vacation, relax, then I'd be ready to get to work again. He didn't believe I meant it. That's who I was expecting that day I heard the vehicle outside the window. Curry will track me down, try to convince me to come back. I left a trail leading to Greece, then circled around and came home. Came home and started hurting everyone I care about.''

"Creed, no," she said, getting to her feet and dropping the doll to the floor. She went to him, circling his waist with her arms and leaning her head on his back. "You haven't hurt anyone except yourself. You believed in what you were doing for your country, but it's over. You can fill the emptiness within you with a new life, purpose. You're not lost. You're

Creed Maxwell Parker. And you're home. I don't hate you for what you've done. I love you even more for having the strength to walk away from a life that had become a nightmare for you. I do love you, Creed.''

With a strangled moan he turned and pulled her roughly to him, holding her so tightly she could hardly breathe, as he buried his face in the fragrant cloud of her hair.

"I don't know who I am, Dawn," he said, his voice a hoarse whisper.

"You will. Time and trust, remember? You asked them of me, and I agreed. Now you've got to grant yourself the same request. Give yourself time. Trust in yourself, believe.'' If only he would cry, she thought, her heart aching. He needed to cry, to cleanse his soul. Yes, he was lost, but he had to fight, win, find Creed Parker again. Then, and only then, would there be any hope, any prayer, of his loving her, staying with her.

"I don't deserve you," he said, "but I don't want to let you go. Oh, Dawn, why is it you can accept what I told you, but I can't?''

"You lived it, Creed, I didn't. I can only imagine what those years were like for you. The only part that's real for me is the man I met here on the farm, the man I fell in love with. Nothing you have said has changed how I feel about you.''

She lifted her head to smile at him, a warm, tender, loving smile, and Creed's heart thundered in his chest as he gazed down at her.

He hadn't lost his Dawn! his mind repeated over and over. She still loved him! If he declared his love, asked her to marry him, she'd be his forever, his wife, his gift. No! No, he couldn't do that, not yet. Maybe not ever. He'd be taking everything from her, and giving nothing in return. The inner battles were still his to fight. Alone.

"Kiss me, Creed," Dawn whispered. "I really need you to kiss me."

"Dawn," he said, then claimed her mouth.

The kiss was urgent, rough, speaking of Creed's turmoil, anger and frustration. Then slowly it gentled as the taste, the feel, the aroma of the woman in his arms swept the evil forces into a dusty corner of his mind. There was only Dawn. His hands roamed over the material of her robe to come to the sides of her breasts. He filled his palms with their lush fullness as his manhood stirred, strained against his jeans.

"Dawn," he gasped, tearing his mouth from hers.

"Yes?" she asked, taking a shaky breath.

"The word is 'no,'" he said, smiling slightly. "This is hardly the time or the place. But I do want you."

"And I want you, Creed."

"Listen to me," he said, gripping her by the shoulders and moving her away from him. "Even though I've told you what I did, some things haven't changed. I still have nothing to offer you. I can't make plans for my future, until I've dealt with my past."

"I understand."

"I think it would be best if we stayed away from each other for now."

"What?"

"This isn't fair to you. I can't keep taking from you. And I do take, Dawn. I use you to escape from myself. I fill the emptiness with you, warm the aching chill inside of me. No, I'm not going to touch you again until I—''

"Now, you just hold it, Parker!" she interrupted, planting her hands on her hips. Creed's eyebrows shot up in surprise. "I happen to have something to say about this. Your noble gesture stinks!"

"It does?" he said, frowning again.

"Darn right it does! In case you haven't noticed, there is a major battle going on here. I'm up against your past, years of it, with ghosts and horrible memories. That is a formidable opponent, but I have every intention of fighting for you."

"But—"

"Quiet. What you view as wrong, I see as very, very right. I help warm the chill within you? So be it. Ice that melts is gone forever. Quit being so stubborn. There's no law written that says you have to struggle alone. Dark tunnels aren't nearly so frightening when there's someone with you. I'm sticking like glue, Creed Parker, because I love you!"

"Whew!" he said, a smile tugging at his lips. "You're a tough lady."

"You'd better believe it. I'm not standing meekly by, wringing my hands, wondering if you'll ever kiss and hold me again. I might lose, but I intend to put up one heck of a fight!"

"Yeah?" he said, grinning at her.

"Yeah," she replied, folding her arms over her breasts.

He chuckled and shook his head. "You're really something."

"Yes," she said, appearing rather pleased with herself, "I am."

"It's wrong, though," he said, frowning deeply again. "I should work this through alone."

"You're giving me the crazies, Creed Maxwell!" she yelled. "And get your big foot off my doll!"

"What? Oh, sorry," he said, stepping back and picking up the doll. "Hey, this is really cute. I like the freckles."

"Freckles are very popular. I get a lot of orders for freckles."

"You're incredible," he said, placing his hand on her cheek.

"Because I make cute freckles?"

"Yep, and that's not all you have going for you," he said, leaning forward and brushing his lips over hers. "I've got to leave. I'm due at the hospital to see Max."

"Tell him I love him, Creed."

"I will, and I'll speak to whoever is in charge about letting you visit."

"Thank you."

"No, Dawn Gilbert, *I* thank *you*. For everything. I'll see you later."

"'Bye," she said, smiling at him, then turning to watch as he strode from the room. Picking up the doll from the rocker, she ran her fingertip over the freckles she'd sewn on the chubby cheeks. Sudden tears blurred her vision, and she took a wobbly breath. "I can't lose you, Creed," she said to the quiet room. "I can't. I love you too much."

The cardiac care unit was in the form of a circle, with the nurses' station in the center. From that vantage point the monitors above the door to each patient's room could be clearly seen.

Creed entered Max's room and pulled a chair next to the bed, sitting down and gazing at his sleeping father. As if feeling his son's presence, Max slowly lifted his lashes to reveal cloudy blue eyes.

"Hello, Dad," Creed said, smiling. "Fine kettle of fish you've gotten yourself into."

"Did it up right, I guess," Max said, his voice weak.

"Everyone sends their love. Dawn, Elaine, Orv are all thinking about you. Don't worry about the farm. Everything is under control."

"How you doing, Creed?"

"Me? Fine. You're the patient, remember?"

"Creed, I know the truth about you. Have for a long time."

"What?" he said, stiffening in his chair.

"Curry told me."

"He did what?" Creed said, his jaw tightening.

"When your mother was ill, I kept phoning the State Department, but no one seemed to know who you were. Late one night, Curry called."

"We'll talk about this later, Dad," Creed said, covering Max's hand with his. "I don't want you to upset yourself."

"I'm not upset, son. I'm the proudest father in the state of Wisconsin. Curry explained everything. He said he'd find you himself, and get you home as quick as he could."

"Yeah, he came and..." Creed started, his mind racing. Max knew? Had known for five years? Was proud of the fact that his son was a killer? Hell, this didn't make sense! "Dad, I've killed men. I've shot them with a gun that was never inches from my hand."

"I know that, boy. You put your life on the line for this country, for old men like me, for women like Dawn. Curry swore me to secrecy, but I was bursting with pride."

"Why didn't you tell me that you knew?"

"Wasn't my place. I'm only saying it now 'cause I don't know if I have a tomorrow. It's over for you now, isn't it, Creed? You can't do it anymore. I've seen the pain in your eyes. You've twisted what you've done, and turned it on yourself like a knife. Don't do this to yourself, Creed. It's over. Finished. It's time to look ahead to new things, new hopes and dreams."

"I don't know if I can do that," he said quietly. "I really don't."

"You will. You're a Parker; my son, Jane's son. You're a stubborn, strong-willed man. You'll beat this thing that's haunting you. In the meantime, get me out of this place and take me home."

"Dad, I—"

"Greetings, gentlemen," Dr. North said, coming into the room.

"You're just in time to say goodbye," Max said. "I'm going to my farm."

"That a fact?" the doctor said, chuckling as he flipped through Max's chart.

"That's a fact," Max said.

"In a few days maybe," Dr. North said. "Max, here it is, up front. The tests show your heart is severely damaged. I'll give you medication to control your blood pressure, but that's all I can do. Rest is the key. You can take short, very short, walks but other than that, you sit. Agreed?"

"No," Max said.

"Yes," Creed said.

"Hell's fire," Max muttered.

"If your heart stays stable for the next three days, I'll let you go home. Creed, you're going to have your hands full with this old coot."

"I'm bigger than he is," Creed said. "Don't worry about a thing."

"Five more minutes, Creed," the doctor added. "Then Mr. Personality here has to rest. You can come back tomorrow."

"Doc," Creed said, "those people that were here with me would like to visit Max."

"No can do. The rules here are stricter than San Quentin. Tell your friends to gear up for the arrival of the prisoner. Five minutes," he said, leaving the room.

"Well," Creed said, "you heard the doc."

"I'll do as I please with my own life."

"We'll come to blows about it later. Dad, I don't know what to say to you about you knowing the truth for all these years."

"Then don't say anything. Never could see you in those fancy clothes, sipping tea with your pinkie in the air. I'm a proud father, Creed."

"Thanks, Dad. It's not a big enough word, but it's all I have. I love you very much."

"Fair enough, and I love you. You'll find your peace. I know you will."

"I'll let you rest," Creed said, squeezing his father's hand, then getting to his feet. "I'll see you tomorrow."

"Come back at midnight and sneak me out of here."

"No! Goodbye."

"Hell's fire!"

As Creed emerged from the woods, he saw Orv and waved. The older man stopped and waited for Creed to join him.

"How's Max?" Orv said.

"Ornery."

"Good sign," he said, pulling open the back door. "Elaine, set another place for dinner. Creed's here."

The two men washed their hands, then returned to the kitchen.

"Hello, Creed," Dawn said, smiling at him.

He nodded, then their eyes met and held in a long moment.

"Land's sake," Elaine said, "kiss her, Creed, and be done with it. I can't get this food on the table with the two of you blocking traffic."

"Yes, ma'am," Creed said. He reached for Dawn, bent her backward over his arm and planted a loud smacking kiss on her mouth. "I do everything I'm told," he said, close to her lips.

"Oh, good grief," Dawn said, blushing crimson as Elaine and Orv laughed in delight.

During the meal, Creed brought the Gilberts up to date on Max's condition, telling them the visiting regulations could not be broken.

"Can't see Max just sitting," Orv said, shaking his head.

"My father knows his own mind," Creed said. "He made a decision a year ago when he had that first heart attack, and I'm sure he isn't sorry. I'll caution him to a point about taking it easy, but it's really up to him. No man should be forced to live a life that isn't right for him. Max will decide how he wants to play this.''

"He could kill himself if he pushes," Elaine said.

"Then he will have died happy, tending his land. I won't try to stop him. I respect him too much. He granted me that same respect five years ago when he found out I made my living wearing a gun, not a tuxedo.''

"Creed!" Dawn said, shock evident on her face.

"He knows, Dawn," Creed said. "Max has known ever since my mother died. He's proud of me. Can you believe that?''

"Yes," she said softly, "I can."

"Elaine, Orv," Creed said, "a few hours ago I snapped at Dawn, said I could never tell you this sitting around the kitchen table, but that's exactly what I'm going to do. It's time you knew the truth.''

Dawn sat with her hands clutched tightly in her lap, her eyes riveted on Creed's face as he once again told his story. His voice was flat and low, and she saw the pain flicker across, then settle into his expressive blue eyes. She blinked back her tears, willing herself not to cry.

"God bless you, son," Orv said, when Creed finished speaking.

"My poor boy," Elaine said, dabbing at her eyes with the corner of her apron.

"I chose my own direction, Elaine," Creed said. "The mistake I made was in not turning back before it was too late.''

"What will you do now, Creed?" Orv said.

"Take one day at a time for a while. Max needs me, and this time I'm here. I thank you for your understanding. Everyone has been very accepting of what I've done.''

"Except you," Dawn said.

"Yeah, well, I'm my own worst enemy, I guess," he said, getting to his feet. "Great dinner, Elaine. Dawn, want to come help me milk the cows?"

"Go," Elaine said. "I'll tend to these dishes. Creed, I'm glad you told us. It explains a lot."

Creed nodded, then extended his hand to Dawn and led her out the back door. In the woods, he pulled her into his arms and kissed her. Dawn circled his neck with her arms and returned the kiss in total abandon, savoring the taste of Creed, his special aroma, the feel of his rugged body pressed to hers.

"So much for never touching you again," Creed said, his breathing ragged.

"I told you it was a lousy idea," she said, trailing her hands slowly down his chest.

"Cows need milking."

"I know," she said, undoing two buttons on his shirt and kissing the moist dark hair on his chest.

"Ah, man," he gasped, "don't do that."

"All is fair in love and war," she said, pushing another button through the hole.

Creed chuckled. "As a very wise man once said, 'Fair enough.' I'll concede this round to you, Miss Gilbert, *after* the cows are milked."

"Fair enough," she said merrily, linking her arm through his. "Shall we go, Farmer Parker?"

The first colorful hues of the summer sunset were streaking across the sky when Creed and Dawn left the barn and made their way through the woods to the swimming hole. There, on the plush carpet of grass, they reached for each other with an urgency that engulfed them both. They kissed and touched until they could bear no more, then became one in a journey of ecstasy. Dawn declared her love for Creed over and over. He whispered his love for her in his mind.

Sated, they lay quietly, close, allowing the tranquillity of the setting to cloak them in contentment.

"Elaine and Orv aren't blind," Creed said finally. "I'm sure they know there's something happening between you and me. They might not approve after what I told them."

"Don't be silly," Dawn said, snuggling closer to him. "They love you, Creed. If they're concerned, it's for you. They knew something was wrong the minute you arrived home."

"Remind me never to play poker. I'm apparently very transparent."

"It's your eyes. Your eyes mirror your feelings."

"Oh, yeah?" he said, rolling on top of her. "And what do you see?"

"Shame on you! That's a very naughty message you're delivering."

"And?" he said, lowering his mouth to hers.

"I accept delivery."

Much later, Creed escorted Dawn through the woods, kissed her deeply, then waited until she was safely inside the house. He returned to the back steps of the Parker home and sat down, watching the fireflies dance through the darkness. The events of the day replayed in his mind, and settled over him in a heavy depression.

The term "odd man out," applied to him, he thought. He was surrounded by people who fully accepted, seemingly understood, the path he'd chosen

for his life. Proud, his father had stated adamantly.
Proud of his son who killed. Once, whenever it was,
Creed, too, had registered a sense of pride at serving
his country in such a specialized, crucial role. He'd
rationalized it all with a sense of patriotism. Then it
had all caught up with him. The devil had wanted his
due. And, oh, Lord, how dearly Creed was paying.

Creed took a deep breath, filling his lungs with air,
inhaling the scents of the farm. Rich scents, earthy,
real. Tomorrow he'd finish plowing the field, he decided, then start painting the house before driving to
Madison in the afternoon to see Max. In a few days
he'd bring his father home to this land. Then he'd
step back and allow Max to make the choice whether
or not to follow the doctor's orders. Out of love and
respect, Creed would leave him alone to make the
decision.

As quickly as the depression had crept over Creed,
it disappeared. He had a full day ahead of him tomorrow, he realized. A productive day, with a sense
of purpose that would produce visible evidence of his
labors. And tomorrow would start with the beauty of
a dawn, and with *his* Dawn. His lovely, wonderful
Dawn.

For the first time since Creed could remember, he
felt a sense of anticipation for the new day ahead.

"Damn it, pig, back up," Creed said. "I can't get
to the trough to feed you when you're leaning against
me! Move!"

Creed stiffened as he heard a noise in the woods,
then relaxed as Dawn emerged waving and smiling at
him.

That was all the pig needed.

As Creed raised his arm to return Dawn's greeting, the hog leaned its two hundred pounds farther into Creed's knees.

"Oh, good Lord!" Creed yelled, then down he went, flat on his back in the mud. The expletives that reached Dawn's ears were very colorful.

"Well, hi!" she said brightly, climbing up on the fence and peering at Creed. "How's life?"

"Damn it!" he said, struggling to his feet in the slime.

"That good, huh?" she said, her laughter bubbling through the air. "I missed you at the swimming hole this morning. There I was, naked as a jaybird, with no one to keep me company. Such a shame. I don't think mud is your color, Creed. It's rather icky, you know what I mean?"

"Zip it, Gilbert," he growled, sloshing to the trough and dumping in the bucket of slop. "Damn it, pig, move!"

"I think she likes you."

"Pork chops and bacon," he said. "Hear that, hog? And thick ham sandwiches. And sausage!"

Dawn dissolved in a fit of laughter.

"I'm warning you, Dawn! Knock it off!" Creed roared.

"It's just so-o-o funny! You should see yourself."

Creed turned and advanced toward her, arms raised, hands curled into clawlike fists. He walked stiff-kneed like a robot, growling ferociously.

"Oh, no!" Dawn said, jumping down from the fence. "Don't you touch me with that mud on you! Don't you dare, Creed Parker!"

"Grrr! Kiss me!" he rumbled.

"No way!" she said, taking off at a run toward the house.

Creed put his hand on top of the fence and vaulted over in a smooth motion, sprinting forward the second his feet hit the ground.

Dawn didn't stand a chance.

Large muddy hands gripped her waist, spun her around and flattened her against a rock-hard body.

"Oh, blak!" she said. "Oh, yuck!"

"You're so articulate," Creed said, then kissed her very thoroughly.

"Just look at my clothes!" she shrieked, when Creed finally released her. "The kiss was super but, darn it, I'm a mess!"

"No problem," he said, grabbing her by the hand and hauling her across the lawn. "I'll fix you right up. What we need here is a little water."

"Bad plan," Dawn said, attempting to dig her heels into the grass to halt her flight. "Terrible. Not good. I'll go home and take a shower."

"I wouldn't hear of it," he said, grinning at her. "I always clean up the messes I make. And you are definitely a mess."

Creed turned on the faucet, picked up the hose and drenched a sputtering Dawn from head to foot.

"Give me that," she said, snatching the hose from him. "Now it's my turn."

"Be my guest," he said, holding out his arms. "I'll just stand here and enjoy the view."

"The what?" she said, then glanced down at herself. The thin material of her wet blouse clung to her breasts, outlining them to perfection. The buds grew taut under Creed's scrutiny, and a burst of laughter escaped from her lips. "How much did you pay the pig to knock you over?"

"Ten bucks. It's worth every penny."

"There's a name for people like you."

"Innovative. Brilliant. Then there's— Aaagh! That's wet! And cold!"

"Close your mouth before you drown. Hey, this is fun!"

And it *was* fun. Their laughter intermingled and sparkled through the air. The hose managed to change ownership several times, until Creed finally turned off the faucet. He lifted Dawn off her feet and held her high on his chest.

"You're so good for me," he said. "You make me laugh right out loud."

"I love you, Creed," she said, then lowered her lips to his.

He slid her slowly, sensuously down his body, their lips never parting. When her feet reached the grass, his hands moved to nestle her against him, to feel the hard evidence of his arousal.

"But you just had a cold shower," she said breathlessly.

"Tells you how much cold showers are worth," he murmured, trailing a ribbon of kisses down her neck.

"Oh, Creed," she said, desire swirling throughout her.

"Right," he said, stepping slowly away from her. "Duty and chores call."

"Yes, I have to get back, too. I promised Elaine I'd pick the raspberries. I came over here to ask you if I could ride into Madison with you. I need to deliver an order of dolls to a shop there."

"Great. I wish they'd let you visit Max."

"So do I."

"I'll pick you up about two. Well, I'm off to plow the field."

"Soaking wet? You'll be a mudpie again."

"Know anyone who might volunteer to hose me down?"

"Nope."

"Kiss me, Gilbert."

"Oh, Parker, how can I resist such a romantic request?" she said, slipping her arms around his neck.

"That wasn't romantic? What if I said 'please'? Please kiss me. Please take off your clothes. Please ravish my body until I'm too weak to move."

"Go plow a field," she said, then kissed him. "Now, I've got to go home," she said, taking a deep breath as she slid her hands down his wet shirt. "I'll see you at two."

"I'll be counting the hours, minutes and seconds," he said, covering his heart with his hand.

"Now that was romantic. See ya."

Creed watched as Dawn hurried toward the woods. He whooped with laughter when he heard her parting words.

"Thanks, pig," she called. "You just became my best friend!"

Seven

Creed folded his arms over his chest and nodded in approval. He'd finished painting half of the front of the house, and it looked good. The blue was a perfect color, blending into the setting. Max, he hoped, would be pleased.

A half hour later, Creed had showered, then dressed in dark slacks and a yellow shirt open at the neck. He slid behind the wheel of Max's truck and drove to the Gilbert farm to pick up Dawn. He parked in front, shouted a greeting as he entered the living room, then stopped in his tracks.

"Good Lord," he muttered, as the blood pounded through his veins.

Dawn had halted halfway down the stairs, her hand resting on the banister. Her white dress was a peasant style made of gauzy material, with brightly embroidered flowers at the scooped neckline and around the hem. Her three-inch heels accentuated the gentle slope of her calves. Coral ribbons had been interwoven through her hair, which was braided, then coiled onto the top of her head.

Creed cleared his throat roughly. "You are the most beautiful woman I have ever seen," he said, his voice slightly gritty. "You are lovelier than the dawn and sunset combined. There aren't enough words to describe... Well..." His voice trailed off, and he appeared slightly embarrassed as he shoved his hands into his pockets.

Dawn moved gracefully down the remaining steps, a soft smile on her face as she stopped in front of him, placing her hands on his cheeks.

"Thank you," she said, then said no more, as her throat tightened.

They stood, not moving, each seeming to memorize the moment, etch it indelibly in their minds. The warmth from Dawn's fingertips sent whispers of heat throughout Creed, igniting his desire. He kept his hands in his pockets, fists tightly clenched, as he resisted the urge to pull Dawn into his arms and bring his mouth down hard onto hers. He was acutely aware of his own strength, and the fragile beauty of her lissome body. His manhood stirred with the need, the want, to bury himself deep within her honeyed femininity. But he didn't move.

Dawn tilted her head slightly to the side, an expression of near-wonder on her face, almost awe. She moved her fingers over Creed's face in a feathery exploration of his rugged, tanned features, tracing each in turn. She inhaled his fresh soapy scent which was the mingling of a woodsy after-shave with an aroma that was simply male. She anticipated the sensual pleasure of tasting him, feeling his mouth on hers, the sweet torture of his tongue dueling with hers. Her breasts grew heavy, aching for his tantalizing touch. The coil of need deep within her ignited a rambling flame of passion throughout her.

Dawn sighed, marveling at the beauty of this man, marveling at the intensity of her love for him. They weren't even touching, except for the tips of her fingers, and he excited her like no man before.

She slid her hands to his shoulders, feeling the muscles tremble under her foray. His sharp intake of breath matched the discovery of his male nipples beneath her palms as her hands moved lower.

"Dawn," he gasped, "you're driving me crazy!"

"You are so beautiful," she said, then pressed her mouth to his.

Creed's hands whipped out of his pockets to grip her upper arms. He hauled her against him, his mouth crushing hers. Dawn moaned in pleasure, returning the kiss in total abandon, savoring every sensation that rocketed through her. She leaned into him, relishing his heat, his strength, the power within him that he held in check.

Creed struggled for control as he felt himself slipping into oblivion. Dear Lord, how he wanted this woman! He would kiss every inch of her velvety skin, bring her to a height of passion never before experienced. Nothing would exist but the two of them, and the ecstasy of their union.

"Dawn!" he said, tearing his mouth from Dawn's. "We're in Elaine and Orv's living room!"

What did that have to do with anything? Dawn thought dreamily, slowly lifting her lashes. So what if they were...

"Oh, dear heaven," she said.

"Man," Creed said, running his hand down his face, "another minute and it would have been too late. What you do to me is unbelievable."

"Dawn?" Elaine called from the kitchen. "Did I hear Creed drive up?"

"Oh, Lord," Creed said, grabbing Dawn by the shoulders and spinning her around. He placed her directly in front of him, her back to him, his hands resting on her shoulders.

"What are you doing?" Dawn said, her breathing not yet steady. "Are we posing for a picture?"

He chuckled. "I certainly hope not."

Creed pressed against her, and Dawn's eyes widened as she felt his manhood.

"Well, there you are," Elaine said, bustling into the room.

"Yes, we certainly are," Dawn said, then giggled. Creed groaned.

"Are you leaving for Madison now?" Elaine said.

"No!" they said in unison.

"In a minute or so," Creed said. "I think. I hope."

"You'll have dinner with us, won't you, Creed?" Elaine said. "I'm making raspberry cobbler for dessert."

"Thank you," he said. "Sounds great."

"Creed will be ready for a good meal," Dawn said. "He's had a *hard* day."

"I'm going to wring your neck," he muttered under his breath. She giggled again.

"Fine," Elaine said. "Well, have a nice trip into town, and give Max our love."

"See ya," Creed said, as Elaine hurried back to

her kitchen. "Let's get the hell out of here," he growled, striding to the door.

Dawn laughed merrily as she picked up her purse and a large shopping bag containing her dolls. Creed was already behind the wheel of the truck, and she slid in next to him, placing the bag against the door.

"I feel like a fifteen-year-old kid who got caught kissin' in the parlor," he said. He turned the key roughly in the ignition and drove away from the house, a stormy expression on his face. "I need, I want, to make love to you, Dawn Gilbert! I'm going to pull off the road and take you in a damn corn field!"

"Goodness, how very bohemian."

He shot her a dark glare, then a slow smile crept onto his face, finally erupting into laughter. "This is crazy," he said, serious again. "We're adults, not children. I want you in my bed, Dawn. I want to make love to you at night, and wake up next to you in the morning."

Then marry me, you dunderhead! Dawn thought. Should she say that out loud? No, it was definitely beyond her scope of liberation. Creed had never even said that he loved her. Those precious words had never been spoken by him.

"We have other people to consider, Creed," she said. "I can't just pack up and move in with you."

"I know," he said, sighing deeply. "But, damn it, I was milking cows this morning while you were at the swimming hole. When, where, are we going to make love?"

"Do you really hate having to do those chores?"

"What? Oh, no, not at all. It feels good tending the farm. There's a reason, a purpose, for everything a man does. I got half of the front of the house painted, too.''

"I'm supposed to help you!"

"There's plenty left to do, believe me. The blue is great. Nice color. Once I reach an understanding with that pig, I'll have everything under control.''

"Then you're enjoying what you're doing?''

"Yeah, I said I was. Am I being interviewed?''

"No, but when you came home I don't imagine you expected to take over running the farm. I just wondered how you felt about it. It's a very different life-style.''

"From what I was doing? True. The farm is proving to be exactly what I need right now.''

Right now, Dawn's mind echoed. Swell. But what about the future, the forevers? Did Creed envision himself as a farmer for the rest of his life? Everything was in limbo, a twilight zone. He was a prisoner of his past, functioning in the present in a role his father needed him to be in. But what would tomorrow bring? He wanted her to be his lover. Her dreams encompassed marriage, children, life on the farm together.

"You're awfully quiet all of a sudden,'' Creed said, glancing over at her.

"Things are very complicated at the moment. So much has happened very quickly.''

"Yes, the good with the bad. You are on the top of the good list. Things will smooth out once Max comes home. This dashing into Madison every day isn't normal. I'll get a routine worked out that will definitely include some private time for you and me. Somehow. I would have liked to stay in Madison and take you to dinner, but I have to milk the cows. I'm such a dedicated farmer,'' he said, chuckling softly.

But for how long? Dawn's mind screamed. Oh, enough of this. She was going to totally depress herself. She had Creed all to herself for the next few hours, and she intended to enjoy!

"How does this sound?" Creed asked. "Instead of splitting up, you come to the hospital with me. They don't let me stay very long. Then we'll go deliver your dolls together. Treat me right, and I'll buy you an ice cream soda."

"Fantastic," she said, her buoyant mood restored. "I adore ice cream sodas."

"And I adore you. Lord, what a dumb word. You're turning me into a romantic."

Dawn laughed, then leaned her head on Creed's shoulder. Her distressing thoughts were pushed away, and a smile stayed on her lips during the remaining miles into Madison.

At the hospital, Dawn settled onto a leather chair in the waiting room after telling Creed to give Max a big hug from her. A few minutes later, Dr. North came in.

"Dawn Gilbert?" he said.

"Yes," she said, getting quickly to her feet.

"I know when I'm outnumbered. I'll give you five minutes with Max. If anyone asks, you're a heart specialist from Burbank or wherever."

"Oh, thank you! How is Max doing?"

"Much better than I'd hoped or expected. He's a tough old bird. He also lights up like a church whenever he speaks of Creed. I take it that Creed just arrived home?"

"Yes, he was away for many years."

"Well, he's the best medicine there is for Max. A patient's mental attitude can have a great deal to do with their recovery. I hope Creed plans on sticking around."

"I'm not really sure," Dawn said quietly. "He's just taking one day at a time for now."

"That's understandable under the circumstances. This situation with Max is shaky. Although, if he follows my orders, I think he has a good chance of coming through this."

"Max is stubborn. His farm is his life, his world. Creed feels that Max has the right to make his own decisions."

"That's true," the doctor said, nodding. "Well, time will tell. Go give the old buzzard a big kiss. Third door on the right."

"Thank you again. I've been so worried about him. I really appreciate your letting me see him."

"Max is a lucky man to have such loving family and friends. 'Bye for now."

Everyone was interested in Creed's plans, Dawn thought ruefully, as she walked down the hall. The frightening part was, she didn't think Creed himself knew. He might wake up one morning and decide it was time for him to move on. Would he really do that? Just pack up and go? Leave her? Well, why not? He'd never said he loved her. Smile, she told herself firmly. Smile for Max.

"Hello," she said, poking her head in the door.

"There's my little girl," Max said. "Come in, come in."

Dawn walked to the edge of the bed and hugged him. "Oh, Max, I was so worried," she said, "but you look wonderful. You're probably just staying here to bat your beautiful blue eyes at the nurses."

"I'm bored with that, so take me home."

"Here he goes again," Creed said, rolling his eyes.

"You'll be home soon, Max," Dawn said, taking his hand in hers. "The raspberries are ready to pick, and Elaine is starting out with cobbler, with lots of goodies to come."

"Raspberry jam," Max said, "on homemade bread. Sounds mighty good to me. All I've had in this place is Jell-o and watered-down soup."

"Well," Creed said, "get used to less than fancy meals, Dad. I just became the chief cook at the Parker farm, and my culinary expertise consists of very strong coffee."

Max chuckled. "You used to make a pretty decent peanut butter sandwich when you were a boy."

"I can probably still stick one of those together," Creed said, smiling. "You'll have to view this as an experience."

"If my heart doesn't get me, the cooking will. As long as I'm back on my farm, I won't complain."

"Won't be long," Creed said, getting to his feet. "Our time is up. I'll see you tomorrow."

"Goodbye, Max," Dawn said, kissing him on the cheek. "Behave yourself."

"Goodbye, Dawn. You're pretty as a picture in that dress. You look like a bride."

"Save your blarney for the nurses," she said, laughing. "See you soon."

"'Bye, Dad," Creed said. "I'll spring you from this joint as quickly as possible."

"Fair enough," Max said.

Pretty as a bride, Dawn thought, as she and Creed walked down the hall. Now all she needed was a groom. Maybe she'd whop Creed over the head and drag him to the courthouse.

"Max looks good, don't you think?" Creed said in the elevator.

"Yes, he really does. His color is normal, and he's certainly feisty. Creed, do you think he'll disregard the doctor's orders once he's home?"

"I don't know," he said quietly. "Max is the only one who can decide about that."

"Yes," she said frowning, "I suppose so."

"Hey, one day at a time, remember?"

"Okay. Listen, there's no reason for you to cook. Elaine makes tons of food every day. I'll pack a basket and bring it over to you and Max. Or I could do the meals right at your house. I'm very good in the kitchen, but Elaine loves to cook so I don't get much of a chance."

"No, I don't think that's a good idea."

"Why not?"

"I can't ask you or Elaine to take that on. Max and I will muddle through. I'll get the hang of cooking. It can't be all that tough. Where to, Miss Dawn's Dolls?" Creed said, as they walked outside.

Dawn absently gave Creed the directions to the boutique she needed to go to, then climbed into the truck. Her feelings were hurt, she realized. She *wanted* to prepare Creed and Max's meals, move around in that kitchen, provide for the Parker men. It would be like playing house, pretending she and Creed were married and she really belonged there. But independent, stubborn Creed, was going to do it all himself. Perhaps the thought of her functioning in that role made him uncomfortable, presented a picture of a little wife in the kitchen, and he wanted no part of that scenario. Well, fine! She hoped his peanut sandwiches stuck to the roof of his mouth!

"So there!" she said.

"What's your problem?" Creed said, as he maneuvered the truck through the traffic.

She burst into laughter. "I'm just throwing a mental tantrum," she said. "I'd really like to cook for you and Max, and since I didn't get my own way, I'm pouting."

"Dawn, try to understand. I'm so afraid that I'll allow myself to concentrate only on you, and not the problems I have to deal with. You would look so right in that house cooking meals the way Elaine does in hers. I could get caught up in the fantasy and never face reality. Look, if it turns out that I'm close to poisoning Max, I'll reconsider. Okay?"

"Okay," she said, smiling brightly. Creed *did* see her cooking for him in his home. It wasn't that he didn't want her there, it went back to that damnable past of his. Well, he was going to get a handle on all of that. Oh, dear heaven, he just had to!

The boutique was in an affluent section of Madison, and was one of several small shops situated around a grassy area with trees and a fountain.

"Megabuck folks," Creed said, as they approached the store.

"Yes. You wouldn't believe what they charge for my dolls. It's ridiculous, but you'll notice that I don't object when they hand me my check. Are you coming in?"

"Sure. I want to see you in action, high roller. Besides, I'm carrying the babies."

In the boutique, Dawn was greeted by a pleasant woman in her forties named Gwen. Dawn introduced her to Creed, then presented Gwen with the new supply of dolls.

"And here is your check for the others," Gwen said. "They sold in ten days. I could use twice what you bring me. Oh, here he comes. Dawn, that man walking across the courtyard wants to see you. I told him you'd be in this afternoon, and he said he'd be back."

"Who is he?" Dawn asked.

Before Gwen could reply, the man entered the store. He was dressed in an obviously expensive three-piece suit, and had perfectly groomed gray hair.

"Good timing, Mr. Matts," Gwen said. "This is Dawn Gilbert of Dawn's Dolls, and Creed Parker."

"Paul Matts," he said, smiling and shaking hands with Dawn, then Creed. "I was hoping to have a word with you, Miss Gilbert. Perhaps we could go out under the trees and sit on one of those benches."

Dawn glanced at Creed, but he had no readable expression on his face. Apparently, he was not going to step into her world of Dawn's Dolls.

"What did you wish to speak to me about, Mr. Matts?" she asked.

"It's Paul," he said. "Shall we go outside?"

"Well, I guess so. Goodbye, Gwen. See you soon. Creed?"

"I can wait in the truck."

"No, please join us," Dawn said.

"All right," Creed said. Matts was in his early fifties, he mused. Tan was natural, not a sunlamp number. Loose gait. Athlete. Kept himself in good shape. And he was loaded with money, according to the sheen on the suit, the well-groomed haircut, the quality of his watch. So, what did the hotshot want with Dawn?

"Miss Gilbert," Paul Matts said, after the three

were seated on a bench, "I own a promotion firm here in Madison, with branch offices in Milwaukee and Chicago. My secretary purchased one of your dolls, and the other women in the office were enchanted with it. My professional ears perked up, and I did some investigating, which led to you. The whole concept of Dawn's Dolls is marvelous, and I congratulate you on producing a unique and very marketable product."

"Well, thank you," Dawn said.

Smooth, Creed thought. Very smooth. The guy had class.

"What I would like to do," Paul continued, "is promote you through my firm. I know that each of your dolls is handmade, and no two are alike. I don't wish to tamper with that at all. What I'm talking about is an extension of Dawn's Dolls in the form of a line of little girl's clothing, lunch boxes, dishes—the list is endless."

"Good heavens," Dawn said.

"And then, there's the promotion of you."

"I beg your pardon?" Dawn said.

Here it comes, Creed thought, frowning.

"Gwen told me that you were a pretty young woman," Paul said, "but that hardly describes you. You're very beautiful."

"Oh, well, thank you," she said, smiling slightly.

Brother! Creed thought, shifting his weight and deepening his frown.

"The American people love a success story," Paul said. "Here you are, a lovely woman living on a farm, sewing your dolls, and suddenly you're a highly successful businesswoman. I can get you on talk shows, interviewed by top magazines, newspapers, all of which will further promote the Dawn's Dolls products. I can also see autograph sessions across the country, where the little girls will want to meet Dawn herself. It will call for very careful planning and timing, but I assure you I know how to do it. My reputation speaks for itself. We both stand to make a great deal of money, plus you'll gain public recognition.''

"Oh, Mr. Matts, Paul, I really don't think I—"

"Don't give me your answer today," he interrupted. "Here's my card. I realize I hit you with a great deal at once, and you need to think it over. I'll expect to hear from you within the next two weeks. You're welcome to have your attorney examine our contract before you sign it. We want you to be comfortable with us, Miss Gilbert. I can guarantee you a very lucrative and exciting future. I'll wait to hear from you," he said, getting to his feet.

Dawn and Creed also stood, and handshakes were exchanged. As Paul Matts walked away, Dawn sank back onto the bench and stared at the card in her hand. Creed leaned his shoulder against a tree and crossed his arms over his chest. A muscle twitched in his tightly clenched jaw.

Damn it! he thought. Dawn had just been offered the world on a silver platter! Money, travel, everything. *And* recognition for something that she had accomplished on her own, that was totally hers. This was her ticket off the farm, a chance at an exciting new life she'd created, earned. But, ah, no! He didn't want her to do this! Yet he sure didn't have the right to say a word. He loved her, but couldn't tell her. Wanted to marry her, but couldn't ask her. He had to keep his mouth shut!

"Did that really happen?" Dawn asked, shaking her head. "This is unbelievable."

"You can check the guy out, but I'd say he's on the level. So? What do you think?" Creed said, keeping a casual tone in his voice.

Dawn looked up at him quickly, shock evident on her face. "I wouldn't even consider it, Creed."

"Why not?" he said, pulling a leaf from the tree and studying it. "It's a wingding offer."

"I lived in the fast lane once, remember?" she said, getting to her feet. "I hated it."

"That was your parents' world and money. This is different. You've done this on your own, and you'd be in charge of things. Matts can't force you to do anything you don't want to. Where you went, what you did, would be up to you."

"You sound as though you want me to do this," she said. Oh, no, she thought. What about them? Their future together? Did he really want her to pack up and go to a glitsy world, leave the farm? Leave him? Maybe so. After all, he'd never said that *he* was staying on the farm. And he'd never said he loved her.

"It's not my place to express an opinion," he said, lifting his shoulders in a shrug, as he tore the leaf into small pieces. "It's like this thing with Max. You have to make your own choices regarding your life. We all do. The bottom line is, it's up to you."

"I see," she said quietly, sudden tears prickling at the back of her eyes. "You're right, of course. It's my life to do with as I choose. However," she said, her voice trembling slightly, "I would think that the fact that I love you would play some importance in my plans for the future."

Every muscle in Creed's body tightened as his heart pounded in his chest. A trickle of sweat ran down his back as he forced himself to concentrate on shredding the leaf. There were tears in Dawn's voice, and he didn't dare look at her, see the hurt and confusion he knew would be in her eyes. He wanted to rage in anger, shout at her, tell her she was his, and he loved her. He loved her and she wasn't going anywhere without him!

But he couldn't say those things, because he hadn't earned the right to declare his love. He had felt the beginning of a small sense of peace within himself as he'd labored on the farm, but it wasn't enough. He wasn't healed, whole, complete. He was less than a total man, and Dawn deserved better. Maybe, just maybe, the farm and its way of life were to be his salvation. But he didn't know yet!

"Creed?"

"Matts offered you a hell of a lot," he said, dusting off his hands. "I have *nothing* to offer you." He turned slowly to face her, his muscles actually aching from tension. "Want that ice cream soda now?"

"Do I want an ice cream soda?" she said, an incredulous expression on her face. "Doesn't it matter to you that I could leave the farm? Doesn't my love mean anything at all? Your one-day-at-a-time philosophy works very well for you, doesn't it? Provided, of course, there's some sex thrown in to each of those days!"

"Damn it, don't talk like that!" he said.

"I don't think it would bother you one iota if I accepted Matts's offer," she said, her voice rising. "I could write letters home about the fancy places I'd seen, but at least mine would be true! You got very good at lying, didn't you, Creed? You told me how much you care for me, how happy you are that I came into your life, and I believed every word. I can understand your hands-off policy in regard to Max. But I can't understand a man who claims to have deep feelings for a woman, who would stand silently by and watch her walk out of his life!''

"He does it," Creed said, his voice low as he drew a shuddering breath, "if he has no right to ask her to stay."

"No right? Or no reason? There's a tremendous difference between the two. Which is it, Creed?"

"I've had enough of this," he said tightly. "Let's go home."

"Answer me! Which is it?"

No right! his mind screamed. But to say it out loud, at that moment, would sway her decision regarding Matts's offer. That answer would give her the hope that he would beat the insidious ghosts of his past and come to her. That answer asked for more time and trust from her, with no guarantees as to the outcome. That answer wasn't fair to her; it wasn't his to give.

And so Creed said nothing.

He knew how well Dawn could see the pain in his eyes, so he shoved his hands into his pockets and stared at the ground. And said nothing. The knife of loneliness twisted in his gut, the dark tunnel moved in around him, the emptiness screamed at him in a multitude of voices. Sweat poured down his back and chest, as a cadence beat unmercifully against his temples. Seconds ticked by, each measuring a greater distance between him and the woman he loved. His precious gift. His Dawn.

Dawn stared at him, mentally begging him to say

he wanted her to stay with him, but felt he had no right to ask it of her. He *did* have the right, because she loved him, would put him first, forsaking all others and all things. But that love had to mean something to Creed. It had to touch his soul, his heart, his mind. His silence beat against her, caused unnoticed tears to spill onto her cheeks, spoke volumes with its stillness.

She had lost.

Whatever ember of caring he'd had for her had been crushed into dust by the heavy burden of his past. And he *had* cared for her. Her harsh words accusing him of lying to her about his feelings had been spoken in anger, without thought. What they had been building together had been real and honest. But it had been put to the test before its time, before the present could outweigh the past, then grant them a future.

What Creed had reached for so tentatively with her, he was now retreating from, refusing to pay credence to. He stood alone again, enclosed in the unyielding walls of his dark tunnel. She loved him, but it hadn't been enough to win the battle.

She had lost.

"I'd like to go home, please," she said, her voice no more than a whisper.

Creed nodded, then walked slightly behind her as they went to the truck. The drive back to the Gilbert farm was made in silence; icy, heavy silence. Dawn glanced down at her pretty dress, registering an irrational feeling of amazement that she was still wearing it, that this was the same day she had walked down the stairs in the warm glow of Creed's appreciative gaze. They had stood there in a moment that had held greater awareness, discovery, an increasing intensity of what they shared. And now it was over, splintered into a million pieces and whisked into oblivion, leaving no trace but the ache in her heart.

In front of the Gilbert house, Creed stopped the truck but didn't turn off the ignition.

"Tell Elaine thank-you," he said, his voice flat, "but I'll start practicing my cooking tonight."

"Yes, of course," Dawn said tightly, opening the door.

"Dawn, I..." he started, then stopped speaking.

"Yes?" she said, not turning to look at him.

"Nothing."

A few moments later the front door banged behind her as Dawn ran into the house.

"Nothing," he said to no one, "except I love you and I'm sorry. I do love you, Dawn."

He drove home slowly, then walked up the stairs to his bedroom with dragging steps. He changed into old jeans, then went back outside. There, until it was time to milk the cows, he blanked his mind and painted. He painted the house the delicate shade of blue that matched Dawn's satin ribbon.

Eight

"Ah, man!" Creed said, waving his arms in the air to clear away the smoke. "That's not an egg, it's a hockey puck!"

"Good morning," Elaine said, coming in the back door. "Call the fire department yet?"

"Cute. The first three eggs were runny. The last three were bricks. The hell with it. I'll have pie and coffee."

"Would you settle for warm biscuits?" she asked, handing him a basket covered with a towel.

"You're a sweetheart," he said, pouring a cup of coffee, then sitting down at the table.

Elaine scraped out the frying pan, then broke four eggs into it.

"Dawn told us about Paul Matts last night," she said.

"I assumed she would."

"She said you feel it's her decision to make alone."

"That's right," he said, starting on his second biscuit.

"Mmm."

Creed waited for Elaine to speak again, glancing over at her where she stood by the stove. She placed a plate of eggs in front of him, refilled his coffee cup, then loaded the dishwasher. When she had filled the sink with hot sudsy water, he'd had enough of her brand of silence.

"Damn it!" he shouted, smacking the table with his hand. "Knock it off!"

"I haven't said a word," she said calmly, scouring the frying pan.

"You can say more by not saying anything than anyone I know," he said, none too quietly.

"That didn't make a bit of sense. But then, what should I expect coming from a man who doesn't make a bit of sense at all? I thought Max was stubborn, but you take the cake, Creed Maxwell. It will be the comeuppence you deserve the day Dawn packs her bags and goes traipsing across the country with that Paul Matts."

"Like hell she will!" he roared, instantly on his feet.

"Mmm."

"Where is she?" he yelled.

"Tending her chickens."

The screen door hummed on its hinges due to the force with which Creed slammed it as he went barreling out, heading for the woods at full speed. Elaine lifted the frying pan for inspection, and the shiny surface reflected her wide smile.

Dawn placed the sixth egg in the sling she had made with the bottom of her cotton blouse. She cradled her arm beneath her fragile cargo as though nestling a baby below her breasts. After bidding her clucking friends adieu, she stepped out of the enclosure and latched the gate.

"Dawn!" a deep voice bellowed.

As she turned, her eyes widened when she saw Creed thundering toward her. His expression was as menacing as a winter storm, and her eyes grew even wider.

"I want to talk to you," he said, pulling up short in front of her. "Right now!"

"Goodness, you must be in excellent shape. You ran all that way, and you're not even winded," she said, smiling up at him.

"Dawn!"

"Oh. What was it you wished to speak to me about, Creed?"

"Matts. And his Dawn's Dolls's ideas," he said, volume on high. "Do you really want a picture of your dolls on a lunch box? Do you? Do you want to live out of suitcases, sleep in sleazy hotels?"

"Sleazy?"

"Yeah, sleazy! There are users, takers, out there, Dawn. Everyone will want a cut of the pie, some of the action. It's cutthroat big business, and no one will give a damn that you're the most trusting, the most wonderful woman on the face of the earth. You'll be in a hot tub, instead of the natural beauty of a swimming hole where you belong!"

"Well, I—"

"And furthermore," he continued, beginning to pace back and forth with heavy strides, "I don't want you to go! I have no right—catch that?—no *right* to say a word, but I have to, or I'll pop a gasket. Aren't you happy on the farm? Yes, damn it, you are! Any idiot can tell that. You belong here, Dawn. This is the world for you, not the flash and dash that Matts is dangling under your nose.''

"But—"

"Would you just listen?'' he shouted, stopping in front of her.

"Yes, of course,'' she said, nodding solemnly. "But do you have to holler?''

"Yes! You think I don't have a *reason* for wanting you here? Wrong! I do! I love you, Dawn Gilbert! I love you!''

Dawn gasped, then a lovely smile came to her lips as she gazed up at a scowling Creed.

"You do?'' she asked, her voice hushed. "You love me, Creed?''

"I didn't mean to say that,'' he muttererd. "But, yes!'' he went on, yelling again. "Yes, I do! Ah, the hell with it,'' he growled, then hauled her up against him and brought his mouth down hard onto hers.

Eggs have never been known for the durability of their shells.

As Dawn was crushed to Creed's body, so went the eggs. Her eyes shot open and she stiffened in his arms as a crackling noise reverberated through the air, and a warm, sticky substance began to soak through her blouse.

"What in the...'' Creed started, then his mouth dropped open as he looked down.

Dawn drew her arm away and as if in slow motion the eggs, slightly scrambled, slid off the material, landing with a plop on the top of Creed's shoes. Neither Dawn nor Creed moved. They simply stood there, staring at the gooey mess as though they had never seen an egg before in their entire lives.

"I can't believe this," Creed said, shaking his head. "This isn't happening to me. I tell the only woman I have ever loved that I love her, and it turns into a situation comedy."

"This is the most romantic, the most wonderful moment of my life," Dawn said, flinging her arms around his neck and molding herself to him. "Oh, dear," she said, an instant later, jumping back. "Now I've gotten eggs on your shirt and jeans!"

"They'll wash. Come here, Dawn," he said softly. "I really do need to kiss you."

Forgotten were the eggs, the eggshells and the condition of their clothes. Forgotten were the hurt and confusion of the previous day, and the long, sleepless night both had endured. There was only the kiss. Sensuous and sweet, then deepening in its intensity as their tongues met, the kiss took their breath away. It spoke of love, and trust, and commitment. It heightened their passion, caused heartbeats to quicken, and pulses to skitter. It went on and on. It was Dawn and Creed held tightly in each other's arms, oblivious to anything other than the one they loved. The kiss was sensational!

"Good Lord," Creed said, taking a ragged breath, "first in a living room, now by a chicken coop. One of these days I'll really forget where I am when I'm kissing you and land in jail."

"Please say it again," Dawn whispered. "Tell me that you love me."

He cradled her face in his large hands. "Oh, Dawn, I do love you so very much. I didn't feel I had the right to tell you, I still don't. Look, we need to talk. Have you finished your chores?''

"I certainly have," she said, peering down at her blouse.

"Go change, and I'll hose myself off. We'll walk down to the swimming hole.''

"Which is so much nicer than a hot tub," she said, smiling at him. "I'll be right back."

Ah, man, Creed thought, watching Dawn run to the house, what had he done? Some secret agent *he* was. He'd just spilled the beans about something he'd had no intention of making known. But oh, what a beautiful glow had come to Dawn's face, such happiness had shown in her eyes when he'd said that he loved her. He had brought her that joy. Him! Creed Maxwell Parker, who saw himself as only a taker, had given to his Dawn. It felt good, and right, and real. It was too late to turn back. He'd declared his love, and there was nowhere to go but forward.

"So be it," he said decisively. "Oh, Lord, where's the hose? This junk is grim!''

Dawn stripped off her clothes and dressed in blue shorts and a blue and white terry-cloth top. Creed loved her! her heart sang. It was glorious! Nothing could beat them now. Nothing. The ghosts of Creed's past didn't stand a chance because they were together, united, in love.

Dawn brushed her hair to a shimmering, honey-colored cascade that tumbled down her back. With a smile on her lips she dashed from the room to go to Creed.

He stood waiting for her, his clothes and shoes soaked with water, and circled her shoulders tightly with his arm as she moved to his side. They shared a warm smile, a tender gaze, then walked without speaking through the woods to their private place by the swimming hole. Creed pulled her down next to him on the plush grass and kissed her deeply.

"I want to make love to you," he said, close to her lips, "but we have to talk."

"Couldn't we talk later?" she asked, undoing the buttons on his damp shirt.

"No!"

"Pooh."

"Dawn, I want you to understand something. I didn't intend to tell you that I loved you until I was free of my past, was a whole man again. I also realized that it might never happen, that I might never find the peace I'm seeking. But now everything has changed, because I *did* tell you how I feel."

"Thank goodness," she said, leaning her head on his shoulder.

"I've got that Ping-Pong ball in my head again, but at least it's slowing down a little, giving me a chance to catch my breath. I've had a glimpse of it, Dawn, the peace, here on the farm. Being with you, working the land, has given me the beginning of a sense of purpose. I'd decided that allowing you to warm my inner chill was wrong, totally unfair to you. I'm probably right, but I can't stop it from happening."

"It isn't wrong, Creed. You give that same warm glow to me."

"Yeah, well, you were doing all right before I got here. I arrived in the form of an empty bucket. I'm still not in that great shape. You've got to realize that a section of me is dead, gone, lost. I want to be complete for you, but it might never come to be. All I have to offer you is what's left, what you see, part of a man. That's it. That, and my love.''

"Oh, Creed," she said, tears shimmering in her eyes as she lifted her head to look at him, "I love you so much. We can find your peace together, put the past away.''

"Maybe not! That's the point, don't you see? I've got to know that you understand that it might not happen! You'd be waiting, watching, for some signal that everything was suddenly terrific. I need you to accept me just as I am right now, because this might be the best I can do. I may have to live with my past for the rest of my life. Can you do that, Dawn? Share me with ghosts?''

No! her mind said.

Yes! said her heart, and Yes! said her soul.

And Yes! said the very essence of her being, which loved Creed Parker with an intensity that was beyond description in its magnitude.

"Yes, Creed," she whispered.

He drew a deep breath and stared at the sky for a long moment. "I don't deserve you, your love," he said, his voice gritty, "but God help me, I can't let you go. I want so much more for you. I'll try to make you happy, I swear it. Dawn," he said, shifting toward her and cupping her face in his hands, "I'm hoping you won't go with Paul Matts. Stay with me, please? Dawn, I'm asking you to marry me.''

"I—"

"For better or worse," he rushed on, "and I'm afraid you're getting the worst. I'm not leaving here, Dawn. I'm going to tend the land, work the farm like a true Parker son. And that's another thing. With me, you get Max. I don't even know how much care he's going to need or... Ah, hell, you'd be out of your mind to marry me!''

"Then color me crazy, Parker!" she said, smiling at him.

"I beg your pardon?" he said, squinting at her. "Does that mean you will? You'll marry me?"

"Yes." She kissed him. "I will." She kissed him again.

Then *he* kissed *her*.

With a moan that rumbled up from his chest, Creed's mouth swept over hers as he lowered her to the plush grass. He drank of her sweetness as his tongue met hers. The shudder that ripped through him was one of desire, need, want. The kiss grew urgent, frenzied. They moved away only long enough to shed their clothing, then reached for each other.

Then Creed slowed the tempo. Mustering every ounce of his control, he kissed and caressed Dawn in a languorous journey over her satiny skin. He thought only of her, placing her pleasure before his own, wanting to give, *give*, to this woman who had given so very much to him.

"Oh, Creed!"

"Soon," he said, drawing the bud of her breast into his mouth.

His muscles trembled from the effort of his restraint, his body shone with glistening perspiration, his heart thundered in his chest. But still he held back.

Dawn tossed her head restlessly as her fingers dug into Creed's corded shoulders. Heat licked throughout her, igniting the flame of passion. She moaned in mingled pleasure and pain, and called Creed's name in a voice husky with desire. She needed him *now* to fill her with his masculinity, consume her, quell the fire that burned within her.

"Creed!"

"Yes!"

He entered her with a smooth, powerful thrust that took her breath away. She arched her back to meet his driving force, matching his rhythm, taking him deeper and deeper within her. She was him. He was her. They were one. And it was ecstasy.

Seconds apart, the crescendo was reached in a maelstrom of sensations that rocketed through them. The earth beneath them seemed to shift, tilt, hurl them into an abyss of splendor from which they did not wish to return. They held fast to each other, lingered there beyond reality, then slowly, reluctantly drifted back.

Creed pushed himself up to rest on trembling arms, then kissed Dawn's lips, cheeks and forehead, before moving away and pulling her close to his side.

"Incredible," she said softly.

"Beyond words," he said, sifting her hair through his fingers.

They lay quietly, bodies cooling, heartbeats returning to normal levels, as the sounds of nature serenaded them.

"Creed," Dawn said finally, "why were you in such a hoopla over Paul Matts?"

"Elaine said it would serve me right when you packed up and went with him. I freaked out, I guess. I couldn't handle the thought of you leaving me."

"But I told Elaine and Orv at dinner last night that I had no intention of accepting that offer. Did Elaine actually tell you I was going?"

"Yes. Well, no, maybe not. I think I was had."

"And I'm glad. It brought you storming through the woods like a crazy man and you told me that you love me. What more could a girl want?"

"A baby."

"What?!"

"Sorry. My mind is jumping all over the place. I was thinking it would really be something if you and I had a baby. Am I rushing you?"

"Just a tad," she said, laughing softly. "We're not married, remember? I have a tendency to be slightly old-fashioned about motherhood. Not prudish, you understand, simply conventional."

"Good point. We'll get married right away. But, Dawn, I'd never want our child to know that his father had been a... I couldn't tell him."

"Say the word, Creed. Say, 'killer,' and then really listen to it. It indicates a cold-bloodedness, a ruthlessness, a total disregard for human life. The title doesn't fit you. It doesn't! Yes, you killed with that gun, but only to stay alive. You acted on behalf of your country, on assignments given to you by your government. You did nothing wrong, except not listen to your inner voice when it said you'd had enough. That was your only mistake, Creed."

"You don't understand," he said, sitting up and reaching for his clothes. "I felt nothing toward the end when I killed those men. I just walked away as though it had never happened. That makes me a killer, Dawn, so don't try to pretend otherwise. Facts can't be changed."

"But men can change, and you did. You came home."

"With the ghosts."

"Yes," she said, sighing, "with the ghosts."

"Hey," he said, pulling her up to sit beside him, "let's give all this a rest. This is supposed to be a happy occasion. We're in love, we're going to be married, and make beautiful babies together."

"You betcha, Farmer Parker. Oh, Creed, I do love you so much."

"And I love you," he said, kissing her deeply. "Come on," he added, when he finally released her, "let's go find Orv and sneaky Elaine, and tell them the good news. You realize, of course, I'm only marrying you because I can't get the hang of this cooking number."

"Sure, I know that."

"And because," he said, serious again, "you are the most wonderful thing that has ever happened to me. You are my gift from the dawn, and I will love and cherish you for the remainder of my days."

"Oh, Creed," she said, blinking back her tears. "Let's go home."

It almost seemed like a dream.

Dawn stood staring out of her window at the night, unable to sleep. The events of the day replayed over and over in her mind, and a smile came to her lips. She was going to marry Creed Maxwell Parker. He wanted her to stay with him on the farm, marry him, have his baby. It was glorious!

Elaine and Orv had been thrilled. Elaine had, Dawn mused, been slightly smug, as if she were taking credit for the whole thing. And Max. Dear, sweet Max had gotten tears in his eyes when she and Creed had shared their news when they'd visited him. Even Dr. North had looked happy, and said Max could come home the next day, ahead of schedule.

Dawn and Creed had gotten blood tests at the open clinic at the hospital, then had gone for the postponed ice cream soda to discuss when they could get married. Max's health had been an important consideration, they both agreed, and they'd settled on asking the minister who had the small rural church if he would perform the ceremony in the Parker living room. The clergyman was on vacation, the secretary had said, but she would write the Parker wedding on the calendar.

"Two weeks," Creed had grumbled. "Ministers aren't supposed to go on vacation. What if somebody dies, or has a problem, or…or whatever?"

"Or wants to get married," Dawn had said, laughing.

"Yeah! Exactly. The man has a responsibility to his congregation!"

"The man has a right to a vacation like everyone else."

"I waited thirty-five years to get married, and I want to do it now!" Creed had said fiercely, then ordered another ice cream soda to make himself feel better.

And then the wedding rings. Lovely brushed-gold matching bands, Creed's twice as wide as Dawn's, and both nestled in a blue velvet box. Dawn had held them all the way home, then pouted when Creed said to cough them up until he could officially put hers on her finger.

The dinner at Elaine and Orv's had been festive, then Dawn had come back to the Parker farm with Creed to help him milk the cows. Then in Creed's bed, where she had first seen him as the beautiful bum, they made sweet, slow, sensuous love. With obvious reluctance they got dressed again and Creed walked her home through the woods, mumbling about the irresponsibility of ministers who went on vacation. After one last searing kiss and shared declarations of love, they parted.

Now, near midnight, Dawn was unable to sleep. An infinite joy filled her, an indescribable happiness. Everything was wonderful, fantastic, marvelous.

Except for Creed's ghosts.

She sighed, then crawled back into bed. It wasn't fair, she mused, that a man who had given so much to his country should suffer such an aftermath of pain. Creed deserved to be free of his past, to move into his future whole, as he yearned to do.

At the swimming hole, Creed had sounded almost resigned to his fate of living with demons, as though he were giving up the battle against the dark tunnel. No! He couldn't do that! It wasn't just for herself that she wished him free, but for Creed. And she would help him. Somehow. He'd said she warmed the icy misery in his soul when he was with her, but she knew it crept in around him again when he was alone. It had to be conquered once and for all. She couldn't bear the thought of him suffering. She just couldn't.

"Oh, Creed, I love you so much," she said to the night. "So very, very much."

Creed too, was awake. He lay in his bed, missing Dawn. Her aroma was there, the memory of their lovemaking was there, but *she* wasn't there.

What a day, he thought ruefully, running his hand down his face. A crazy bunch of hours, and the bottom line was, he was getting married. Unreal. And fantastic! Lord, how he loved his Dawn, and she loved him, she really did. He also knew that marrying her was probably the most selfish thing he had ever done. That thought caused the knife to twist in his gut again. How strange life was at times. Years ago he had chosen a path, and his lies had protected his parents from knowing the truth about their son. No one had been hurt. Except himself, of course.

But now? Years later, Dawn was paying the price for his actions. Into their marriage, their private place, their union, he would bring his ghosts. Damn! Why wasn't he stronger than this? Why couldn't he shut the door on his past once and for all, and forget it? He could still feel the cold, heavy metal of that gun in his hand. Dawn deserved better than what he was! And he was going to marry her anyway.

"You're a lowlife, Parker," he said aloud.

With a mumbled expletive, he rolled onto his stomach and finally drifted off to sleep.

"Mighty pretty blue," Max said, standing in front of the house the next afternoon.

Creed chuckled. "Well, don't look at the sides. I have a ways to go yet. I'll do the porch railing and trim in white."

"All spruced up for your bride. That's good, Creed."

"Let's get inside, Dad. It's time you put your feet up."

In the living room, Max settled onto his favorite chair and waved Creed onto the sofa opposite.

"I have questions for you, son," Max said. "I'll only ask them once, and I want straight answers. Fair enough?"

"Yes."

"Do you love Dawn?"

"Yes."

"Do you truly want to stay on the farm?"

"Yes."

"Is a sick old father going to be in your way here?"

"No."

"Have you buried the past, Creed?"

"No, sir, I haven't."

Max nodded, then a silence fell between father and son. Creed waited.

"Fair enough," Max said finally, then got to his feet. "I think I'll go up and rest a bit."

"Dad?"

"Yes?"

Creed pushed himself to his feet and walked to where his father stood. "It's going to be good, Dad," he said quietly. "I love Dawn more than I can tell you, and she loves me. She understands about my ghosts. This home is going to have laughter in it again."

"And children?"

"We hope so."

"Always wanted to be a grandpa. You're taking on a lot of people to love, Creed," Max said, starting up the stairs. "Best do some dusting and cleaning of your soul, so you have room for everyone."

Creed shoved his hands into his pockets and watched until his father disappeared from view.

"Hell of a man," he said under his breath. "Maxwell Parker is something."

"Creed?" Dawn called from the kitchen.

Creed strode into the kitchen, pulled her into his arms and kissed her until her knees trembled.

"Hello," he said, not releasing his hold on her.

"Goodness," she said breathlessly, "that was quite a greeting."

"I missed you. It's been hours since we were at the swimming hole."

"True. How's Max?"

"Doing fine. He likes the blue paint. He went up to his room to rest."

"He volunteered?"

"Yep. I don't think there's going to be any problem with him taking it easy. Seems he always wanted to be a grandpa."

"Really?" she said, laughing in delight. "Sounds good to me. Oh, Creed, I'm so happy, and I'm so glad Max is home where he belongs."

"A lot of new brides wouldn't be so generous about having their father-in-law live with them."

"I love him."

"And I love you. Come sit down at the table. Dawn," he continued, when they were seated, "I called Washington this morning and made arrangements to have my belongings shipped out here. I do own more than one suitcase full of clothes. Truth of the matter is, I have quite a bit of money accumulated. I never had anything to spend it on. I want you to redecorate the house in your own tastes. New furniture, drapes, whatever."

"Your mother put this home together, Creed."

"But it's yours now. Max will want to keep his favorite lumpy chair, but other than that, he won't mind. Will you do it?"

"Well, yes, I guess so. Don't you want an opinion on the furniture I choose?"

"Nope, as long as it's sexy satin and leather. Oh, and maybe a furry rug."

"Sick!"

"I was in this place in Belgium once that… Forget it. Lord, I have a big mouth. Want some lemonade?"

"What I want is to hear about Belgium," she said, squinting at him.

"Naw, it's a boring story, really dull. Want to help me paint for a while?"

"Okay. I'm sure your Belgium adventure couldn't have been any racier than mine in India," she said, getting to her feet. "That place was amazing. Absolutely amazing. I was having a marvelous time, until it got raided. Oh, well. Do you want me to paint the porch railing?"

"Raided?" Creed said, a deep frown on his face as he pushed himself up to loom over her. "Why? What kind of place were you in?"

"It wasn't listed in the tourist guide book, I'll tell you that!" she said, laughing merrily as she scooted around him and went out the back door.

"Dawn Gilbert, you come back here!" he yelled, following close behind.

Creed demanded to know all the details about Dawn's escapade in India. She cheerfully refused to utter a word. He waggled a finger at her. She stuck her tongue out at him. He kissed her until she couldn't breathe, and India and Belgium were forgotten. Then they painted the house.

An hour later, Creed came around from the side to where Dawn was standing on the porch painting the railing.

"Nice," he said, nodding. "You do good work."

"I have many talents, Parker," she said, smiling down at him.

"Oh, I know, Gilbert, I know."

"I make cute dolls with freckles, I can cook, the list goes on and on."

"Do tell," he said, chuckling.

"I wouldn't dream of it. There's certain things a lady doesn't discuss while standing on the front porch."

"There's a car coming," he said, raising his hand.

"I don't see... Oh, yes, now I do. You certainly have good ears. Who do you suppose—" Dawn stopped speaking as she looked at Creed, a knot tightening in her stomach as she saw the hard set to his jaw, the rigid, coiled readiness of his muscled body. He'd crossed his arms loosely over his chest, but his hands were clenched into fists. "Creed?" she said, setting down the paintbrush.

"Go in the house, Dawn," he said, his voice low.

"No. I'm not a child, Creed. I'm going to be your wife."

"Go in the house!"

"No!"

"Damn it!"

The black car stopped and a man got out, glancing around the farm as he slammed the door, then started slowly in Creed's direction. He was wearing a tan suit that stretched tightly over a well-muscled physique. Around forty, he had sandy-colored hair peppered with gray, and was perhaps two or three inches shorter than Creed. His features were ruggedly handsome, except for a scar that cut through one eyebrow, and a slight bump on a previously broken nose. He walked with an easy rolling gait, and with each step,

Creed grew more tense, his eyes icy chips of winter-
blue, as a pulse throbbed in the strong column of his
neck. Dawn wrapped her arms around her elbows and
chewed nervously on the inside of her cheek, as her
gaze flickered back and forth between the two men.

The stranger stopped about three feet from Creed,
glanced at Dawn, then the house.

"Nice place," he said. "Doing a little painting, I
see. Pretty color."

Creed didn't speak.

The sound of Dawn's heartbeat echoed in her ears.

"You led me a merry chase to Greece, Creed," the
man said, a casual tone to his voice.

"You can go to hell, Curry," Creed said, his voice
ominously low.

Nine

Curry! Dawn's mind screamed. Oh, dear heaven, no!

"Now, now, let's not use such language in front of the lady," Curry said, unbuttoning his jacket and shoving his hands into his pockets. "I assume she's your lady, Creed?"

"Not that it's any of your business, but Dawn is about to become my wife," Creed said tightly. "Are you getting the message yet? I'm finished! Done! There is nothing you can say that will change my mind, not this time."

"I see," Curry said. "Well, perhaps Dawn will excuse us so we can discuss this privately."

"No way," Creed said. "She knows what I've done. I told her, just the way you chose to tell my father."

"So, now you're just one big happy family," Curry said. He smiled, but no warmth reached his dark eyes.

Dawn shivered. "Very touching, Creed," Curry continued. "Killer turns farmer. What's next? You sit in a rocker on this pretty porch of yours and write your memoirs?"

"Shut up and get off my land," Creed said, his eyes narrowing. "Now!"

"Hey, is that any way to talk to a man who saved your life a couple of times?"

"And I saved yours! We're even, Curry. All the way across the board. I don't owe you a thing. I walked away from the stinking world you live in, and I'm not going back!"

Yes, that's right, Dawn thought frantically. Creed was home, and he was staying on the farm! Curry had to go away! Go away and leave them alone!

"I'm beginning to think you mean it, ole buddy," Curry said, pulling his hands from his pockets and crossing his arms over his chest. "Thing is, the slate isn't as clean as you think. I never thought you'd cop out leaving a debt, Creed. I never thought you'd do that."

"What in the hell are you talking about?" Creed growled.

"You do remember that last little fiasco we were in, don't you? Sure you do, because that was when you lost it. The kid cried his little heart out and you let him off."

"So? Let the courts handle him."

"I was yelling at you to shoot him because my gun had jammed. Didn't you hear me?"

"Not really, and I'm not listening to you now."

"You should have killed him, Creed," Curry said, shaking his head. "I saw in his eyes what you would have seen if you hadn't been strung out. The kid was crazy, a fanatic. You know how to tell the difference, but you weren't paying attention. You left unfinished business behind. Because of you, Parker, people are dead!"

It happened so quickly, Dawn hardly saw it. Creed's hands shot out and gripped the lapels of Curry's jacket. In the next instant, Creed slammed him roughly against the porch railing, causing Dawn to gasp and jump back in surprise. She stared at the two men, her trembling fingers pressed to her lips in fear.

"I won't fight you, Creed," Curry said. "You're the only man I know who can take me out. Busting my jaw won't change the facts."

"What facts?" Creed said, his voice icy with rage. "Spill it! Fast!"

"Your crybaby escaped two days after you left. He rounded up some sweethearts, and they went on a binge. Bombs, Creed. Bombs in government cars, mail pouches, you name it. Men are dead because you froze, because you didn't shoot that sniffling lunatic when you had the chance! You've got a debt to pay. He's out there, and it's up to you to bring him down!"

"No," Dawn whispered. "Oh, no, please."

Seconds ticked by as emotions played across Creed's tight, angry features. The fury slowly changed to the haunting pain that settled in his eyes. Then a weariness seemed to sweep through him, as he slowly released his hold on Curry and stepped back, taking a shuddering breath.

Curry pushed himself off the railing and straightened his jacket. The silence hung in the air like a crushing weight, and Dawn could hardly breathe. Her mind screamed at Creed to tell Curry to go away, to catch the terrorist himself, and leave them alone! Creed had given enough! Dear heaven, he'd given them his soul!

"I knew you'd want to do the right thing," Curry said. "I'll meet you at Central Headquarters in three days, then we'll go find your friend. See you soon, Creed. Pleasure meeting you, ma'am," he said, glancing at Dawn.

Dawn hardly heard the sound of Curry's car starting, then being driven away. She stared at Creed, searching his face for some clue as to what he was thinking, feeling. His expression was blank, unreadable, telling her nothing. On trembling legs she moved off the porch to stand in front of him.

"Creed?" she said, her voice a near-whisper.

He looked down at her as though surprised to see her there. "What?" he said.

"Creed, it's a trick, don't you see?" she said, tears filling her eyes. "Curry is trying to lay a guilt trip on you so you'll come back! If you do it, he'll never let you go. There will be another assignment, then another. He can catch that man. Don't let him do this to you, to us! Creed, please! Say something. Talk to me!"

"I'm very tired all of a sudden," he said slowly, as if speaking were a tremendous effort. "Would you mind checking on Max while I put the paint away?"

"Creed!" she said, a sob catching in her throat. "Please!"

"Check on Max, Dawn. Go on."

Tears blurred Dawn's vision as she stumbled up the stairs and into the house. Max was sitting in his chair.

"Oh," she said, coming to a halt and taking a deep breath, "hello, Max. I, um, did you have a good rest?"

"Come sit down, before you fall down. I saw and heard it all, Dawn."

"Oh, Max," she said, walking across the room and sinking onto the sofa, "Curry was so cruel. He... No, this is wrong. You mustn't upset yourself."

"Hush with that nonsense. I'm not the one in trouble here, it's Creed."

"Creed is acting so strangely, Max, like he's numb, in a trance. I don't know what to do! Oh, God, what if he goes? What if he listened to Curry, actually believes it's his responsibility to find that man? I can't tell what he's thinking! Max, we have to stop Creed. We can't let Curry take him from us, because we'll never get him back!"

"There's nothing we can do."

"Don't say that!"

"Dawn, it's up to Creed. Leave him be. He's fighting the toughest battle of his life right now, and he has to do it alone."

"Oh, Max," she said. She slid off the sofa and sat at his feet, resting her head on his knees. "I love him so much. I don't want to lose him."

"I know," he said, stroking her hair. "I know."

A silence fell over the room, then a few minutes later it was broken by the sound of Dawn's crying. She wept as though her heart would break, and Max allowed her to cry out her misery and fear. What she didn't see were the tears shimmering in his blue eyes.

Creed lay on his back on the grass by the swimming hole. He watched the sun skitter through the leaves of the trees, then saw a bird land next to another on a branch. A few moments later they flew away, together.

Every muscle in Creed's body ached, and he ran his hand down his sweat-soaked face with a weary sigh. He had never been so tired, so drained. Breathing was an effort. Curry's words slammed against his brain with an unrelenting force, pounding into his head. He wanted to run, but couldn't move. Had to think, but no thoughts came through the cacophony of Curry's accusations. He needed Dawn, but didn't remember where she was.

With a strangled moan of agony that ripped at his soul, Creed covered his ears with trembling hands.

Tears spent at last, Dawn got to her feet, then hugged Max.

"Thank you," she said. "I'll wash my face and get started on dinner."

"I doubt if Creed will be in, Dawn."

"Maybe not, but I'll have it ready. Besides, you're overdue for some decent food. I'll call Elaine and tell her I'm staying."

Dawn was positive that Elaine was aware that something was wrong, but the older woman didn't press for answers. Dawn left it at that, knowing her tears would begin again if she attempted to discuss what had taken place. She concentrated on the preparing of the meal, glancing out of the window many times for any sign of Creed. He was nowhere to be seen.

The meal was consumed in nearly total silence, except for Max's compliments on the fine cooking. He sipped one last cup of coffee while Dawn cleaned the kitchen.

"The cows are bellowing," she said suddenly. "I forgot about them needing to be milked, and apparently Creed has, too."

"I'd say he has other things on his mind."

"Yes, of course, he does. I'll go tend to the cows right now."

"I wish I could help you, Dawn."

"No. I'm a great cow milker. One of the best. I'll be back in soon, Max," she said, going out the door.

In the barn, Dawn stopped, her breath catching in her throat as she saw Creed. He had a milking stool in his hand and was walking toward the stalls. He spun around as he heard her enter, then stood perfectly still. Their eyes met and held in a long moment, then without speaking he moved toward a cow and settled onto the stool.

Fighting back her tears, Dawn picked up another stool and went to the end of the row where she began to milk. She had seen the fatigue etched on Creed's face, the depth of the pain, deeper than ever before, in his eyes. She longed to run into his arms, beg and plead with him not to go, not to listen to what Curry had said. She wanted to declare her love in a voice loud enough to drown out the echoes of his past. But she had to leave him alone in his battle. She had done all she could do, and the rest was up to him.

I love you, Creed, she whispered over and over in her mind. I love you.

The milking was completed, the cans filled and set in the cooling room. Dawn washed her hands, then stepped aside to give Creed access to the sink. The silence screamed.

"What's that noise?" Creed asked suddenly, causing Dawn to jump in surprise.

"I don't hear anything except the cows," she said.

"I do. It's over by that stack of hay. Stay here."

"Forget it," she said, falling in step beside him. "I don't take orders from you, Parker." Oh, how annoying, she thought. The man had enough problems without her sassy mouth.

"I noticed that, Gilbert," he said, smiling at her. Dawn's heart melted right down to her socks.

Creed hunkered down by the pile of hay and brushed some aside. Dawn peered cautiously over his shoulder, deciding that if there was a snake in there, it would be kinder not to scare it to death. She then silently admitted that she was lying through her teeth. Snakes were not her cup of tea.

"Well, now," Creed said, "look at this."

"A kitten!" Dawn said. "It's so tiny! How do you suppose it got in there? It's eyes aren't even open."

Creed cupped the kitten in his hands and pushed himself up, holding it at eye level.

"It's sick, not breathing well. The mother probably brought it here to die. Animals have an instinct, they know when something is hopeless."

"Then I'm glad I'm not an animal," she said, looking at him steadily. "I won't give up on something or someone I believe in."

"Maybe you should," he said quietly.

"No, Creed, I won't. I love you more every passing minute. That's all I can say to you. I love you, Creed Parker. I know you're in terrible trouble because Curry came here. I also know that I have to leave you alone to deal with it. Just remember…" She brushed a tear off her cheek and continued with a tremor in her voice. "Remember that I love you with every breath in my body. You are my love, my life. Forever."

"Dawn, I..."

"Now then!" she said, averting her eyes from his. "Let's see what we can do for this baby. Okay? We'll take it up to the house."

"Dawn, the kitten is dying."

"Well, it's not dead yet! Do you want to help me or not? I'll take care of it myself if you're not interested."

"Lead the way," he said, grinning at her. "I wouldn't dream of crossing you when you're in this mood."

"I should certainly hope not," she said, turning and marching toward the door. She needed him to hold her tightly in his arms, she thought. But at least he was there. And he'd smiled. Oh, Creed!

Dawn was trying so hard to be brave, Creed thought, following her out of the barn. He'd disappeared for hours, hadn't talked to her about Curry, hadn't shared any of his reactions. He was such a louse. The Ping-Pong ball in his mind had gotten a dozen more for company, and he'd finally had to tune out before he lost his sanity. His life, his world, was splintering, crumbling into pieces. Pieces he had so carefully, tentatively begun to build there on the farm with Dawn. What in the hell was he going to do? Bottom line: who owned his soul?

Max was sitting on the back steps and got to his feet when Dawn and Creed approached.

"Sick kitty," Dawn said.

"Yep, looks puny, all right," Max said, peering at

the furry bundle in Creed's hands. "Might surprise you, though. Loving goes a long way."

"My sentiments exactly," Dawn said, pulling open the door.

Creed frowned. "You people take a correspondence course in innuendos?" he said.

Max laughed softly. "Well, I'm off to bed. Good luck with the patient."

"Good night, Dad."

"'Night, Max," Dawn said.

"Oh, and, Creed?" Max said, stopping at the kitchen door and turning to look at him.

"Yes?"

"I'd have bet my last ten dollars that you could have knocked Curry out cold. Would I have won?"

"Yes."

"Figured as much. Don't forget about that dusting and cleaning you're supposed to do. 'Night."

"Dusting and cleaning?" Dawn asked, looking up at Creed.

"Of my soul," he said quietly. "Why don't you get a towel for this poor thing, and we'll see what we can do for it."

A half hour later, they sat at the kitchen table staring at the kitten. Creed had brought a gooseneck lamp down from his bedroom, and bent the arm to provide warmth. After Dawn heated some milk, he placed it carefully in the kitten's mouth with an eyedropper.

"What do you think?" Dawn asked.

"It's a fighter, hanging in there. I'll give it milk every half hour."

"All through the night?"

"Well, yeah. It doesn't have enough strength to

take much at once. It's the only way. It's going to have every chance to live. I don't want it to die.''

Dawn looked at Creed, the kitten, then Creed again. Something was wrong, she told herself. There was a franticness to Creed's voice, a desperate edge, close to panic. But he was the one who had said the kitten was as good as dead. Now he was acting as though the animal was the most important thing going on in his life! Were his emotional burdens so great that he was ignoring them, directing his mental energies toward this helpless creature instead? What was happening to her beloved Creed?

"We could take turns," she said. "Sleep on the sofa in shifts."

"No, I'll do it. I want to."

"Yes, all right," she said, a knot tightening in her stomach. "I'll sleep here on the sofa if you don't mind. I told Elaine I was staying."

"What? Oh, sure, fine," he said absently, his eyes riveted on the sleeping kitten.

Two hours later, Dawn walked wearily into the dark living room and sank onto the sofa. Two hours, and Creed had not spoken to her, nor acknowledged her presence in the room. His attention had centered on the kitten. He had coaxed it to eat, that same frantic edge to his voice when he'd talked to it. It was frightening and confusing, and Dawn was shaken to the core. But in spite of the turmoil in her mind, the events of the exhausting day played their toll and she drifted off to sleep.

"Damn you! No!"

The sound of Creed's voice brought Dawn sitting bolt upright on the sofa. She somehow registered the facts that the clock on the end table said 1:00 A.M., she was on Creed's sofa and he was yelling. She scrambled to her feet and ran into the kitchen.

And then she stopped.

"No," Creed said, placing the kitten gently in the towel and covering it over. "I didn't want you to die. I never wanted anyone to die! I just did what I had to, understand? Do you understand?"

"Creed?" Dawn said, moving to his side. "Creed?"

He turned his head to look up at her.

And he was crying.

He reached for her, circling her waist with his arms and burying his face in her breasts. She cradled his head in her hands as silent tears ran down her face.

"I was doing a job, Dawn," he said, his voice breaking. "I did the best I could. The men I killed wanted to destroy everything this country stands for. God help me, but if I had it to do over, I would."

"Oh, my Creed," she sobbed.

"I will tell—" he drew a racking breath "—I will tell our children that I fought for my country with bravery and honor. And then, when it was time, I came home. My war is over."

He lifted his head to look at her, tears streaming down his face, and shimmering in his eyes. Eyes that were warm, loving, tender, gentle. The winter chill was gone. Creed was free.

"I love you," he whispered.

"Oh, and I love you. Welcome home, Creed Maxwell. Welcome home, my love."

He stood and pulled her to him, holding her tightly. He simply held her as their warmth and strength weaved back and forth one unto the other. It was a moment of sharing like none before, as time lost meaning. The silence was gentle, comforting. They were at peace. The emptiness, the dark tunnel within Creed, had filled with love. They were one.

"Come with me, Dawn," he said finally, "to the swimming hole. We'll take the flashlight and bury the kitten in our private place."

"Yes."

"And then we'll make love under the stars. Oh, Dawn, you've given me so many gifts. Even the gift of learning how to cry the kind of tears you told me about. The kind that cleanse a man's soul. I can love you now, as you deserve to be loved, and I do."

Dawn couldn't speak past the lump in her throat, so she shared a smile with Creed, then he picked up the towel containing the kitten, and they left the house.

Their lovemaking was exquisite. There were only the two of them in a place far removed from reality. Again and again they reached for each other to join as one in a celebration of ecstasy. They slept at last, close, relishing the heat and aroma of each other. The first light of dawn woke them and they greeted the new day filled with the hope and promise of their tomorrows. After dressing, they walked through the woods toward home.

"Creed?" Dawn said.

"Hmm?"

"Since everything is perfect now, I'm feeling guilty about one teeny-tiny, itzy-bitzy thing that I didn't quite tell the truth about."

"Oh?" he said, raising his eyebrows.

"Nothing major, you understand, but maybe it

would be better if I were honest about it. Not that it matters, but—''

"Dawn! Spit it out!"

She took off running.

"I've never been to India!" she yelled. "See ya!"

Creed whooped with laughter and started after her, anticipating the moment when he would catch up with his Dawn; his love, his life, his gift.

* * * * *

*For more delightful romance
from Joan Elliott Pickart,*

look for Baby: MacAllister-Made,
Silhouette Desire #1326,

part of THE BABY BET *series,
on sale October 2000.*

Beloved author
JOAN ELLIOTT PICKART
reprises her successful miniseries
THE BABY BET
with the following delightful stories:

On sale June 2000
TO A MacALLISTER BORN
Silhouette Special Edition® #1329
The Bachelor Bet's Jennifer Mackane proves more than
a match for marriage-wary Jack MacAllister.

On Sale July 2000
THE BABY BET: HIS SECRET SON
Silhouette Books®
A secret son stirs up trouble for patriarch
Robert MacAllister and the clan.

On sale October 2000
BABY: MacALLISTER-MADE
Silhouette Desire® #1326
A night of passion has bachelor Richard MacAllister awaiting
the next bouncing MacAllister bundle!

**And coming to Special Edition® in 2001:
HER LITTLE SECRET.**

Available at your favorite retail outlet.

Silhouette®
Where love comes alive™

Visit Silhouette at www.eHarlequin.com   PSBET

Duets™

**Don't miss
an exciting opportunity
to save on the purchase of
Harlequin and Silhouette books!**

Buy any two Harlequin or
Silhouette books and save
$10.00 off future Harlequin
and Silhouette purchases

OR

buy any three
Harlequin or Silhouette books
and save **$20.00 off** future
Harlequin and Silhouette purchases.

**Watch for details
coming in October 2000!**

PHQ400

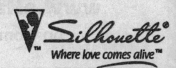

HONORABLE, LOYAL...AND DESTINED FOR LOVE

These are the  **M E N** of Belle Terre

Bestselling author

BJ JAMES

brings you a new series in the tradition of her beloved *Black Watch* miniseries.

Look for the adventure to begin in August 2000 with **THE RETURN OF ADAMS CADE** (SD#1309)

And continue in December 2000 with **A SEASON FOR LOVE** (SD#1335)

Men of Belle Terre
only from

Silhouette®

Desire

Available at your favorite retail outlet.